Candi Kirk:
GRID VICTIM

By Patricia Florray

This book is a work of fiction and any similarities to people, life events, or circumstances is pure coincidence. It is based on true stories of slander and conspiracy. Information about world religions is from authenticated sources.

The author has been a victim of hackers since 2011 that caused her to declare two bankruptcies.

The author worked as a computer programmer from 1982-1998, a licensed real estate agent in Georgia, USA from 1997-1999, a substitute teacher from 1999-2001, and a waitress from 2001-present.

PRELUDE

In the year 1474   *The Teepee*

The Native American woman who called herself Yellow Flower awoke from a good sleep and saw that the bearskin tarp had already been pushed aside. The weather was warm and sunlight filtered through the woods. A crow cawed loudly from one of the trees. She got up from her mat and went outside to find her husband, Great Thunder, sitting upon the tree stump at the lower ground; he was carving sticks into points. She went and put her arms around him; they loved each other very much.

Suddenly there was a loud cracking noise and then a few seconds later, a giant crash onto the top of the teepee, which fell over in a crunch. On top of the teepee lay a gigantic branch that had fallen thirty feet from the top of the pine tree.

Great Thunder and Yellow Flower were astonished at what had just happened and were unable to speak for a moment.

Yellow Flower asked, "What are we going to do now? I love it here. The rabbits, raspberries, and pecans are plentiful."

Great Thunder replied, "My wife, I want to move to the area by the river where there are ten teepees or more. It is half a corn husk's time away. Would you be willing to try it for a while?"

CHAPTER 1

In the year 1985   *Watch your kids*

     Ben and I have been married for a year now and
I'm happy. Of course, I can only speak for myself.
     We don't have excess money, which is very stressful, but we both
have good jobs and are hopeful that one day we will be able to have
less stress and some financial security. Right now we are focusing on
making payments on Ben's college loan, car payments, and saving to
buy a house. We are renting one side of a duplex but have been told
that investing in a house is a good investment. We are in our 20's,
have a healthy 1-year old son named Lee, and are hoping for a good
life. We listen to and admire people who we believe have good values
because we both had good mothers and good fathers who loved us,
never abused us, and taught us good things such as it is a sin to harm
other people or their property and it is good to try to help other
people.
Both of our fathers served in the United States military and we
proudly fly the U.S. flag on July 4th because we like our country. We
believe in the freedoms given to people living in the U.S. and the
standard of living. There are many great countries in the world, but
we were born in the U.S. so this is where our lives are and we want to
make the best of our lives.
     So Ben Kirk and I have lived for only twenty plus a few years. Our
short lives have been good. We went to good schools and churches.
We have good families and friends. We always had food to eat. We
both started working jobs when we were 16 years old or even
younger when we babysat, cut grass, or washed cars to earn money.
There has been peace in our lifetime so far and we do not take it for
granted.
     Although we are proud to be Americans, we think about the
situation in North America over 200 years ago when the British,
French, Norse, and Spanish explorers were having conflicts with the
Native American Indians, fighting for territories which resulted in
the Native Americans being pushed westward. Although we did not

even exist 200 years ago, it gives us sad feelings to think about all of the lives that were lost in those wars. I do not think that the Native American Indians should have lost most all of their lands. Whatever happened 200-500 years ago in North America, I do not think that the Native American Indians got a fair deal. According to researchers, Lenape Native Indians from Asia came to North America over the Bering Strait to Alaska and onto the continent about 15,000 years ago.

Ben and I both believe in an unseen God and that is one reason why we are together; we both wanted to marry a person of faith. We have discussed who we think God is and we think that God is loving and kind and wants good things for everyone on Earth. We wish that all people on earth could have a nice place to live, good food to eat, family and friends, access to good medical care, opportunities for education, freedom to read books and review public media, and freedom to work at a craft or job that they enjoy.

While watching news broadcasts on TV, we heard about religious violence, sexual predators in religious entities, and preachers who stole money from their congregations. Why are people killing each other over different beliefs about Our Creator, prophets, and messiahs? It is the year 1985. Jews, Christians, and Muslims have been fighting for 2,000 years for no good reasons except each religion believes that their religion is the only truth. The people who believe in the middle-eastern religions should realize that half of the world are Asian people who believe in the Buddha Self or the teachings of Siddhartha Gautama Buddha, the teachings of Confucious and Lao Tzu who were Chinese, and the teachings of Oyasama who was a Japanese peasant woman. The ancient scriptures of the Asians are as old as the ancient writings of the Jews. Many people believe that all the religions are praising and thanking the same Creator of the Universe.

We heard on the news about boxing matches in arenas where humans are beating on each other's bodies for a money prize; is this ethical and why are humans supporting such a sport? It is a big world with many opinions.

The Greeks, Romans, Egyptians, Persians, Indians, Chinese, Mongolian, Korean, Japanese, Aztec, Native American Indians, Inuit Eskimo, Norse, Eastern Islanders, Australian Aborigine Tasmanians, and African people all had spirituality and religions before scriptures were written on papyrus during the first and second millenniums. After papyrus was invented, scriptures were written down for the Jewish Torah, the Christian Gospels, the Chinese Tao Te Ching, the Persian Zoroastrian Avesta, the Hindu Vedas, Upanishads and Gita, the Buddhist Lotus Sutra, the Catholic Vulgate (earliest Bible that combined Jewish Torah and Christian Gospels), the Greek Septuagint (also early scriptures of the Jews and Christians), the Muslim Koran, the Japanese Kojiki, and the Sikh Adi Granth. All of these holy books were written thousands of years ago or hundreds of years ago.

I think the purpose of religions should be about giving thanks and praying to the unseen Creator of the Universe, friendships, good things, and helping each other.

Also, about 2000 years ago, it is thought that people were called by one name or maybe two names to designate a tribe or a land. Now, there are so many people in the world that people have first and last names, or maybe three or four names.
In the Bible there is Jesus and there is also Jesus Justus mentioned in Colossians 4:11.

I was out jogging one Saturday afternoon when I saw my neighbor's 7-year old son start to descend a steep driveway on a skateboard toward the street; he was laying on his stomach with his arms outstretched. A car was coming down the road. I stopped running and stood in the middle of the street, waving my hands and signaling with vertical palms for the driver to stop the car, yelling "Jason, Stop!" to the boy. The driver slammed on the brakes of the car and by this time, the skateboard had reached the street. The car's front tires stopped a few inches from Jason's head. He rolled off the skateboard and started crying. Then his father came running out of the duplex saying, "I saw what just happened and you are in trouble, young man. I told you not to play outside of the front yard." He spanked Jason on his derriere, not once but several hard blows.

I was so grateful the car had not run over the young child; I was quite shaken up. The driver of the car, looking frazzled, waved to us and drove away.

I wondered why what just happened had to have happened. I wondered if God placed me in that exact position on the street that day to intervene in the situation. Or maybe it was just a coincidence. If I had not seen the car and stood in the middle of the road, I wonder what would have happened. I wonder if the car would have whizzed by and missed colliding with him by microseconds.

I also wondered if the spankings were necessary; 7-year old kids will be 7-year old kids but I have been hearing lately that spankings do not really accomplish anything. However, people have different opinions about spankings. Maybe just one spank, but why many hard spanks?

My parents never spanked me, but they did yell at me or lecture me at times.

I went into our side of the duplex. Lee and Ben were just waking up from an afternoon nap. I fixed a sippy cup of apple juice for Lee but I always added in a little water to dilute it a bit because fruit juices are high in sugar and too much sugar is not good for the teeth or the body because it can cause tooth decay, blurred vision, and diabetes. Sometimes I fix him a sippy cup of only water. Ben and I are young and learning how to be good parents; we are not perfect but we are trying to be the best parents we can be.

We took Lee to a little neighborhood park that had swings and a ball field, swung him in the toddler swing and ran around the grassy area a little bit with him and took some pictures. Then we went to eat dinner at a local Mexican eatery. On the way home, we had to stop at the grocery store to buy a few things. On the way into the store, we found a wallet in the parking lot that contained more than $200 in cash that we brought into the store and gave to the store manager. When we got home, we read a few books to Lee and tucked him into his bed that still had guardrails to prevent him from falling off.

Once in our own bed, I think Ben and I fell asleep in less than 60 seconds. One time I was so tired I went to sleep in my clothes without getting into sleep attire.

CHAPTER 2

1986   *Wednesday night church supper*

My babysitter Shelley opened her front door with a smile as she did most every morning. Her personality had a cheery disposition. Depending on which day of the week it is, she babysits two or three kids in addition to watching her own son Nathan who is 3-years old and her daughter Amy who is 1-year old. Shelley has two friends who live nearby who also watch kids to earn an income, and I have met her friends many times and they are nice people. They get together often so the kids can play together on backyard swing sets, play kickball, play with toys, or watch television. Shelley has been watching our son Lee for over a year now and I trust her completely. Her husband Mike is also a loving father and loving husband.

"Candi, don't forget about the spaghetti supper at the church tonight," Shelley said to me. "And Nathan's birthday party for the kids is this weekend."

"No, I haven't forgotten and Ben said he is coming to the church tonight, too. Thank you for inviting us." I replied.

I hugged and kissed Lee goodbye and turned around to exit through the door, nearly tripping on a stuffed monkey laying the floor. I picked up the toy and voiced a monkey chirp while scratching the top of my head at the same time, trying to mimic a monkey, and the kids laughed. Shelley said "Bye, Candi. Be safe out there." Shelley did not like to drive in heavy traffic so much and she usually drove on back quiet roads, unlike myself who had to drive interstates to get to work. After saying goodbye to Shelley and wishing them to have a good day, I drove to the subway train station. Thirty minutes later, I was seated at my desk working on computer programs, converting mainframe computer Assembler sequential batch programs into COBOL. I had mentally 'switched gears', as the analogy goes, from being a mom to being an employee. My IT (information technology) job involves developing and maintaining a computer user billing and accounting application. Computers are changing rapidly; just 5 years ago, computer programmers had to type computer instructions on punch cards that were fed into a card reader. Now program instructions are typed into a memory location on a board inside a computer monitor and the operating program reads the memory; this is much better because if you dropped punch cards on the floor you had to put them all back in order again before you put the stack back into the card reader.

My first job out of college in 1982 was developing a hotel reservation system on a mini-computer. However, I took my current higher-paying IT job simply because Ben and I want to buy a house. All of the work factors of my first job were good, such as work location, commute time, benefits, salary, people, opportunities to learn new skills – but we needed more money for our dreams so that is why I took the new job.

A work factor that I love concerning my present job is that every programmer on our team has a back-up programmer who knows the nature of what is going on with the other's programs. Therefore, if my child is sick and I miss work, my back-up should be able to handle a problem. Several times, I have also been awakened by phone calls in the middle of the night to handle my back-up programmer's program problem or my own. Once I even had to get dressed in the middle of the night and drive downtown to the city to get on my desktop computer and fix a problem. Thoroughly testing a program will avoid many problems, such as endless loops when your program performs the same few lines of code repeatedly over and over again because you forgot to tell the computer to change what it is doing. For an example, your code instructions tell the computer processor to read a file of records but you forgot to tell the computer to proceed to the next section of code when it reaches the end-of-file; this could cause an end-of-file error or an endless loop, depending on the code logic. Another kind of error code could be if your program is expecting to read numbers only and the record contains alphabetic characters, spaces, or other special characters. These types of errors caused the computer to appear as if it is doing nothing or produce wrong output. The input data that was input to the computer is only as good as it is; if the data entered is a jumbled mess, the output data will look like a jumbled mess. So that is why there are programs in our IT department in 1986 that 'edit' or read data and 'error out' data to reports that specify how to correct the data.

For the basics, our computer program printouts show the files input to and output from the program processing, all of the memory locations that we have reserved, our program instructions, and an optional memory printout called a memory dump showing IBM EBCDIC characters. The times we requested memory dumps were if we were testing our program or it was running live in production mode but crashed and we could not figure out why the program was erroring so we needed to see what values were in what fields. For example, if my program is erroring out when it is doing a numerical calculation, I can check to see if there are numbers in all of the numeric fields because you cannot add an alphabetic character or a special character to a numeric character in our programs. For our numerical calculation, according to the IBM EBCDIC chart, the fields should all be showing F0 through F9 for the hex values, so if we saw anything other than F0 through F9 that could be causing the problem. We would have to write a short utility program to correct the bad field and run the utility program on the file with the bad record and then restart the program with the corrected file to see if the program would then run without crashing (erroring).

A nightmare on my first job was that after our company had installed a hotel reservation system in the hotel's computer, unbeknownst to us, the hotel was undergoing a renovation and had physically changed some of the room numbers. Because some of the room numbers had changed, unfortunately our computer app was checking people into some rooms that were already occupied. It took 2 days to straighten out that mess. I just kept thinking that 'Humans make mistakes; no one is perfect except for God.' When I told the hotel manager this, he did not appreciate my humor. Nevertheless, it was only partially our fault because they did not tell us that they had physically changed some of the room numbers.

On the train going home that day, I lucked out because a man sitting next to me gave me a newspaper to read when he got off at his stop, so I had something to read. Ben and I had stopped the newspaper delivery to our front door in order to save more money for the down payment for our future house, if it happens. Lately I've been interested in the comics because I appreciate the witty humor that people think of; I certainly could not do it. I think comedians are very smart people. I was talking about the topic of humor with one of my coworkers who told me that comedy is a very hard profession because people have different opinions about what is funny according to their individual experiences in life. There are cultural differences about what people consider humorous or not. And people may consider something funny or not funny depending on what kind of mood they are in at a particular moment. For stand-up comedy shows, the mixture of personalities and moods of the people in the audience at the time of the show may have an impact on how the comedian's jokes and stories are accepted.

Some people do not like humor, laughter, smiles, or hugs.

I had cut out several comics and taped them to the metal cabinets in my office cubicle as a reminder to myself that I wanted a little bit of humor to be a part of my life and personality because my older siblings liked to joke and they had made me laugh many times when we were growing up. When I was 8 years old, I remember my 17-year old brother would give me a nickel to make him a bologna sandwich or rub his shoulders for a few minutes. He said he was teaching me the ways of the world but I laugh when I think back to how many sandwiches I made for him and I think he was just manipulating me but maybe he was sincere. I had a girlfriend who also made sandwiches for her brothers; she said her brothers were helpless and did not know how to make a sandwich so that is why she did it for them. But even in high school she still made sandwiches for them so I didn't believe at that time that her brothers could not make sandwiches.

The little comics would give me a little chuckle and a little diversion from all of the technical computer programming languages and manuals that I had to read all day on my job. Also, humor and laughing can cause your body to produce endorphins which are the body's natural pain killers and which produce a general sense of well-being and may boost the body's immune system.

One of my coworkers had a daily calendar on his desk that had daily comics. Another coworker had a daily inspirational calendar with a profound verse for each day such as 'A journey begins with the first step.' Another coworker who loved nature had put up posters of flowery plants, birds, wolves, mountain views, and beachfront coastal scenes. Another coworker liked sports and had put up logos of all of his favorites sports teams. One co-worker had his childhood teddy bear on top of a cabinet in his cube.

One of my favorite comics shows a mouse hiding behind an arched opening in a wall while the owner of the house is standing at the front door talking to a deliveryman who is saying: "Someone at this address ordered 10 lbs. of cheese." That comic of Ziggy by Tom Wilson would make me laugh for thirty years and forever.

I drove from the train station to Shelley's house and picked up Lee and followed Shelley and Mike in the car to their church, where we met up with Ben.

The spaghetti supper at Shelley's church that night was lovely. It was $3 a plate for adults and $1 a plate for children. Lee was wearing a red shirt that day so if he splashed some spaghetti sauce on his shirt, well, it was a lucky break because the sauce would blend right in with the pattern. People were having conversations about happenings in their lives and some people were reminiscing about church attendances. An older couple was seated next to the table where Shelley, Mike, Candi, Ben and all of their children were seated. The older man said to Shelley: "I remember when I was a young boy and my parents took us to church every Sunday, my mom would bake 4 honey buns and put them in a pan and we would each eat one of them on the way to church. And there was a fountain outside the church on the sidewalk where we would rinse our hands and take a sip of water before we went into the church."

And then a woman at another table turned around and shared a memory that she had: "My church would have a pancake breakfast or pancake dinner every fall before a fall festival where people could sell crafts and Thanksgiving and Christmas decorations."

Another woman said: "I remember my mom always dressed me and my sister in matching dresses for the spring Easter service."

"My mom said a bird flew into the church through the big double doors at the front of the church on her wedding day and the wedding was delayed for half an hour until they finally managed to make the bird leave by swatting a broom in the air at it," a man said.

Another woman said, "My church would have a holiday cookie bake as an activity for children one afternoon in December. Our church had a kitchen so we would bake the basic butter cookie dough that we cut into shapes of stars, bells, trees, and angels and then let all of the children decorate 4 cookies each to take home with them in foil or holiday plastic wrap. The kids could have milk with the cookies if they wanted. The dining hall doors led out to the children's playground so they could play for a while after they decorated the cookies."

Candi interjected: "When I was a kid one winter my mom let us decorate our bedroom doors and I remember I covered the entire door with silver wrapping paper and glued cotton balls all over it to make it look like snow."

A couple sitting nearby told everyone that they were Hindu and their child, Jarak, who was sitting beside them, attended the day care school at the church. "We don't eat a lot of spaghetti," the mom said, "but we thought we'd try a few bites." The family was sitting at a table with their neighbors who were Christians whose son Mark also attended the daycare. Both of the boys were 3 years old. 'I love curried peas and paneer cheese,' said Candi, referring to a popular Indian dish, and the Hindu couple smiled and nodded.

Another person reminisced about Vacation Bible School, which was a week during the summer school vacation where children could go to the church and learn about bible stories and how to handle life situations that might have moral dilemmas.

Another person told about a reenactment at Easter time of Jesus' crucifixion and said "I felt like I was in a time thousands of years ago."

"Well, that's better than someone bringing a rattlesnake into a church service to test your faith."

Another person said something I found very interesting. They explained about Maundy Thursday. A lot of Christian churches in the Catholic, Episcopalian, Lutheran, and Methodist denominations offer services on Maundy Thursday in a special service to reenact the Last Supper before Jesus was betrayed by Judas. A tradition in the Maundy Thursday service is to strip the altar at the end of the service as the congregation and all clergy watch in silence. The persons removing all items from the altar store them in a room away from the altar. When the altar is barren, everyone leaves the sanctuary in total silence. The barren altar represents ideas such as Jesus' life was taken away and we are left empty, hurt, and grieving. Then the altar is redecorated on Trinity Sunday when Jesus rose from the dead.

Another person said, "This is a true story. I remember one time at my church, when the service was over and everyone was leaving, all of a sudden, we heard a woman give a startling cry. Her husband had been sitting beside her in the pew and had died while sitting there."

Then there was some talk about funerals for a few minutes.

I said, "The thing about funerals that I don't understand is that, usually at funerals, people show up that you haven't seen for twenty years and you may not even recognize them. I just wonder why they wait until after someone dies to come see them. If they really cared about the person, why didn't they come visit them before they died?"

"Probably because most people are just so busy with their own lives but they still want to come show their respect for the life that just ended," Ben said.

"Maybe people should make better plans to try to see their friends occasionally," I replied.

There was a piano in the fellowship hall and they played some hymns. We were singing 'Let us gather at the River' and 'Amazing Grace.'

The church had seen many baptisms, services, weddings, and funerals. They are a good group of people, the people at this dinner.

There are groups of friends at gatherings in all religions around the world and the friends cherish the happy moments.

CHAPTER 3

1986   *Humor*

Humor can be dangerous because humor can cause hurt feelings, even though most people intend for humor to be harmless.

There are different types of humor. Some people think it is hilarious to smash a pie on a human face but some think it is not funny. Sometimes words are said as sarcastic humor in response to something said or done to the person who said the sarcasm.

Humor can be a stress-reliever.

Humor does not physically kill a person but humor can crush a person's ego, so be careful what you say.

Suppose a friend goes shopping and buys a new car, a new house, gets a new haircut, prepares a special meal for you, or does something nice for you and wants to share their new 'trophy' with you, that they are very proud of. If you say something humorous or critical to bring them down, it just hurts their feelings. The best thing to do is not voice your opinion if there is a possibility it could hurt their feelings. Say something nice and thank them for their effort. Everyone on this earth is struggling to find his or her way and survive physically and emotionally on the planet.

Some people speak honestly and bluntly at all times, but many believe that it is wise to think before you speak. Every human being has their own unique emotional foundation; you cannot know everything that another human being has experienced in their mind and what information they have retained in their memory. So when people speak to another person, they should not assume that the statement will be processed and received with the exact meaning the statement was intended to have.

CHAPTER 4

1987   *Corporate Security*

"It's your responsibility to monitor the 40,000 employees of this company and report back anything of significance," said James Labrand, a corporate Vice-President, to Ken Smarr, the head of Corporate Security.

"Does this include putting cameras and listening devices in the bathrooms?" asked Ken.

"We will never have this discussion again. Just get with Building Maintenance and Engineering and get it done. The IT unit of Corporate Security goes into effect today."

The word got out through 'the grapevine of the people' that everyone was being watched through hidden cameras in the elevators, hallways, bathrooms, and the cafeteria.

James Labrand himself was unaware that an obscure group of people had placed listening devices throughout corporate buildings. Bigger spies spied on lesser spies.

A coworker, Max, down the hall from me, dropped by my cubicle and told me to not pick my nose or adjust my skirt in the elevators because now there were hidden cameras everywhere. I just laughed and said he was crazy. I told him "There are no hidden cameras" and returned to reading my 20,000 lines of computer logic and programming code.

The next month I noticed a computer journal among the popular magazines and newspapers laying on the tables in the employee break room. I opened the computer journal and read an article about computer surveillance involving tiny cameras being connected to computer hardware and software and something called *pixels* enabling images to be seen on computer monitors (screens) in addition to text letters. So it must be true, I thought, *spying with cameras.*

I wondered briefly for a second if my coworker Max had been spying on me while I was working in my cubicle. ? 'I hope he didn't see me putting my hand down my shirt to scratch my breast when it was itching,' I thought to myself.

That night, the local city news on the television featured a segment about a property owner who was being sued by a tenant for having had placed hidden cameras throughout the apartment he had rented out. Ben was sitting next to me on the couch so we both saw the news segment at the same time. We just looked at each other, shaking our heads, not really knowing what to say. I personally felt disgusted that someone would spy on a person to watch their actions in the privacy of their own apartment. The thought made my heart break, that humans could be so evil as to watch an innocent person unaware that they were the target of a spy. How embarrassing for the tenant to have been seen having sex, going to the toilet, eating an entire bag of potato chips, or making rude remarks that were not intended to be heard outside the walls of their home. Of course, that depends on whether the spy had audio as well as visual capabilities.

"Thank God for the freedom of the media in the USA, right?" I said to Ben. "Or we might not have known about the spying."

"Yep," was all Ben said, as he looked deep in thought.

The next week we went to buy a new television. We had been using an old TV set from 1970 that showed images in black and white. We were amazed to see that the new TVs came with battery-operated remote controls with buttons that enabled channels to be changed; we had never seen this kind of technology in our lives before and we were amazed!

The electronics and computer industry was thriving.

We ate some pretzels and drank colas while watching TV that evening, watching episodes of Gilligan's Island and Star Trek.

CHAPTER 5

1988   *Modern Housing*

We found a great deal to build a new home and the real estate agent on the neighborhood property said, 'For options, you get to pick out what you would like for the bathroom shower and floor tiles, kitchen floor vinyl, carpeting, and light fixtures. All of the interior of the house will be painted in the light beige, but you may pick out the exterior paint colors for the wood siding and the color of the brick for the front of the house.'

Ben and I were thrilled to purchase a home finally. It was a small 3-bedroom ranch with huge vaulted ceilings in the main living areas and 9-foot ceilings in the bedrooms. The master bedroom had a special cantilevered ceiling with a ceiling fan and a bathroom with a huge garden tub and a shower. We were planning on living in the house for the rest of our lives. Ben wanted to pay extra money to have the backyard deck enlarged and that turned out to be a great idea because we spent a lot of time on the deck. We would go out there at random for a moment of peace; the deck was like an extension of the great room and kitchen area and was built along half of the back of the house. Even our cat wanted to wander in and out. Double glass doors with wooden panes graced the deck from the kitchen that was next to the great room.

I thought about the sliding glass doors at the house owned by Ben's parents, which were nice, but the double glass doors with wooden panes in our house were nice, too. One time in my life, I walked into a sliding glass door and bumped my face on it, and I have heard of others who have done the same thing, so an advantage of the double glass doors with wooden panes is that there is less chance that you will accidentally walk into them. Some people put a sticky item on the sliding glass door for people to notice so they will not walk into it.

Sliding glass doors also made me think of some Japanese houses that I saw in movies and on TV that have sliding wooden doors to enter the rooms.

There is much beautiful architecture in homes and buildings all over the world, different designs of beauty from all the various cultures.

Sometimes we would sit on the deck at night, leaving on the recessed lighting over the kitchen sink; the soft lighting filtered through the glass doors and gave the deck a cozy atmosphere for relaxing with a drink, talking or cuddling, or listening to the crickets or rolling thunder far away. When our kids were afraid of thunder, we told them what our parents told us: the angels are bowling so that is what is causing the thunder.

The builder had to cut down many trees and grade the land since it was a wooded area.

We learned at a street party where everyone brought a food dish that the neighborhood was diverse; we had Jewish, Christian, Muslim, Greek, Catholic, South African, Russian, and Chinese neighbors. There were expensive and inexpensive cars. I learned that some people liked ice in their drinks and some people liked no ice in their drinks; some of it was a cultural preference. I was talking to a Chinese man about how warm the weather was getting and he said the seasons are like Yin and Yang; warm and then cold; he said it was a Taoist principle. A Greek woman and a South African woman had started a playgroup, alternating in their homes on occasional weekend afternoons so the kids could play together.

One neighbor had been in an accident while walking her dog; the leash was wrapped around her wrist and her big dog suddenly bolted forward after a cat and she was catapulted to the ground. She said she finally got the leash untangled so the dog could not drag her further. Luckily, she was not seriously hurt but she had to have a cut in her chin closed with four stitches at the emergency room.

One Jewish neighbor invited us over at Hanukkah to see their Menorah and to eat sandwiches, and the same couple brought our kids candy on Valentine's Day and Halloween because they had leftover candy after their grandchildren came to visit.

The neighborhood association had put together a neighborhood directory that included names and telephone numbers of households in the neighborhood who wanted to be included; some households declined. We opted to have our names included in the neighborhood directory.

Ben and I were elementary-school-aged kids in the 1960's and we both experienced school desegregation in the USA, which is why we probably noticed the diversity of the neighborhood. Changes in laws removed racial barriers so people of any skin color could live in any neighborhood, attend any public school, eat in any public restaurant, etc. The civil rights laws were great for the United States of America because the laws promoted equality for all.

Even after the Civil Rights Act of 1964, people continued to segregate by race or native ethnic group in private social groups such as 'African-American Real Estate Agents of such-and-such city', 'Indian Dentists of such-and-such city', 'British Bee Keepers of such-and-such city' or BET Black Entertainment TV, because people do not want to dismiss their heritage because it gives comfort. Some think such social groups are counteractive to eliminating racial and cultural barriers but they do offer support and comfort.

We liked the neighbors very much and were fortunate that our fate brought us to a nice neighborhood. In some parts of the world, people cannot even enjoy their lives or sleep well due to crime and wars.

CHAPTER 6

1988   *Modern Societies*

Our 2nd child was born the next year. We called her Valerie. I was very impressed by the procedures at the hospital where our children Lee and Valerie had been born. Ben had a better experience during the birth of Valerie and did not almost pass out as he had almost done when Lee was being born. During Lee's birth the nurses had to give him some orange juice to drink and put a cool cloth on his forehead because he almost hit the floor at one point when the doctor had to perform an episiotomy on me. When Lee was born, he depressed my tailbone and you could hear it pop in the room but the doctor had predicted this might happen which is one reason why I opted to have an epidural and pain medication. Occasionally it will flare up and hurt but it was worth it to have a baby born. I sometimes wonder if my children's births should have been C-Sections but that kind of delivery may be risky, too. Men should realize that women's bodies may go through a lot in order to bear children and keep the human race in existence.

The hospital had a program where staff took pictures of the babies the day after they were born; we were so grateful for the pictures.

Once I walked through a cemetery near the university I attended and noticed many baby graves that were dated in the 1800's. Medical procedures like removing the baby from the womb with forceps and C-sections have enabled many babies and women to live whereas 100 years ago, some babies and mothers unfortunately died during childbirth.

I thought about doctors and medical staff, hospital emergency rooms and emergency medical assistants who offer their services to help human beings stay alive and well. I thought about good human beings who offered medical help to others as civilization has progressed over the past 2000 years. People did not have to help others but they made a choice to help others.

Was there ever a time or place on earth when a doctor refused to help a woman deliver a baby? Or refused to help her deliver a baby unless she could pay first? I considered myself lucky to live in a time and a country on earth where I could get medical help. I was glad for the painkillers that helped me cope with the pains of childbirth although I admire women who can deliver a child naturally without any drugs.

Of all the times in history that I could have lived, for some reason God let me be born in 1962, and I lived in a time and a place in civilization where humans in society offered services to help other humans. The founding fathers of the USA made choices to make our society what it is. From what I read about some civilizations a long time ago, if you were not a queen or a king or living in the castle then it was hard to get help if you were just a peasant living on a small farm. The Founding Fathers of the USA declared Independence from King George III of Great Britain on July 4, 1776 and the document was drafted by John Adams, Thomas Jefferson, Benjamin Franklin, Roger Sherman, and Robert Livingston and was signed by 56 delegates from all 13 colonies: Georgia, North Carolina, South Carolina, Maryland, Virginia, Pennsylvania, Delaware, New York, New Jersey, New Hampshire, Massachusetts, Rhode Island, and Connecticut. Patrick Henry, Samuel Adams, Thomas Paine, John Hancock were active in the American Revolution. John Locke of Great Britain was an English philosopher who believed in representative government and protection of basic rights and freedoms, such as freedom of the press, freedom of religion, and human rights. The United States Constitution was signed on September 17, 1787 by 55 delegates from 12 of the 13 colonies. Rhode Island did not send delegates. Seven men who were very active in drafting the documents and forming the US government were John Adams, Benjamin Franklin, Alexander Hamilton, John Jay, Thomas Jefferson, James Madison, and George Washington. George Washington was the first to sign the US Constitution as President and deputy from Virginia. John Adams, James Madison, and Thomas Jefferson also served as US Presidents. Benjamin Franklin was an American diplomat. Alexander Hamilton was Secretary of the Treasury. John Jay was the first chief justice.

I thanked the entire hospital staff who helped me give birth to our kids, cleaned up the delivery room and afterbirth placenta, and took great care of our infants, me, and my husband. The hospital also served me delicious food. When we left the hospital, we were given a box of infant diapers, free samples of infant formula for feedings, a little suction syringe that would suck mucous out of a baby's nose that the nurse said not to overuse because it could interfere with the baby's eardrums, and instructions for new parents. A nurse told us "I tell all my new parents to remember to never shake a baby because it could physically hurt it and if you need help, ask someone for help. Parents can get physically and emotionally exhausted but please never hurt your child." My first thought was that I was offended that she thought I would ever hurt my child, because I would rather punch a pillow instead of hurting my child, but I thought about it later and realized that the nurse just loved babies and was doing a good thing by reminding parents to never shake a baby. I think you are never supposed to shake any human being, no matter what their age is, because it can damage their spinal cord. We also left the hospital with several containers of flowers, congratulatory and welcome baby cards, and balloons that people had sent.

Twenty years later you would have the option to have your child's placenta cryo-frozen and stored for potential future medical purposes but that option was not available at the time our children were born.

I was also so grateful that Valerie was born healthy. Pregnant women need to be very careful because their balance can be off; I fell going up the stairs at the train station once and I was scared the baby had been harmed in my womb but she was not.

Pregnant women are supposed to avoid trampolines, skydiving, skiing, surfing, certain processed luncheon meats and cheeses, drugs, alcohol, extreme temperatures, tight clothing, high heels, caffeine, cigarette smoking, and more. Pregnant woman should drink water but not too much water. I knew a few women who avoided all caffeine during their pregnancy and even delivered their child naturally without taking painkillers and I admired them a lot.

My sister hosted a baby shower for Ben and I after Valerie was born, as she had when Lee was born. One of the neat gifts we got was a toddler booster seat to put on top of a regular dining room chair to boost the child up so they could eat properly at the table. It brought back memories of when I was a toddler; my parents boosted my siblings and I up by sitting us upon several merchandise catalogs like Sears and JC Penney and telephone books so we could eat from our plates at table level.

CHAPTER 7

1988   *Is Goodness innate?*

Where did kindness begin for human beings? People have wondered about this; is kindness and caring for others innate, genetic, or spiritual?

I think I read somewhere that some scientists are looking for a 'good' versus 'violent' gene influencing the brain. Some people who believe in evolution believe we may have some violent or territorial genes in our genetic makeup that are natural; maybe in the future we won't need them anymore! I believe in evolution and God; to me, the human species is just a part of the great big mystery of the whole entire universe.

Religions have put emphasis on doing good works and prohibiting bad works. The ancient religious symbols and scriptures renew the mind and spirit and give us hope and new beginnings in our attitudes. I read that religions helped to stop human cannibalism. Modern humanity has evolved over a span of about 40,000 years, according to evolutionists.

How does a spider know how to build a web? How does an ant know how to build an anthill? How do birds know how to build nests? How do many animals and plants know to 'recreate' in the springtime? How do bears know to hibernate? How do lobsters know to line up next to each other when it comes time to march in migration? Humans have always wondered these thoughts.

I have noticed that family members can have very similar handwritings and I have wondered if it is the same 'thing' as the spider making the web or the bird making the nest.

Where did spirituality begin? Some people just believe in the holy book of their religions and think that human civilization started with their religion, but archaeologists have found evidence that spirituality existed before the invention of paper and holy writings on paper. Archaeologists have found cave drawings, totem poles, and jewelry and items buried with bodies in tombs in many parts of the world. I also read that archaeologists have found rocks with starches on them that might indicate unleavened bread was baked 30,000 years ago. They have found fig fossils buried with cooking artifacts in the middle-eastern regions around the Mediterranean Sea that have been dated to precede biblical times.

I also read a theory by evolutionists who theorized that when the first human species was evolving, they were talking and making sounds but their brains did not realize or comprehend that they themselves were the ones talking and they may have thought that the sounds of their own voices were coming from 'above' in a spiritual sense.

The human brain is an evolving organ by itself. Throughout our lives, our brain is developing itself. Scientists think magic psychedelic mushrooms may have enhanced consciousness in the brain.

When I was 16 years old, I thought I knew everything. Later I realized that I did not know everything and I opened up my heart and mind and I learned new things from other people. I have been trying to improve myself all of my life, hating myself for the times that I have thought bad thoughts and have even done some mildly wicked things, for example, the time when I was 6 and my sister was 4 and we traded some Halloween candy and I talked her into letting me have all the M&Ms and later she cried. Someone told me that I am too hard on myself, that no one is perfect, and that I should try to like myself. I do not like myself when I have bad moments. I want to be a good person, only do good things, and only think good thoughts. Plus, I was always taught to be humble like Jesus. I have read some articles written by psychologists that said that Jesus should not have said to be humble all of the time because people have to stand up for themselves and fight for their rights and human dignity.

Years later after I read major world scriptures and attended worship services at many religious congregations, I am glad that, as a child, my parents and the church I went to did not teach me radical things such as 'Every word of the King James Bible is the pure truth' and 'Our church is the only true church' because there are nice spiritual people in all religions. My parents took us to church, taught us to say prayers every night, to be thankful for food, to be nice to others, to be honest and work hard, but they were not adamant about specific beliefs about God. No one actually knows who God is.

CHAPTER 8

1988   *Good Parenting Techniques*

Ben and I have argued about if we should tell Lee that Santa Claus is not real or not tell him. I do not want to tell Lee that Santa is not real; I want him to figure it out on his own because he will eventually figure it out or one of his friends will figure it out and tell him. I want Lee to know what 'imagination' is versus reality. Ben said that his parents never let him believe in Santa Claus; they told him when he was 3-years old that the Christmas gifts were from them and that parents are 'Santa Claus' who is just a character in a book. Ben does not want Lee to believe in fairy tales or things that are not real. Then I argued back that I thought it was harmless to let Lee have a little imagination in his childhood. Imagination is what scientists say led to many great inventions for humanity; it is what enables humans to think 'outside of the box', as the popular saying goes. I said we have to be flexible sometimes, like Gumby. Ben said Lee was his child, too, and I had no right to force my opinion on Lee. I suggested that we flip a coin to decide. Whosever side the coin landed on, we would follow it. He agreed. We flipped a quarter and I won. So Lee would not have to be told that Santa Claus was not real yet. He was only 4-years old. But when we played with his toys and watched TV or movies, we told Lee that the super hero figures were not real, that they were just imaginary, and I stressed this to Ben so he would not hold a grudge on me about the secret of Santa Claus.

One evening Ben and I took the kids for an evening walk after dinner. It was a beautiful summer evening and the sky was twilight. We were walking along the street with the baby daughter sitting upright in her stroller and Lee, our 4-year old son, was walking beside us. Ben and I were looking at trees and discussing if we wanted to plant any special trees in our yard when suddenly Lee grabbed my arm and said "Mom, watch out, there is a snake in the road." We stopped in our tracks. About 4 feet ahead of us lay a copperhead snake in the middle of the road. Ben directed me to take the kids back home and he knocked on a neighbor's front door. The men killed the copperhead with a shovel. The neighbor said that when woods are cleared to build houses, it is natural that there will be animals being scattered. Several times in upcoming years I reminded my son of the day he 'saved his baby sister from a snake bite' because we might have strolled right over it if my son had not intervened. And, like several times in my life before, I wondered if God had intervened…'out of the mouths of babes' as the Bible verse says.

One of my sisters had children about the same age as my children and she lived in the same city, so me and my sister got together often so the cousins could play, have slumber parties, or we would watch each other's children if we had errands to run without children. We taught our children not to say 'Shut up' to each other because our parents did not like us to say that to each other. We taught them to say 'Please stop saying that.' If one of the kids was being bothered, we told them to leave each other alone and go find something else to do; there is no sense in fighting. Often we would find an activity to do and play with the kids ourselves, supervising. One time we built a city out of play dough on our kitchen table playing with the kids. Or we would play with them out in the yard on the swing set or toss a ball. Basically, all of our kids played well together and there was very little fighting or arguing.

I tried to mop my kitchen floor often when I had crawling babies and young kids because they played on the floors with their toys. Once when I was mopping, I had positioned the chairs to block off the dinette area where I had mopped and I told the kids to stay away from the wet floor, but my son ran through the kitchen area anyway, slipped and bumped his head on the concrete floor quite severely. I rushed him to the doctor and they took X-rays but thank goodness, he did not crack his skull. He did have a nasty bump on his forehead for the next few weeks which worried me but it healed up nicely.

Our house was built on a concrete slab with imbedded piping instead of raised wooden planks and I have heard people say that there are advantages and disadvantages to both. For example, a wooden foundation can rot or be eaten by termites; and concrete foundations have to be drilled through to fix broken imbedded pipes.

One night I went to take the kitchen trash out to the large curb can in our garage and I screamed as I saw a strange animal in our garage. I jumped on the back hood of my husband's car. Ben came running out of the house and saw a possum running out of the garage. "You afraid of a possum, girl?" he laughed at me. I had no idea what a possum was because I had never seen or heard of one before. That was the day I learned about a possum.

That night I was a lover in addition to being a mom, a college alumni, a sister, a friend to my friends, a member of a nice neighborhood, a computer programmer, and a U.S. citizen (who gladly pays taxes because I appreciate our police, roads, dams, state parks, firefighters, government and public officials, etc.) One person has many roles; I've been hearing about this concept lately. I was very happy to be snuggly warm in my bed with my husband in our cozy home with our little ones tucked in their beds. But I was like many parents; the minute your kids go to sleep you cannot wait for them to wake up; you miss them while they are sleeping.

Our neighborhood association sent out a flyer saying that they recommended a trash service that also offered recycling pick-up. So we had another can in our garage for No. 1 & 2 plastics, bottles, metals, and cardboards. The orange Hefty Recycling bag is for No. 4, 5, and 7 plastics. Many people in the world are trying to improve things. People are working hard to do good things. I was inspired by such people.

Once when we were pulling weeds in the backyard and digging in the dirt, trying to decide where to put in a flower garden, we found an arrowhead that could have been crafted by an early American native. I imagined that perhaps 500 years before us, a teepee could have been anchored in the exact spot or area where our ½ acre was located, with maybe a family of natives, rain dancing or smoking herbs on this very land.

I read a modern best-selling novel that mentioned about electricity in the human body. It said that humans are losing their natural connection to the earth because we are wearing rubber soles too much. If you stand barefoot on the earth or in leather-soles shoes, earth neutrons will come up and blast apart inflamed cells with a positive charge, working like an anti-oxidant. A person could also bend down and touch the earth with their hand to be infused with powerful earth neutrons. We evolved from the earth infused with electricity in our bodies. So I shared this idea with Ben, the kids, my family, and our friends and neighbors.

Computer images on the internet showed a brain before standing barefoot in the grass and after standing on the grass. After standing barefoot in the grass, the brain was more lit up.

CHAPTER 9

1990   *Soul Connections*

At least two times in our lives, my sisters and I had telepathic moments. One time I picked up my land-line phone receiver to dial her number and call her and I was astonished to hear her calling my name; I had picked up the phone receiver apparently one second before it should have rang on my end. This happened to me and another sister at a different time. Also, it happened on at least two occasions where I would call my sisters in the evening and we had both fixed the exact same meal for dinner.

I've heard when you find a 'soul mate' that you can quite often know what the other is thinking or about to say and you might say the same thing at the same exact time. It's like you feel you have known the person forever or you feel connected to them immediately.

It is also neat to think about twin and triplet births, and the commonalities in their lives.

There have been moments in my life when I have prayed for divine guidance and asked God to please be in my thoughts and my heart or for God to use me for a divine purpose if I was needed. And then after a period of time something would happen that made me feel I had experienced a charismatic 'GOD MOMENT' which is hard to explain except you feel that God answered you and it is mysterious and will make tears come to your eyes because it feels so real.

One time I had been praying because I was very stressed and wanted for God to be with me and when I went grocery shopping my bill was $8.88. Then I woke up in the middle of the night to use the restroom and my digital bedside clock read 4:44am. Then the next day I was in my car and when I looked at the clock it said 2:22pm. Then a few nights later, I woke up in the middle of the night and my clock read 5:55am. Then when I was grocery shopping again, the message at the bottom of my receipt said that I had saved $8.88. This week was the week that I should have been in Vegas playing slot machines! Several times over the next years I would get triple numbers when I prayed for God to be with me.

CHAPTER 10

1990   *Craziness*

Once I spent four hours driving to 3 different shoe stores looking for the perfect pair of shoes to go with a dress I found. Maybe I should have just bought the first pair I found at the first store that were on sale for $19 instead of paying $80 for a pair that I had found at the third store. I really could not afford the $80 pair, but I just 'had to have them.' This incident caused me much spiritual stress. That night Ben heard me out and he looked much frazzled when his wife talked for 30 minutes about shoes and ladies fashion. "Can we please stop talking about this?" he begged. I gave him a nice neck and back massage. While I was rubbing his back I was thinking about the $ 80 pair of shoes that I had bought. Well, I sighed to myself, I will enjoy wearing them. But I resolved that the next pair would be a bargain pair and a purchase based on cost and not just my preference, in order to save money. As the saying goes, I was thinking I could live a champagne life-style on a beer budget. Wine is more expensive than beer because grapes are more expensive than barley, hops, and wheat. Champagne is wine that is fermented a second time to create bubbles.

I read in a magazine about the concept of *wabi-sabi,* which is the Japanese concept of beauty among imperfections caused by time, such as cracks in wood, dried-out-leaves, liver spots on skin, or rust on metal. It helped me realize not to discard household items or clothing just because of small scratches or stains. Holes in jeans and clothing became a fashion trend that went in and out of fashion beginning in the 1970s and 1980s and people began to wear clothes with holes in them or small stains on them instead of tossing them out. I've heard people say that nothing is perfect except for God, so why do people waste so much time and energy on perfection? Some things have to be perfect but some things do not have to be perfect; I think it's about putting things in perspective.

Humans have two brain hemispheres – a left brain that has more logical processing and a right brain that is more passionate. People that are very passionate, angry, having crazy moments, or suffering from addictions need to realize that they should not let their right brain dominate their thinking. Humans can make conscious choices about their actions and can choose good actions. The left brain is good at math and logic and controls the right side of the body. The right brain is good at creativity and coordinates the left side of the body.

God set boundaries between day and night. Also, there are boundaries between the seasons of spring when the plants turn green and blossom, summer that has the great warmth of the sun, fall when the time length of sunlight is diminished and the plants that are not evergreens turn into brilliant orange, red, purple, and yellow colors, and then winter when many plants lie dormant. Maybe people who suffer from addictions and obsessions could ponder about God's natural boundaries and realize that there is a time to say yes and a time to say no, like day and night - the boundary concept could help give them some personal strength and help them with their addictions. Habits are a hard thing to improve or change because they are in our personal comfort zone and thus a part of our personality.

I read an article that a person may have to try different things if they want to try to break a habit or change something. The article said to do something over and over and expect different results is insanity.

In my life, I have set small goals and tried to reach them. For example, times when I wanted to lose a few pounds. Instead of skipping meals or cutting out favorite foods, the goal was to eat less. Instead of two plates, just eat one. Get up from the table and go do something else.

Ben and I were trying to be conservative and not crazy with our money. Several times when our family was out doing errands we would see people on street corners asking for donations for their organizations or cashiers asking if we wanted to up our purchase by a dollar for a donation to a charity. Sometimes we would give a dollar and sometimes we would not, depending on how much money we had at the time. We hoped that those asking for donations were legitimate organizations; they are supposed to have a solicitation license in order to stand on street corners and ask for donations. Once there was a family in front of grocery store with a sign begging for food money; Ben and I gave them $40 and wished them good wishes that their financial situation would change. The man of the family said to us "Thank you so much; we appreciate your assistance." I appreciated what he said to us because one time I had a neighbor call me and ask me for a ride to the store because her car was broken. After I took her to the store and drove her back to her home she told me "Thank God, I knew God would provide for me a ride to the store." Her statement made me wonder and think, as I thought that my choice of actions was as much a part of the good deed as God was. But she did not personally thank me for the ride I gave her to the store. But she was nice and I liked her.

I pray for God to be with me and all people and guide us, but I am not sure that God is in all actions on earth, because violence and murders do not make sense if God is everywhere and everything is preplanned by God.

Thinking about God gives humans much to think and talk about.

Later that night when Ben and I were discussing our monthly budget, we decided not to have the driveway pressure washed for $50 because we had given the $40 to the starving family. We would do the pressure wash next year.

CHAPTER 11

1990   *A Defining Moment*

My husband Ben left for work. Then Lee, my son who is our oldest child, left for school on the bus. Luckily the bus stop is right in front of our house. I put Valerie, our 1-year old daughter into her car seat in the mini-van and strapped her into it. It was our daily routine every morning at the time. I went back into the house for a minute or two to make sure the coffee pot was off and to grab my purse. That morning I had to get a slice of toast out of the toaster to eat in the car along the ride. Suddenly, I heard the squeal of brakes. What? I said to myself. I walked quickly to the garage and was astonished to see an older Caucasian woman reaching into the mini-van towards Valerie.

"Excuse me?" I said, thinking 'What are you doing? Who is this woman? What is happening?' The woman looked at me, turned around and started running out of the garage. "Wrong house," she said.

I ran after her but stopped halfway down our driveway as it sloped downwards and I was wearing high heels and felt wobbly. Within a few seconds, the woman drove off in an older white car. I craned my neck to read the license plate but bushes were in the way and by then the car was gone.

I didn't know what to do. I was thinking many thoughts. I looked to the sky, saying 'God, you have spared us from a horrible fate. Please guide us.' I did not call the police because I did not see the license plate. Also, the thought crossed my mind that if this was a pre-planned kidnapping, maybe some corrupt police were waiting for a call indicative of a botched plan. Maybe the woman in my garage did not know my name, only our address. My daughter was safe. I felt like this was a very sinister and evil thing. I got into my car and drove Valerie to the babysitter's and then got myself to work.

I told my coworker Greta about the attempted kidnapping. She told me to be careful and watch my back. And she had a serious and baffled expression on her face. Her words of wisdom would guide my thoughts for the rest of my life.

That night I told Ben about the attempted kidnapping. He was an attentive listener. We could not believe that human beings could be so evil to other human beings.

I told Ben that maybe we should not have put our names and address in the neighborhood directory. Or maybe just have given our last name and address to be listed and not the names of the children. Now I understood why some people did not want all of their private information in the neighborhood directory.

What kind of evil person kidnaps another human being and takes their God-given life away? Only the most vilest people on earth. Or maybe the kidnappers are insane and mentally ill, to ruin another human being's life.

When you think about how mean and cruel other people are, it makes you feel a little bit better about your own self. As ugly and bad as I feel about myself sometimes, I know for a fact that I am better than the cruel people who are kidnappers, thieves, liars, and murderers.

Ben hugged me and the kids tightly that evening while we were relaxing after dinner and playing with the kids. Ben doesn't express a lot of his innermost feelings so sometimes it is hard to know what he is thinking about. Me, sometimes I talk too much; I need to think and listen more and talk less.

CHAPTER 12

1993   *Family Life / Work / Religion*

The next 3 years were very busy. We had a third child, a son that we named Will. Will was born at the same hospital as Lee and Valerie.

Shelley had 2 more children, a boy named Isaiah and then a girl named Hope. And she was still watching our children. She wanted to stay home and raise the kids.

I contemplated staying home but our mortgage was high so I made the decision to keep the corporate job and let the kids stay with Shelley. My children truly loved Shelley; she was like their second mother.

And I compensated Shelley well, more than an average baby-sitter because I felt like we were all raising the children together in the situation and Shelley and Mike were trying to save up to buy a house as well. I had briefly tried to babysit a few children for 6 months after Lee had been born, but I was not making enough money. Years later, I would regret not staying home with my children, but it was our financial situation that required two-incomes.

 A lifetime can be somewhat planned out. A parent can stay home with the kids and have a career later on if they want to; it may be necessary to obtain new training or education to meet job requirements. In the 1950s thru the 1970s in America employers paid one parent enough money to allow the other parent to stay home and raise the kids, but then the women's liberation movement of 1968 became a major topic of discussion and women fought for rights to work in professions that were once only dominated by men; news broadcasting, journalism, and advertising were some of the professions. Around 1972 the schools in the United States allowed girls to wear pants to public schools instead of only dresses.
By the 1980s the idea came around for women to have careers; childcare became a big business and most families relied on two-incomes. Twenty years later, I think maybe society should reevaluate;

people are becoming too robotic; life has become all about paying bills, huge profits, and family values are in jeopardy.

Shelley was so good to us. One time I was delayed by thirty minutes because we had a problem at work. When I arrived at Shelley's, Lee and Valerie were seated among her own kids around the dinner table, eating chicken-n-dumplings with a side of green beans, which was one of Shelley's favorite dishes to make. She invited me to sit down and eat dinner also. I was so grateful for her friendship, I was so hungry, and it was delicious. She even poured me a glass filled with ice cubes and her famous sweet tea. But the children were drinking water because we tried to minimize the amount of caffeine that they drank so if they had sweet tea at lunch then they had to drink water at the next meal.

Shelley told me that earlier that week one afternoon Nathan had been choking on an ice cube when they were on their back porch. Mike threw Nathan against the railing of their porch so that his abdomen hit the railing and the ice cube came popping out. I read that this is a technique that people could use if they are alone and are choking – they could try to throw their abdomen against the edge of a railing or table to try to dislodge the item in their throat.

The Heimlich maneuver for choking was invented by an American Jewish Thoracic surgeon named Henry J. Heimlich who was born in 1920 in Wilmington, Delaware. The Heimlich maneuver has also been used on animals, such as a dog who choked on a tennis ball.

CPR, or Cardio-Pulmonary Resuscitation to save a human life was also a great invention. CPR was invented by Austrian Surgeon Peter Safar who was born in 1924.

LifeVac invented by Arthur Lih in 2014 is a non-power portable suction device developed for clearing the obstruction from an upper airway in a choking victim.

Being a parent, I have also appreciated the zinc oxide diaper rash ointments and sun protectant lotion that were invented by geniuses.

You could spend a lot of time thinking about all the inventions that changed humanity – creating fire, the wheel, tools like knives and hammers, boats, glass, mattresses, eating utensils, water wells, water wheels on rivers that were set up as mills to grind corn and wheat into flour, antibiotics, bicycles, carts with wheels, cars and airplanes, electricity, phonograph to record voices, telephone, television, refrigeration and freezers, indoor plumbing and kitchens, boxed cereals and cake mixes, electric washing machines and dryers, frozen dinners, air conditioning and heating, microwave ovens, Velcro, lava lamps, computers and cell phones, submarines, space rockets, and much more.

At our house one evening Ben and I were playing a board game with the kids and Will was being difficult, giggly, and hiding a game piece. I was at wit's end and couldn't get him to cooperate. I went to the telephone and called Shelley and asked her what I should do. I figured that she spent so much time with Will that she would know how to reason with him. She told me to tell him that he had one more chance or he had to go to timeout for ten minutes and sit in a chair. I hung up the phone and said to Will: "Shelley said you have one more chance." Maybe it was a peer pressure thing from being with all of the daycare kids at Shelley's or maybe he had been put in the ten-minute timeout chair, because he fully cooperated and gave us the game piece. It was funny. Will asked us, "Shelley said she is the head boss at her house. Who is the head boss at our house?" Ben and I laughed and I said, "Both of us are head bosses, but just be a good boy and there won't be any trouble from us."

I started telling my kids that the tickle monster would get them if they did not do what we asked and we did have several tickling sessions.

I tried to negotiate with my kids if they had a request or refused to cooperate; I didn't always have to win. Our life was also our kids' life. For example, if they asked for five more minutes to play in the bathtub, I would let them have a few more minutes to play in the bathtub if we had time. But if it was late, I would say 'No, not tonight because it is late.' I tried to be a good parent but I was learning at the same time. I tried to be like a mother duck to my little ducklings. I am not perfect, though. I remembered one night when Lee was almost a year old and Ben was out of town, Lee started crying the middle of the night and I tried for an hour or more to comfort him; it was 4am and I had to go to work the next day so I finally put him into his crib and he cried himself to sleep after 20 minutes. The next afternoon, I took some leave time and left early from work and to take Lee to the pediatrician, who said that Lee had an ear infection. I felt so bad. From then on, if the kids kept crying in the middle of the night, I would take them to the children's hospital emergency room. I didn't know to take them to the emergency room in the middle of the night for an ear infection until the pediatrician told me to do it. I knew that if a baby had a very high fever to take them to the emergency room in the middle of the night. But some say that a fever is the body's natural way of fighting an infection and some experienced parents or individuals will give a fever a day or two before going to the doctor to see if the body will heal itself on its own. Each individual and family becomes familiar with what is normal or not normal for them.

We learned that if we had a sore throat, we could gargle with lightly salted warm water before we went to bed and many times it cleared up our sore throats.

One time I was grocery shopping with my two youngest kids and the kids used to love to sit inside the shopping cart while we were grocery shopping, so I let them if we were only buying a few items. My daughter Valerie suddenly stood up in the shopping cart and fell out and landed on her head. Thank goodness she was not hurt. I felt so bad. This was before someone invented the shopping carts that have a little cab in the front for the kids to sit in and pretend that they are driving; I would like to thank the person or persons who invented those nice shopping carts for kids to ride in! The diaper-changing stations in public bathrooms became popular around the same time and they were a phenomenal invention also so I would like to thank those inventors also.

When we were in the mini-van driving, I started giving the kids the option of listening to the radio or music cassettes or sometimes I would ask: 'Do you want to listen to the radio or just have peace and quiet?' And they would make choices. Sometimes we would listen to a song or two and then have peace and quiet. We would talk about what songs we each liked. We would talk about a variety of different things. It was interesting to learn their moods and their interests. I realized that our life wasn't just about me; it was about all of us.

I want to read the book written by a First Lady of the United States, Hillary Rodham Clinton, entitled <u>It Takes A Village: And Other Lessons Children Teach Us</u> published in 1996.

One night I was late coming home from work so Ben handled picking up the kids and cooking dinner. I snapped at him because he didn't start the laundry, too. Ben just looked at me and didn't say anything back but he looked flustered and hurt. I had hurt his feelings. I felt awful – my husband was a wonderful helper and I was being too snappy, like a snapping turtle. I would snap and have an ugly expression on my face; I'm sure this was not appealing to him. Once you say something, you cannot take it back. I would try to do better. I didn't want to be a wild stallion; I wanted to be sitting on a branch like a wise owl. I needed to tame myself, which I have heard is that I need to use my left brain more because the emotions of my right brain are dominating. I must have some dragon genes in my human Animalia chromosomes. Or it could be my female hormones; I read that the changes caused by the female hormones each month greatly affect how a woman feels emotionally and physically. I am doing the best I can, considering everything that I have lived through in my life and considering the things that I am dealing with in the present.

I had read somewhere that for every time you think a bad thing, you are supposed to think a good thing. For example, if you find a bad quality in someone or yourself, then you are supposed to find a good quality in someone or yourself. Or if you get discouraged, think of something encouraging. This is supposed to 'keep it real'.

I made a promise to myself that I would quit being so fast to criticize another person; people try so hard to do good things and then they are brought down in one second by someone saying mean things to them. I would try in the future to appreciate people more and think before I spoke. I felt so awful for saying mean things to people for no reason; maybe too much caffeine, stress, hormones, and too little sleep are making me snappy. Someone said Satan is the cause of all evils but I shudder to think that I would let Satan take over my thoughts and actions. My sister told me to say "Satan, be gone!" whenever I felt agitated but I'm not sure crankiness is caused by Satan. One thing for sure: I am an exhausted parent. Plus, sometimes we are getting late fees on our credit cards which is stressful. One time I slammed my fist on our kitchen table because I was so mad at the huge late fees charged by credit card companies. Then I realized how stupid I was, because if I had broken my wrist, it would have made things WORSE!

Sometimes I have said stupid things which have bothered me for a long time. Sometimes I have felt like I have said too much or too little which has also bothered me. I shouldn't let things bother me so much. I need to learn to focus on good things and progress to move forward. I know a person cannot forget about experiences that they have actually lived through but they have no choice but to move those feelings aside in order to focus and achieve tasks that need to be done in order to make progress and move forward in time. If you think about this in the great scheme of things and in the great timeline of eternity, this is how human beings have made progress throughout the past millenniums, centuries, decades, years, weeks, days, and hours. Sometimes things are so confusing or baffling that you cannot emotionally handle but one thing at a time or take life a few minutes at a time but then hopefully things will seem better or actually get better and then you can emotionally handle more things together. There have been times when I have been so frazzled that I picked up the phone and called family and friends to talk things out to help clear my mind.

Ben said something to me that made a major impact on my life; he said for me to stop being a perfectionist unless it was something where absolute perfection was required. Brain surgery and some engineering or manufacturing may require perfection, but it does not matter if the French bread grilled a little darker than we usually grilled it. Ben said I was driving him crazy when I agonized that my cooking was not perfect all of the time. Ben liked to cook also and sometimes he overcooked the hash browns on a weekend morning but he said that he wasn't even going to agonize over it because it did not matter. That is one thing I loved about Ben, that he could be easy-going. But I still think that I was more concerned about our financial situation and the attempted kidnapping of our child than he was. Ben said to forget about the attempted kidnapping but I could not forget about it.

I was just trying to be the best person I could be, living the life that I had, and trying to make things the best I could. Nobody is perfect, I was not perfect, but I felt bad about the bad things. I wanted to have a good balanced life but my life had too much stress and I was overtired. I believe in God but why is life so stressful and does God plan our lives?

My parents brought me and my siblings to church many Sundays of our lives. I remember sitting through many long sermons which made the church service longer than one hour. When the service was too long, as a kid I would sit there and look at the back of the heads and shoulders of every person sitting in front of me in the pews of the church, looking at their hair, hats and clothing, and wondering about who they were and what their lives were like and if they would go to heaven or hell; I thought that the people here had come and brought themselves 'before God' at the church, displaying their best and trying to open their minds and hearts to God.

Sometimes priests and nuns would come to our house for lunch or dinner. One time when I was about 8, I remember we had a dinner party and a priest was dancing among other guests in our living room. So I learned as a child that priests and nuns can dance, too. I learned that the Catholic Church allows deacons who are married with families to serve in the church.

When I was an adolescent, I was invited to a movie theatre with a school friend to see a Christian movie. After the movie, a Baptist preacher walked up on the stage at the movie theatre inviting anyone in the audience who wanted to be saved to go down to the front of the theatre. So, I went down to the front of the theatre with my friend and we were declared 'saved.' My parents and school teachers had always taught good values and I was glad to have been 'saved' also. But I had already been 'saved' in the Catholic Church when I had been christened as an infant and dedicated to the Lord and when I received my First Holy Communion at age 8 when I was 'dedicated to follow Jesus' so now I had been double-saved. So, I tried to be good and not have any sins on my soul. Now, when I yell or say something mean, I feel so bad and guilty that it takes me a long time to accept my sins of imperfection. I read that all humans make mistakes, and no one is perfect so we can consider many of our actions to be mistakes rather than sins, so it should make us feel better. In my life, sometimes I have felt so bad saying something that I later felt was inappropriate that I have driven a few people crazy by apologizing too much. If you want to save yourself some stress, do not get angry about things that aren't worth getting angry about.

I think about the Caucasian lady that was in our garage and tried to kidnap Valerie. How could a human being be so cruel to our family and to our child? God intended for the baby to be a part of our family, not for the kidnapper. The kidnapper was not a person of God; they were filled with Satan.

You have to watch the kids every minute out in public or in the privacy of home. You must watch your children out in public so they do not get abducted, bitten by spiders, hit by baseballs, harmed by coyotes, pythons, alligators, or snapping turtles near lakes, or a million other things. Toddlers have been known to unroll entire rolls of toilet paper streaming them down hallways and to write on walls with crayons. Once when we were unloading groceries, when Will was a toddler, I think he took a brand new tube of toothpaste still in the box and put it in the trashcan because I remember he was holding the toothpaste and I happened to find it later on in the trashcan.

I realized how tired I was being a working mother, getting up at 5:30am each day and going until midnight most nights. So, because I have a sleep deficit, I need to be aware of my thoughts and actions. On weekends, often Ben and I will take turns getting up with the kids and let the other have a few extra hours of sleep.

I admit that Ben handles fatigue and stress better than me; he shrugs many things off and says 'There will be more time in few years when the kids get older to do what we want to do but right now let's just focus on the kids.'

All was fine except bills were piling up. We weren't big spenders but we probably could have been thriftier in some things. Looking back, we definitely spent too much money on toys and birthday parties. We had big birthday parties for each kid for every birthday and we loved taking photographs and we had lots of pictures. We wanted to preserve the fun memories.

I was very concerned that we were spending too much money, though, and one time Ben and I had an argument because he bought the kids a lot of toys during a month when there were no birthdays; he should not have spent that money. I thought he spoiled the kids too much; I was told 'No' sometimes by my parents so sometimes I told my kids 'No'. But I tried to be nice to my kids and reason with them and explain things to them. Like when we were shopping and they wanted something, many times I would say 'We cannot buy everything you want all of the time because we don't need it and we should save some money." One of my girlfriends said that you should never tell a child about having to pay bills or it will cause a child stress but I disagree; I think you can talk briefly about money with a child occasionally so they will know about it. Sometimes when I was young I heard my parents talking about saving money and I don't think it hurt me. But I think my girlfriend did have a valid point in that a parent should not stress their child out all of the time with adult topics.

A few months after Will was born, I realized that I had gained 30lbs. of fat which was totally unacceptable to me. I went on a strict diet for 2 months; I did not deviate from it and I lost the weight. I would eat breakfast and lunch but only a few bites for dinner and I would enjoy a cup of hot tea later in the evening.

Once or twice a week I would leave Ben eating at the table with the kids and I went to our bedroom, where I used the time to clean out my closet, my dresser drawers, my makeup drawer, or sleep for thirty minutes. I discovered that I had accumulated 14 pairs of sunglasses over a 15-year timeframe; I had a sunglass collection and didn't even know that I had had one. Ben knew that I was trying to not eat so much at night and he said he would be glad to make sure the kids ate some dinner so I could focus on getting the weight off. Sometimes I went for a walk or a ten-minute jog. I would also use the time to clean the bathrooms or clean out the children's closets, dresser drawers, the toy closets, the books on the kids' bookshelves, etc. I stayed focused and luckily, I was able to lose the weight.

Having a child is hard on a woman's body. It is freaky to see the stretch marks on your abdomen, but then I would think about how lucky I was to be a female and have the experience of bringing a human life into the world. Some women's bodies bounce back to their normal size quickly but I had to work harder. My eyesight changed during all of my pregnancies and the optometrist said changing hormones could affect eyesight and the changes were probably just temporary. One time when I drove into the garage, I hit the toy box and one of the sharp edges bashed a hole into the sheetrock of the garage. Ben was upset. It could have been a change in my depth perception but it could have been just plain fatigue! It took a few years for my eyes to adjust. My feet went up 1/2 size after my pregnancies. My hips expanded an inch after my pregnancies and never went back. These facts bothered me out at first, but when I thought about my children and how happy we were that they were here, it didn't matter. Husbands should be nice to their wives after they give birth because the changes to their bodies can take time to adjust to. Also, Ben was mean saying that I was crazy because I had driven into the sheetrock and he never apologized which I considered to be a sin on his soul. The Catholic Church ranked sins –

some sins were mortal sins but some sins were less serious. My opinion is that God ranks the sins but I do agree with most people that murder, theft, deception, and kidnapping are heinous crimes.

Ben's sister had a good idea about saving money on toys. She said when her kids lost interest in a toy she put it away in a closet. Then, she wrapped it up and gave it to her kids again a few years later. You can get away with this while the kids are still young; older kids might be able to recognize old toys. Is this a sinful tactic?

Ben and I had our children baptized at a local Christian church that we were attending. I had heard people say that humans are born with original sin because of Adam and Eve, but I refused to believe that. In fact, I never believed that. I believe that all children are born beautiful and innocent. My kids were born sinless.

Ben and I taught Sunday school for 2 years at the church we attended. Our youngest son, Will, was in our class. The church was very nice to have the curriculum ordered from a Christian education resource provider, so all we had to do was pick up the handouts from the church education office in addition to bringing juice and a snack for the children. The topic of one class was Noah and the flood; one of the 4-year olds asked Ben if Noah had a jet-ski and Ben laughed and said "No, Noah lived about 3,000 years ago and there were no jet skis." Children can make precious delightful comments.

Once at Sunday school, I was pouring juice into the plastic cups for the kids and I got distracted by something and over-filled a cup, the juice pouring onto the counter. At this exact moment, the Sunday school supervisor, Fran Whitter, happened to be standing in the doorway waiting to pick up the attendance sheet. She frowned as she saw me pouring the juice on the counter. I was just overtired and was quite embarrassed for her to have seen the little fiasco.

That winter it snowed, and Ben and I and our 3 children were warm and snug inside of our home. At one point we were all standing by the tall back windows looking over the snowy backyard, enjoying a fire in the fireplace. We had made hot chocolate in colorful mugs covered with images of snowmen, penguins, and polar bears. Our daughter, Valerie, ran to some windows that looked over the front yard and exclaimed gleefully: "Look, y'all, it's snowing in the front yard, too!" We laughed at the wisdom of our 5-year old. Lee rolled his eyes and teased his little sister.

In the spring, I planted sunflowers in a sunny spot beside the front walk and was astonished to see them grow to be 5 feet tall! I did not know that sunflowers could grow to be so tall. The kids called them 'silly big.'

On weekends sometimes one of my girlfriends or one of Ben's college buddies would come visit for an afternoon or spend the night. One of my friends was very energetic the weekend she came and she offered to vacuum my house and fold the laundry while I was cleaning the kitchen, which was very nice of her!

Sometimes when I put the kids to bed at night, I would ask them how they wanted to be woken up for school, as my father had sometimes asked me and my siblings when we were young. "Do you want me to gently nudge your arm and say your name, do you want me to turn the light on and off, do you want me to shake your bed, do you want me to moo like a Cow, or do you want me to turn on the music?" The kids laughed a lot about this question and we had many funny moments. They would often climb into bed with us on weekends to wake us up.

Raising children with both parents working was especially tiring but we worked hard to get as much done as we could. We were basically happy and our children seemed to be happy.

Several times Ben saw my fatigue or stress expressed in a bad way when I would curse hardships, but in front of the kids I always tried to be happy and parent-appropriate. Ben handled stress in a different way from me; he would start smoothing down the back of his hair when he got uneasy feelings or he would just quit talking for a while. This year he suddenly grew a beard for several months and then shaved it off; I wondered if he was having an affair because he kept putting me off when I wanted to be with him. I asked him but he didn't respond; he just looked out the kitchen window.

Also, he was working late a lot of nights.

CHAPTER 13

1993   *Spooky Feelings*

I noticed a strange man on our floor at work walking down the hallway past my cubicle and my co-worker Greta's cubicle. She said that she didn't know the man either. The next day my boss told me that he was moving me and Greta to different cubicles but he didn't give a reason; he also took down from our cubicle walls our name tags that identified our cubicles and said it was because we were getting new ones soon. I wondered if something was going on.

The next day, I noticed that my binder with my work calendar was missing from my office. It had also contained many notes, associate names, and telephone numbers from various corporate meetings that I had attended. I told my boss that my scheduler binder was missing and also asked him "Is there something weird going on?" My boss just looked at me and said "Nothing weird is going on that I know of. If you didn't misplace your binder, it could've been stolen." I almost fainted.

I was getting a little stressed regarding the incident 4 years earlier when the woman tried to kidnap Valerie out of the mini-van in the garage. It was unexpected and still puzzled and bothered me. Now there was a strange man walking down the hallway at work and Greta and I were moved to different cubicles. I was experiencing anxiety alongside my happiness. Sometimes my anxiety would cause me to pick at my fingernails, which I did not like.

I read an article where an author said that a little bit of stress can be good for you, supposedly because if you are too complacent all the time, then some things may never be strived for, changed, or achieved. The article also said that if a person sticks to the facts of a situation, it can help to control anxiety and stress because facts are things that are real and not imagined. But I feel like the stress that I have had to deal with in my life, such as being financially poor or lacking, living paycheck to paycheck with limited options, and now having to deal with the fact that an unknown woman almost kidnapped my baby has been too much and overwhelming.

Sometimes at home in the evening we would get some telemarketing phone calls on our home landline asking if we would participate in brief surveys giving our opinions about political candidates, if we wanted to subscribe to season tickets for the orchestra, ballet or sports leagues, do we need insurance or a realtor, or did we buy certain products. If I wasn't busy I would take time to answer some of the questions. But one night a woman wanted to know the ages of the adults and children in the house. Remembering the attempted kidnapping of my child, I just told the telemarketer that all of the children in the house were grown and had moved out. Sometimes you just should not give out personal information to people that you do not know.

CHAPTER 14

1993   *An argument*

Ben worked on a project for his job that required him to travel a lot for 2 years. One night when Ben was expected to return from a trip out of town, I ate a good dinner with the kids, bathed them, read them books, kissed them and tucked them into bed, left the little night light on in the hallway, checked the laundry, checked the kids' school backpacks to get them organized for the next day, and then I decided to do something I had not done in ten years – smoke a few puffs of a cigarette. Earlier that day, I had bummed one cigarette from Shelley, who was a light smoker but was considering stopping. I've smoked a few cigarettes in my lifetime, but on rare occasions; sometimes I just like a few puffs. I am the same way with alcohol and rarely drink. I've heard that smoking cigarettes causes lung and throat cancer and drinking alcohol causes liver damage and kills brain cells, so that is why I have never been a heavy smoker or a heavy drinker. But I have been stressing lately and just wanted a few puffs of a cigarette. Sometimes I chew sugarless gum to relieve stress, but sometimes I chew it after eating because it is supposed to be healthy for your teeth and gums to chew gum for a few minutes.

I was sitting on the back deck of the house puffing the cigarette when Ben opened the back door, arriving home from his business trip.

"Welcome home," I smiled, because home was a safe haven to us and we loved our home and family life.

His response was that he got angry and said: "Why are you smoking? Put it out. I hope the kids didn't see it. This is so bad."

I was startled by his attitude. "The kids are sleeping. I just felt like smoking a few puffs. Why are you so mad about it? God, I am a 34-year old woman," I asked.

Ben said "You are crazy" and went inside the house.

I wondered what was going on inside his head; he has been very distant to me for the past year. I guess I've been distant to him also. Actually, we are just very busy being working parents and raising kids and I think we have neglected our husband-wife relationship.

A few minutes later I went into the house, turned off the recessed lighting over the stove, made sure all the doors and windows were locked, and went upstairs to our bedroom. Ben was just getting under the sheets, his luggage lying near his dresser waiting to be unpacked the next morning.

I brushed my teeth, pulled my hair back in a headband and rinsed my face with warm water and patted my face dry with a hand towel, took my headband off and brushed my hair, and changed from my clothes into a nightgown.

Then I wandered down the hallway to check on all three kids; Lee, Valerie and her favorite stuffed puppy that was a hand-me-down from Lee, and Will and his stuffed bear were all sound asleep in their beds. Will's bed still had guard rails to make sure he didn't fall off.

I went back to our bedroom and got into the bed next to Ben, saying "Are you awake?"

"What do you want?" Ben replied.

"Listen, I don't know why you are so mad. You know good and damn well that this is the first time that you have ever seen me smoke a cigarette and you know it, and we've been together for 15 years now. Ben, you are not the one who is the victim of a setup by a mafia or whoever it is who tried to kidnap our baby. I cannot believe Valerie was almost kidnapped. You know good and well that if Valerie had disappeared, then I would have been the prime suspect. Ben, something is *very* wrong. Today at work I could not find my calendar binder in my office – I think someone stole it from my cubicle."

"Well, right this second, we are all fine," said Ben. "Please don't become a smoker. I don't want you to become a smoker because it is a disgusting habit. And I'm sure you just lost your calendar."

"Ben, I am not going to become a regular smoker. I only smoke about one cigarette every 5 years or so. But I just felt like puffing a few puffs so it is no big deal."

We were both quiet for a minute and then I said to Ben, "Ben, Jesus said a person is supposed to forgive another person 7 x 70 times, so you are supposed to forgive me 490 times." I had been taking a few notes of the Bible and read this in Matthew 18: 21-22.

Ben just sighed and turned his back to me. I felt like he was angry, not amused. I was just trying to make my case.

"What's been going on with the kids for the past few days?" he asked.

I told him about the kids' schoolwork. I told him I found the electric bill that Will had taken off of the kitchen table and had hidden from us. The kids like to help get the mail out of the mailbox sometimes and one day I had lifted Will up so he could take the envelopes out of the mailbox and he carried it into the house and placed it on the kitchen table. But then he took one of the envelopes and ran off with it, laughing. I chased him but then the land-line phone rang and I got distracted and forgot about the envelope that he had taken. I told Ben about it but we had forgotten to look for it. Then I remembered a few days later and I found it behind the couch in the living room and put it neatly in the stack of bills on the top of Ben's dresser, where we kept the stack of bills that needed to be paid.

Of course, the kids would be thrilled to see that Ben was back home when they awoke the next morning; Ben was like a big cuddly teddy bear to them. The kids were often cuddled with Ben at night in the huge lounge chair or on the couch while they watched a TV show or two. I was usually doing the dishes or other cleaning, but sometimes we switched and I relaxed with the kids while Ben did the dishes. But ever since the attempted kidnapping, I usually did the dishes because I had so much nervous energy that it was hard for me to relax; I kept wondering what evil person had almost kidnapped Valerie. I was also bothered that both Greta and I had been moved to different cubicles; did it have to do with the strange man walking around the floor at work? What was going on? Maybe nothing was going on but I felt like some weird things were happening.

"Ben, you need to *repent* from hating me and forgive me right now," Candi said half-jokingly to her husband lying next to her, "because you know that I am a good person in a strange situation." But Ben was sound asleep and Candi only heard a soft snore returned. She thought about a time when she and Ben were dating when they were ages 19 and 21 and went to the beach for a few days with his brother and his girlfriend. While his brother was driving the car, she and Ben were cuddled in the back seat of the car; they kissed and cuddled for 5 straight hours during the drive! They often laughed about that memory!

As tired as I was that night, it took me awhile to fall asleep because I was so uneasy about the spooky things.

As a matter of fact, I had a lot of nights where I could not sleep and one time I actually went for a drive to try to relax and one time I paced the floor for several hours, wondering who had tried to kidnap Valerie.

Sometimes I have thought of answers that I needed when I was in the shower, driving, jogging, or sitting on the pot.

However, there were no answers about the lady in my garage that had almost abducted my child.

CHAPTER 15

1993   *Thoughts*

Through media like newspapers, magazines, and radio, I read or heard about hypothetical situations that invoke a person's thought processes, such as:

If you had to spend $20,000 a day,
how would you spend it?

If it was your last day on earth,
what would you do?

If you could choose your time and circumstances
of death, what would they be?

If you could travel backwards or forward in time,
what century would you visit?

If you were offered the opportunity to go to Mars
would you go?

Do you think other life exists in the universe?

What are humans going to do if a big asteroid
is heading towards earth; could we destroy it?

Why don't humans need their appendixes
anymore?

If you see your best friend's mate cheating on them,
should you tell them or not?

Can live humans communicate with the spiritual realm?

What is your dream job?

If you could be invisible for a while and then reappear, would you do it?

All of these questions would interest me and help me to keep a perspective on my life.

It is my opinion that if astronauts take animals and plants to Mars to start a new human colony, I hope they do not bring certain snakes, spiders, scorpions, rats, bats, alligators or poisonous plants like poison ivy, or plants that eat animals like Venus fly trap, pitcher plant, or sundews. I hope God of the Universe forgives me for stating this.

CHAPTER 16

1993   *A snake crawled under our door*

I pulled into the driveway after work with all 3 kids in the mini-van on a summer evening. I had picked them all up from a local summer school. Shelley was not babysitting our kids this summer because she wanted some time off and there was a local day school nearby and my children enjoyed it. My niece had watched the kids the summer before but she had been invited to Europe this year to work at an internship in England.

Our family schedule at the time was that I picked the kids up and was the first one home, with Ben usually arriving home within ten minutes of our arrival. But when school started, the schedule would be for Ben to pick up Lee and then I would pick up Valerie and Will from Shelley's house. It sounds confusing but we work it out and our household and life run quite smoothly. I would say that we are a happy family and laugh a lot.

Sometimes I drink too much caffeine to keep going; I drink coffee in the morning but then I have coffee or a cola in the afternoon around 4pm. On the weekends, if I skip the caffeine in the afternoon, I get headaches and nausea. It took me awhile to realize that I was abusing caffeine and that it was not good for me. I said to myself: I will try to do better and improve myself. They say the most important thing is to realize there is a problem, 'pinpoint and define the problem', and then make plans to correct a problem, then actually 'do the work and correct the problem', and then progress will be made. I want to be good person and go to heaven in the afterlife, so I am trying to be a good person. By heaven, I mean maybe there will not be 'streets of gold' like described in the King James Bible Book of Revelation 21: 18 but our spirits and the spirits of my mother and father and all departed souls will be with God. No one knows for sure what is beyond our lives on earth.

An orthopedic doctor ordered me to have an MRI after I went to see him for neck pain. He said I have a bulging disk and he scheduled physical therapy with a neck therapist who guided me with exercises that were supposed to strengthen my neck muscles. The doctor said that carrying babies around on my hips and carrying heavy diaper bags on my shoulder for the past ten years might have something to do with it. Also, driving in the car, having to keep looking over your shoulders to make sure no cars are in your blind spots may have contributed to the problem. I do use my side mirrors to see what cars are driving beside me but I drive on interstates that have 3 lanes going the same way, so I need to glance over my shoulder to see what I'm dealing with. I also went to see a chiropractor who took an x-ray of my spine and he scheduled me for several spinal adjustments. Ben also had back pain from an old injury.

Almost ten years later, when the kids were older, I still had a mild pain in my shoulder blade that ricocheted straight through my torso into my breast. Someone suggested a back-massage therapist, so I scheduled an appointment with a massage therapist. She had powerfully strong hands and she worked my back over good. She told me that my pain was the result of a pinched nerve and my back might be sore for a day or so. The result was that the massage therapist cured my back pain that I had had for ten years; I was so happy to have that little nagging ache gone. She said even infants could possibly have pinched nerves and that may be why some infants cry all the time.

On that evening when I pulled into the driveway and pushed the button on the remote controller inside the mini-van to open the garage door, I saw a snake crawling under the door to go into our house. 'Did I just see that?' I asked myself. "Kids, we are going to stay outside on the driveway and play for a few minutes until Dad gets here." I said, praying that Ben would be on time. He is usually very punctual. And then I was so grateful when he pulled into the driveway a moment later. I quietly told him what I had seen. He said "Let's not keep the garage door raised anymore for the cat to go in and out anymore." He grabbed a shovel, went into the house, and found a green garden snake under our washing machine. The kids never knew about it because luckily, I found a bottle of play bubbles in the garage so we stayed out in the yard making soap bubbles with the wand. Ben took the snake out to the furthest edge of the yard and put it over the fence.

It was very traumatic for me to forget about a snake in my house; I kept on thinking what would have happened if I had not seen it crawl under the door. When would it have been discovered? The thought would send chills up my spine. I was having spooky feelings about the house. I had some mild panic attacks but Ben was not very supportive emotionally. He began pulling away from me. Looking back, I think I did dwell too much on it and was probably getting on Ben's nerves. But in front of the kids, I tried to be happy and a good mother.

In the back of my mind, I was still wondering about the woman who had tried to kidnap my daughter; this incident would be a missing puzzle piece in the puzzle of my life forever. I also thought I recognized that a car might be following me home from the train station on different days and I told this to Ben. I told Ben that maybe we should move to a different house but he said I was crazy for wanting to move. We had an argument and Ben punched me on the arm but I let it go; we had been together for fifteen years and this was the first physical strike ever from either one of us. I considered and wondered that whoever had tried to kidnap Valerie might now be turning Ben away from me or maybe Ben didn't love me anymore.

That night I was crying in my bedroom from all of my confusion and anxiety and my daughter Valerie had gotten out of her bed and walked into our bedroom. I didn't want her to see me crying but I told her that I was fine. I hugged her for a minute and put her back into her bed saying, "Go back to sleep, Doodle Bug," She is a sweet little girl.

CHAPTER 17

1993   *Good Values*

   All of my children are precious to me and I am thankful that I am a mother. Having kids and being a parent changed the way that I looked at the world.

   Kids are totally innocent. I feel that it is my duty to teach my children good things and keep them safe from harm. I hope when they grow up that they will have happiness and good lives.

   I thought about my own childhood. I am so lucky that I had good parents who never abused me, never taught me to be a racist, a hater, a killer, a thief, or a jealous person. Wouldn't it be great if everyone on earth could have a nice life? My parents taught me to share my toys with my brothers and sisters, help with household chores, listen to my teachers at school, be respectful, do my schoolwork, try hard, stay out of trouble, ask an adult for help if I needed help, be nice to our cat and dog and do not hurt them, and to pray. When I was very young, I was taught to not put dirt in my mouth, to not go far from home, to stay away from strangers, and to not break another child's toy. I was also taught to not pick up dead animals because once I brought home a dead lizard that I saw laying by the side of the road when I was a young child walking home from the school bus.

   When I was a young child 35 years ago, it was a different world in the United States, many children played about their neighborhoods, running from yard to yard and house to house with other kids, often barefooted, and we would play outside for hours. My father would step out onto our front or back porch and whistle through his fingers; three whistles was our signal to come home for dinner or bedtime, and I could hear him from the next street when I was playing in my girlfriend's yard. He had a loud whistle and it was his own, not a metal whistle. If we didn't hear the whistle, of course my parents would call on the landline telephone to our friend's house and he would ask to send us home. Or other parents would call our house to send their kids home for dinner. Sometimes a child would be invited to have dinner with their friend at their house. Nowadays it is not safe to let your kids play by themselves around the neighborhood because there are evil kidnappers, drug dealers, and sex offenders lurking around. Parents should always know where their children are. Even if you have a backyard and the kids are playing near your house, you should still watch them carefully.

My parents fed us excellent meals and they were both good cooks. My father's specialty that he loved to cook was split-pea with ham soup. My mother's specialty was stuffed cabbage leaves that were stuffed with ground beef, rice, onions. She added a can of tomatoes and some sauerkraut. They were boiled in a pot and then simmered. Later, she skimmed off the fat from the top of the broth. The dish was an ethnic Slavic dish. She cooked the family a variety of meals including baked chicken or pot roast, sirloin steak, collards, mashed potatoes, fried potatoes with onions and paprika, baked potatoes, cooked carrots, boiled beets served hot or cold, broccoli, Brussels sprouts, lima beans, navy beans, macaroni and cheese, homemade chicken soup, bread and butter, pineapple upside-down cake, canned Chinese foods because our family was often on a food budget and the canned Chinese food was cheaper than Chinese delivery, salads, corned beef hash, tuna casseroles, sandwiches of all kinds even peanut butter and jelly, turkey and stuffing for Thanksgiving and Christmas, open-faced turkey sandwiches with brown gravy on white bread made from leftovers, a leg of lamb at Easter with scalloped potatoes, green beans, cucumbers seasoned with corn oil or olive oil, apple-cider vinegar and salt and pepper. My mom had canned sardines for herself, which was a little snack that she loved, but we kids would not eat them. For snacks to eat, she let us have popcorn, chips, fruits like apples, oranges, and grapes, and cottage cheese in a little bowl dolloped with sour cream. In the summer, we usually made homemade ice cream once or twice, and ate a sliced huge watermelon, usually on the back patio outside our home and we were allowed to invite friends over to share. I also remember our mom and dad spraying citronella around our legs so the mosquitoes would not bite us. Usually there would be fireflies zipping around the back yard and we had so much fun chasing them and catching them in glass jars with holes poked into the lids so the fireflies could have air to breathe.

Our mom was very nice to us; when she made grilled cheese sandwiches, she made some with grilled tomatoes and oregano on top and some with just plain cheese so we could choose. However, sometimes she would just make dinner like she wanted to cook it and if we did not want to eat a certain food, she would tell us to try a bite of something new to taste it and try not to complain about food because there are many starving people in the world. She couldn't cater to our individual tastes all the time.

Looking back, I also realize how good my parents were by fixing us a good breakfast before we went to school. They let us eat the boxed cereals with milk and sometimes they would slice fresh bananas or strawberries over the top of the cereal. We liked Cheerios, Apple Cinnamon Cheerios, Rice Krispies, Chex, Shredded Wheat, Sugar Pops, Alphabets, Captain Krunch, Fruit Loops and many others. Many cereals were fortified with vitamins and minerals. Frosted Mini Wheats were invented in 1969. Sometimes my mom would make us soft-boiled, hard-boiled, or scrambled eggs with bacon or sausage with buttered toast or a bowl of hot oatmeal and juice like orange, apple, or tomato. On weekends, we were allowed to have the sweeter toaster pastries like Pop Tarts. My dad loved fried egg sandwiches. My mom's family were big hot tea drinkers, so my mom often made hot tea for us children. We added a little milk and sugar to the hot tea so that is a tradition that I carried in my heart with me all my life. I do drink plain tea sometimes, but some traditions are somewhat hard to break. I also drink southern-style sweet iced tea with a lemon or peach flavoring but I prefer it to be decaffeinated. I also learned that grits is a food of the south because my parents said there were no grits in New York, that they grew up eating Farina.

CHAPTER 18

1993   *Crying Spells*

Candi did not know that Corporate Security spies had been spying on her home from computer screens in their offices; fiber optics and IP addresses (Internet Protocol addresses) is the technology that made it possible and was in the wiring of their new home. Candi was quite naive in her mind. Candi might have considered that someone had been spying on she and Ben, but didn't take it seriously because she thought spying on people in their homes was so evil that she honestly thought good humans would not do that.

Once she told Ben that she would only have sex under the sheets or if they got a canopy bed with a curtain that went all around the bed, because they could be giving a live-sex show to someone who might be watching them, even from halfway around the world on the internet. She had read in a computer journal that the internet was an upcoming public technology, but Ben said she was crazy. Once she suggested that they have a rendezvous in their bedroom closet.

"You need to shut up about what you are thinking," Ben told Candi.

"I will never shut up because someone tried to kidnap our daughter and they obviously set me up to be the suspect. I am a victim of a conspiracy, Ben. If they wanted to, they could have shot me dead with a gun and then kidnapped the baby, but they didn't. They wanted to leave me as the suspect. Maybe there is already a dead baby buried in the backyard of our home?" Candi replied back.

"Candi, you need help," Ben said to me.

One time I was home and busy cleaning up the kitchen and family room and had started a load of wash but forgot to put the clothes in. Ben just happened to be walking through the laundry room when I was standing there, crying and staring at the empty washing machine.

"What is wrong now?" Ben asked me, looking annoyed.

"I wasted a whole washing machine full of water and suds because I forgot to put the clothes in. And I wasted 20 minutes." I was so tired; I was crying.

Ben just looked at me and walked away.

I stood there and cried for another minute. Then I put in another load of laundry.

Candi almost started panicking at the thought that someone could be spying on her and her family in the privacy of their own home. For what reason would they be spying on her family? Candi went to the kitchen, opened a kitchen cabinet door, and reached high up on the shelf for a bottle of whiskey that had been opened a few months before. Candi and Ben rarely drank but Candi just wanted a spoonful of whiskey to calm her nerves. After she drank the spoonful of whiskey, the land-line telephone rang.

"Hello?" Candi asked.

"Hello, this is Mr. Whiskey asking parents to not drive when drinking," the male voice said. And then the line hung up, a prank phone call.

A chill went down Candi's spine. The phone call that had just occurred could not have been a coincidence. Someone had to have been watching her in her own kitchen; maybe or maybe not. Maybe they should invest in one of those caller display gadgets and not answer the phone unless it was a recognized telephone number. But, even telephone numbers on a caller display can be faked by computer hackers.

Candi and Ben found out years later that there are companies that offer homeowners services to come out to your house to search for hidden cameras and microphones and check to see the type of wiring used in the house. There are also companies that will come to your house to check for dangerous radon gas and carbon monoxide gases that are both odorless. EMF experts can come to your home to check for concentrations of electromagnetic waves that may induce you to move or rearrange furniture. In some cases, entire small neighborhoods have been torn down because of concentrations of EMF waves, dangerous gases, or buried toxins.

Candi told Ben about the shot of whiskey and the immediate prank phone call that had occurred afterwards, but he would not listen to her and said to quit bothering him about weird things.

"Maybe a weird neighbor is watching us through binoculars," Candi said. Candi's heart was breaking that Ben would not listen to her concerns. Her own husband was not being emotionally available to her to listen to her concerns. Ben was being mean to her and she was not being mean to Ben.

After dinner that night, she was doing dishes in the kitchen while Ben was watching TV with the kids. There was enough light in the kitchen to see even though the sun was setting so Candi flipped the light off to save some electricity; they had to watch their bills. She did so many dishes that she could do dishes in her sleep, she thought. Ben came into the kitchen a few minutes later on his way to the garage. He stopped and looked at Candi and he looked angry. "Why are you doing dishes in the dark?" he gruffly asked.

"There's still plenty of light for me to see. I just flipped off the light to save some money on the electricity bill. I'll turn it back on in a few minutes if we need it but I am almost done. Why are you harassing me?" she asked him.

"You are getting really crazy," he replied and went out into the garage.

After a moment of thinking, she became angry. Candi went out into the garage. She walked right up to him and pointed her finger in his face. But then she decided not to say anything. She just gave him an ugly face and turned and walked away. A sin on his soul, she thought, because I am not bothering him and I was just trying to save a quarter on the electricity bill.

Later that night, before Candi got into bed, she placed a flashlight on her bedside table. She had a candle and matches on her dresser in case the electricity ever went off, but she had decided a flashlight would be good to have in case the electricity went off in the middle of the night and she could get to the kids quickly if they needed her.

"Why do you have a flashlight on your table?' Ben asked.

"I just think it would be a good idea to have a flashlight near our bed in case the electricity ever went off. If the kids need us, we can get to them quickly," I replied.

"You know, you are getting weird," Ben said back.

"I am NOT," I replied back. "And I'm going to get a flashlight for each of the kids to keep on their bedside tables."

"You are going to make the kids paranoid," Ben said.

"No, I am not! Ridiculous for you to say that. If you love your kids you are supposed to go over a fire escape plan at least once a year. We've never even rehearsed an escape plan with them. There is nothing wrong with teaching safety to your kids. I always encourage the kids to wash their hands before they eat but I don't tell them to wash their hands a hundred times a day. If I was paranoid, I would make them wear masks on their faces every day that filter out all germs in the air and make them wear gloves if they touched anything out in a public place, but our kids are healthy. If I was paranoid, I would sanitize the doorknobs and car door handles every day, but I only do it about once a month. So, quit saying that I am crazy, Ben. I'm getting a little bit perturbed at you."

CHAPTER 19

1993   *The Mental Hospital*

"Why are you doing this to me?" I asked Ben, as we drove a few days later to an appointment to see a psychiatrist. I had fully agreed to go and talk to the doctor that someone had recommended to Ben.

"Because you need help," he said.

We arrived at the office of Jill River, Psychiatrist, and she spoke to both Ben and I together at the session.

"What's going on with you?" she asked me.

I told her that I was experiencing some anxiety because I was not happy with our current living situation and I was thinking about looking for another house. I also told her about the Caucasian woman who had tried to kidnap our daughter 4 years earlier. I also told her that sometimes I felt that I might be being followed by a strange car and that I might have had some strange things happen.

"Your husband says that you have crying spells."

I told her that I did have a few crying spells, but not in front of the kids. I told her I was functioning and working close to normal.

We had been talking for less than ten minutes.

"You are seriously mentally ill. You are a paranoid schizophrenic and if you do not go to Viewpoint Mental Facility now, I will have the police escort you," she said to me and she walked out of the room.

"I didn't know they were going to do this to you," said Ben, looking at me.

Inside I started panicking. "Well, you are my husband and you live with me. And you have known me for 15 years. So tell her that I am not crazy." If anything, I may have a sleep deficit and I heard that it can cause a person to 'dream while they are awake' which could lead to irrationalities, but I am not crazy or a paranoid schizophrenic. Sleep deprivation can be a serious condition. I also have stress but who doesn't. Basically, I think I am a good person, an excellent mother, a good wife, a good friend to my friends, good to myself, and a good citizen. 'This psychiatrist is crazy, not me' I thought to myself.

Doctor River entered the room again with a handout giving directions to the mental facility, which she handed to Ben.

Ben and I didn't know that we could have gotten an attorney to confront the psychiatrist; someone told us years later that we could possibly have sued for medical malpractice.

I was admitted to the mental hospital and kept behind locked doors for 10 days but it seemed like 10 years. Doors at the end of every corridor were locked. It was very scary. I did the best I could to try and concentrate and participate in the group discussions and the individual therapy sessions which were helpful and offered subjects such as anger management, self-awareness, personality types, hobbies, conflict management, decision making, music and art therapy, and how to control addictions and substance abuse. The facility had all of the patients on a strict schedule; we were awakened at 6am and every hour of the day was planned out for us. In my free hour I read a novel that I had brought with me to the hospital, watched television, or walked around the little outside courtyard to get some exercise.

One of the psychiatrists at the hospital asked me why I thought someone was spying on me and my family. I told the psychiatrist that I did not actually know that someone was spying on me and my family. He said I had indicated on the questionnaire that I had filled out for Dr. River that I thought someone was 'following me and my family' and I replied "But that didn't mean that I thought my house was bugged. It is possible for someone to find out personal information without them actually spying on you in your home. I never said my house was bugged because I do not know if my house is bugged or not."

I was not forced to take medicine because of state laws but I cooperated and took the medications. The medicines prescribed for me were Haldol, Zyprexa, Tofranil, Ativan, and Fiorinal and the medicines made me sleepy and sluggish. Haldol and Zyprexa were anti-psychotics for paranoid schizophrenics or bipolar disorder. Tofranil was an anti-depressant. Ativan was a tranquilizer. Fiorinal was for headaches. After taking the drugs, I could barely raise my arms and my tongue felt heavy. After a few days my stomach began to hurt. I asked the doctors if they could lower the dosage of the prescriptions. I figured that people with lower body weights might need less dosage than people with higher body weights. But the doctors said that all people needed the same dosages of the psychiatric medicines, but this did not make sense to me because, for example, children have smaller bodies and their dosages are smaller.

I also was such a total nervous wreck that I could not relax to pee; it would take me several minutes to be able to relax and pee and this condition stayed with me for almost a year because I was a complete nervous wreck due to being thrown into the mental hospital and being labeled crazy.

The mental hospital requested a patient to fill out forms about their entire medical history and they asked many questions. I was even forced to take an IQ test; why? I told the psychiatrist that I had occasional headaches but that I had finally realized that they could be being caused by my drinking too much caffeine in a week and then going through caffeine withdrawal; so that is why I thought I really didn't need the Fiorinal.

I didn't need the anti-psychotic drugs either; why were the psychiatrists saying that I was crazy? Something was wrong and I became very afraid. This was the result of a mafia or whoever tried to kidnap Valerie, I thought to myself.

I am neither a paranoid schizophrenic or have bipolar depression. I do not see bugs on the wall or believe I can fly from a roof so I am not a paranoid schizophrenic. Bipolar depression means a person has extreme highs of mania or elation and may suddenly switch to extreme lows of depression. How can a psychiatrist who has only known me for 10 minutes make such a serious diagnosis about me, I wondered? Also, life situations, hormones, music, drugs, or caffeine withdrawal may cause a person to experience emotions, so why are psychiatrists just blaming a person's emotions on the left and right hemispheres of the brain and insisting that medicine is the only cure? There are times when I have listened to music that has caused me to dance around my house like a person on uppers but I do not do this around my kids. If I want to dance around in private, that is my business. I think that if a person is depressed but they do not know why they are depressed, then they may need medication to help the chemicals in their brain. But if a person is depressed because of a situation, then the person should try to find a solution to improve their situation to make them happy again. The psychiatric medicines and the dosages of the medicines that are supposedly being prescribed to millions of patients can cause damage to vital organs of the body.

When I arrived back home after being released from Viewpoint Mental Facility, I would start to shake at times and experienced major anxiety because of the weirdness of the situation; the psychiatrist was a criminal because I am not crazy and she had no basis for throwing me into a mental hospital. I told Ben that something very evil and sinister had entered our lives. Ben knew that I was not a paranoid schizophrenic and he told me so. Also, my anxiety got worse. Years later, I read in a pill book that certain anti-depressants can cause anxiety. I had also been prescribed drugs that should not have been mixed together.

"It is a bad 'mafia' of a sort – a bad group of people who have set me up to make me look crazy. This has got to be connected to whoever tried to kidnap Valerie," I told Ben.

I prayed as I was going to sleep. When I woke up, my first thought was that I wondered if our house was bugged with hidden cameras and listening devices. I believed that whoever had tried to kidnap Valerie knew that she was in the garage while I was in the kitchen. Or maybe someone from another house in the neighborhood could have been watching with binoculars. Or maybe a random person who knew where we lived was the culprit. Maybe the kidnapper knew someone I worked with, or someone Ben worked with, or someone from the church, from the public school system, or maybe a neighbor. I was thinking it through from different perspectives, trying to analyze it. I told this to Ben, but he said I was crazy. I told him I was going to smash the huge wall mirror in our bathroom with a hammer to see if there were any hidden cameras behind it. He said "You are insane. Do not smash that mirror." We looked up at the stippled ceilings and Ben said "Builders could hide cameras in the stippled ceilings very easily probably. Who knows?"

I went back to work immediately, resuming my normal work schedule and our family schedule, because we had several thousands of dollars of credit card debt which needed to be paid.

I was sitting on the subway train platform one morning waiting on the train that would take me to work when 60 yards down below into the parking lot I noticed a car park behind my mini-van. A man was walking around my mini-van and then he stopped in the middle of the isle and started waving his hands. I was stunned because I did not recognize the man and I had no idea who he was. The next moment the train pulled in; I got on and went to work. That evening,

I told a train station police officer what had happened and asked if he could look at the camera recordings and get the license plate number, but he just said "I am sorry. I know nothing about that." I told the facts of the incident to Ben, but he just said I was crazy. Emotionally, I felt very much alone. Our life was generally exhausting, so the exhaustion alone may have compounded my anxiety but something was very wrong when my own husband would not quit calling me crazy and now a strange man was looking into my car at the train station parking lot. Four months later, after me and Ben had an argument and he kept calling me crazy, and in a bad emotional moment I took 2 sleeping pills and told Ben I did not want to live anymore because I knew it was a mafia interfering in our lives but Ben did not believe me; it was a very bad group of people. I know it was bad to say that I didn't want to live anymore but I really didn't mean it – I was frustrated and just wanted Ben to listen to my concerns because they were real to me because I was the one who was experiencing weird things happening, not Ben. There were several nights when I could not sleep and I was awake in the middle of the night, pacing the floors. He thought I had taken the whole bottle of sleeping pills. He called the psychiatrist and they put me into the mental hospital again for 10 days. Another psychiatrist named Tom Satchez spoke with me. Tom Satchez also told me that I was psychotic and a paranoid schizophrenic and prescribed me Paxil, Depakote, Zoloft, and 4 little pills of Lithium. Paxil was an anti-depressant, Depakote was anti-convulsant, Zoloft was an anti-depressant, and Lithium is an anti-manic and antipsychotic. Lithium is a metal that is a natural earth element.

When I opened the vial of pills that contained the Lithium and saw that there were only 4 little pills, I called the pharmacy to see if it was a mistake, but they said that it was the correct prescription that the psychiatrist had prescribed.

But the psychiatrists would not answer my questions about why Ben was calling me crazy when I know that I am not crazy?
Ben was being mentally abusive to me.

I was angry at my brother and sisters when they came to the mental hospital to see me because they know I am not crazy but they would not insist that I be let out of the hospital. And no one was addressing the issue that Ben kept on calling me crazy, when I was not doing anything that put any one else in danger. Why couldn't they analyze Ben's mind also?

I was kept locked up again for 10 days against my will. The state I lived in had passed a law that said a mental patient has to be released from a mental hospital after three days if there is no evidence that he or she is a danger to themselves or anyone else; I would like to know how harmlessness is assessed because I was talking to another mental patient who said she was admitted to the mental hospital by her family because she was having trouble sleeping and the mental hospital did not let her go after 3 days. The woman was very upset that she was being kept in the mental hospital against her will which is what had happened to me. I think it should be a state law that anyone who is admitted to a mental hospital has free access to telephones and lawyers.

Somebody told me that judges have the power to send people to the mental hospital, even for just raising your voice in court. For some reason, when a person goes into a courtroom, the judges want no emotions to be expressed. Judges need to realize that innocent persons who are victims of crimes and slander might be a bit emotional and that doesn't mean the person is crazy or has mental problems.

In the state where I live, if three of your family members think you are acting strange, they can throw you into a mental hospital but you are supposed to be set free after 3 days if you are not expressing a desire to hurt yourself or anyone. Mental patients should have immediate and free access to telephones and lawyers at all times because patients admitted to mental hospitals need to have witnesses who know the date and time that they are admitted to the mental hospital or they need to be able to retain contact with somebody. I read an article that said it is very possible that some people could be easily murdered in mental hospitals with drugs and the mental hospitals would simply explain that the patient was crazy and killed them self or that the patient had a fatal reaction to a drug.

I read in a novel a story about a mental health patient who was murdered with psychiatric drugs; once the patient had been on the psychiatric drugs for several weeks and the drugs were in his bloodstream, someone slipped pseudoephedrine into his coffee at work and the man instantly died of a heart attack because of the interaction of the two drugs.

I cooperated with the psychiatrists, psychologists and counselors for several months, but I got very frustrated because they all thought I was psychotic and had mental problems. No one seemed to care that a Caucasian woman had tried to kidnap my baby several years before. I thought to myself, this situation might be about some real powerful people who are just very evil, unethical human beings. Or this could be some kind of cover up, maybe by the government or rich real estate people; maybe they are calling me crazy just to cover up espionage in the United States. There is no reason why they should be writing on paper that I am a severely mentally ill person. Candi acknowledged to herself that public surveillance might be deemed necessary to catch terrorists and villains who tried to harm the public, to catch bank robbers and thieves, and to assess other situations like traffic jams.

One day, I realized that I had to save myself from a bad situation.

I took myself off of all psychiatric medications after a few months because it was making me sluggish, bloated, sleepy, and my stomach hurt. The psychiatrist refused to lower the dosages. I asked myself: 'Why am I cooperating with a psychiatrist who says I am crazy when I know that I am not crazy?' I have no intentions to hurt anyone, I do not believe that I am seeing monsters crawling up the walls of my house, I am not standing on the roof thinking that I can fly off the roof, and I am working as a computer programmer and taking care of my family, myself, and the cat. Why are they saying that I am crazy?' What is going on?

I read an article that warned psychiatric patients to not mix certain decongestants like pseudoephedrine with certain psychiatric medicines or it would cause an instant heart attack and possible death.

I realized that I was becoming a victim of a very bad group of people who may have initially tried to kidnap my daughter. Maybe they were trying to get rid of me because they thought I saw the license plate of the woman in the white car but I did not see it. The problem was that it was obscure and I did not know the identities of the predators. I kept trying to express my feelings to Ben, but he just kept on calling me crazy.

I did the best I could to take care of and love the kids, take care of household duties, perform my job well at work, and take care of myself. Ben and I were drifting apart, although I still loved him very much and I loved our life together. I felt like my world was beginning to crash. I did have brothers and sisters, the siblings of my childhood family, but we all lived independent lives so I felt like I couldn't really go live with any of them because they all had their own family matters and money problems to deal with without adding my own problems.

I did not know that, behind my back, Ben was calling all of my brothers and sisters, friends, and neighbors and telling them that I had mental problems and was acting crazy. One of my brothers flew in from another city and came to visit me, expressing his concern for my 'mental state.' I will never forget the look in his eyes when he stood in our kitchen and looked me over from the tip of my head to my feet, and then kept staring me in the eyes with a quizzical look in his eyes asking himself if I was crazy.

Ben and I had another argument about my mental health and for the first time in our relationship, I punched Ben on the arm because of a lie he told to my family. I am not proud of it, but now we are even because Ben previously punched me on the arm one time and now I punched him on the arm. Years later, I would think about this physical violence. Moses' law said 'an eye for an eye and a tooth for a tooth'. Jesus's law said to 'turn the other cheek' and forgive. Mohammed said that Jesus should have fought back and not turned the other cheek. Buddhists say to not retaliate because you are supposed to detach your mind from the world and retain your good life. So, people have many different opinions about how to handle situations. I personally felt very bad after punching Ben on the arm, but he should not have been calling my friends and family to tell them that I am crazy! By telling my friends and family that I am crazy is assaulting me in an emotional way and it hurts as much as a physical attack. I was suffering from anxiety.

Addictions, hording, and anxieties are types of mental conditions that could be included in 'mental illness' but it does not mean the person is crazy or a bad person.

In the 1970s our culture treated alcoholism as a mental illness and many alcoholics were admitted to mental hospitals.
Then the Betty Ford Center was established in 1982 in California by First Lady Betty Ford (wife of President Gerald Ford), Leonard Firestone, and Dr. James West for people suffering from addictions.

I was glad our insurances covered the entire mental hospital bills.

But my anxiety was causing me to feel shaky and I could not concentrate very well sometimes. I kept telling myself that I had to be strong to survive this nightmare of corruption surrounding our lives. I prayed many seconds of each day and night, praying for God to be close to me and guide me in this dilemma.

Candi and Ben never knew that Viewpoint Mental Facility received a $40,000 payment to label Candi as severely mentally ill as a result of the dealings of vile people who had an espionage ring going on in the city. Four hundred houses in a 200-square mile area had been bugged with hidden cameras and listening devices and spies were monitoring families who were unaware of being watched as they were innocently living their personal lives.

CHAPTER 20

1994   *Kids have hectic schedules*

We did a lot of activities with the children. We took them swimming at the neighborhood pool and played tennis with them at the neighborhood tennis courts. Sometimes we just volleyed the ball across the net and didn't keep score.

One summer evening there was a neighborhood pool party and we ordered a pizza and had it delivered to the pool. I gave the delivery teenager a $20 bill as a tip and later that night Ben and I had an argument because he said that was too much of a tip to give for delivering a pizza but I told him that we had not gone to church in several weeks and so we did not give any money as church offerings, so that is how I justified giving a $20 tip. Everyone needs money and gas is expensive to buy so I felt like the delivery teenager deserved a big tip. It's not like we tip that big all the time, but sometimes you just do it to help others. Ben was right that it was probably too big of a tip but sometimes you just do things like that 'to give back to the community' is the way I've heard it on the radio and have heard people say it.

We liked to play in the yard on the swing set with the kids. We also took them to ride their bikes along the side streets. We played with them on the driveway with the basketball and other soft rubber bounce balls. The kids were all on kid soccer leagues or basketball leagues. We had gotten the kids a telescope and we sometimes pointed it towards the moon and let them see close ups of the craters on the moon. Our kids smiled and laughed a lot. They did their homework, were making good grades in school, and visited with friends at their friends' homes and at our home. Our kids attended at least one birthday party a month, it seemed.

Although Ben and I were not very active in the school PTA (Parent-Teacher Association) because we already had extra full schedules with both of us working and teaching Sunday school for two years now, I did volunteer to be a teacher-helper and committed to twice a year to help the teacher for 2 hours. One time I took a half a day off from work as part of my vacation hours and the second time I took off an entire day from work as part of my vacation hours.

Both Ben and I have a little notebook that we keep with our bills that notate all of the hours that we have taken off from work. Our employers give us both 14 vacation days, 5 personal days, and 5 sick days for us to use but they will still pay us our salaries even though they allow us this time off. With 3 kids, there are times when the kids do not feel well and if they have a fever or a contagious cough, they are required to be kept home from school. So, it is a juggling act between Ben and me to see who can stay home if one of the kids gets sick but thank goodness our kids have good health and rarely get sick. Plus, we are grateful that both of our employers are understanding and the nature of both of our jobs is that if we cannot go to work during the day, we could go later that night to do our jobs. If we were brain surgeons or engineers at construction sites and had to coordinate the tasks of many people at certain time frames, things might not go so smoothly for us. Both mine and Ben's jobs are primarily research and development positions which allow us some flexibility in our schedules but we do have to support projects that are in production mode also. And with both of our jobs, we are not the exclusive specialist; we both work on a team of people who know the nature of our jobs so if we cannot do our job on a certain day, thank goodness that there is more than likely another member of our teams that can handle a problem.

Some jobs on earth are so complicated and stressful and may require years of education and years of school loan payments; that is why some people elect to not have children. I did not think about things like this when I went to college, wondering what I would major in. I didn't really plan to earn a business degree because I wanted to be a librarian, but I had some college friends who were excited about computers and that is how I ended up taking some computer classes and switching my major to business. I had one friend who told me that she thought I should major in education but at that time computers were more interesting to me. But after having had children, I thought about my friend's advice because if I had become a teacher, my work schedule would have coincided more with my children's schedules and it would have been more ideal for a family life.

For the first volunteer session Valerie's teacher requested that I come to the classroom and tell the children about the great artists of the world. With most small children, you have to keep it simple, so I just presented information on Leonardo da Vinci, Claude Monet, and Vincent van Gogh. I had found a few books at the library on the artists and then I went shopping at a huge interior decorating bargain retail warehouse where I found 3 posters of famous paintings by these artists that were print reproductions. I went to local print shop and made some flyers with the famous paintings on them that I planned to pass out to each kid in the class. At the end of my presentation, I asked the students to guess a number between 1 and 100, and the student who was the closest to the number I had picked won a poster; I let them pick which poster they wanted. We did that 3 times until all three posters were won.

The second volunteer session the teacher asked me to come to the class and assist with International Food Day. On the day I went to volunteer it was Mexican Food Day. I went shopping at a bargain shop and found a sombrero hat to wear. A sombrero is a hat worn in Mexico which has a wide brim to shield your face, neck, and possibly the tops of your shoulders from the sun. It has a chin string to hold the hat in place. The teacher wanted me to bring chicken enchiladas. Another parent brought a bowl of white rice that had bits of sautéed tomatoes and onions and corn added to it. Other parents were bringing tacos, refried beans, a cake made with *leche* which is the Spanish word for milk, and flan which is a type of custard dessert. Since the food event was scheduled for 10 AM in the morning, the teacher had notified the principal to switch the lunch hour for the 4th graders that day to 1 PM instead of 11AM.

Regarding the topic of international foods, I read an article about ice cream because it is a very popular dessert in many countries but many people may not know that ice cream is not eaten in every country in the world.

I like to read and listen to people talk about many things; I may not be willing to change my opinions or preferences but I am at least willing to learn. It has made me realize what a huge world we live in. It has been estimated that there are over 6 billion people on the planet in over 200 countries. It is amazing what humanity has brought us to in the current century, all of the perseverance and hard work of the people that lived before our current generation and how they were able to endure what they endured and achieve what they achieved.

Sometimes I like to think about history from the beginning. I imagine our Creator overseeing all of the progress that has been made since the beginning of the universe which scientists believe to be between 8 or 14 billion years ago but they think our solar system was created about 4 billion years ago. The human species has been around for about 40,000 years and is not guaranteed; flesh eating bacteria, fungi, an asteroid hitting the planet, or the moon drifting away could wipe out the human species. How do we know the sun will keep shining, for it could go out any day? Scientists say the heat deep inside the earth would remain for millions of years.

When I think about the human species on the timeline of all eternity, I am grateful that I am living in a modern time. People a long time ago had it much harder; I couldn't imagine not having modern plumbing with clean water, toilets, nice showers and tubs, washing machines and dryers. Water faucets connected to the exterior of homes allow water hoses to be attached to them to water the yard, wash cars, and attach sprinklers so our kids can run through the sprinklers in the summertime while wearing their bathing suits. Frozen pizzas, rock and roll music, toothpaste and toothbrushes.

At a local park, there is a sign posted beside a gravel parking lot that explains ways that humans can help to clean up the environment. One way is to not wash your car on your concrete driveway because if you live in a neighborhood that has curbs and drains, then most likely all of the soap runoff from washing your car will run down your driveway into the drains that carry the soap to the local water filtering facilities. If you wash your car on a grassy or gravel area, the soap will filter down into the soil instead. Many people will be concerned that the soap would kill their grass, but natural citrus-based soap could be used instead of soaps with phosphates. Also, medicines, drugs, and alcohol should not be flushed down toilets or put down the drains of sinks. If everyone helped a little bit, the public water supply could be cleaned up. This is just like air pollution guidelines that have been put into place in certain countries in order to improve the quality of the air that people are breathing.

They say the world is becoming a 'concrete jungle' because there are so many roads, parking lots, and buildings upon the planet. Maybe we should have some more dirt roads.

Thank the ingenuity of human beings who invented forks, knives, spoons – a long time ago, humans ate with their hands only.

When we had extra money, we took our kids to specialty museums to see science or art exhibits, to the nature center that had an interesting mini-zoo and a boardwalk that went along the river and through the adjoining woods, on nature hikes, or to the botanical gardens. One spring we drove 80 miles to see a botanical garden that I had always wanted to visit. I told the kids that we were going to see so many azalea bushes in bloom that they would be amazed. When we arrived at the gardens, there were no azaleas in bloom so we inquired at the visitor center and they said to come next week to see the blooms. The kids laughed in the car about it, saying "Sure, mom, we were amazed at all of the azaleas in bloom. Thanks for driving us 80 miles to see the green bushes with no azaleas." And they reminded me about it several times on the way home, being the silly kids that they were. They learned about sarcasm that day.

One summer we decided to take the kids peach picking. We drove 40 miles to a peach orchard and bought a large-sized bucket because we planned on giving some of the peaches to family and friends. We walked with the children through several rows of peach trees until we started picking peaches and the kids were amazed to be standing in the middle of a grove of peach trees.

One museum offered trains that were once powered with steam engines fueled by coal but were now retired to the museum. It is amazing to think that in some places of the world, engineers are constructing modern trains that cruise at speeds of more than 100 miles per hour.

Once I read an article that said some engineers were thinking of constructing a train that went around the entire world. There is the train that goes under the English Channel between France and England.

We liked to play cards and board games with the kids, take them bowling, watch TV with them, read books to them, and even play video games with them. Some of the video games were so fun that you could get addicted to playing them. We set up a ping-pong table in the garage for a while and had many fun ping-pong volleys. Many times, we did not keep score; we just pinged it back and forth.

Sometimes I would put our dinner in a big pan and leave it cooking in the oven or I would fill the crock pot and leave it cooking for several hours and I would take the kids for a walk or down to the tennis courts to hit a few tennis balls with them. Then, when we came home, our dinner would be all ready, except to warm up dinner rolls if we wanted them warmed. Sometimes we ate them plain out of the bag. My next-door neighbor had the unfortunate circumstance of starting her washing machine and then leaving her home to run an errand and when she came home, she realized that the water hose behind her washing machine had burst and water had flooded her floors. She told me that it is best to never leave any appliances running when you are not home, just in case of flooding or fires.

We did take our kids to some fairs, water parks and amusement theme parks that offered roller coaster rides, house of mirror walks, and sky bucket rides. I was forced to ride a roller coaster with Lee that zoomed in an upside-down loop because Ben doesn't like roller coasters. I was very afraid but did it anyway but it turned out to not be that bad; the roller coaster ran very smoothly and I was impressed at the engineering of the design. While on the roller coaster that day, Lee lost his favorite baseball cap that he had been wearing. I wondered if we could inquire about a lost and found department and we could come back next week to see if Lee's hat had been found. When I explained my idea to Ben, he just laughed and said that I was crazy and to forget Lee's favorite baseball cap because he didn't want to drive 30 miles to come back for a baseball cap. It is sad to think about all of the items that get thrown into the trash or end up in Lost and Found at theme parks, restaurants, and travel hubs.

On the way home we played Guess What It Is? I said Guess what is round and jiggles? Ben and the kids suggested marbles, cheerios in a bowl, soap bubbles, a belly button but the answer was hula hoop.

I read an article about humans and what they are thinking about in one moment of time. People can choose what they want to think about. Sometimes people are thinking only one thought, but people can be thinking about many different things at one time.

People are the result of everything they have interacted with up to the current moment of their life. I am lucky that I have interacted with good people up to the current moment of my life, except for the corrupt woman who tried to kidnap my child, the psychiatrist who said I am crazy, and Ben who is calling me crazy. But I am trying to remain optimistic and have a positive attitude.

CHAPTER 21

1994   *Trying to make it all work*

One weeknight I stayed up until 1am to catch up on housework while Ben and the kids were sleeping. I tiptoed around, folding and putting away all of the laundry. We're good at washing laundry, but we don't always have time to fold it and put it away. Instead, it often ends up in a big pile in an easy chair in a corner of our bedroom.

I admit I have sent the kids to school in their favorite tee-shirts that were wrinkled-looking, but I had no time to iron them. But what's important is that at least the kids made it to school.

Ben writes out the paper checks from the checkbook to pay the bills and balances the checkbook. He stays up late at least twice a month in order to do this. Sometimes we were so busy and tired that we bounced our checking account. It sounds like an excuse but sometimes we were so tired that we didn't write all transactions in the checkbook every single night which is what we should have done.

And Ben and I are making our life work – we go to work and put forth our best efforts, try to pay the bills on time, ensure that the kids get good nutrition and exercise, have playtime with cousins and friends, and keep up with their schoolwork. I have sometimes stayed up at night typing Lee's homework if the teacher required for it to be typed. If Lee was very tired, I would read through his handwritten draft and make sure I could read all of the sentences before I sent him off to bed and then I would type it. We had purchased a small personal computer with a word editing software application. We also still had an old manual typewriter with a spare box of ribbons. And we take the kids to church at least once a month since we are not teaching Sunday school this year and don't have to go every week. We speak to the kids about good values.

We are still listed in a neighborhood care group at the church and once we were contacted and asked if we could provide a hot meal for a couple in our neighborhood whose husband had just been released from the hospital. I called the couple and they told us to just bring some chicken, potatoes, and vegetables and we did.

We have a cat and a fish aquarium. We had a turtle but Lee would not help clean out its tank, so we let the turtle out by the creek. But I heard on the news that people should not let exotic pets like iguanas, pythons, and alligators out in the woods or lakes in domesticated areas. The exotic pets that escaped from pet stores on the coasts that were destroyed in hurricanes and the exotic pets that people let out of their care into domesticated areas are causing dangerous reptiles like the pythons and alligators to become a big problem because the reptiles keep migrating further inland. I heard on the news that some local governments are paying reptile hunters to go into woods and swamps to kill some of these dangerous reptiles because they are becoming too populated.

Our cat can act mysterious at times, like it knows what you are thinking. Once my brother's dog ran to their front door and sat there for 5 minutes until his wife pulled into the driveway; they say that dogs can hear different frequencies than humans and we wondered if their dog could hear his wife's voice or car engine from a few miles away. They also say that some animals can probably see images in different colors than humans do.

We only change the sheets on the beds about once a month because the kids are all potty-trained now. We keep our house reasonably neat and tidy.

Ben does most of the yard work but I have even mowed the grass a few times. We had some wild onions growing in the yard, and they smelled so good when we cut the grass. Many people love the smell of freshly cut grass or the smell of colorful flowers.

Ben plays racquetball with friends sometimes. I also had occasional lunches or dinners with college girlfriends until they began to act strangely towards me regarding my dilemma about the strange woman in my garage and my stay in the mental hospital; then my friends quit returning my phone calls.

We had some neighbors over to play cards one night for a few hours while our kids went to my sister and brother-in-law's house to have a slumber party with their cousins.

Tonight, I cleaned up the toy closet and put all game pieces back into their proper boxes. I even got down on my hands and knees and crawled around until I found a missing game piece under the couch and I put it back into its proper box. So, the next time my kids play the game, all of the pieces will be there for them. And many times, I play the games with them, so I am saving myself stress in advance.

When I clean out the kids' school back packs, I prefer for the kids to help me. Then I can ask them what is important and what they do not need anymore. I am trying to teach them responsibility and to be organized.

We try to keep all bedrooms and closets clean and organized.

I clean out the mini-van every single night and remove all trash.

Ben and I know exactly what is in the attic and what is in the garage, and we have removed all excess and all trash.

The kitchen drawers need to be cleaned out but I will get to that. At least once a year or two, I try to empty the drawers, wash the silverware organizer and the inside of the drawer, and then put everything back inside the drawers. But I admit the silverware drawer is not usually organized; when I empty the dishwasher, I usually just dump all of the silverware into the drawer which really bothers Ben. He told me I was being slack not to organize all of the spoons together, all of the forks together, and all of the knives together, but I apologized to him and told him that I didn't have time to worry about that right now but if he wanted to organize the forks, spoons, and knives each day, then he could certainly do it. I told him that maybe in the future when the kids got older and things slowed down a little, then I would have more time to organize the silverware draw, but right now I was just concentrating on getting everything done that needed to be done.

Our other kitchen drawer is not organized that contains that little miracle invention called a 'vegetable peeler' that easily removes the skin off of cucumbers, potatoes, and carrots, our potato masher, our garlic press, our plastic suction thing-a-ma-jig that can take the grease off the top of casseroles or other stuff, the rubber-plastic jar openers that were also a miracle invention, the pot holders so you can remove pans from the oven without getting burned, the cookie cutters, and the wine opener for the rare occasion when we drink wine. Ben and I rarely drink alcohol. We might drink one beer or one mixed drink or one shot of whiskey a year but that is all.

All of the items in our kitchen were offered by good humans to other humans to help them; if you look at the world this way, you can truly see how far humanity has come and what a good species we are. The items were not just for sale in a store, they were offered to us to help us.

Before we went grocery shopping, we tried to look in the pantry and made a list of what we needed and what meals we would like to cook that week. We made a list because it saved us time, stress, and money. So many times I would have to go back to the grocery store because I forgot something, so I learned that making a list was very helpful.

Sometimes I would read the packaging on food items to learn about the nutritional content and where the product was manufactured. The variety of packaging and the creativity of the marketing artists was astounding and beautiful.

Many times, we saved the plastic containers and used them to put leftover food in them. Candi did not buy plastic wrap for a year – she made it a point to try to reuse all of the plastic containers. For example, if only a half of an orange or banana were used, she would put it into a reusable plastic whipped topping container and put the lid on it. Popcorn could be put into the reusable containers. She reused small plastic cups from drive-thru fast-food chains or recycled them.

She acquired a collection of plastic utensils and small salt and pepper packages from fast food orders and threw them all in one big container; then when she and Ben had a dinner party or an afternoon get together with family and friends, she didn't have to buy plastic utensils each time. Ben asked her, "Don't you think you're being a little miserly and crazy?" to which Candi replied, "Well, I'm just trying to be a little conservative instead of wasteful. We don't have to be so formal for our family and closest friends. But, Ben, another thing we could use the saved plastic utensils for is in case the water gets turned off for some reason, at least we would have some extra eating utensils on hand. What if our country has a nuclear or neutron bomb dropped on it and we survived the attack? I heard it in the news that everyone should get prepared and try to be self-sufficient to try to survive. There are so many people in the world that the governments cannot take care of everyone. Ben, please quit saying that I am crazy. I am just thinking of the kids if our country is attacked or if there is a pandemic, about how we could survive." He responded by kissing me on the side of my neck, which surprised me. He said, "You're thinking too much."

Once I took an inventory of the cereal that we had in the pantry, and we had 14 boxes of cereal, most of which were halfway full. This was way too many boxes of cereal for a family our size. Our cereal inventory was way out of control. But I need to explain how we acquired 14 boxes of cereal; twice at the grocery store, the kids threw some boxes of cereal into the shopping cart when either Ben or I did not see them doing it and one time one box of cereal got placed on a different shelf in the pantry so at the next trip to the grocery store, another box of the same cereal was bought again because it was thought that there was no cereal of that kind but then the lost cereal box was found. Then, one morning Ben and I discussed that we needed some cereal, milk, eggs, and bananas for breakfast the next day but it got confused about who was going to the grocery store, and that evening coming home from work, we both stopped at the grocery store and came home with cereal, milk, eggs, and bananas. (This was life in 1994 before everyone had their own cell phones.) From now on, we would have to do better.

One thing we did do that was good was that when we ordered a pizza, we did keep the leftovers and would microwave it for a few seconds the next day to have it for lunch. When we ordered a pizza for the kids, we often tried to serve a tray of sliced celery, carrots, green peppers, cucumbers, green or black olives, or grapes with it. We encouraged our kids to eat some plain vegetables like celery or cucumber stalks or fruit along with their slices of pizza so that they would have adequate fiber in their diets. The kids would also like to dip celery and carrots in ranch, Italian or some other kind of salad dressing. Another reason why we did this was because the kids would only eat cheese pizza or pepperoni pizza; we tried to order a supreme deluxe pizza with meats and vegetables but the kids would not even take one bite. We tried to teach our children to eat 'balanced' so they would not just eat carbohydrates which are converted to sugar. Our children grew up learning to eat salads which are low in fat if you don't eat it with too much salad dressing and vegetables like broccoli, green beans, cauliflower, red and green and yellow peppers, squash, potatoes, tomatoes, pinto beans, white beans, lima beans, green peas, Brussels sprouts, and corn. I would try other vegetables but I am listing the vegetables that they would eat. They would eat fruits like oranges, strawberries, grapes, pineapple, apples, and meats like turkey, chicken, beef, and pork. Some people in the world do not eat meat but we grew up eating meat so we fed meat to our children. Many people substitute oatmeal or bean proteins for meats. The kids would eat fish sticks but they would not eat grilled fish. My kids would eat tuna salad and tuna casserole when they were toddlers but they would not eat it when they got older because their friends wouldn't eat it. Lee, who was our oldest son, did eat fish when he became an adult. We let our children have sugary snacks like candy, cookies, and ice cream but we would also give them snacks like chips or celery strips filled with cream cheese, pimento cheese, chips, or peanut butter with raisins on top that has a cute nickname of ants-on-a-log.

One interesting fact that I had read about is that paper can be made out of the leftover part of the sugar cane plant after the plant is processed for sugar. Trees are not the only source for making paper. Paper has also been made out of rocks.

In case of WWIII which we hope never happens or in case of any other type of disaster or pandemic, for emergencies we have on hand several 24-packs of bottled water, candles and matches, several flashlights with batteries, cat food, toilet paper, toothpaste, paper towels, peanut butter, protein and granola bars, a bag of assorted flavors hard candy, a worldwide hand-crank radio with a rechargeable battery, a medical kit (that included gauzes, rubbing alcohol, iodine or an antiseptic lotion or cream, antibiotic cream, and hydrogen peroxide), vitamins, a calendar, a clock that runs on batteries. No one needed special prescription medication. We also have a compass and a few cigarette lighters that we could use like matches. We should probably add some more food items to our stash.

We have a spare tire that is in good and working condition, a jack to support the car, a lug nut wrench, and battery cables in the trunks of our cars, and we have a spare car battery that we put in the trunk if we drive long distances.

We also have had a carpenter bumblebee drill a hole in the door framing for the kitchen door that leads to the back deck, so that problem needs to be fixed. My sister and her husband had a family of squirrels get into their attic; she thinks they came in through a hole that a woodpecker drilled into an upper plank of their cedar home. We actually laughed about the family of squirrels because they had a hard time getting them to leave their attic. I imagined the squirrels talking to each other, saying they didn't want to leave because the nice lady who lived in the house threw seeds and breadcrumbs out for the birds which they could also eat and the nice lady's children often left half-eaten cookies out on the deck when they were finished with them and they could eat them also. And they had a hard time getting the woodpecker to stop drilling holes in their home, and they were becoming agitated because they were paying a $1400 home mortgage payment each month because they were trying to pay their mortgage loan off in 15 years instead of 30 years so they didn't have a lot of extra money to make expensive home repairs. One of their neighbors finally suggested that they go buy several large owl statues and put an owl on top of their roof edge and on their deck in order to scare the woodpeckers off and it worked. You should also have your house regularly checked for termites because they can eat up your house.

Home maintenance can be expensive and time-consuming.

One spring there were many rains. One day the kids were playing in the back yard; I could watch them from the kitchen but many times I was sitting on the deck or I would be out there playing with them or talking with them. Will ran up to me and said he wanted to show me a big hole in the ground. I went to investigate what he was talking about and I was astonished to see a sink hole nearly three-feet in width and it looked deep. I was so glad that Will or any other child had not fallen into it. Ben arranged to have a landscaper come look at it and they recommended that we have the entire back yard back hoed and graded and we did. Apparently, some builders bury a lot of debris after they build new houses and if the debris is in big pieces, the landscaper said it could cause big sink holes later on. The landscaper had plowed up some big pieces of wood, roof shingles, and even soda bottles which must have been left over from the workmen's lunches.

We loved to play in the backyard with the kids. Because the back of the house had several huge windows that overlooked the back yard, we could keep a close watch on them if we were in the great room or the kitchen. One time I was cleaning and had put on the radio to listen to while I worked. I stopped for a moment to dance to a song and suddenly I heard a knock. I realized it wasn't coming from the front door. I turned around to look out the back window of the great room and all 3 kids and Ben were staring at me and laughing and they all started dancing in the back yard. They were making fun of me; it was a funny moment. Well, I am glad my kids were dancing because they say dancing is a good exercise. Plus, I love music and

Ben and the kids love music so it is good for their spirit and brain. I read that when you do things you love, endorphins are released in your brain that are good for your well-being.

When Ben and the 3 kids came into the house, Will said "Mom, you are crazy because you love to dance and sing all the time." I said to Will: "I like music but I do not sing and dance all of the time because I also cook, vacuum, do dishes, do laundry, play with you, go to work, brush my teeth, and sleep so I cannot be singing and dancing all of the time." We hugged each other.

We brought chalk and drew squares and numbered them and played hopscotch on the driveway. Also, Valerie's class made the cat-in-the-cradle string toy and she brought it home from school in her backpack and we had fun playing that. I remembered I played cat-in-the-cradle string game when I was a child also.

I loved going through the children's schoolwork and backpacks. They say that by reading your children's schoolwork, you can refresh your entire education and learn new things. Lee's science books had some new facts about the solar system that I had not learned when I was his age, such as the number of moons that Jupiter and Saturn have.

We invited Shelley, Mike, and their kids to enjoy our neighborhood pool with us one weekend afternoon. All of the adults were talking around one of the umbrella tables when suddenly Shelley jumped up and ran and jumped into the shallow end of the pool. Her 11-yr old son had tip-toed towards the deep end and was struggling to keep his head above water. Thank goodness that Shelley had seen him. There was a lifeguard on duty but Shelley knew her son better than the lifeguard, which is why she suddenly jumped in to rescue him.

One Friday night after a busy week, Shelley, Mike, Ben, and I took the kids to a bowling alley and helped the kids bowl two games. Nathan and Lee could pick up the 7-lb. balls and roll them down the lane themselves. We had to help the other kids roll the balls down the lanes but they enjoyed it the same.

Sometimes on weekends Ben and I would take the kids to a small regional airport that had an outdoor observation deck where you could sit and watch the small planes and jets take off and land. There was also a small playground for the kids to play on and a restaurant where you could buy lunches and eat at tables near big windows where you could also watch the runway.

One spring we took the kids to a local plant nursery and let each of them pick out a flower to plant in our backyard flower garden. We had fun that day in the back yard, planting daffodils, tulips, and pansies and playing in the back yard. Ben's parents had also given us a honeysuckle vine that we planted near the deck by some bushes.

Lee, Valerie, and Will are very enthusiastic and energetic kids. Sometimes all three kids will want something at the same time and they will ask Ben or I to hug them, hold them, swing them, wrestle them, read to them, or get them a snack and I will laugh and tell them to be patient, explaining to them that I only have two arms and two legs and am not an octopus so I can only do one thing at a time.

But one afternoon I was cleaning the kitchen and then I needed to vacuum the entire house. The kids were being good kids playing in their rooms with some friends. Ben was playing tennis with friends. Will came to me asking, "Mom, can we have some apple juice?" So, I had to stop what I was doing to pour some drinks. The kids drank it down and went back to Will's room to play. I had a bad moment and swore under my breath that kids can be annoying because they always come first and you always have to stop what you are doing because the kids come first. But the ugly thought was erased from my mind in the next second; I asked God to forgive me for what I just thought and I believe God did forgive me. God knew that I loved kids; I was just very tired, overworked, overstressed, and I was having a bad thought because I was trying to get all of the housework done. I had been a mother for over ten years now and I had been working straight through either full or part-time for seventeen years without a break, since I was a senior in high school, so to be emotionally and physically exhausted was to be expected. Many Americans work all of their lives at least 40-80 hours each week just trying to survive; very few people can afford to work only part-time or not at all.

We certainly could not afford maids to come in once or twice a month to mop and vacuum, which would have been a luxury.

One time our kids had spent the night at my sister's house with their cousins and she was driving them home to us the next day. Ben was out with a friend. I laid down for an afternoon nap for an hour but overslept. When I woke up, it was dark and I got confused, thinking it was morning. I went to the kitchen and began preparing breakfast. Then, when I went to awaken the children, they were not in their beds. At that moment, the doorbell rang because my sister was returning the kids. I laughed to myself but I felt so weird to have gotten the timeframe all mixed up. This happened to me a few times in college also when I was very overtired and had a very hectic schedule. We ate the breakfast for dinner; it was no big deal.

I went out on the deck for a moment to talk to myself. I told myself that I was lucky to have healthy and wonderful children, a nice family and friends, a wonderful and ethical husband (except for calling me crazy), good health of my own, a beautiful home in a peaceful neighborhood, food, clean water and clean air, and a good and interesting job. I shouldn't be taking any of this for granted. I am so lucky that we could afford to have cars and, if I wanted to, I could get the kids in the car and we could drive to any of the nice nearby stores, restaurants, or playgrounds if we wanted to. We could drive a few miles or 400 miles to see family, whereas just 100 years ago, it wasn't this easy for people. Most people had horses and buggies and to travel hundreds of miles was a major event. I could pick up the phone and call anyone I wanted to, even in other parts of the world; just 150 years ago, it wasn't this easy. People communicated by telegraph until the telephone was invented. And before that, people communicated by sending letters by a carrier on a horse. And centuries before that, some sent scrolls of parchment that were tied to a string to a carrier pigeon.

I told myself that I am lucky to have lived in the decades that I have lived in and I shouldn't be complaining. And the reason why I have so many modern conveniences is because of good, brilliantly smart humans who invented all of the things that I tend to take for granted.

I was born in the 1960's in the United States and I have seen a lot of progress and changes that have been made in the world. I have seen the inventions of color TV, remote controls for TVs, seat belts in cars, air conditioning in cars and houses, dishwashers, ice makers in refrigerators (refrigerators used to be called iceboxes and delivery men brought ice to your house to be put in the icebox), prepared cake mixes, frozen foods, microwave ovens, Velcro, personal computer devices and cell phones, public worldwide internet, wireless technology, sticky notes, MRI and medical imaging on computers, GPS, electric hair rollers, electric can openers, and more.

Other progress was that public cigarette smoking in public buildings was banned because cigarette smoke can give lung cancer to people who do not smoke cigarettes. The Berlin Wall that separated the citizens of Berlin, Germany came down. I have read that scientists are concerned about the air quality in high-rise buildings that are built to be air-tight. Some people do not prefer skyscrapers but prefer buildings that are no more than 10 stories that could be built with windows that had a portion of the window could be opened a few inches to let air in without having a danger of someone falling out. I think animal leash laws that prevented dogs from roaming around neighborhoods was a good ordinance and an improvement for our community because me and my friends in my childhood years had a few encounters with dogs when we were playing outside and some of the encounters were scary when the dogs kept growling at us.

I learned that if people have any metal in their bodies, they should not have MRIs because MRIs have powerful magnets which can cause the metals in your body to move and cause internal injuries. Welders could have metal fragments in their eyelashes that could injure their eyeballs if exposed to the magnets of an MRI machine.

When I was a child, we did have a washing machine and a dryer, but my mother and many people still hung clothes on clothes lines with clothes pins to air-dry.

I have also lived through public school desegregation in the United States in the 1960s. Also, I was an 'Air Force brat' and my family moved four times by the time I was 9 years old; I went to 6 different public elementary schools and had to leave friends behind because we moved to a different country and between several US states. I think that living through so many changes has actually made me have anxiety which I do have to monitor although I have read that the more experiences and the more knowledge a person has, it is for the better and makes them stronger but I think statements like this are all relative because everyone on earth has a unique life experience and so we all have unique reasoning logic even though it may be similar to others. Some people love to travel but I only like to go away from my home for a few days at a time. I am the type of person who loves to sit on my front porch or deck for a while and just think.

One time Ben left on a Sunday night to go on a business trip as I was returning to town with the kids from visiting my sister. I was alone with the kids to prepare a meal (I gave the kids their choice and they just wanted soup and PBJ sandwiches), give them their baths, and prepare their backpacks for school the next day. When I went to get the kids ready for bed the beds had no sheets on them. Ben did not tell me that he had stripped all of the sheets from the kids' beds, so I had to put sheets on three beds also. I swore under my breath but let it go. I wonder why he didn't tell me.

CHAPTER 22

                    Flexibility

The next morning, I was standing in the hallway, leaning against the doorframe of the bathroom, watching my two youngest children brush their teeth; they were standing at the sink, smiling and brushing their teeth with orange and purple toothbrushes before the huge wall mirror. I wanted to remember this moment because they looked so cute and our kids are very nice and cooperative kids. We hardly have any trouble from these kids. They are very enthusiastic and have nice personalities. The oldest child Lee just got on his big yellow school bus for middle-school. Lee and I sometimes play Scrabble while waiting for the bus to come if we have 5 or 10 minutes to wait; we watch and listen for the bus from the dining room window where we sometimes keep the board set up for a week while we have a game in progress; once Will was a little culprit and moved some of the letters around because he thought it was funny. We also keep a dictionary on the table by the game so we can learn some new words if we need to or look up any words that we think might be a word but aren't sure of the correct English spelling and we have had a few funny arguments about some words and have ended up in a tickling match. If there is a dispute, I always tell Lee that I am the mom so I can make the final decision but Lee just laughs and says 'No Way.' After I help Valerie and Will get on their bus, I will have to rush to get myself to work downtown. This morning I got up thirty minutes earlier than usual to fix eggs, bacon, grits, and fresh oranges. But I know that many of the boxed cereals have good proteins. I make sure my children try to eat a good breakfast so that they will be able to concentrate on their schoolwork without their stomach growling. I have suggested to the children that sometimes they could have a turkey or ham sandwich, a pizza, or some chicken soup for breakfast but they were not interested.

For some reason, Valerie and Will have been wanting to wear some of the same shirts two and three days in a row. What does a parent do in this situation? I laughed to myself. I don't want their teacher to think they don't have other clean clothes to wear. "Why do you want

to wear the same shirts again that you just wore yesterday?" I asked Valerie and Will. They said, "We don't know; we just want to wear the same ones." So, I let them.
It's just something they'll outgrow in a few weeks I guess, I said to myself.

And tonight, the boys have karate lessons and Valerie has ballet lessons. Later this week all three kids will go to a piano lesson.

This weekend Ben wants to go out of town to visit with his parents, but I asked him if I could please stay home alone this weekend and rest by myself; I need some personal time alone. Ben also has had a weekend to himself when I took the kids out of town to visit my sister who lives in a nearby town.

Ben and I are trying to have a somewhat balanced life.

I was dressed and all ready to leave the house. While brushing my teeth, a small speck of toothpaste splashed directly into my eye and it was burning. I cursed to myself and leaned over the sink, making a cup with my hand to catch water from the faucet and flushed my eyeball several times with water. Then, looking into the mirror, I saw, of course, that my eye makeup was all smudged on that one eye. Well, I didn't have time to refresh the eye makeup on that eye so I didn't care what my eye makeup looked like that day. I didn't have any important meetings at work. I laughed to myself and just walked out of the bathroom, out of the house, and got into the car.

The eye makeup fiasco brought back a memory about one time when Lee was just a small infant, about 3 months old, and Ben and I had just finished taking showers and getting dressed. We had the car packed for an overnight stay at his parents who lived 2 hours away. I was putting Lee into his car seat, and as I lifted him up from his infant carrier, he spit up a large amount of spittle all over my cheek, hair, neck, and shoulder. The spittle felt warm and started dripping down inside my chest from my neck. This was when we were just first learning about babies and being new parents. I just laughed and our trip was delayed by half an hour so I could rinse the spittle from my hair. Another time Ben was holding Lee in his lap, and we didn't know that the legs of the diapers were loose and Lee peed and his warm baby urine went all over Ben's lap and thighs – we were at a wedding and Ben ran home to change his pants and then came to the wedding reception late.

I drove to the train station and parked, retrieved my brief satchel from the passenger seat, took off my high heels and carried them with my fingers and ran in my stockings to catch the train, only to miss it by seconds. 'Damn, now I will have to wait 15 minutes for the next train so I will be 30 minutes late for work,' I thought to myself. I was frustrated and made an ugly face and made a fist. Later, I wondered if the train station police had me on camera, looking ugly. Sighing, I sat down on the concrete bench and put my shoes back on. Thank goodness my boss is flexible; he said that if I am late then I could stay late or take a half hour lunch instead of an hour. So, even though I am stressing at the moment, I am thankful to have an understanding boss and a type of job that allows me some flexibility. If I was a teacher, a surgeon, or a pilot – time requirements might be more stringent. Plus, my boss has kids of his own so he understands the lifestyle of working parents.

I also thought about the quiet moment I had an hour before, watching my children brush their teeth before the huge wall mirror. When I was a kid, 30 years before, our houses had small medicine cabinets with a mirrored front on the door and were attached high on the wall above the sink, so small children could not see their reflection in the mirror. It is amazing the inventions and creations that homebuilders are putting into modern homes. I thought about our modern refrigerator and the automatic ice-cube maker; when I young we had to make ice cubes in plastic trays placed in the freezer. I remember when cake mixes, frozen dinners, and microwave ovens were invented. I have seen a lot of changes in my lifetime. The train I am about to catch runs on electricity; before electricity was invented, train engines worked from burning wood, coal and steam. But, of course, the electricity has to come from somewhere, like from a dam with hydro-turbines with running water, wind turbines, solar energy, or a power plant that is powered by burning coal, natural gas, or by nuclear energy. Humanity has made good progress because of good smart people. It is believed by historians that scientists worked for 2400 years to create and harness electricity, and Benjamin Franklin of USA (1788) is credited as the inventor who finally achieved it. Then Thomas A. Edison completed the work of many scientists including himself that took 75 years to create a long-lasting lightbulb. And Alexander Graham Bell invented the telephone in the late 1880s.

The reason why a bird can sit on an electrical wire and not be electrocuted is because the bird is not grounded. If the bird placed a claw on the ground while it was still sitting on the wire, it would get electrocuted. But since it is just sitting there, it is not affected by the electricity.

I was so deep in thought that I almost missed the next train. One time I fell asleep on the train and missed my stop where I got off to go to work. Luckily, I awoke before the next stop but had to wait on the next subway train; that day I was over thirty minutes late to work. But I was scheduled to come in to work that weekend for a few hours since we had a deadline coming up so it all balanced out and my boss was very understanding since I was a young working parent and was handling many tasks in my life, both at home and at work. I had no idea that life would be so hard, even though there are happy moments.

CHAPTER 23

1995   *Mom's Timeout Weekend*

Ben's parents are wonderful people who live about two hours away. Sometimes they drive to see us but Ben loves to drive to see them because his parents are still living in his childhood home. The home is beautiful and Lee, Valerie, and Will love to go visit. The grandparents have always kept a vegetable garden in the back and the kids love to learn about how to grow vegetables. Ben's parents have always kept an awning with a big bench swing in the back yard and they have had several different ones. Of course, the kids love to swing in it. We have many pictures of them all snuggled into it with Ben's parents and even with their great-grandmother who is still alive; Ben's mother's mother. It is amazing to think about families and generations of relatives. Right now there are five generations of Ben's family alive: his great grandmother, his grandmother, his mother, Ben, and our children.

This Saturday morning I helped pack up the kids' luggage after an early breakfast and helped put the kids and some of their toys that they were currently interested in into the mini-van. Ben was taking the kids to visit with his parents but I would stay home this weekend for some time by myself.

I had planned on doing some cleaning, watching some movies that I had wanted to see, and reading a book while Ben and the kids were away for the night. They would be back tomorrow evening. I planned to go to bed early and sleep in late. Next month I planned on taking the kids to visit my sister and their cousins in a different town that was also two hours away and Ben planned to stay home and rest and have some personal time to himself.

Ben was helping Will, our 3-year old, put on his shoes in his bedroom and I wanted to remind Will of something so Ben could hear it also. "Will, remember this please, when you are going to the bathroom at Grandma and Grandpa's, please pee into the toilet. Do not be looking around and accidentally pee on the floor or onto the walls. Okay? I don't know who is peeing behind the toilet, but if it continues, I am going to make you kids go pee outside in the woods like people used to do a long time ago."

Lately I had been finding some pee behind the toilet in the kids' bathroom; I'm not exactly sure who it was because we had a lot kids using the bathroom when their friends were over, but I instructed both Will and Lee to alert them to pee straight into the toilet.

Will said, "Mom, you are crazy. Nobody pees outside in the woods."

Thank goodness Ben came to my rescue and said, "Yes, Will. Mom is right. A long time ago there were no toilets or sinks or tubs. People had to pee in the woods and wipe with leaves because there was no toilet paper. And people took baths in the river or they had to bring up water from wells with buckets. We are lucky because we live in modern times. A long time ago people had it very hard."

Ten minutes after Ben and the kids drove away, I relaxed while sitting on a stool at the kitchen counter, sipping a cup of hot tea. But suddenly I was overwhelmed by the quietness of the house that I was not used to and burst into tears. I told myself that Ben and the kids would be back tomorrow evening, which was only about 32 hours away, so there was nothing to cry about. Also, I could speak to them by telephone land line in about 2 hours. I told myself that I was being too dramatic!

I got busy and vacuumed the entire house. Then I drove to the department store up the highway because I needed a few things. I found a cheap pair of matching lamps that I loved that were on display at the end of an aisle that I walked by; they were looking right at me so I had to buy them. I also bought a small trash can with a lid for our bathroom for the stuff that I threw into it and for the stuff that Ben threw into it; once at our neighbor's house their dog had dragged everything from the trash can into other rooms of the house and it was not a pretty sight. We also had a big trash can with a lid for the kitchen to try to keep bugs to a minimum. I also filled my cart with some clean sponges and some other supplies. I also got us a big new candle and some matches for emergencies. When I arrived back home, I made myself homemade macaroni and cheese from my great grandmother's recipe because the kids usually only want plain macaroni and cheese.

Grandma Agnes' Lithuanian Macaroni and Cheese

Boil elbow macaroni until it is almost done. In a sauce pan you put a few tablespoons of corn oil in a skillet and sauté yellow or white onions diced into small pieces, along with a few cloves of fresh minced garlic and oregano. Next, open a medium or large can of tomatoes and sauté them with the onions and garlic. Drain the elbow macaroni. Take an oblong or round oven-proof casserole dish and butter inside the bottom if you like. Then place a few large spoonfuls of the tomato mixture on the bottom of the casserole dish. Then put a layer of macaroni over the tomato layer. Then put a layer of medium shredded cheddar cheese on top of the noodle layer. Continue making layers until out of macaroni noodles, tomatoes and cheese. Salt and pepper each layer as needed. Using a spoon to push back some macaroni at side or end of the casserole dish, make an opening and pour some milk into the layers and then when you remove the spoon the macaroni will fall back into place. Cover with tin foil and bake at 350 degrees for about 30 minutes. Remove the foil after 20 minutes if you like so the top will brown a little.

 Today I decided to cook the onions and garlic in a little olive oil instead of corn oil, to break out of my comfort zone and do something different.

I am a person who finds it difficult to change my habits and do different things, so this was difficult for me, but sometimes I force myself to do something different because the experts say it is good for you; sometimes I agree with 'the experts' but sometimes I do not. I think if I wanted to make the same recipe the same way for 60 years, use the same brand of toothpaste, or make sure that all 52 cards-in-the-deck are all accounted for at the end of card games, that is not 'obsessive compulsive behavior'. (I am still angry about the corrupt psychiatrist who said I was crazy.)

Once I cooked some Brussel sprouts but Ben would not try one. I told him I would pay him $5 to try one but he just laughed. For green vegetables, Ben will only eat green beans, fried okra, and lettuce. I am grateful that our kids will eat broccoli and Brussel sprouts – I cooked them on nights when Ben had to work late so that is why the kids will eat them. If they knew that Ben hated broccoli and Brussel sprouts, I bet the kids would never have eaten them either.

Thinking about furniture, I decided to rearrange some pieces of furniture in our bedroom. I placed the new matching lamps on our bedside tables and put our two old lamps in the attic. One of the lamps was Ben's lamp from his childhood; it was a samurai warrior lamp.

I went for a quick jog around the neighborhood and met a new friend. Her name was Aamira and she was planting flowers around her mailbox. We talked for a few minutes and I found out that she was Muslim and from Afghanistan. She and her husband had bought a franchise for a restaurant chain. While we were talking, her next-door neighbor Ramona came out to turn off her lawn sprinkler and all three of us had a nice conversation. Ramona was from Ohio; she had gone through a divorce and moved to our city to be closer to some friends. She said she was not coping very and still adjusting to her new life. She told us that she had worn her hair long for forty years but suddenly kept cutting her hair short and changing the color of it with hair dyes. 'When I look in the mirror, I don't feel like myself anymore,' she said. Aamira and I told her to give it time, that there would be more happy times in her life. I just said that to her because that is what I've heard all my life. But sometimes people have to live with devastating losses the rest of their lives; you just go on living. Ramona said that she had been attending a local support group in the community that focused on people dealing with grief or losses. She said that she had heard many sad stories.

When Ben arrived back home the following day, he had a conniption fit when he saw the new bedside lamps. "Where is my warrior lamp?" he asked.

"Don't panic – I just put it in the attic. Can we please use the new lamps for a year, and then we'll go back to the old lamps for a year? We'll alternate. Is that ok?"

He just sighed. "It's not like we have to show anyone our bedroom, right? It's just mine and yours. Why does it have to look like a magazine picture?"

I sighed and looked at him, saying, "I just think we could negotiate and try to use the new lamps for a while. Is that okay? I know this house is both of ours and we can both decorate it but the warrior lamp is kind of...violent-looking."

Ben replied, "Well, that pharaoh painting that you have hanging in the great room is different."

I went and got out his warrior lamp and replaced it on his bedside table and put one of the new lamps on my dresser. That made him happy.

"Sorry, honey. That lamp is a part of me. It's been my bedside lamp since I was in middle school," he said.

He also told me to quit taking so long to get dressed when we were going somewhere – he said it was not necessary to take one and a half hours to get dressed but that I should be dressed and ready to go in twenty minutes. "Well, if you don't want me to look like the belle of the garden, I'm not going to worry about how I look," I said, laughing. "But there is nothing wrong with trying to be the best you can be."

"It doesn't matter because everyone is a belle of the garden," Ben said, reasoning sensibly. "It is what is inside of a person's heart, mind, and their actions is what matters," he said in a patronizing voice.

It was fun rearranging the furniture in the kids' rooms sometimes, too.

A few days later, Aamira rang our doorbell and I invited her into our home. She had baked some cookies and had put some on a plate for our family; how sweet of her to think of us. I reciprocated by bringing her family a plate of brownies the following week. Her son rode the same school bus as Lee and it turned out that Lee knew her son and sometimes sat by him on the bus.

CHAPTER 24

1996   *The Writing on My Whiteboard*

When my train arrived at my stop, I hurried up the escalator and exited the train station into the building where I worked. Arriving at my cubicle, I put my brief satchel beside my desk and turned around, intending to step into the next cubicle to say good morning to Greta, who was my co-worker and my back-up.

I was stunned to see that someone had written 'Humpty Dumpty will fall' on my whiteboard. I'm sure that my heart skipped a beat. I quickly erased the message. I did not know why someone would be so mean to write such a message.

"Good Morning!" I said to Greta.

"Good Morning, Candi. Do you want to go to a Lunch-n-Learn seminar today?" asked Greta.

"What is the topic?" I asked.

"Self-awareness," she said.

"Sure. What time is the seminar?" I asked.

"12-12:30pm in Conference Room 4-B," Greta explained.

"Sure, I'll go," I said. "That's where we had the meeting to discuss the Y2K program changes. I love that conference room." The Y2K project was all computer program changes needed to accommodate the date change for year 2000. Everyone in the world with a computer wanted to make sure their computer programs would not shut down because of the numbers '2000' for the year of the new millennium. Many computer programs just stored the year as the last 2 digits; for example, '95' for 1995. Some programs had to subtract years from a year to get a count of a number of years. For example, if you subtract 95 from 97 you would get two years, but when year 2000 came around a program would error out having to subtract 95 from 00 because you cannot subtract from 00. Many programs and record layouts were being expanded to include a 4-digit field for the year.

"The tables and chairs are gorgeous in that conference room. And the window looks out over the street so you can count Mustangs and Beetle Bugs," I added.

"Candi, you're nuts," Greta laughed. "The notice says that you have to bring your own lunch to the seminar," said Greta. "And, Candi, don't say out loud in the seminar about counting Mustangs. People at this corporation are very formal so you have to act 'corporate'." Greta was very smart and a nice mentor.
I wasn't planning on saying out loud about counting Mustangs; I was saying a joke to her but I appreciated her advice nonetheless.

At precisely 12 pm, Candi and Greta were seated in conference room 4-B with 20 other employees, eating sandwiches or various other lunches, listening to the commentator discuss the concept of self-awareness.

"Self-awareness is knowing who you are and what your values are, how to describe yourself, knowing what factors make you happy, sad, stressed, interested, etc. Part of self-awareness is knowing how you react to certain situations. Humans have a more logical left brain and a more emotional right brain, and the two sides of the brain work together. People are complex. Self-awareness is an all-encompassing task, being in control of yourself – your emotions and your physical actions. It's making plans and goals, knowing and cherishing what is precious to you, managing your time, getting proper sleep, knowing what is reality versus fiction, perhaps finding a hobby or an interest…knowing what you can and cannot do…being honest with yourself…being able to describe yourself…plan your next day…schedule tasks…how you prioritize…" The topic was interesting.

The commentator spoke for the entire half hour.

Candi counted at least 5 Mustangs and 2 Beetle Bugs in the city traffic. She had a special place in her heart for Ford cars and trucks, because Ford was the first car made on the assembly lines. Mercedes was the first car and invented in Germany, but Ford was the first cars mass produced on a factory line. Her first car out of college was a red Mustang but they traded it in after the baby was born for a 4-door car because it was easier to get the car seat in and out. Ben's first car was a Toyota. Candi had been orphaned at age 12 and she lived with her brother until she went to college. He let her drive his blue VW beetle bug sometimes in high school and it was fun to drive. Her parents and siblings loved each other. In her lifetime, Candi considered herself lucky to have been surrounded by good people who never taught bad things like killing people, robbing banks, doing drugs, committing evil acts, being jealous of another person's good things. Candi had never been sexually or physically molested. All of her uncles and male cousins were proper gentlemen and good family.

Later that day Candi found a paper memo in her IN BOX that was being circulated through the department that explained a new trend for corporations was to enact a MISSION STATEMENT for the corporation's goals. The mission statement for their company was currently being developed, but the company would provide excellent customer service, excellent products, offer employees opportunities to advance to other positions with the company, offer employees technical training, offer employee assistance programs that offered counseling, ways to submit complaints confidentially, personal development programs, and even exercise gyms.

Candi crossed her name off the Reader List and walked into Greta's cubicle and put the memo into Greta's IN BOX.

Candi was impressed that the corporation valued its employees and took an interest in the scope of their personal lives as well as their work expertise.

'So, what I learned today is that human lives are complex, the human brain is very complex, and corporations are complex,' Candi thought to herself.

Riding the train homeward bound, she looked at all of the complex people riding on the train. She was one of them.

Candi did not know that the thug that had written 'Humpty Dumpty will fall' on her whiteboard was a computer geek who simply did not like her because he did not like her; he thought she was ugly and he hated her hair color and he hated her style. Humpty Dumpty was a rhyme in the book of nursery rhymes that she read to her kids. In the next years, as new computer languages and operating platforms developed, the computer geek would follow Candi at random and cause her trouble. He sabotaged Candi's car engine several times by hacking into the engine's computer and changing some indicators, causing the engine light to come on and costing Candi and Ben several thousands of dollars of repairs. But Candi never knew that it was the hacker that was causing them troubles. A few times when Candi was out grocery shopping, her checking account debit card was denied and there was no reason; it was the mischievousness of the hacker. One time the grocery store had to wheel Candi's groceries back to one of the coolers while Candi ran home to get the check book. Candi did not have an extra credit card in her purse because Ben and Candi tried not to use their credit cards and kept most of them hidden at home in a safe place.

CHAPTER 25

1996   *Moments in Time*

Candi awakened earlier than usual on a July Saturday morning and decided to drive to the donut shoppe to buy donuts for her family, writing 'Gone to get donuts' on a piece of note paper and leaving it on the kitchen counter.

Leaving her husband and 3 children asleep and driving over the crest of a small hill within the neighborhood and then down the hill and around a curve, she immediately saw something wrong – the small toddler that she knew lived in the house to the right side of the road was toddling along the road in the grass and there was nobody in site. Candi parked the car on the side of the road and ran after the small boy, grabbing his small arm and stopping to lift him upon her hips. She carried him thirty yards up to his house and rang the front doorbell. A few minutes later a woman opened the door with a puzzled look on her face that immediately turned to relief as she said "Oh My God!" and reached for her child at the same time. "Thank you so much. We didn't even know that he had gotten out. We didn't even hear the door open. We didn't know he could even open it."

Candi said, "I saw him running down the street and I knew he'd gotten out by himself. I was driving out of the neighborhood to go get donuts. I knew he lived here because I've seen you playing on the driveway."

"Thank God you were there at the moment you were!" She paused to kiss her child on the top of his head and give him a hug.

Candi said: "That's what I'm learning about being a parent; you have to watch your kids every minute, like a hawk! When my kids were toddlers and we were in a playgroup, my neighbor told me to make sure my kids didn't open the door by themselves or lean against an opened window screen because they could fall out. I was glad she told me that because I like to open the windows when the weather is mild but I didn't think about a toddler leaning against the screen and falling out."

"Well, my name is Jackie and this little guy is Mark. And we very much appreciate your help today."

Candi said: "It is very nice to meet you, Jackie and Mark. I'm Candi. Hope to see you again." And then she turned around and headed back to her mini-van.

Driving home from the donut shoppe, she felt that a strange car might be following her again. She drove into a different neighborhood other than her own and parked her car by a curb for several minutes before continuing home, in hope of losing the car if it was following her.

CHAPTER 26

1996   *Mom the Parrot*

Returning from the donut shoppe, Candi placed the box of donuts on the kitchen counter and circled into the great room, lying down on the floor beside the bean bag chairs that contained her 3 children. Although there were 3 bean bag chairs, the 3 kids were nestled together across 2 of the bean bag chairs. They looked adorable snuggled together, watching cartoons on the television in their colorful pajamas. Candi sat down on the floor beside them and gave them all a big good morning hug.

Morning sunlight filled the room through the tall windows on the eastern side of the house. One great feature of their house was that the great room and kitchen were filled with sunlight all day because sunlight also came through windows on the western side of the house in the afternoon. The only room in the house that didn't get much sunlight was their bedroom which was on the north side of the house, but the windows were still big enough to let in enough light.

A humming bird was drinking nectar from the feeder at the corner of the backyard deck. Will saw the bird and said, "Look at the bird; it is the same bird that came here yesterday." And Lee laughed and asked Will, "How do you know if it is the same bird as yesterday?"

Ben was lying on the couch with his eyes closed.
Maybe he was asleep. She didn't bother him because maybe he just wanted to lay still and not be bothered.

Candi wandered into the sunny kitchen and put on a pot of coffee. She opened the cabinet to get out her favorite coffee mug, and decided on a mug with a palm tree that was sitting in the back near the winter holiday mugs with snowmen and snowflakes on it. She thought she would drink out of the palm tree mug just for a change of pace because she usually only drank out of her favorite coffee mug. She thought about the cold winter weather and the cheerfulness of the winter holidays. Then she thought about spring and summer for a moment. It's funny how your brain can skip around.

"After breakfast and a few chores, would you kids like to take your bikes to the school and we can ride the bikes around the big parking lot and play on the playground?" Candi asked Lee, Valerie, and Will.

"Yes!" they said together.

Ben got off the couch and went into the kitchen and gave Candi a big hug while she was cooking and joined them for breakfast. He said he was playing racquetball with one of his friends that afternoon.

After they had eaten scrambled eggs, fried potatoes and onions, bacon, donuts, and milk or orange juice or apple juice, depending on who wanted what, she helped the kids get dressed, brush their teeth, and comb their hair.

The kids were instructed that they had to tidy up their bedrooms and help pick up the toys that lay scattered around the house and put them back in their rooms or in the toy closet. The kids were very good not to throw candy and gum wrappers on the floor; they were very good to put the trash in the trash can. Valerie wanted to help run the vacuum cleaner through the great room and the hallway, so Candi let her vacuum for a few minutes. Will was very astute to notice that some of Valerie's books were in his bookshelf and he made it a point of telling Candi and Valerie "Look, Valerie, some of your books were in my bookshelf so I will put them in your room"; he was so proud of himself. And Candi was very touched when Valerie replied to Will, "Thanks, baby brother!" Lee was excited to find a lost belt behind a pile of clutter in his room that he thought he had lost a few weeks ago.

Candi took a few minutes to clean out her purse because sometimes a lot of clutter remained stashed in it because she was on the go so much. One time Candi had seen a TV show where a talk show host surveyed the women in the audience to see what odd items they had in their purses for reasons known or forgotten about, and the results were hilarious. Today she only found a small rock that Will had picked up from the ground that she'd tossed into her purse.

So the kids were back in front of the television for a few minutes.

"Put your shoes on so we can go to the playground," she told the kids, as she went into the garage to load their 3 bikes into the back of the mini-van.

Then, she went to brush her own teeth.

She went back into the great room and noticed that the kids had still not put their shoes on their feet. "Put your shoes on so we can go to the playground, please," she said again.

Then, she went into the kitchen to grab her purse and several water bottles for the kids and went into the garage to put the items in the mini-van. Her neighbor across the street said hello and started walking over to talk to Candi.

"Hi, Tara. How are you?", Candi asked as she noticed that Tara was crying.

"My brother just died." She sobbed.

"Oh my God, no", Candi replied. "The brother that I met last year who visited?"

"Yeah", she said. "He was on chemo for two years and they said the cancer was gone except for a trace of it. He looked fantastic when I saw him 6 months ago and they gave him a prognosis of 15 to 30 years. He said he felt fine, back to normal and his hair was all back and his weight was back to normal. We were so happy. And now he is gone."

"What do you think happened?" Candi asked.

"Not sure. I had a different doctor tell me that if a person keeps on taking chemo treatments, it can kill them because chemo is a poison that kills good and bad cells in your body and that a person should not have too much chemo. I begged my brother to stop chemo for a year and just let his body try to heal on his own, because they gave him his bone marrow back from his transplant. I thought if he ate healthy food and exercised, and maybe received a blood transplant if he needed it, or more bone marrow, that he could live for 20 years. But he would not listen to me. I know it would be a risk and I'm not a doctor. But chemo is a poison and if you are on chemo, you have to drink lots of water to flush out the poison. That's why I think there should be laws to regulate the use of chemotherapy in patient treatment. My family kept saying that I should just, quote, 'Shut up and let him make his own decision' and 'exercise and healthy food would not help', Tara said.

"Oh, I am so sorry", said Candi, "And I think if a human stands in the sunlight for a minute or two a day, and tries to get sunlight on their arms, tummy, or legs, it could help the immune system to kick in, because wouldn't our body try to defend itself from being sunburned? And standing barefoot on the grass is supposed to be very healthy for us. I don't know if you've heard about that."

Tara said, "Maybe. Like I said, I think it was a risky decision and he was at a decision-making point. If he didn't have residual chemo, the cancer could have come back with a vengeance, or it could have stayed in remission, or it could have slowly came back. But if he took the chemo, it would definitely start killing the good bone marrow cells that he just received and that just doesn't make logical sense to me at all." Tara broke down and started crying hard. Candi hugged her and held her.

"Anything we can do to help, let us know," Candi said.

"I'm going out of town for the funeral for a week", Tara said. "Would you mind please getting our mail for me out of our mailbox and I'll come over and get it when I get back? " she asked.

"Certainly." Candi replied. Tara turned around and walked back to her house as she said "He was the best brother in the world. We loved him so much. "

Candi headed into her house. She thought also that computer hackers can hack medical records and possibly numbers in test analyzer machines if the machines are connected to the internet. With chip technology and wireless, it is hard to know what is being hacked. Maybe a person should pay close attention to how they are feeling – if they feel ill, then they could be ill. But if they feel great and someone tells them they have cancer, it may or may not be true.

She went back into the great room once more and the children still had not put their shoes on their feet. "Kids? You silly kids! How can we go to the park if you will not put on your shoes?" She picked up Will's little sporties and placed them on his feet. She helped Valerie put her shoes on. By that time, Lee had put his shoes on.

Candi laughed to herself. This is insanity, trying to get the kids to put their shoes on. No wonder I get emotionally exhausted. I feel like a parrot sometimes, repeating myself over and over. "Kids, do you think I am a parrot? Why do I have to say to please put your shoes on 3 times? Did my words go in one ear and out the other?" They laughed. Lee said, "Well, we heard you but we were busy." Valerie said, "I think I heard you say that."

I asked the kids: "Are you trying to drive me crazy?" I laughed as I hugged them.

They had a great time riding bikes around the big school parking lot and playing on the playground. When Candi was a kid, it was just swing sets, slides, and sandboxes. Now, modern playgrounds were amazing engineering designs that included swinging bridges, forts, and tunnels in addition to swings, slides, and sandboxes. And nowadays the grounds of many playgrounds were covered with barks or plastics; when Candi was a kid the ground was loose dirt or grass, although dirt or grass was fine to her, except after raining, the water left the playground a muddy mess. 'It is just amazing, all of the creativity in the world,' she thought to herself.

When it was time to leave the playground, she told the kids: "It is time to get into the Golden Pumpkin so we can drive home." The kids laughed and Will said: "Mom, it is not a golden pumpkin! It is just a min-van." Valerie said: "Mom, stop being crazy!" and she laughed.

On the way home they listened to a children's cassette in the car, singing songs about monkeys, lions, and bears. Candi and Ben loved to sing children's songs with the kids. Some other songs were Twinkle, Twinkle Little Star, Three Little Monkeys Jumping on the Bed, This Old Man, The Alphabet Song, The Wheels on the Bus, and more.

Later that night, Candi set the table in the formal dining room, lit candles, turned the chandelier illumination down low, and they ate mashed potatoes, broccoli-carrot-cauliflower-yellow-and-red-peppers-and-grilled-onions medley and steak cut into very small pieces for children on the fine porcelain dishes. Fresh peaches were in season, and peeled, cut up and placed in a bowl, they made their own juice and were delicious with shortcake and whipped cream. Candi put a Bach CD in the CD player and a few moments later 4-year old Will asked; "Mom, what kind of music is this and why are we eating with candles in a dark room?" This made Ben smile.

"This is called a fancy dinner and this music is classical music from about 300 years ago. And people dressed up in fancy clothes just to eat dinner."

"But why are we doing it?" Will asked again.

"Just so you will know that it is a fancy dinner with candles and Bach music. Some families have fancy dinners for holidays or on the weekend. It is different from eating at the dinette table near the kitchen like we usually do during the week."

"And maybe we could eat a meal out on the deck sometime,"

said Ben. But we didn't have a table and chairs out back on the deck. Patio furniture was on our wish list.

CHAPTER 27

1996   *Does the Lord plan everything?*

"Candi, I need your list of programs and program changes needed for Y2K," said Greta as she walked into my cube.

"I've got it ready," I said, looking through my IN PROGRESS shelf of my desk organizer to find it. "Let me go make a copy." I went to the copy room and made a copy; a piece of the crisp warm paper that came out of the copier gave me a paper cut on my finger. Ouch! I had been injured by a piece of paper. I went back to my office and gave my analysis to Greta.

My desk telephone rang and I picked it up. It was my husband Ben who worked as an industrial chemist in a large laboratory.

"Candi, it's me, Ben. Oh My God! You won't believe what just happened. We were working in the lab and a man fell thru the skylight and crashed to the floor. There are brains and blood splattered everywhere."

"Oh no," I replied to my husband. "Are you okay?" I said, knowing that he would naturally be shaken up.

"I'm okay but I can't believe it. We all know the guy. He works here. He was up on the roof a lot. They don't know how it happened."

"I'm so sorry," Candi said. "Be careful driving home today. Try to focus on driving so you don't have an accident. Are you going to be okay to pick Valerie and Will up from school?"

"Yes, I will pick them up. Don't worry. Love you."

"Love you, too," Candi said and hung up the phone.

She told Greta what had happened to her husband's coworker.

"You never know when or how the Lord will take you back," said Greta.

Both of us were quiet for a few seconds.

"Do you think God took his life by letting him fall through the skylight or do you think it was a human accident?" I asked Greta.

"God told Noah to build an ark because He was planning to destroy the earth with a flood but Noah would be saved," replied Greta.

My brain felt confused. I said, "Well, I have a hard time believing that God would harm people or cause them pain to bring them to heaven. I wish someone would write a modern book and add it to the end of the Bible for the year 2000."

Greta laughed. "No. It is written that nothing can be added or subtracted from the Bible."

"But the King James Bible was translated in the 1600's and when it was written and typed it only included the beliefs of the Jews and Christians."

A moment later a Hindu co-worker named Deepak came walking into my cubicle, saying: "Candi, can I see one of your programs? I need to check a file layout to see how your program is passing it to one of my programs?" Deepak's programs involved corporate tax information.

"Sure," I said, nodding and motioning with my hand towards the bookshelves where I kept the latest printouts of my programs.

"What do Hindus call heaven?" I asked him.

"It's called nirvana. It's when the *atman* or *buddhi* which is what Jews, Christians, Muslims, Shamans, Jains, and Sikhs call the *'soul'*, finally stops reincarnating and reaches its ultimate highest state."

I thought about what Deepak had just told me.

"Maybe we could go to the cafeteria one day for lunch if you'd like and you could tell me more about Hinduism" I said to Deepak.

The corporation was big and it was not unusual for people to have many snack break and lunch buddies. Candi felt like the employees who worked there were friendly, good people and she liked the corporate values that the executives directed to the employees, except the gray area of corporate spying and the mystery of who had tried to kidnap her daughter from her home was still bothering Candi.

"Sure," Deepak replied. "We also have Sai Baba, who is like the Christian Jesus. Sai Baba had an unending casserole dish that fed starving people. Candi, are you going to be doing any data bases for your applications?"

"Yes, I have one program that we will be adding in a data base for a corporate report that will be used by the Sales Division." I had attended the 4 mini-classes that had been offered to the computer programmers at our company because data bases were evolving in information technology. All of our programs involved sequential batch processing because they processed millions of records and it was necessary for all of the data on all of the records to be read each processing cycle because many different types of data files were produced and needed by many types of programs. But I was responsible for one application that produced sales data on paper reports which my boss told me that, because of the new technologies, could now could be stored as a data base and viewed on a computer screen by sales representatives in another division of our company in another city and that division was requesting on on-line data base for their reports. So, one project I was working on was adding logical code to one of my programs that would store the data in a data base and that is why I had attended the data base classes.

For example, say you want to know the population of the United States and you have a computer file with 50 state records stored in a sequential order and sorted in alphabetical order by state name and the records include a field that contains a population estimate for that state. In sequential processing, a computer has to read through all 50 records and add each state's population estimate field to a U.S. total population field that a computer programmer has reserved in the working memory section of their program. Then, when all 50 records on the file have been read and the computer is at the 'End of File' or EOF, then the computer programmer writes the logic to print out the U.S. population total field on a report. But data base languages were developed that allow data to be stored in a way that enables grouped data to be read more quickly such as in columns and in this example the computer programmer would code computer instructions to 'write' or 'store' the state population estimates in a data base column. Then, a computer user who was a member of the sales team at Candi's company, could 'query' the column of data that was reserved for the 50 state populations and the total U.S. population could be calculated in one command. So, in other words, if a person just wanted the sum total of all state populations, the computer does not have to read all columns of information about all of the states like the number of cities, the number of bridges, the number of dams, the number of lakes, the number of interstates, the number of state parks or other data about the state.

For another example, if someone wanted to know the population of Oregon, in sequential processing the computer has to read through all records until it reaches the record for Oregon, but when reading a data base, the search can go directly to Oregon because an indexing key can be placed on the state name column; that is why data bases are usually faster than sequential processing.

"How about you, Deepak?" I asked, "Do you have to make data base changes?"

"Yes, I will have to make changes to my programs for some data bases. I am also thinking about becoming a data base manager."

"What is a data base manager?" I asked.

"At this company, a data base manager is a person who is responsible for overseeing the specifications and the space allocations needed on the mainframes for the data bases. For example, Joe Landor is the person that will handle the creation of mine, yours, Greta's, and anyone else in our computer system who needs to build data bases. And Joe knows our computer system well; he will try to avoid redundancies if possible. For example, if the data base that you build and the Sales Division will use – if another department requests data that could be satisfied with the data from your data base, then your data base will be recommended."

"I remember in one of the classes the instructor said that we would have to submit the specifications to reserve the space on the computer but I didn't grasp the importance of Joe Landor's job or the extent that his work reached. Thanks for explaining it to me, Deepak."

"Sure." He spent a minute looking at a few pages in one of my computer printouts. "I found what I needed."
He put the binder back on my shelf and said "See you later" as he left my cubicle.

Then Greta walked into my cubicle again to see if I wanted to attend a lunch and learn about UNICODE and I marked my calendar to reserve a lunch to attend the UNICODE mini-seminar with her. UNICODE is a coding convention for computer characters that began around 1991. UNICODE can support over one million characters for scripts for languages all over the world. UNICODE has 96,000 characters for scripts for languages all over the world that are enabling computers all over the world to be able to communicate with each other. We would not have to worry about UNICODE at our company because our company was processing with IBM mainframes that used EBCDIC or ASCII in the platform which means the operating system.

I enjoyed the lunch and learn seminars that Greta asked me to attend with her. Greta used to work in the computer mainframe data processing center as a console operator but then applied for a position as a computer programmer and was accepted. My degree was not a Computer Science degree but a Business Management Degree that included some computer programming classes. I was hired by our corporation as a computer programmer because companies were desperate for many IT employees to read all of the program code to check for the upcoming Y2K changes for when the year changed from 1999 to 2000 because the 'SEARCH' commands had not been invented or finalized yet for the programming utility commands and companies needed employees to read thousands of lines of programming instructions to prepare for the year 2000 change.

A few employees in our department were actually trained biologists and school teachers but our company trained them to be computer programmers on our company's computer platform.

CHAPTER 28

1997   *Knock Before Entering*

Valerie had her friend Melinda over to play and they were in Valerie's bedroom along with Will who wanted to build a city and play with trains and cars. I had also helped them erect a tent in the bedroom with a queen-size sheet that was held in place by some books on the top of her dresser, her lamp on her bed table, some books on top of her bed, and one end of the sheet was draped over and tied to her desk chair. So, the three kids were sitting under a sheet in her bedroom pretending they were on a camp out.

Ben had gone to pick up our oldest son Lee who had spent the afternoon playing at a friend's house.

I was doing laundry and was carrying a stack of clean dish towels to the kitchen when I stumbled into my neighbor Joe who lived across the street. Joe was Melinda's father.

Apparently Joe had let himself into our home unannounced and without knocking. I was puzzled because I usually kept the door locked.

I confronted my neighbor and he admitted that he had entered our home unannounced and without knocking.

Even though Ben and I had good relationships with our direct neighbors living on all sides of us, our relationships were respectful and we knocked on each other's doors. The only person I knew who gave me permission to enter her home without knocking was my sister, and I gave her the same permission to enter my home without knocking. But Ben and I customarily always kept the doors locked when we were inside the house.

"I came to check on Melinda," he said but he turned and left our home, closing the door behind him. I was upset so I didn't go after him to try to speak to him further.

The kids played for about thirty more minutes and then Melinda went home at the agreed upon time. I reminded her to look both ways before crossing the street and watched to make sure that she crossed safely to her house. The street we lived on was a quiet street in the back of the neighborhood and there was little or no thru traffic but we are still careful. Joe opened their front door and welcomed Melinda in, waving to me from across the street.

When Ben came home bringing Lee with him, I told Ben in private what had happened. "It's okay," he said.

"No, it's not okay," I said to Ben. "Something is wrong and something weird is going on. Normal people do not break into other people's homes and start wandering around. How did he get in? I'm sure the door was locked."

The next month Valerie invited her friend Hannah from the soccer team spend the night at our house. Hannah's mom Suzi was one of the soccer coaches for the girl's team. When Suzi came to pick up Hannah, I was rolling up sleeping bags and packing Hannah's backpack.

Suzi said she would wait in her car. A moment later when I brought Hannah's sleeping bag outside, I found Suzi going through the interior of my car which was parked on the driveway. I was dumbfounded; why was Suzi, whom I barely knew, searching my car? What was she looking for or was she putting a listening device or a GPS (global positioning chip) in my car?

When I took the cat earlier this month for rabies vaccination, the veterinarian recommended a GPS chip insert for our cat that would enable computers to locate the cat if it ran away, so I agreed to the service. That is how I learned about GPS chip location positioning.

After they left, I told Ben what had happened but he said it was okay. I told him that it was not okay. I told him that I wanted to call the police about Joe being in our house and Suzi being in my car, but Ben said not to. My stomach was in knots.

CHAPTER 29

1998   *I am not crazy*

I asked Ben for a divorce because he keeps on saying that I am crazy, and people are doing some strange things around me and Ben is not concerned. I need to get away from this situation.

If weird things are happening and I am supposed to be crazy, then maybe it is safer for me to get away and be alone.

I feel that this situation is very serious. I have spoken with some of my coworkers and they told me that many people who are diagnosed as paranoid schizophrenics end up in prison for crimes that they probably didn't commit. For example, if a person is said to be crazy, some criminals could come into their home and kill everybody in the home, and then put the gun into the supposedly-crazy person's hand and everyone would think that the supposedly-crazy person killed everyone.

 I am 'crazy on paper' as written on the paper of the psychiatrist in her office. I have been slandered by words on paper.

It is very bad that the psychiatrist has ruined my good name by labeling me 'crazy.' I wrote letters to state and national psychiatric associations to request a hearing on my case but was denied.

Ben and I discussed a possible divorce. I have no problem with him having custody of the children. I would love to have custody of the children, but I am a modern-thinking woman and someone has to be the non-custodial parent. If he won't give in, then I will give in.

Also, right now Ben is the assistant coach of Will's and Valerie's soccer team, which is how Ben knows Suzi, and Ben is the assistant coach of Lee's church basketball team, so it will be easier for Ben to be the custodial parent. Ben and I have been together 20 years so I trust him and I'm sure our divorce will go smoothly as we have agreed. I do not want to stress the kids out because I know kids have hectic schedules just like adults do, so even if I could see them once a month for a nice dinner or an afternoon outing, or an overnight stay, it will be fine. Meeting with the children in a public place will be the safest thing for everyone.

It is sad, but I cannot stay with a man who keeps on calling me crazy. The situation is so bad, and I am so scared, that it feels like I have been turned to stone. I can barely concentrate but I am trying as best as I can.

Somehow, I have to survive.

CHAPTER 30

1999   *The Truth*

I left my job in IT because I was getting spooked. Like the time there was a strange man on our hallway and even Greta did not recognize him. One coworker told me that he heard a rumor that an employee at another company affiliated with our workgroup had been shot to death in his cubicle and no one realized it for many hours. And someone left a note on my desk that said, "You cannot fight this." I showed the note to my boss and asked if he could explain who would have left me such a note. He just shrugged and said "I do not know. But I will tell you something – my house burned down last year." I asked my boss, "What has this got to do with me?" But he just shook his head and said, "We cannot talk about this." So I quit. That night, Ben said I was crazy to quit a $55,000 job.

One night after Ben and I had put the children to bed and finished cleaning up the kitchen from dinner, I went for a ten-minute night jog on our street; I did not go far but just kept to the streets near out home. I had been doing this for several years so I was familiar with the neighborhood. The neighborhood had street lights so the areas in the streets were not very dark, they were fairly well-lit. There was a strange car that I did not recognize driving too slowly down the road; I hid behind a tree for several minutes until I felt the car had left our part of the neighborhood. My knees were shaking but I told myself that this car probably had nothing to do with me so I pushed away my feelings.

My reality was that I had actually experienced some strange happenings, yet Ben thought I was crazy and he had told everyone that I was crazy. So many people thought I had severe mental problems. My life was falling apart.

I began contacting local churches and support organizations, begging for help. Somehow. I ended up working as a waitress in American, Greek, or Korean restaurants. My American boss would sometimes bring donuts or order the employees pizzas to share in the breakroom. My Korean manager Jenna once brought in a box of ice cream cones and offered us a free snack, saying "Fill this with ice cream and enjoy!" and we did. At another restaurant where I worked, our Japanese boss cooked the employees pasta with shrimp for a snack one afternoon. My income dropped drastically but I was still making good money. I met some very nice people who listened to my dilemma. I enjoyed working in restaurants except usually you have to work on weekends and holidays with very little time off. Also, it is hard having to look at delicious food all day long. Waitresses in many restaurants also have cleaning duties, such as sweeping and mopping the floor or vacuuming, dusting the light fixtures, sanitizing tables and chairs, door handles, cleaning windows, and maybe even stocking or cleaning bathrooms. Once I had just arrived at work and began to sanitize all the chairs and tables in my section, when some of the bleach water splashed into my eye. Although my eye makeup was going to be smudged, I quickly ran into the bathroom and flushed out my eye with water from the faucet. One time while I ws cutting lemons, a lemon squirted me in the eye and I had to flush my eye out with water.

At one restaurant, another waitress and I clashed in personality. There were a few times when I was late for my shift by 5 minutes and the other waitress hated me for it and we had several heated moments. One time she said to me, "I wish you would leave. I am going to do everything I can to have you fired." I told this to my boss and my boss said "Ignore her. She is a little bit crazy." The other waitress kept bullying me so another waitress and I reported it to my boss. My boss spoke to her and asked her to not speak to me. I just kept ignoring her. I could have retained a labor lawyer to help me sue the restaurant but I did not get one. I think the waitress who kept on bullying should have been fired but they did not fire her, even though several people were complaining about the bully.

One time I saw the bully waitress in the computer room at the library by the restaurant. I was trying to be courteous to her, so I said hello but she ignored me. I kept hoping she would stop bullying and be friendly, but she kept being mean.

When it was my turn to make the buckets of soapy water and clean water for us to mop the floors with, many times I saw the bully waitress eating fried chicken or pieces or oranges and she did not pay for it. Even our manager saw her do it. That was so hypocritical of her. She would complain if I clocked in 1 minute late, but she was stealing snacks and not paying for them.

At this same restaurant, we had gotten a cute new toothpick holder which was a toucan bird. You pressed the bird's head down and it came back up with a toothpick in its beak. Everyone was laughing about it when they saw it. One day the toothpick holder disappeared and my manager assumed that it had been stolen. About a month later, one of our customers brought an identical toothpick holder in for us and told us that she had ordered us a new one from the internet.

Also, one time a customer named Don sneezed so loud that most everyone in the restaurant laughed and looked at the customer who had sneezed and someone said loudly, 'God Bless You!'.

There was one customer who liked to joke around with the waitresses and he said some funny things. Once he told them that he had an excellent memory and he even remembered being born! One customer said the USPS mail carrier noticed that he had not checked his mailbox in several days so he knocked on his door to check on him to see if he was okay.

Several customers came to eat at the restaurant every day and often talked to the waitresses and the manager about their personal lives. Sometimes it felt like a big happy neighborhood at the restaurant. Customers would share stories about their vacations, their illnesses and problems, their gardens, and their blessings. Some would tell a weird dream they had while sleeping. Sometimes people talked about flying saucers, spaceships, and aliens. Some shared TV shows or movies they had seen, books they were reading, sports they were following, news items, and lotto games. One lady told a story of going to an apple orchard an hour away with another lady and a male friend who was a senior citizen. The man drove back to town, leaving the women stranded and they had to call for a ride. Apparently the senior was having memory problems.

Sometimes small children would fall asleep in a booth after a busy day. One time Candi waited on 2 adults and a 4-year old child. When she went back to check on the table, when she asked "How is your meal?" the adults were chewing food and the 4-year old answered "Fine, thank you." And everyone laughed.

A few times customers brought service dogs into the restaurant. One woman had a tiny white maltese. One service dog was a springer spaniel.

There were two employees at the restaurant who were fighting addictions, and both went to rehab. Two employees had an argument about using the dishwasher when they tried to use it at the same time. "I have to go home in a few minutes, so let me use it first," said a male dishwasher. "No, I was here first and I have to get back on the floor," said a female waitress. They argued for several minutes, wasting time.

There was one man at the restaurant who would always bend his spoon so the base was at an almost 45 degree angle to the handle to eat his soup. He said he like to do it because he saw some spoons like it at the Chinese buffet. The owner finally asked him to stop bending the spoons or to not come back to the restaurant.

One time a customer stood up in the restaurant and played the harmonica for a few minutes. Everyone clapped.

I worked at a restaurant owned by a man from Greece. In that restaurant, some customers got into a big argument about politics and he had to ask one customer to leave and not come back. But, a few months later the customer came back and apologized and was allowed to dine there again. The owner told the employees to never discuss politics, sex, or religion in his restaurant and to just talk about the weather.

At another restaurant where I worked, I was in the ladies room. I had just finished washing my hands when a man walked into the ladies room with a newspaper draped over his hand. I imagined that he was holding a gun under the newspaper but I do not know if he was actually holding a gun. I said 'This is the Ladies Room' and quickly ran past him. I told my boss and we wrote down the man's license plate but I never heard anything more about it.

Once when I was filling my car with gas, two men on the other side of the pump walked around to the back of their truck to put a can of gas in the back. I heard one of the men say 'She doesn't want to die; she's too young' and he glanced at me. I did not take it personally, and I did not tell Ben. Or was this some kind of threat? Maybe someone thought that Ben and I were going to try to sue a builder or someone and claim that our house was bugged or had hidden cameras.

I tried to write down as many theories as I could about who had tried to kidnap my daughter, why a psychiatrist felt it necessary to label me a paranoid schizophrenic, and who had written the Humpty-Dumpty-will-fall message on my whiteboard in my office but I came up with no answers. I went to the police with all of the information, yet there were no answers.

Ben and I were on the deck when he suddenly took both of my hands and said, "The truth is that I love you and you love me and there is no reason to get a divorce. Let's stay together and fight off this satanic evil situation."

I didn't know what to say, because inwardly I was still perturbed that he had been telling everybody that I was crazy.

"Let's talk about it when we get back from vacation," I said. Ben and I had arranged a 4-day vacation which we were looking forward to; the first day to travel, two days to enjoy the beach and the surrounding restaurants, shopping, nature centers, and entertainment that was offered, and the fourth day to travel back home.

We left the garage door up about 6 inches so the cat could go in and out of the garage, but this time we put a barricade of an old towel against the bottom of the door so no snakes or bugs could crawl under the door, even though Ben had placed rubber sheathing under the door. After we had barricaded the door of the laundry room that led into the garage, we exited out of the front door which also had adequate rubber sheathing on the bottom.

I emptied out the refrigerator of any leftovers so nothing would be moldy by the time we got back. Ben turned the air conditioning system up to 80 degrees while we were gone.

We called my sister and his parents and gave them the number of the hotel that we were staying at with our children. We sang '99 Bottles of Beer on the Wall' on the way to the beach with the kids, counted VW Beetle Bugs of every color and tickled each other when we saw one, and played all sorts of games on the way to the beach. We listened to children's music, surfed radio stations that were broadcasting, and listened to some oldies cassettes and even some Beatles songs. Ben did most of the driving, but I drove for 2 of the 6 hours on the way to the beach and on the way back from the beach. For a while we turned off the radio and the children were just quiet, looking out the windows of the van. We passed some cows and horses in some beautiful farmlands and some chicken farms. Once I sat in the back of the van with the kids and Will slept with his head against a pillow that was leaning against my arm. The kids were very good and did not keep asking 'Are we there yet?'

We told some jokes in the car.

'What is yellow and goes up and down?'
A banana in an elevator.

'What goes up and never comes down?'
Your age.

'What is green and flies?'
A super pickle.

'Why is a teddy bear never hungry?'
His stomach is stuffed.

Another game we played sometimes was 'Quit saying everything that I say.' This is when one person keeps on repeating everything a person says and keeps on doing it until they get tired of repeating.

We went through a fast-food restaurant chain to get a meal and the kids were delighted that peel-off temporary tattoos were the kid trinket that came along with the meal. When we got to the hotel, we had fun putting the tattoos on their arms.

The second night, Ben and I were sitting on the hotel balcony looking out at the ocean. We were on the second floor and it was a magnificent view. We cancelled our divorce plans. Earlier that day we had crazy fun on the beach, building sand castles, running around in the surf, and sipping cold drinks under a big beach umbrella. We made sure to apply sunscreen lotion before we went out on the beach. We took the kids to a nice restaurant and we sat on an open porch and saw a beautiful sunset and there was a light warm breeze coming in from the ocean.

When the sun set, we took the kids on the beach with flashlights because Ben liked to do this; he liked to see the sand crabs crawling around but it kind of scared me so we were only out there for fifteen minutes and then I gave the ultimatum to go back to the hotel.

The third night at the hotel, the phone rang at 2am. Ben picked up the phone and I gathered that he was talking to my sister. "Oh, no," he said. "Unbelievable." I heard him thanking her and he hung up and turned to me.

"Our house just burned to the ground. Your sister said we could stay at their place after we drive back." Our neighbor Tara had called my sister to report the fire.

Ben and Candi were glad they had left the garage door cracked and hoped their cat would be unharmed.

CHAPTER 31

1999   *Shelley and Mike's divorce*

"Hi, Shelley, I haven't heard from you in a while. How are you?" I said to my former babysitter as I answered her phone call. All of the kids were older now and in the public school system so now our visits Shelley and her kids were usually just once or twice a year. Will and Valerie still went to some after-school programs when I had to work and Lee had learned to let himself in the house after he arrived home from school. Lee would be at home alone for about an hour before Ben or I got there. I really do not like for Lee to be a latchkey kid but Ben and I still need two incomes.

"It's not good. Mike and I got a divorce but he is telling all kinds of lies about me to the judge through his lawyer and the judge awarded custody to Mike and says I have to have supervised visits with the kids. And you know that I don't need supervised visits with the kids! I am just beside myself. I cannot believe what is happening. Mike and I have been together for 20 years and now he is trying to turn the kids against me and my family. It's all on paper – pure lies! And then he said I needed medication because I am 'irresponsible' just because I left a pot of water on the stove to boil and forgot about it and that happened because I am so confused right now about why he wants a divorce and all of the water boiled out of the pot but I caught it in time before the pot melted which may have started a fire because I always check the kitchen before I go to bed and I also make sure the windows and doors are locked."

"Shelley, that is so awful. Well, I will certainly agree to be a character witness for you if you need one. But, for now I think you should agree to the supervised visits. And I'll be happy to be a supervisor if Mike would agree for me to be one."

The reason why they had gotten a divorce was that Mike would not quit smoking his occasional marijuana. Mike was a great husband and a loving father but he did have a few friends who broke the marijuana law. Shelley could smell it on his clothes. She begged him to only smoke marijuana when she and the kids were gone out of town because she did not want her kids around it, it is illegal, and they could not afford it but he would not comply.

It was so wrong that Mike was telling lies about Shelley and using the kids like property just because he wanted a divorce. He was putting slander of pure lies onto pieces of paper. Mike was being evil. The kids belonged to both Shelley and Mike and both parents should be able to have a good relationship with the kids; they both had been together and parents for 16 years.

Shelley even called Mike's family and begged them to tell Mike to quit telling lies, but they said that the divorce was between her and Mike and they did not want to take sides and they hung the telephone up as she was speaking.

What Mike was doing to Shelley on paper is similar to what the evil psychiatrist Jill River had done to me – putting slander down on paper. I was still angry and scared about what the psychiatrist had written on paper about me; Dr. River only knew me for 10 minutes and she was wrong to call me a paranoid schizophrenic after knowing me only a few minutes. And, just because she wrote it onto a piece of paper, some people would think it was true.

"The main thing I've been doing lately is taking lots of nice warm showers. I just stand under the water crying. I cannot believe Mike is telling all these lies about me and people are believing it," Shelley said.

"I can't believe it either, Shelley," I said. "People are so cruel to other people. It is unbelievable what humans do to each other. I still can't believe that woman tried to kidnap Valerie."

"Yes, that was very weird and unexpected," Shelley said.

"Shelley, have you tried to speak to the police or the FBI about all of these lies and the unfairness of the judge?" Candi asked.

"I did. They don't care. They just say it is a civil issue in a family court that is jurisdiction of the individual states and not a criminal issue."

"Well, I disagree. I think when someone lies and ruins your reputation, it is criminal." I said.

"There are slander laws, but you have to file a lawsuit in a civil case. Maybe I should file a slander case. They put the cart in front of the horse about me and it has ruined my whole life. Candi, you know it is a lie – I watched your kids along with my own for 10 years."

"The facts are true that you were a mother for 16 years and a babysitter to many children, all without any bad incidents. You'd think there could be a jury to hear your side?" I asked.

"I wondered about that also. I don't know why they didn't give me a jury. The judge did not care about the fact that I was a good mother for 16 years. He's not a fair judge."

We said our goodbyes and hung up the phone call. I accidentally knocked some papers off the countertop that fell to the floor and my eye caught a piece of paper swirling to the floor in the sunlight coming through the window. I thought of a bird flying through the air. For some reason I thought about the Japanese culture – the Japanese were creating beautiful art forms like birds by folding a piece of paper which is called *origami*. Other people were recycling paper. Other people were printing news items and advertisements on pieces of paper called newspapers, handouts, and magazines. But Mike was using court papers as a weapon. And Dr. River used her authority as a mental health professional to ruin my reputation because now Ben and my siblings were questioning my mental health because it was written on a piece of paper that I was a nutcase.

Like many people, I have a Bible. I picked up the Bible, opened it, fanned through the pages, smelling the paper. I think the Bible was supposed to be good words written down on paper and I still had not read the Bible cover to cover and I was nearing 40 years old. I wondered how people could be so evil to other people. Why did Mike want to ruin Shelley's reputation? Shelly was a love of his life and the mother of their four children. Why did the psychiatrist want to ruin my reputation? I did not do anything acutely strange to deserve the paranoid schizophrenic diagnosis that the psychiatrists had given me.

Mike and Shelley went to church at least once every two months with their children. Mike proclaimed to be a Christian and believed in Jesus, so was why Mike being so mean to Shelley and determined to ruin the good relationship that Shelley had with their children? I haven't read the entire Gospels of Jesus, but I'm sure Jesus would not want Shelley and the kids to be estranged from each other.

It was good that Shelley's girlfriends were sticking by Shelley's side because they had been together many times over the past fifteen years while they were watching children together and they knew that Mike was telling complete lies about Shelley. It also broke Candi's heart to hear that Mike had told Nathan, Amy, Isaiah, and Hope that 'Shelley and her family were out of their lives.' Candi had driven to a southern-cooking restaurant to meet Shelley and her girlfriends for dinner and conversation. It hurt Candi to see that there was so much sadness in Shelley's eyes, not to mention tears that were streaming down her face as she told Candi and the others how much she missed being a mother. 'You are still the kids' mother,' everyone told her, 'and one day the kids will know the truth about how bad Mike treated you.' But these types of statements did not comfort Shelley.

"The time that I am not spending with my kids is lost time that I cannot ever get back," Shelly cried. "The kids are beginning to grow apart from me, I can feel the distance widening, and it hurts."

"It is said that a kid would search the world over or even fly to the moon to find their parents," another one of her girlfriends interjected.

And the women spoke about Candi's situation regarding the attempted kidnapping for a while and agreed that Candi's life had become as emotionally difficult as Shelley's.

The restaurant was a buffet and the women made themselves plates from the hot and cold bars that included a variety of different foods on different days of the week such as fried chicken, baked chicken with onions and carrots, cole slaw, mashed potatoes, white rice, hamburger steak and brown gravy, turkey and cornbread dressing with cranberry sauce, grilled tilapia fish, baked whiting fish, fried catfish, hush puppies, boiled cabbage, boiled collards, boiled squash, cauliflower, corn, rutabagas, spinach soufflé, pinto beans, yams, lima beans, white beans, butter beans, garbanzo beans also called chick peas, green peas, green beans, black-eyed peas, broccoli-cheese-rice casserole, fried green tomatoes, sliced onions, beets, lettuce, assorted salad dressings, fresh vine ripe red tomatoes, cucumbers, green and red peppers, broccoli salad with raisins and walnuts and mayonnaise, apple salad with raisins and celery, crackers, fruit salad that contained cantaloupe, honeydew, grapes, pineapple, and oranges, egg salad, tuna salad, cold potato salad, cold macaroni salad, banana bread, banana pudding, chocolate cake, vanilla cake, coconut cake, strawberry shortcake, strawberry gelatin, bread pudding with raisins and coconut, peach cobbler, apple pie, cherry pie, chocolate or vanilla pudding, ice cream, fresh hot yeast rolls, honey butter, buttered corn bread, chicken and dumplings, vegetable soup, deviled eggs, sweet and unsweet tea, coffee with caffeine and decaf coffee, lemonade and sodas. On some days, the buffet had other food such as cold crab salad, fried squash, tacos, baked ziti, spaghetti, cold curried chicken salad, sauerkraut, chicken pot pie, BBQ pork and chicken, cheesecake and more.

While they were filling their plates, a commotion occurred. A person who was filling their plate with strawberry shortcake was scraping the whipped cream topping off of the entire cake onto their plate, leaving the rest of the vanilla cake without icing. Another customer saw it and was saying: "Fool, stop that. Look what you did? Now there is no more icing on the cake for the next person, you idiot! Don't you have any manners?" A manager was trying to calm them down. I agree, that person was wrong to do that. They could have just asked for some additional whipped topping from the kitchen. To me, the customer who was scraping all of the icing off of the cake at a food buffet was crazy – where is a psychiatrist when you need one? I said to myself.

Upon leaving the restaurant, Candi retrieved her umbrella from the bucket that was left by the door for the customers to put wet umbrellas in so the raindrops would not get the floors of the restaurant all wet. Because it was still raining, Candi opened the umbrella and there was a hole in the umbrella. Apparently someone threw a wet cigarette butt into the umbrella bucket and it burned a small hole in her umbrella. She looked at the stream of water pouring through the hole in her umbrella but she laughed instead of cried.

Candi's college girlfriends didn't know what to think after Ben called them and said that she was acting strangely because they didn't see Candi except once or twice a year, and when they did get together, it was only for an hour for lunch or dinner, so they had not noticed any unusual behavior from Candi. Candi was so heartbroken that her girlfriends were not returning her phone calls for a yearly lunch together, but there was nothing she could do. She had to let her friends go if they did not want to see her anymore so she changed her PO Box Number; it hurt Candi a lot because she valued her friendships very much. She thought her friendships would last a lifetime.

Candi had subscribed to a PO Box after the attempted kidnapping of Valerie. She had read that people can be snoopy and even go through the mail in your mailbox to see your contacts. Since she and Ben were not at home during the day, she thought it would be best to get a PO Box for a while. Ben thought she was crazy, but she did it anyway and used their PO Box for all of their accounts and mail. In Candi's way of thinking, the less people who knew where they lived, the better, so she would give people her PO Box instead of their physical address of their home. She didn't know what evil group of people she was dealing with, but someone had almost kidnapped Valerie so someone somewhere knew something.

Candi looked to the sky, like she had begun doing since she was 9-years old when her father died; a person suddenly realizes a profound change in their life and many people cry for guidance or help from the Lord.

You look to the sky but there are no answers. But Candi thought that this is what faith is, to still have hope in God after you live through difficult struggles as well as in happy times.

The strange circumstances that Candi had been processing in her brain caused anger, sadness, and despair at times. She was also in disbelief that Shelley could not see her children, that someone had tried to kidnap her own child, and that Ben was not supporting her emotionally very well by calling her crazy.

Candi had an appointment with a church counselor who was a man named Ragsdale and he listened to things that were bothering her and he said "You are crazy. I can't help people like you." She saw another church counselor who was a woman who told her she was suffering from factual incidents that were obviously causing her great anxiety. She also saw another psychiatrist who told her "You are a paranoid schizophrenic because most people do not accuse people of spying on them." But Candi argued that she was not accusing anyone but just wondered if her home could be bugged or contain hidden cameras. The psychiatrist said "I am sorry. I cannot help you." Candi decided to have several sessions with the church counselor who recognized that she was suffering was anxiety. It spooked her that mental health professionals could simply label her as crazy when she knew she wasn't crazy. She consulted some attorneys who said they were sorry but they were not interested in her case.

The next morning when she was making a pot of coffee, she slammed the coffee carafe down on the counter in anger and broke it. Then she started crying. Thank goodness that Ben and the children did not witness it because they were still asleep in their beds.

Sometimes Candi woke up thirty minutes earlier just to have a few minutes to think and go over their plans for the day. Today her self-esteem went down the tubes after breaking the coffee carafe.

CHAPTER 32

2000   *Computer Digital Technology*

When our house burned down, we did not rebuild. It hurt us deep in our souls to move because we had loved our home, but we both felt that something was wrong. Instead of rebuilding, we moved to another neighborhood and we installed a wired security system where the monitor would beep loudly if any window or door was opened if it was in the ON MODE. Ben and I had a sense of peace knowing that we were being safely protected by the security monitoring system.

Still being concerned about the attempted kidnapping of Valerie ten years before and the diagnosis of paranoid schizophrenia seven years before, Candi wanted to improve security. They got a miniature terrier dog that got along well with their cat, and Ben bought a gun. Both Ben and Candi became experts on handling their particular handgun and went to the shooting range together to practice. Their children did not even know that their parents had a gun; Ben and Candi kept it hidden and only took it out at night. Ben kept his baseball bat from his teenage years beside the bed at night and in the morning, he put it under the bed. Candi kept a sharp knife on her bedside table but she put it away in a safe place immediately upon awakening so the children could not see it. She also took one of her sharpest kitchen knives and kept it in the side pocket of her car door. She always made sure the mini-van was locked when it was in the garage so the kids or a predator could not get into it. She also went to a hardware store and bought some mace and she kept it in her hand when she was alone in parking lots. Candi tried to be very aware of what was happening around her.

Ben and Candi did not allow their children to stay home alone because the kids were young and because of the strange circumstances in their life. When the children were a few years older, when the children were home alone on rare occasions, and if no visitors were expected, the children were instructed to never open the door and to not answer the doorbell. Candi put curtains on some windows that were uncovered, making sure the windows were covered if she left the kids home alone. Lee was 14 years old now, so he understood his parents' concerns and listened closely. And, in fact, one time all 3 children were home alone for a few hours and the doorbell did ring, but all 3 children remained perfectly quiet and did not answer the door and they heard a car drive off. The kids told Ben and Candi about it, and, after that, Ben and Candi decided to not ever leave the kids home alone again because they had not been expecting anyone to drop by their house; it was just too risky to leave the kids alone.

But it could have happened another way; if a burglar thinks that no one is home, then maybe a burglar would have entered our home. I have heard about 'safe rooms or panic rooms' in houses where people can retreat to safety, much like storm cellars that protect from tornadoes.

They did have a place near the porch where they kept an extra house key hidden, and they taught the kids where the extra key was hidden and all three kids knew how to open the front door to get inside if they needed to get in.

The house that they moved to was very different than the small ranch that had burned down. They had lost everything in the fire, but they had an insurance policy that had paid to replace all of the home furnishings. They had lost all of their pictures, but Candi's sisters and friends sent back to Candi pictures that she had sent to them, and Candi and Ben were grateful to have some of the pictures back. Ben had been wise to place some important documents like the marriage certificate, the kids' birth certificates, the insurance policies, the car titles, the mortgage note, and immunization records in a rented bank vault at their bank. Their cat was safe, so they were grateful for that.

Over the next decade, cell phones and laptop computers became popular worldwide. Many people stopped using land-line phones and relied only on cell phones. But then computer hackers began sabotaging the data in computers and cell phones and stealing people's identities and information. Norton, Avast, Malwarebytes, Microsoft, Apple, Google, HP, IBM, Dell, PC Matic, McAfee and other companies created software to stop hackers from sabotaging computers. Web pages for your business can be backed up and restored in case your website gets taken over by ransomware.

Candi often wished she'd had the opportunity to learn HTML, PHP, PYTHON, and RUBY which are computer languages used to create web pages on the internet. She did not have the opportunity to learn the new computer database languages such as C, C++, Java, Pearl, C#, or others that had object-oriented capabilities. She would have liked to learn cyber security.

Candi relaxed on the couch, closed her eyes, and thought to herself for a while about many things…

Languages and religions have been causing problems for thousands of years, alienating people from each other.

A great thing about modern computers are the language translation programs that are allowing humans to communicate with each other more accurately. Maybe one day in the future many people will speak a common language which will lead to a more peaceful world.

There are many computer apps that allow you to post information about your family tree so you can find your ancestors and reconnect with lost loved ones or people that you didn't know you were related to; but these applications also give strangers or computer hackers access to much personal information.

There are pros and cons to this miracle invention called the internet.

In the USA, many people speak Spanish and Candi remembered a Spanish man told her that he believed everyone in the USA should speak Spanish. His statement mystified Candi because the English language is a more modern language than any other language. For example, in English, a person does not have to know if a door or a car are feminine or masculine. In English, a door or car are not considered to be a 'male' or a 'female.' Many people in the world speak Chinese Mandarin or other Asian languages that have thousands of calligraphic symbols. Candi knew a Japanese man who had been speaking and reading Japanese his entire life and still did not know every Japanese symbol. Candi was amazed at the man's linguistic ability; he could speak English and Spanish as well as he could speak Japanese. Candi had read an article that explained how some people were working very hard to translate language symbols of many languages such as Russian, Greek, Hebrew, Aramaic, Farsi, Sanskrit, and Hindi into the sounds of other languages that used 26 alphabetic characters.

A disadvantage of land-line phones is that wires can be cut that makes them useless. A disadvantage of cell phones is that many computer hackers can listen to conversations and change data in the cell phones. Computer hackers can change the date and time, create text messages and even mimic a person's voice and mimic cell numbers to create completely false conversations. Hackers can control your cell phone calls and voice mail.

Candi told her children: "If you get a text message or a phone call from me and I tell you that I am picking you up in my car, and you see my car drive up, make sure you look into the car and make sure that it is actually me picking you up" because computer hackers can create all kinds of trickery and steal people's identities.

There is a movie called 4closed produced in 2013 with actress Marlee Matlin that has a computer hacker character scare a family that moved into a house that he lived in but was foreclosed on. The computer hacker also hacks the teenager's cell phone. The Net 1995 with Sandra Bullock shows identity theft. TV show Hawaii Five O episode named Akanahe is about a computer hacker who hijacks an airplane en route to Honolulu from LA. Author David Baldacci wrote King & Maxwell about a computer hacker who hacked a car engine. There are many productions showing how dangerous computers can be. You would think the public would protest that we are being forced to use technology that is so easily hacked.

Ben and Candi read that security systems can be hacked. Computer hackers can 'freeze frame' a picture on a monitor; for example, a person can be looking at a picture of their baby asleep in a crib, while in reality, someone is sneaking into their baby's room and kidnapping their baby right out of their crib.

Using GPS positioning, computer hackers can stall your car, cause a person to have a car accident, or locate you by the location of your cell phone and kidnap you.

Computer hackers can change engine light indicators and cause them to run off of the road and crash into each other. Computer hackers can cause airplanes to crash into each other. Car manufacturers have produced cars that are driven by computer for thousands of miles to make a delivery with no human driver driving the vehicle and a hacker can make these vehicles crash into other vehicles.

Many people feel that the internet should be optional in cell phones, personal computers, TVs, and car engine parts. Why are people being forced onto the internet? The old desktop computers in the 1980's and early 1990's did not have internet components inside them so data was more secure.

Candi did not like banks forcing accounts on the internet because she did not use on-line banking but one reason they put everyone's information on the internet is so that all of the ATM's in the world could be connected and work together. For all the conveniences that computers have given us, the unethical hackers have compromised everyone's safety. There are possible nightmares for everyone. Candi thought: A computer hacker could empty my bank account if they wanted to, know the exact location where I live, flip my car, and steal my identity. Cash could be loaded to a reloadable card not connected to my bank account but then you may not have transactions recorded like on bank statements.

In theory, if my house was properly wired for the internet and had hidden cameras or wireless cameras, an unethical hacker could film my family in motion, 'photoshop' in different features or faces, and create a movie and I wouldn't even be aware that it was happening.

Having everyone's accounts on the internet enables law enforcement agencies and credit agencies to freeze the accounts in a second if they wanted to, to help catch or stop criminals, so this is a good thing about the internet.

Ethical hackers are the computer forensic experts who help the police find and stop criminals.

Also, I was told by a doctor in the USA that all patient medical records were required by law to be put on-line and he disagreed with that law.

Maybe one day people could be offered intranets of cities or states if they do not want to be connected to the world-wide internet.

Many schools and colleges are forcing computers to be the main mode for learning and test-taking for students that is all hackable. Many people still like to learn from books.

Many schools are not teaching cursive writing anymore because they just want children to type on computer keyboards and many people disagree with that decision.

Many people are concerned that all world languages are in danger of destruction because of all the abbreviations being used during texting like LOL which means Lots of Love.

If computers were safe, I would have a different opinion. But computers are hackable and I even met a hacker who said that she could hack anything she wanted to, that she knew all of the technologies.

Computers can do wonderful good things. For example, a surgeon in one country can perform robotic surgery over the internet to operate on a patient lying on an operating table in another country. Computers have enabled humans to retrieve data in a matter of moments instead of hours. Computers are enabling people to connect globally and information can move quickly. But the evilness that computer hackers are capable of needs to be considered.

A computer hacker could change the logic for a gift card so that every time the gift card holder made a purchase with the gift card, the balance is refreshed to the original amount or the amount deducted each time was less than the amount purchased.

Many people are trying to figure out how to fight computer hackers. People have been putting their actual pictures on social media and connecting with their friends and business associates but now some people have taken their pictures off of social media. Some people post old pictures or pictures of a favorite item instead of their photo, or a half-picture of themselves or a picture with sunglasses on; this may protect a person from computer apps that pull up information with facial recognition data. Some people use pseudonyms or misspell their last names on social media on purpose.

Computer experts may potentially know every single thing about an individual and they can manipulate lives. Some people are not bothered by it and do not care if the computer experts know everything about them. Maybe the people who are in charge of operating the local computer servers should be voted in as if it were a publicly held office. Maybe the people should be able to know who the spies are and vote them in, but it wouldn't stop the evil computer hackers. Maybe computers will just be declared junk and nothing important will be kept on computers anymore. No one is exactly sure what is going to happen in the computer industry, but people must be educated as to the advantages and disadvantages of computers; otherwise in the future very naive people or people with no knowledge of computer technology will be at risk.

A cell line that is used for internet communication could be separate from a cell line that is used for talking. That way a computer hacker may know all about someone from following them on social media, but in reality, the computer hacker may not know all of a person's plans because a person could have a second or third cell phone that they use to actually make plans with family or friends. And that cell phone number could be changed periodically.

If you do not store the contact list of your friends' phone numbers in your cell phone, it makes it harder for a computer hacker to victimize; you could keep a piece of paper in your wallet with phone numbers written down on it with names or initials beside the phone number. The computer hacker would have to work harder to victimize.

If a computer hacker put a 'bug' which is also called a 'virus' on your phone, it means that there is a computer algorithm which is also called a computer program that the hacker left on your phone or computer; you could reset your laptop or cell phone to its original factory settings. Computer hackers can place viruses in the pixels of pictures; so it may be hard to get rid of viruses. Unethical hackers can put permanent viruses in the ROM operating systems of your electronics that are still lurking even if you reset the computer to factory settings which is why some people have smashed their laptops or cellphones with a hammer and went out and got a different device.

Friends could have a pre-arranged place to meet at the same place and time every month and discuss life or make plans in person. Some may arrange to have private talks while on hikes in parks or mountains, on the beach, walks around a mall or city sidewalks. People could write messages on paper for a friend to read, and the friend could write a message back.

If you feel like you are being followed by a computer hacker or a predator, it is said that you should not make yourself an easy target. For example, do not park in the same place each day. Do not take the same route every day, driving or jogging. Make plans to protect yourself.

If you are jogging or biking in a remote area, you are making yourself an easy target. Perhaps have mace or a knife with you and be prepared to use it. If your car is parked in a busy parking lot and you are approached by a stranger, put up your mental wall of defense immediately; the person may be asking for help or donations but the person may have evil intentions. Also, do not linger in a parking lot; when walking to your car, have your car keys ready, look into the back seat of the car and make sure no predator is in your car, get in your car and go. Do not make yourself or your children an easy target.

Some people say you should never go to a very remote place in a park or other place alone or with people you do not trust. People have been known to disappear from remote places and even in very crowded places.

Many people desire cars to be manufactured that have no computers in the engine parts. Many people desire for TVs to be manufactured that have no computers in the TV. Some think that people are looking back at you from a camera inside the TV while you are watching TV. Some people want to go back to analog TV with antennas.

Some people are not bothered at all by the computer technology but maybe they have never been the victim of a computer hacker.

Some people think that the bitcoin (a unit of internet money) will control the world someday but others think that paper money and gold ingots will always be around because some people do not want the internet and computers to rule the entire world.

Computer hackers can create false news accounts on the internet so some people want to follow local new broadcasters on television or read paper newspapers.

After thinking for about 15 minutes, Candi got up from the couch and boiled a can of Campbell's Cream of Celery soup, poured it into a bowl on the table, sprinkled some black pepper on it, and relaxed looking through a few magazines that Ben's mother had given for her to read.

CHAPTER 33

2000   *Lunch with Greta*

Although it had been almost two years since I left my job in IT, I still kept in touch with Greta. She invited me downtown to the building where I used to work and where she still worked so that we could have lunch together and talk. It felt strange riding on the subway train to go downtown; part of me felt like I had done this a long time ago and part of me felt like I had done it only yesterday.

Greta told me that all of the computer systems had transitioned well with the Y2K (Year 2000) revisions that we had researched and begun working on in 1990, ten years prior to the change. They had had only minimal problems with the new program implementations.

One big change that she showed me was that all of the reports that had been previously been printed out on paper were now available on-line to look at on computer cathode ray tube monitors if the programmer or user did not want a paper printout. I was amazed at the graphic interfaces on the monitors because when I left only text characters appeared on the screens of the monitors.

Part of me missed my IT job very much, but thinking about the lady in our garage who had tried to kidnap Valerie, the strange man in the train parking lot, the strange message on my whiteboard, my missing scheduler binder, and the psychiatrist who said I was crazy gave me shivers. I felt a panic attack coming on but asked God to help me get through it. Why had my life taken such a bad turn? The main thing I kept on telling myself and thanking God for was that Valerie was safe and doing fine.

Greta told me that she had attended family reunions on both her mother's side of the family and her father's side of the family. Both reunions were big events and at least 100 relatives came to both reunions. She showed me a stack of photos that she'd taken at the picnics. I was happy for her. She said that both of her families had the big reunions every 5 years, without fail, because most of her relatives lived within 100 miles of each other.

After lunch, Greta took me back to the office with her so I could say hello to my former boss and coworkers. I enjoyed the afternoon very much and felt so fortunate to have known such a great group of people. One of our other coworkers had accepted a job at Google and was going to be work on the Google Maps application. "I'll be a test driver to test the app," I offered and we all laughed. I wondered if I should seriously consider that!

I drove home a different route from the way I had driven downtown and was surprised to see how much things had changed in 2 years. Several homes and shopping centers had been torn down and many new structures had been built.

When I got home I said to Ben: "Ben, I don't like this house. It is too dark with not enough sunlight and it is too close to the road and you hear a lot of traffic. Sometimes I need silence. I'm sorry but I think we made a big mistake buying this house. I want to try to work with a real estate agent and maybe try to move to a different house."

Then Ben said, "I regret buying this house also. It's way different from our first home and I'm not happy either. But we don't really have the money to move right now so can't you just try to adjust to it for a while?"

"What harm would it do to try to move? Maybe we can find a situation where we can just move with no big out of pocket cash expense?" I said back. He didn't say anything.

'Marriage', I thought! Well, I am not perfect and neither is he. But we do love each other. At least, I love Ben, but maybe Ben doesn't love me anymore.

It happened that a few months later, we sold our house to a friend of one of our neighbors who wanted to move to be near their friend, and we found a great deal on another ranch house owned by a man who wanted to sell quickly because he wanted to retire to Australia to be with a woman he loved. It worked out for all.

One night I had been listening to some of Lee's alternative music CDs that he had bought with his allowance money. He was away spending the night with a friend, and I sat on his bedroom floor until 3am listening to his music CDs because I wanted to hear some alternative rock music groups such as Nirvana, Metallica, Green Day, Third Eye Blind, Smashing Pumpkins, and Foo Fighters.

Lee was only 12 when he first acquired some alternative rock music and once, I thought, is this kind of music too much for a 12-year old? but I think kids are growing up much faster than we did when I was 12 which was over two decades ago.

When I went and climbed into bed, Ben asked me why I had stayed up so late so I told him I had listened to some of Lee's alternative rock CDs. He said, "You are crazy." 'Hmpf', I said to myself. Ben will only listen to James Taylor, the Eagles, and Dan Fogelberg. I like all 3 of these also, but I am branching out on what types of music I will listen to. If nothing else, it is something to talk about with my teenager.

CHAPTER 34

2005   *Shelley was slandered on paper*

The time period from 2000-2005 was a nightmare for Shelley. Mike would not let Shelley or her family visit with Nathan, Amy, Isaiah, and Hope. They would not give Shelley any pictures of the children or any of their schoolwork. When Shelley tried to call on the telephone to speak to the kids, she was immediately hung up on. Shelley experienced anxiety, confusion, anger, and sadness. She had trouble concentrating. She did not understand how a judge could ruin a parent's life for no valid reason. She kept records on paper; she had only spoken to her kids 4 times in 5 years by telephone and had only seen them twice in the 5-year time frame for 2 hours each time. Nathan, Amy, Isaiah, and Hope were becoming detached from Shelley and did not hug their mother like they used to before the divorce. The children were being brainwashed against Shelley because of the lack of regular visitation.

The church that Shelley and Mike had attended gave her a job working in the preschool so she did have support from the women and men at her church. Mike stopped bringing Nathan, Amy, Isaiah, and Hope to the church and Shelley had no idea if the children were attending a different church.

When I spoke to her on the telephone she said: "I wake up every morning feeling like I want to cry. I cannot believe what has happened to me. I cannot believe a judge can just ruin your whole entire life based on lies."

I told Shelley: "I cannot believe it either. I cannot believe judges have the power to ruin your life and your relationship with your kids for no reason. Nathan, Amy, Isaiah, and Hope love you and there is no reason why they should be denied visits with you and your family, and even Ben and me, Lee, Valerie, and Will. This is absolutely inappropriate, slanderous and evil." I became angry and hit my fist on my kitchen table. I was so angry at the judge who had entirely ruined Shelley's life and her children's life for no reason. "Shelley, I know you are a good and excellent person and I know you believe in God. God knows everything that is in every person's heart, mind, and soul. God knows the truth. Maybe God will fix this. But I believe that maybe God cannot fix everything on earth because God is a spirit. Why do innocent people get robbed or murdered for no reason? Do you understand what I am saying? Maybe God cannot intervene physically on earth but just knows everything that is happening. Oh, Lord, I feel so bad for you. Shelley, if you want to come live with us in our extra room or if you ever want to stay with us for a few days, you are welcome. We love you." I started crying for my friend. I felt so bad for her. I was stunned that the divorce court had entirely ruined her life because of the callous personalities of the people running the court system in their county. Candi wondered about the judge who ruled over Shelley and Mike's divorce proceeding; she wondered if the judge practiced a religion. The majority of their county was Christian denominations and Roman Catholic. If the judge believed in God and Jesus, Candi did not understand why a judge would treat Shelley so bad.

Shelley saved up for an attorney who filed a contempt motion asking for the judge to intervene and consider the terms of the divorce. The attorney provided Shelley's testimony to the court that Mike had smoked marijuana on occasion in their backyard and this habit was inappropriate for a parent. Candi, Ben, and Shelley's babysitter friends all testified on Shelley's behalf that Shelley was a loving and responsible mother who did not need supervised visits, loved her children, and should be able to see her children.

Mike's attorney put one of Mike's friends on the stand who testified that Shelley had mental problems because she was jealous and had 'stalked' Mike when he was out on a date, when the truth was that Mike kept hanging up the telephone when Shelley tried to call the kids so Shelley tried to confront him in person to ask him why she could not speak to the kids. The witness was a complete liar but the judge didn't know that.

The judge still imposed supervised visits on Shelley, and Shelley was at least glad that Judge Cameron had decreed supervised visits again. But her nightmare continued because Mike refused to allow her to have supervised visits with the kids again. Shelley was completely perplexed and aghast at the strange divorce that was ruining her whole life. She had given birth to four children and had been a wonderful mom for 16 years and now suddenly she was completely blocked from seeing her kids; her heart was broken because she was not being able to help to continue raising her children.

Candi and Ben had tried to contact Mike several times to try to arrange visits with the kids so Shelley could see them, but Mike kept hanging the phone up when they called him. Candi could not believe that Mike would not let Shelley see the kids with herself and Ben. Nathan and Amy had spent the night at their house for slumber parties with Lee and Valerie as often as Lee and Valerie had spent the night for slumber parties at Mike and Shelley's house, so Candi knew that Mike was just playing a silly game in their divorce. What Mike was doing to Shelley and her relationship as a mother to their children was purely ridiculous. Candi had no idea why the judge was doing what was he was doing, but the judge was ruining Shelley's entire life. Candi could not believe the evilness.

Shelley and Candi checked the city ordinances and decided to picket outside of the county courthouse where Shelly and Mike had gotten divorced. Shelley's friend Barbara also wanted to picket with them. Candi had spent the previous evening and spent the night with Shelley and they made big poster boards that said STOP UNFAIR DIVORCES IN THE USA and I AM A VICTIM OF LIES and HELP A GOOD MOTHER. Candi and Shelley ate nachos with the 7-layer Mexican dip they loved that had ground beef, onions, jalapeno spices, refried beans, cheese, tomatoes, lettuce, and sour cream and had a few daiquiris while they were making the poster boards. Candi drank two daiquiris, one strawberry and one green apple. When she woke up the next morning she felt queasy but still decided to picket. During the first hour, she had to run down the street and vomit into some bushes that were in front of a parking lot. Then she chewed on a mint.

"You okay?" asked Shelley, concerned for her friend.

Candi replied, "Yeah, thanks. I'm not much for alcoholic drinks. I should have only had one drink. Every time I drink too much, I get sick. Maybe it's because of when I had my appendix out as a child."

A few attorneys stopped by and chatted with them, wanting to know the details of the divorce. One attorney suggested a lawsuit against the state. Another attorney suggested that it should be a civil right to be able to see your children if there were no allegations of abuse. They picketed for 2 two hours, had lunch at a nearby sandwich shop, and picketed for another hour.

Later that night, Ben said that Shelley and Candi were being radical but Candi just smirked and said 'No.'

She said to Ben, "Ben, this is no joke. Shelley was a good mom and the justice system should not allow her relationship with her kids to be ruined. That's not good. What planet are you from? Honestly?"

"Well, you don't have to embarrass our family by picketing," he replied.

"What? Ben, we have the freedom to protest in the USA. All we did was stand on the sidewalk and peacefully plead our cause – if the cops asked us to leave, we would have left. This is wrong what the judge did to Shelley and lots of other parents of divorces in this country. Think about the kids also. Did Shelley's kids deserve to have been estranged from Shelley?"

Ben said, "You and I have different personalities in some ways. I would never picket in public. I would just try to talk to lawyers."

They decided to take a walk. While walking, Candi thought to herself, children of divorces have to suffer the consequences as much as the parents; the children's relationships with other children their age may change or be discontinued and children have to deal with the changes emotionally. Children also are forced to deal with changes when their parents change jobs and move to different places or just move to new places. Some parents consider the opinions of their children and some parents do not. Children whose parents serve in the military are often uprooted and moved to new places, and these children, who are often called 'military brats', are forced to deal with sudden changes.

It is sad for both adults and children to move to new places and have to leave friendships behind; in modern times, communication and travel arrangements are much easier that enable people to keep in touch, but it is still not the same as being able to be with someone face-to-face and have a conversation or enjoy a meal or take a walk with them. A long time ago, before telephones, when people packed up and left, you might or might not ever see them again.

Ben and Candi invited Shelley to go with them on vacation one spring for a few days to the beach. They could see the complete sadness and hopelessness in Shelley's eyes. Shelley was a wonderful person, a fantastic mother, a great friend, and a reliable and good babysitter who did not deserve what Mike and the judges had done to her; they had put her in the worst situation imaginable for a divorcing parent. Even Lee and Valerie were confused and asked Shelley: "Why didn't Nathan, Amy, Isaiah, and Hope come to the beach with us?" which broke Shelley's heart. Shelley was honest when she answered their questions: "Mike is being mean and unfair to me in our divorce. He will not let me or my family visit with Nathan, Amy, Isaiah, and Hope. It makes me very sad and breaks my heart." Valerie was very sweet; she came over to Shelley who was sitting down in a chair and she laid her hand on Shelley's shoulder and Valerie said: "Shelley, it breaks our hearts, too."

Shelley had been estranged from her children for five lonely years now.

CHAPTER 35

2005   *Candi's Soul*

Candi had lost both of her parents by age 12, so she felt very alone in the world. She had spent her whole life trying to look into the mirror and 'beyond the mirror' to get a grasp on life, trying to 'find herself' and direct herself in life, wondering who she was and why was she left alone with difficult feelings to deal with. She had had a great childhood and loved her parents, and her parents loved her, and then she had lost everything. Her brother took her in for six years until she turned eighteen and left for college; if he had put her and her younger sibling into the foster care system or an orphanage, her life might have gone in a different direction. Candi was grateful that she was not separated from her family. She had always heard that families that stay together and pray together can have good results. As the saying goes There is no place like home. She looked at the good things that other people were doing and she decided that she wanted to do good things and she consciously made choices to direct her life in good ways. She read an article about Scientology that said that people have a 'spirit' that they need to control, so Candi tried to take control of her spirit and guide it to be a good person. Years later, she realized that 'to guide one's own spirit' is a major tenet or doctrine of many world religions.

Once again, Candi wondered how evil people could kidnap people, like the woman who almost had tried to kidnap her baby. She also wondered how Mike could destroy Shelley's whole relationship with their children – Mike proclaimed to be a good soul yet he was doing evil to Shelley and this made no sense to Candi. And Shelley, Ben, and Candi were still flabbergasted about the evil psychiatrist who said Candi was crazy for no good reason! Candi wanted her soul and spirit to be as pure as possible when she died so the Lord would save her soul. Candi was not perfect but she was trying to make herself a better person each day, that way her soul and conscience would have more good things on it than bad things.

Candi was thankful that she always had good teachers at the schools she attended. She reminisced about an elementary school teacher. If the class was being good, the teacher would draw a star at the top corner of the chalkboard but if the class was being too rowdy, the teacher would draw an unhappy face at the top corner of the chalkboard. If a student was really being bad, the teacher would write the person's name at the top corner of the chalkboard under the unhappy face but she would erase the name if the student corrected their behavior and stopped being rowdy. And there was the 'star of the month' student who was picked by the teacher for doing something exceptional and they always got to go first at the monthly show-and-tell day. Show-and-tell was when any student who wanted to could bring an item to class like a favorite toy, family relic, or favorite book or tv show and share it with the class. The student could stand by their desk or go to the front of the class and speak about the topic they wanted to share. Candi once went to the front of the class and shared a piece of volcanic rock that her father had collected when he went with the US Air Force to Greenland; the piece of rock was passed from hand-to-hand around her entire third-grade class. She told the other students what her dad had told her; the rock at one time had been molten hot lava inside the deep caverns of the earth but had been ejected out onto the upper surface of the earth and had cooled.

Candi missed her parents so much. They were loving, kind, patient, and taught good things. Her dad would let her do dishes with him sometimes; this was in the 1960s before electric dishwashers were common household appliances. He would let her stand on a chair beside him because she wasn't tall enough to reach into the sink. He gave her a mini-physics lesson when she was only 6 years old; he told her when they were doing dishes that cold water was heavier and hot water was lighter because hot water is starting to get steamy and it evaporates into the air. Her mom and dad were loving parents who Candi could always count on for a big hug. When Candi was 4-years old, she got sick in the middle of the night the week of Jesus' birthday called Christmas and her mom took her to the bathroom where Candi vomited from an upset stomach; then her mom carried her downstairs because it was the night that Santa Claus came from the North Pole and her mom let her pick out a present and open it in the middle of the night; Santa Claus brought her a big doll. Then her mom carried her back up to bed and let Candi sleep with the doll.

In the fall, Candi's dad let her and her younger siblings help him rake leaves and pine straw in the front yard of their home. But the rake was too large for the kids to handle well, so Candi's dad finally told the kids to gather the pine cones and put them in a pile.

Candi had lots of good memories growing up as a daughter of a U.S.A. Air Force sergeant. Her father had taken them to swimming pools, libraries, bowling alleys, movie theatres, grocery stores, retail stores, air shows, tours through actual airplanes on the tarmac, and even a faith chapel on U.S.A. Air Force Bases. Not all bases had the same things, but the family had moved several times to different places. But her father retired because he was suddenly stricken with cancer and was preparing for his death. Candi did not know why her father had retired until her brother told her when she got older.

When Candi was nine years old, she began to have upset stomach a lot. Once when the family was out shopping and they were driving in the family's station wagon, Candi told her mom she felt like she had to throw up. Candi just happened to be sitting in the back hatch of the station wagon and her mom pushed the button to the electric window at the back and it rolled down and Candi stuck her head out the back of the station wagon and vomited; her mom had stopped the car in the parking lot near the grass. She continued having pains in her lower abdomen and began vomiting up green slim stuff called bile. Her family rushed her to the U.S.A. Air Force Base Hospital and the doctors performed an emergency appendectomy which saved her life. Candi felt small in that huge hospital bed. All of the medical staff was very nice to her. She remembered how it felt to be left alone in a big hospital; this was before hospitals offered cots so that family members could stay the night in the rooms with the patient. She remembered thinking about the change in the hospital atmosphere from the busy rush of the daylight hours to the quietness of the night hours. She remembered thinking how interesting it was that there was recessed lighting in the halls; the nurses had left her door open at night. The recessed lighting reminded her of her own family's night light that they turned on each night as they all went to bed; the dim light helped them to see if they had to get up to use the bathroom during the middle of the night. She remembered thinking that she felt special, like a queen, when the cafeteria attendant placed a breakfast tray on the moving table that slid over the bed and then punched a button and the back of the hospital bed came up so she could sit up and eat in bed. She had never had breakfast in bed before but had only heard about it! She was the only sibling to have been hospitalized at the age of 9 to have had an emergency appendectomy. She remembered thinking that she definitely had to tell all of her neighborhood friends about her hospital experience, and maybe share it with the third grade class on show-and-tell day. It was when Candi got older and she was in her 50's when she actually realized how fortunate she was to have lived in a country where people care about other people; she realized that the U.S.A. Air Force doctors had saved her life at the age of 9 from the emergency appendectomy, which brought back another memory. When Candi was only 3 years old, she was sitting on a blanket in the front yard with her younger sister, enjoying some sunshine. Then, the next memory is of her and her father at the U.S.A. Air Force base hospital emergency room; she had been bitten by a spider on the back of one of her legs and her leg was swollen; the doctors were squeezing the leg pretty hard, trying to squeeze out puss and venom. Candi remembered her father was standing next to her with his arms around her. Her leg eventually healed but the spider bite left a white-tinted crater scar.

Candi thought of an emergency incident involving Ben. When Ben had been 19, he had been working in a carpet mill and accidentally brought his arm down onto a pair of scissors; he ruptured an artery. He managed to press the emergency button and other workers ran to his aid and put a tourniquet on his arm. An ambulance rushed him to a nearby hospital and doctors saved his arm and his life. If this had happened 100 years ago, he might have died because there were no ambulances, no emergency call buttons, no telephones, and no sutures.

Candi remembered as a child that her family had attended a service about Jesus at the faith chapel that also displayed the U.S.A. flag, the U.S.A. Constitution, and pictures of the founding fathers of the United States of America who were Christians of European descent. But her parents also took the family to a Catholic church and a Greek Orthodox church which were located off of the base in the city. Her brother had told her when she grew older that her mother was raised Roman Catholic but her dad was raised Greek Orthodox so that is why they would go to the two different churches.

Candi's family lived outside of the U.S.A. in a different country for 2 years when she was approximately kindergarten age so she had a sense of the international world at a young age. In the Roman Catholic church that she attended, 'Kumbaya' was a popular hymn sang during the services. 'Kumbaya' is an African saying that means 'We join hands in agreement.'

Candi learned later in life that hospital chapels and U.S.A. military base chapels are neutral and are supposed to be available for prayer for all human beings.

Candi had gone to church with many of her Christian Protestant friends who attended Baptist, Methodist, and Church of Christ denominations. She also had a girlfriend who was a Mormon. She also went on a few dates with a young man in college who was Jewish, who wanted to go watch a college football game on a Saturday even though he was actually prohibited since it was the Jewish Sabbath but the man said he was not an Orthodox Jew (traditional Jew) but a reformed Jew. She also had enjoyed a few dates in high school with a Chinese boy who was very interested in classical music and he said he wanted to make orchestras his life ambition but Candi felt like she could not communicate with him that well but they remained friends and Candi liked him very much. Candi also thought of a time in high school when she and other girls and boys drove 2 cars to a drive-in movie and had fun eating popcorn and drinking colas in the car; the group of kids were decent and there was no drugs or sex, just good fun.

Candi told her children to date several people in high school and college and to try not to get too serious too fast. Candi told them that as their American mother, she realized that they had the freedom to date or marry a person they wanted to, but she had learned from others that it is beneficial to marry someone who you have a few things in common with because it might make living together easier. Once the thrill of the honeymoon is over and real-life sets in, sometimes couples can become bored with each other's company so it helps to have some common interests to share in life. But some couples enjoy being together every minute they can and are never bored with each other. But Candi knew many people marry their first love and remain happily married for their entire lives. Candi told her children that they may or may not want to have children but in their old age it is nice to have a spouse that might enjoy doing some of the same things together like hiking, traveling, cooking, painting, reading, watching TV or movies, etc. She also told her kids that life is shorter than a person realizes; that even though some days seem long, the years go by fast, so they should enjoy their lives and make things the best they can be. She told them to stay out of trouble, to not be jealous because jealousy is a waste of time but focus on your own life with God, to find things that interested them and made them happy, to be honest, to wish others well and try to help others if they had time, and value friendships but realize that some people like to keep in touch during a lifetime but some people do not like to keep in touch and want to go their separate ways.

CHAPTER 36

2006   *The kids are teenagers*

Ben tried to do some special 'boy stuff' with the boys like buying worms and fishing rods and fishing in the creek, but Valerie wanted to do everything her brothers did so she went fishing with them practically every time the boys went with Ben. I tried to do some special 'girl stuff' with Valerie like taking her shopping and trying on clothes, baking cookies, or going to have our fingernails painted at a salon. The boys like to help bake cookies and cook also.

Sometimes we went to play miniature golf and a few times we went to the golf course.

One weekend we all went camping for one night in the late summer and made smores over an open fire and went hiking. The campground had a public restroom and shower facility.

I borrowed a sewing machine that me and my sisters all shared; we passed it around when we needed it and it also gave me and my sisters time to chat and discuss the events happening in our lives. Valerie and I had fun making a quilt together. And Lee and Will also wanted to try to use the sewing machine, so I taught them how to sew some of the quilt squares and they enjoyed doing it. The main thing about the sewing machine that I told the kids was to be careful not to place their fingers under the sewing machine needle because it can go straight through your finger. Then, we would probably need to go see about updating their tetanus shot. Also, I learned to not use upholstery thread in my home sewing machine to sew a quilt because it does not work correctly unless you adjust the tension so it will sew without bunching up. I bought the upholstery thread once because I didn't read the label; I was only looking at the color of the thread. But it is not a total loss because I can use the upholstery thread for hand sewing jobs.

Ben put our family name down on the roster sheet for the Booster Club at the high school, so many times we were volunteered to help at fundraisers. Many people may not know that the uniforms that athletes wear at school events are not paid for by public taxes so funds must be raised by the schools to pay for the extra things that students need in the various sports leagues, musical bands, and clubs and many times the student must pay for the uniforms and instruments themselves. Businesses and private individuals may donate monies to the schools to support the extracurricular events. Some people think that all activities that are considered to be social and not academic should be taken out of public schools. Extracurricular activities give students opportunities to find new interests and meet new friends. The important thing is to make sure students know that each student is important because each student is a unique human being who will live their own unique life in the world; no two human beings are exactly alike, just like there are supposedly no two snowflakes that are exactly alike. The school administration acknowledges the students with top academic excellence but all of the students attending the school should be valued. The students who do not care and do not try may have personal problems that need to be addressed in order to help these students succeed in life. The public schools are for students of all levels of intelligence; the public schools are not just for the students who excel to the highest grade point averages. People have different learning curves and people may have great intelligence in different ways. Some people have intelligence that allow them to read books and do math, chemistry, and physics to become doctors, dentists, lawyers, politicians, scientists and engineers while other people have intelligence that allow them to be great at woodworking, fixing cars, cooking, cutting hair, designing and decorating, mining, soldering metals, singing or acting, religious leader, working with animals, caring for children or seniors, cleaning, driving or piloting, plumbing, electrician, musician. There are many professions in the world. Some require more book learning than others.

Lee, Valerie, and Will were good students. They paid attention to their teachers, studied hard, asked for help when they needed help and gave help when others asked them and Ben and I were proud of the kids for staying out of trouble. We told them 'Thank you for being good kids.'

I have noticed that Lee's handwriting looks exactly like Ben's handwriting and Valerie's handwriting looks like mine when I was her age. My own handwriting has gotten very scribbly looking as I have gotten older because I am usually in a hurry. I wonder if handwriting and coordination abilities are genetic traits. I have spoken to other people in the restaurants where I work about handwriting because sometimes I have had to stand behind the front counter and cashier and I noticed that some parents and their children had very similar signatures.

I have had some interesting conversations with customers in restaurants. When I had a desk job in IT, I worked with many of the same people for almost 20 years and the conversations were mainly about computer programs and getting the work completed. When I began working in restaurants, I saw hundreds of different people each day and this opened a new door for me because it was when I learned how different people are. I remember when I learned that many Asian people do not eat butter on their toast and they do not know what butter is. Some people drink their coffee or tea very sweet and add 10 packs of sugar or sugar substitute while other people drink it plain or just add a little sweetner. And, around the world, the clothing that people wear is of great variety and people have their own styles and mannerisms.

If you take time to look at all of the people in the world, then you realize what a big world it is and how we are all different. Sometimes when I go to the mall or a park, I like to sit down for 5 minutes on one of the benches and observe people. Looking at all of the other people in the world and seeing what others are doing can make you a better person.

I saw one mother slap her child and it made me mad. There is no reason to slap a child; you can pick up the child and give them a kiss on the cheek and try to talk to the child to try to understand why they are misbehaving. I don't think I ever spanked my kids. There were times the kids irritated me but I never felt like hurting them.

CHAPTER 37

2008   *Shelley's Miracle*

Shelley tried everything she could think of to get help to visit with her children. She filed a formal complaint about the judge but the complaint committee denied her request. She contacted Family and Children's Services which was a government agency at the state level and the national level, but they said they could not help. She kept calling various legal aid organizations, lawyers associations, human rights associations, and newspapers but she could not find help. She wrote letters to her state and federal congressman, asking them to draft legislation to make divorces fair in the United States of America, but no laws were enacted.

She called the local police, the state bureau of investigation, and the FBI but Shelley was told that her case was a civil case and not a criminal case. Shelley contacted the Civil Rights Division of the U.S. Department of Justice but Shelley could not find help to be able to visit with her children. She also contacted the governor of her state, the state attorney general, the county commissioner of her county, the county attorney, and two U.S. presidents and was continually told that her case was a civil case and nobody could help her.

Shelley was generally a happy person who liked her life and was grateful for all that she had. She was a reasonable and personable woman. She was a family person and her friends and family were the most important and cherished things in her life. Even in hard times, Shelley was the kind of person who made the best of it and went on living, smiling the best she could. But now she was beginning to feel hopeless. She joined some divorce support groups and learned that many other parents' lives had been totally ruined by lies and slander and unfair judges. She met a man and a woman who had both been denied supervised visits by the same judge as herself. Something was wrong, Shelley thought.

Shelley told Candi about other parents she had met in a support group who had been estranged from their children for no good reason except lies. One man had decided to leave his church; the man was a Jehovah Witness but decided he wanted to go to a Baptist Church. He said his wife divorced him, accused him of a bunch of lies involving violence, and he didn't get to visit with his kids for eighteen years. His father, the children's grandfather, still attended the Jehovah Witness church so the grandfather kept the father informed about the children and the grandfather showed the father pictures of the children. But the children had been brainwashed into believing that their father was a bad person because he had left the Jehovah Witness church.

Another woman had been caught having an affair at a hotel with a man who was not her husband; her husband was angry and hurt because they had agreed on a monogamous marriage not an open marriage where some couples allow affairs. Her husband forged her handwriting on some checks drawn on his company's business account and accused her of theft. The judge sent her to prison for 2 years for theft which is also called larceny and she was totally innocent. Her life was totally ruined because of slanderous lies. Her husband went to church every Sunday, yet he didn't care that he had destroyed her reputation.

Another woman was also slandered by her husband. Her husband, who was a follower of Jesus, told the judges lies about her, that she was crazy, jealous, violent, and might kill someone, and the woman did not get to see her children for 10 years even though she was not any of what she was alleged to be. After 10 years of being denied visits with their mother, the children were brainwashed against their mother and would only see her occasionally in a public place. The woman, who was totally heartbroken, hoped that one day her children would have more confidence in her because her entire relationship with her children had been skewed, like her entire life had been struck by lightning. Everything felt 'off.' The mother was barely functioning. But she kept her faith in God or the divine realm and she honestly felt like a good spirit would be with her. Her apartment manager had told her that a spiritual woman had lived in her apartment and had died there before the woman moved in; maybe it was the ghost of the former tenant watching her dilemma. She could not believe the cruelty and immaturity of her ex-husband. She and her husband had been together for 20 years, yet he had totally ruined her life and her relationship with their three children. She had carried the children collectively in her womb for 27 months. Physically she went through a lot to bring the three children into the world. And then she had worked hard in the household raising the children for 13 years. And then, because her husband wanted out because he was in love with another woman, he had totally ruined her life and her good relationship that she had had with her babies. She said that he had cheated on her before in college and she should have broken up with him then because it was clear then that he was not satisfied with her when he was telling her lies and cheating on her in college. The woman said they should have just agreed to not be exclusive but date several people before agreeing to be in a serious relationship.

Shelley's father met an attorney who was experienced in federal courts as well as in state courts who became interested in Shelley's case. Shelley contacted us, and Ben and I were called as character witnesses and we testified that Shelley had watched our children for 10 years with no incidents indicating that Shelley was crazy or had mental problems. Shelley's other friends who also had daycare businesses in their homes testified that they had shared in the raising of the daycare children for 10 years with no incidents indicating that Shelley was crazy or had mental problems.

Finally, a miracle happened. The lawyer filed a class action lawsuit for Shelley and the other parents that Shelley had met in the divorce support group against the Civil Rights Division of the United States Department of Justice, for crimes against humanity and for mental abuse to parents and children of divorces who had been denied supervised visits with each other after divorces.

The Supreme Court of the United States heard the case in 2007 and passed a judgment that laws should be enacted in all 50 states that would enable fair divorces by ensuring visitation to non-custodial parents even if supervised visits were imposed or agreed upon during the divorce proceedings. If the custodial parent insisted on imposing supervised visits on the non-custodial parent and could not agree on an appropriate supervisor, then the custodial parent would have to pay for a family visitation room at the courthouse with a court-approved supervisor. If there was factual evidence that a child had been abused but the abuse did not warrant the parent to be prosecuted, the presiding judge would decide if the non-custodial parent would be granted or denied supervised visitation and attend a seminar about good-parenting techniques. Any parent of minor-age children who made slanderous accusations against the other parent might risk felony charges for slander with prison time. Couples who were going to divorce had to attend a divorce seminar before a divorce but each could attend separately. The intention of the U.S. Supreme Court was to protect the child-parent relationships from slander. The fifty United States of America were given a ten-year deadline to enact fair divorce guidelines or the federal government would intervene.

By this time, Nathan was 23, Amy was 21, Isaiah was 17, and Hope was 14. Shelley was broken-hearted that she did not get to help raise her children when they were teenagers. Isaiah and Hope would be graduating from high school soon. Nathan and Amy were almost ready to graduate from college. Shelley felt like a stranger to her kids.

There was nothing Shelley could do; Mike had turned into a vicious liar just because he wanted the kids all to himself. Shelley was much more mature than Mike; she knew that the children shouldn't have been treated as 'property'. The kids belonged to both of them, but Mike had been totally selfish and now the kids were brainwashed against her and her family. For all of Shelley's hard work giving birth to her four children and then raising them in their early childhood and working as a babysitter while Mike worked outside of home to help meet the family budget, now she felt lost and alone and estranged from her kids. When she did see them now, for Mother's Day or hers or the kids' birthdays, or at Christmas, the kids were only 'halfway there'. A part of their life living together and knowing each other in a close way was gone forever. Living with each other or visiting with each other at length is different from short one or two hour visits, which is the only time that Shelley had had for 8 years. In her kids' perspectives, Shelley was their mother, but their whole relationships had changed and the kids did not feel the warm love and affection toward Shelley anymore; all of their warm and cozy feelings were for their father, Mike, who had completely dominated their lives for the past 8 years. Mike had completely ruined Shelley's entire life for no reason.

Candi and Ben felt very sorry for the way that Mike had treated Shelley. They had tried to talk to Mike to try to convince him to stop the foolishness and let Shelley see their kids, but Mike simply did not care. Why his personality had changed baffled Candi and Ben. Ben said maybe it was the influence of the new woman that Mike had been seeing, even though he did not remarry. The new woman had two children of her own and all six children had enjoyed a lot of time together.

Shelley did the best she could to take care of herself even though she was barely functioning. Her parents were emotionally supportive to her and loved her immensely but they were as broken-hearted as Shelley was that they had been denied visits with their grandchildren for 8 years.

Shelley's girlfriends who had shared the kids in daycare together were as baffled and dismayed as Shelley and her parents were about the unfair divorce. What had once been beautiful relationships between a parent and children had been destroyed.

The kids suffered emotionally in that they were forced to leave behind a loving relationship with their mom; they had been forced to let go of their mom and focus totally on their dad and his new girlfriend. The kids did not deserve to have had half of their life stolen from them by their father's slander and the unfair ruling of the judge who oversaw Shelley and Mike's divorce proceedings.

Candi and Ben planned a holiday dinner for a Saturday in December especially for Shelley. Shelley drove Nathan, Amy, Isaiah, and Hope and Nathan's girlfriend to the church that Candi and Ben attended to attend a Christmas concert with the choir and an orchestra. Then everyone drove back to Candi and Ben's house and they grilled out shish kabobs on the grill that had chicken, steak, onions, tomatoes, green and red peppers, and mushrooms. Shish kabobs are a middle-eastern food, but an Asian teriyaki sauce was going to be poured on the shish kabobs for those who wanted it but the marinade had been discarded; Candi started doing this because Will could be a very picky eater and wanted everything plain with little seasoning. Shelley had made a Black Forest chocolate cake that had cream cheese frosting in the middle and cherry topping on the top of the cake and there were holiday cookies that Candi and Ben, Lee, Valerie, Will, had made earlier that day. Candi and Valerie had made a pan of scalloped potatoes earlier that afternoon that had been seasoned with cheddar cheese, onions, paprika, salt, and cream, and they took it out of the refrigerator and let it cook in the oven while Ben and Will were on the deck watching the shish kabobs. And Candi put on a big pot of rice to cook for those who preferred rice over the scalloped potatoes. She also put bottles of hot sauce and soy sauce on the table. There were eleven people eating, so Ben put in the middle piece of the table to extend it to full length so that all eleven people could eat together around the table. On top of the dining room table, Shelley put holiday candles and her special cranberry-colored tablecloth that had beautiful floral satin inlays. When you eat foods from different cultures together in the same meal, it is called fusion food.

Candi noticed the change in Nathan and Amy's attitude toward Shelley; they were not as relaxed with her as they used to be when Shelley had been keeping kids in her home and Candi saw them on a daily basis. What can you expect from kids who have been estranged from a parent for over 8 years? Candi prayed that, with time, perhaps things would improve and the children's confidence and total trust in Shelley's character would return. Candi realized how strong in character Shelley was, and Candi admired her.

A surprise was that Lee said he would play some Christmas songs on his guitar and everyone sang along. He had been taking guitar lessons for 4 years now. He also played Led Zeppelin 'Stairway to Heaven,' a short version, and I requested 'Ain't No Sunshine' by Bill Withers which is one of my favorite songs but Lee only sang 'I Know' 8 times each time instead of 26 or 74 like in the actual recordings released by the music companies.

The doorbell rang and it was a pizza delivery man with 3 pizzas. We had not ordered any pizzas. Apparently, it was fraud. Someone had ordered pizzas in our name.

CHAPTER 38

2010   *Studying great religions of the world*

When Candi read the entire Bible for the first time in the year 2010, she read in the Christian New Testament in II Thessalonians 3:6, 3:14 and II John verse 10 that say if a person is not a Christian or not following what Paul said, you were supposed to avoid them. So, Christians were not supposed to associate with non-Christians. And Christians were to be shunned who were not following what Paul dictated, such as women should sit at the back of the church and be quiet. I think it was mean that Christians could not associate with non-Christians, but perhaps all of the fighting 2,000 years ago made Paul decree this to the people in his churches for their personal safety.

If the Bible claims to be a 'good book', then why am I supposed to not associate with half of our world that consist of religions or philosophies originating from Zoroastrian, Buddhist, Hindu, Chinese, Japanese, and Native Spirituality?

In the Jewish Old Testament, Ezra 7:26 says that if a person is not Jewish, they can be imprisoned or killed. Some of the Sanhedrin Council Jewish priests were killing people who were working on the Sabbath; maybe this is why John the Baptist, Jesus and the disciples, and Paul and Stephen and the apostles decided to start a new religion.

Since I worked with computer logic, which has to make sense if you want the computer to compute the correct results that you want, I was confused after reading in the Bible in Ezekiel 33:18-19 which says that a righteous person who sins will go to hell but a sinner who repents will be forgiven and saved; if you think about these statements, they cause confusion, because the two statements contradict each other. Also, if God is all-forgiving, then why were bad angels cast into hell? I guess that readers of the Bible are to assume that God will make *exceptions* for sinners and for righteous believers according to God's judgments, will, and desire.

I did not understand why the Jewish beliefs were called the 'OLD' Testament and the Christian beliefs were called the 'NEW' Testament. I assumed afterwards from thinking about it that when the King James Bible was translated and written on paper and typed in the 1600's that King James wanted the Christians to believe that the Jewish writings were an old belief but the Christian writings were the new belief. Modern Christians still read the Old Testament and follow The Ten Commandments, so the reasoning why King James called it the Old Testament did not make sense to me.

 But another Christian told me that Jehovah God of the Old Testament destroyed the world but saved Noah, Jehovah brought plagues of locusts and frogs, and Jehovah would bring whirlwinds to kill sinners, and Christians after the time of Jesus did not believe that Jehovah God was vengeful and that is why the New Testament was called 'New.' Also, Jesus taught followers to 'turn the other cheek' while Moses taught 'an eye for an eye.' In the Muslim Koran it says that if a peace agreement can be made in a dispute, it is better than 'an eye for an eye.'

Some people believe in the middle-eastern story of Adam and Eve which would make humans 3000 years old, but due to the population count on earth, scientists said that humans have existed for a longer time, probably 50,000 years. Also, the Japanese Tenrikyo religion teaches that the first two humans were born at the Jiba Pillar in Japan.

I am putting my belief with the scientists who postulate that human life genetically evolved; one reason is because I have had my appendix removed and scientists say that it is a useless part of the digestive tract that might have been used a long time ago. Another reason is because there are many similarities in humans and nature; for example, female cows, goats, kangaroos, and humans can provide milk for their babies to suckle and I have read that humans have DNA in common with bananas, lettuce, and chimpanzees. So, I do not believe in the stories that human beings were created by God in one instance but no one knows for sure. Also, I am confused that there are other female animals who suffer birth pains and not just women homosapiens, as God told Eve women would. I do not think the Bible addresses the pains of female mammals giving birth such as cats and horses.

Science articles say that scientists will be able to do miracles with genetic engineering, like genetically modifying or 'editing' T-cells to destroy cancer cells.

Many people are concerned about scientists changing genes in human embryos.

Chimera genetics is putting human genes into animals like pigs such as scientists who are trying to create organs that could be transplanted from pigs into human bodies. Chimera genetics is very controversial.

Scientists have changed genes in plants and foods such as corn.

Some wonder if genetic science has gone too far.

Some think that a woman should keep her pregnancy a secret for 3 months if she is healthy and there is no history of abnormalities. Many think a woman who is delivering a child into the world should try to have a witness with her at the birth of her child, both to witness the event and to help her through the difficulties of childbirth. Hospital workers should make sure babies born in hospitals are not accidentally switched at birth or kidnapped.

Some think it is very important to have a trustworthy relationship with your doctors, medical providers, and hospitals in the modern world, because criminals have become very smart and deceiving. Human trafficking and demands for human organs is rampant. Some think you should not leave family members or friends alone at the hospital.

Candi read an article that said some humans can have 3 strands of DNA or just sometimes have 3 strands of DNA in certain cells and scientists think that it is a new trait evolving in the human species.

Another waitress at one of the restaurants where I worked told me that you can have your DNA sent off to be analyzed and you will receive a report telling you about locations in the world where your DNA originated. She said her report indicated that she had more Neanderthal genes that her sister's DNA showed. The Neanderthal species lived 400,000 to 40,000 years ago in Eurasia. Homosapiens (modern humans) evolved after the Neanderthals. I also saw some commercials on TV that offered and asked for people worldwide to send in a sample of their DNA via saliva or blood so scientists could have DNA to study human evolution.

I believe that there is a 'Creator Lord' of the universe that created all elements, genetics, minerals, and creatures.

If God is the Master Genetic Scientist, are humans supposed to be modifying genes? No one knows.

Scientists say that the human race is not guaranteed and that most species on earth only last 4,000,000 years. The dodo bird, saber toothed tiger, tentree plant are all extinct. Now humans face the dilemma of fighting flesh-eating bacteria which could wipe out the human race. Also, there some fungi organisms on earth that are bigger than blue whales or elephants, making the fungi the biggest organisms on the planet. A climate change that alters the atmosphere could wipe out the human race. Climate changes could be caused by an asteroid hitting the earth, the moon moving away from the earth, changes in the sun, pollution on earth, or the workings of Our Creator. It is believed that fracking for oil or natural gas can cause earthquakes to occur.

CHAPTER 39

2011   *Trying to compile a modern bible*

I got busy and wrote a new, modern bible, but I left out what I considered were bad verses. I considered myself to be the typist and I would interview as many people as I could and try to get volunteers to help give me modern ideas that many people like to discuss. Trying to think of a title, she wrote down about 50 different titles and decided on 2015 Bible or CIVIC, but she knew the title could possibly change as she interviewed people for their opinions. The book was not just about Candi; she considered herself to be the typist or compiler.

I left out the verse that said rich people would have a hard time getting into heaven because I believe that rich people can get into heaven. I also believe that maybe the verse was not meant to be taken literally that rich people would have a hard time getting into heaven but to remind people that life issues mean more than just having a lot of money and possessions. I also don't believe that a person has to give up all of their possessions to follow Jesus.

I left out 4 verses from Deuteronomy 21: 18-21 of the Old Testament in the Bible which say parents shall condemn their son to death by stoning for being rebellious, a glutton, or a drunkard because most people in the world today do not kill their sons.

There is a verse in Deuteronomy 22:8 which says that you 'should put a railing around a flat roof so that no one will fall off' but most builders do not put railings around the edges of roofs today but some do if people have to go up on the roof. I left the verse in but grouped it with some other advice in the Book of Numbers.

I left out verses from Deuteronomy 22: 20-21 which say that 'women who do not have tokens of virginity shall be stoned to death' because, for one example, tampons or medical situations could cause physical alterations to her body. I left out verses from Deuteronomy 22: 22-24 which say 'adulterers shall be stoned to death' because in modern times most people just get divorces in cases of adultery in most countries on earth.

I think an adulterer is a sinner if the marriage partners agreed for it to be a monogamous union and they broke their promise. But there are so many people in the world that court systems don't want to handle such cases. Maybe people should have it written in a marriage contract whether their marriage is strictly monogamous or if it could include extramarital affairs. Sexually transmitted diseases are serious matters and many cheaters are not taking their marriage vows seriously enough.

I left out the phrase from Revelations that says 666 is the mark of the devil because I knew someone who was bothered by this verse. Many do not know the phrase in the Old Testament that says King Solomon got 666 talents of gold from a sale.

Later on, I typed back in all of the verses I had omitted after feedback from Christians who wanted me to simply copy the King James Bible as it was.

As I spoke to many people, the opinions were that some did not believe that Moses spoke to God in a burning bush, that some did not believe that Jesus cured the blind or lepers, that some did not believe angels took the Plates of the Mormons from Joseph Smith's hands, and some did not believe that Mohammad rode a white horse to heaven and got advice from Moses; but many said that such verses about miracles gave people hope.

My personal opinion is that I did not live 3000 or 2000 years ago or even 1000 years ago or even 400 years ago when the King James version was translated, so I actually do not know the truth of anything in the Bible, Book of Mormon, the Q'uran, the Gita, or any of the holy books. I just believe in the Creator of the Universe and being a good person, but those basic beliefs did come from the holy books.

I talked to many people to get their opinion of the Bible and if they would consider a new Bible, what would they like it to contain. Some people said that the Bible should just be left as it is as a historical document and not rewritten at all, but some people said that a rewrite would be acceptable. The problem with the Bible is that some people believe every single word as the truth of God and others do not believe every single word as the truth of God. Most people who read the old verses such as 'a son who is a drunkard must be stoned to death' recognize the verse as an act people did 3,000 years ago but do not do today, but some people still believe in the verse. So, I decided to put in the new Bible information in a section about 'Reformations of Religions' and how people changed their beliefs as time progressed.

I also wondered why the Israeli rabbis will not publish a new modern version of the Torah. The religions of Catholicism, Christianity, Mormon, Islam, Baha'i, Rastafari, Cao Dai, Yazidi, and Druze all include Jewish principles in their respective holy books, and if people are still sacrificing animals to God, then why don't the Israelis publish a new modern Torah? Also, 3000 years ago Persian Zoroastrianism was a popular religion in the middle-east from which Yarsan, Yazidi, and Druze were also created, so I think a new modern Bible having information about all the known middle-eastern religions would be beneficial.

I drafted a modern Bible as best as I could but hoped that, if there was any interest in it, that perhaps some Bible experts could help to create a better version. Someone suggested maybe it could be a token coffee table gift book or a textbook.

Ben asked me, "How did you get such a crazy idea in your head to try and write a modern bible? You should stop and just give it up." But I told him maybe someone would want it, though I did have my own doubts.

"I also have some other crazy ideas," I replied.

"Such as?" Ben asked and raised his eyebrows at me.

"Well, if I could buy the Miss America beauty pageant, I would have the names of the fifty states written on little pieces of paper and put them in a box and then the commentator or another person would draw out the names of the ten finalists, then the five finalists, then the top three. I think to leave it to chance would be exciting because all people in the world are beautiful. Maybe the Miss Congeniality could be voted on by the pageant contestants."

Ben just looked at me but didn't say anything.

"Are you wondering why there isn't a Mr. America?" I asked but didn't let him answer. "Well, I think basically we are living in a man's world and women are treated as inferior to men. In the USA at least this pageant gives women some hope that they are worth something – if nothing else, at least to sell makeup, hair products and clothes to keep the economy going. Women have kept the human race alive because we have babies! Most CEOs of big corporations, politicians, and religious leaders are men."

Ben said, "Men are mostly in power because traditionally women stayed home to take care of children and run the household.

And men had the physical stamina to run the farms and fight the enemies."

"True. That's the way the world has evolved," I said.

I had met a woman who had taken into her household a young mother with a newborn child. The woman rescued the young mother from having an abortion. Fortunately, she had inherited some money and was in a financial position to help the young woman. She helped raise the baby while the young mother found a way to be self-sufficient by taking classes to be a dental assistant. The young woman also met a nice man at a church to which she had been invited and they began dating. The happy ending was that 8 years later the young mother and her boyfriend got married and were in a financial position to create their own household. The two women remained friends for many years.

I typed some information into the modern Bible saying that sexual irresponsibility is not morally ethical and abortions should be a last option. Some ways to stop abortions would be to make available free birth control or give money, medical care, affordable housing, emotional and financial support to unwed mothers. Many people believe abortions should still be legally available to women who are victims of rape. Many people are concerned about the many human embryos that are destroyed in genetic research.

I saved up $800 to have 20 copies of a modern Bible printed out and gave them to some customers at the restaurant where I worked who said they would be willing to read it. Two people gave it back to me, saying that the King James Version was the only true Word of God. Some other Christians told me that I was wrong and that Jesus is the only way to God and evolution is not true. Two people were more open-minded and thought a new bible would be a good idea.

For the people who believe that the King James Bible is the only true Word of God, one thing I thought about was apocrypha, which is books that were included in the Catholic Bible or Jewish Torah but excluded from the King James Version because of arguments by the writers about what stories and reports to include in the books. Apocrypha arguments occurred 1800 years ago and 400 years ago.

I included in the modern bible a chapter that described scientific information about the big bang theory and theories about universal expansion, universal contraction, universal shredding, and parallel universes. I also included a book about safety practices such as:

Do not text while driving.

Do not leave anyone in a locked car in hot or cold weather.

Give someone your hiking route before you go hiking in the mountains and stick to your route.

Know the difference between strangers and friends and know the value of true friendship.

Be cautious when walking to your car in parking lots and have your keys ready to open your car door.

Make sure you turn off the circuit breakers if you have an electrical emergency, need to work on appliances or need to unscrew a broken light bulb.

Lock your doors when you are inside of your house.

If a power line falls onto your car stay in the car until help arrives.

Do not leave anything important in your car in case someone breaks into your car. (Comprehensive auto insurance
may be added to your auto insurance policy in cases of theft, fire, or
vandalism.)

Seniors should take precautions like standing on a rubber mat to prevent slipping in the shower.

Child-proof your homes such as covering electrical outlets, removing small items a child could put in their mouth, removing large items from shelves that could fall over on a child if they reached for them, securing dangerous chemicals, insecticides, and cleaning supplies, securing weapons, securing matches, securing the cords of window blinds, and securing doors that children could open by themselves and get out. Also, watch children when the windows are open because small children can fall through open windows and even push through window screens and fall out.

Do not let small children under the age of 15 roam around the neighborhood by themselves. It is a parents' decision as to how safe a neighborhood is, but children are innocent and vulnerable and predators could be lurking or driving around. Or a small child could come across a snake, a vicious dog, or fall and get hurt.

Some parents think a neighborhood could be safe enough for a child to walk a few houses down to a friend's house, but the parent should stand in the street and watch for the child.

Make sure children and passengers in cars have their seat belts on.

Make sure no one is in front of or behind your vehicle when pulling into or out of a driveway or parking spot.

Never dive into shallow waters or shallow swimming pools.

Never have an MRI is you have metal in your body or have been welding metal (metal flakes could be in your eyelashes).

Never light a match around an oxygen tank.

Never put an electrical appliance in water.

The new Bible also contained modern thoughts and reminders such as:
Think of the consequences before taking any actions.
Try not to be rash and do things in anger. Try not to be impulsive. Many have written that the Rule of Moderation is good which means not to go to the extremes on anything. If you eat too much, you are going to gain weight. If you eat too little, it is not healthy. Eat healthy foods with vitamins, minerals, proteins, amino acids, fats, and fiber to maintain good health.
If you are a workaholic, you may be ignoring family and friends and not be getting enough rest or personal time. If you do not want to achieve anything or do anything, how are you going to survive?
If you are stuck inside the little bubble of your comfort zone and will not open your mind to the rest of the world, you will never experience what the rest of the world knows.
Planning ahead may help avoid procrastination, trouble, and can make things go better.
Some people and babies may be bothered by strong perfumes or the fragrances or chemicals of laundry detergents and fabric softeners put in dryers.
Each human is unique in personality, body, opinions, likes and dislikes.
Can you plan it so the shampoo and conditioner run out at the same time?
Can you get the recommended number of wash loads out of the bottle of laundry detergent?

Some people want to be stuck in their little comfort zone and I think that is fine because I want to be stuck in my little comfort zone. I just want to live my little life but I know that knowledge is beneficial to the mind and can enable negotiation with others.
People have different opinions about how much trust to give strangers and under what circumstances. People have different opinions about everything you can think of; for example, people have favorite colors and color combinations, people may have preferences for geometrical shapes and even geography of the earth, people have favorite foods, and etc. For people who like chocolate chip cookies, some people want 15 chocolate chips in each cookie while some people may want only 2 or 3 chocolate chips in each cookie. You can add almond flavoring to chocolate chip cookies instead of vanilla for a new flavor. You can add mint flavor to brownies for a different

taste. For people who like ice cubes in their drinks, some people like square ice cubes, some people like circular ice cubes, and some people like ice that is crushed into small pieces.

Everyone is unique, and yet everyone is just like every other human being on earth. We are unique and not unique at the same time; this is like a Taoist principle. Also the concept that everything in the universe is linked is in many religious scriptures of the Baha'i and Hindu. And Bible scriptures say that, just as the human body has many parts such as hands, feet, eyes, and ears which all work together, so are humans to God's work. These concepts are in the new modern bible that I typed but I am having a hard time getting people interested in reading it.

It is a fact that if you ask people for their opinion on whatever topic, you may get several different viewpoints or opinion.

For example, ask people to say their favorite colors or color combinations, such as:

Light blue, light gray, and light brown.

Light blue, dark blue, and yellow.

Light blue, dark blue, and white.

Light blue, dark blue, lime green, and white.

Light blue, cranberry, gray, and black.

Blue, white, gray, and yellow.

Blue, gray, orange, and white.

Light blue, black, orange, yellow, and white.

Aqua, black, purple, yellow, white, and gray.

Aqua, black, yellow, and gray.

Aqua blue and orange.

Aqua blue and red.

Aqua blue, green, yellow, and black.

Blue, red, and white.

Black and tan.

Black and white.

Black, orange, and white.

Black, orange, white, pale blue, and green.

Black and red.

Black, red, and yellow.

Black, red, and white.

Black and aqua.

Black, aqua, blue, purple, yellow, and pink.

Black, blue, and white.

Black, blue, yellow, and white.

Black, blue, yellow, white, and red.

Tan and white.

Pale pink and pale green.

Pale pink and black.

Navy blue and violet.

Yellow and black.

Red, yellow, and green.

Red and white.

Orange and white.

Pink and white.

Yellow and white.

Green and white.

Blue and white.

Blue and pink.

Brown and orange.

Brown, orange, and white.

Brown and mint green.

Brown, green, and black.

Cranberry, green, and white.

Pink, red, and orange.

Purple and orange.

Purple, red, and gold.

Purple and pink,

Brown and gray.

Green and brown.

Green, brown and white.

Aqua blue, apple green, navy blue, cream, yellow,
pink, and gray.

French blue, aqua blue, cranberry, white, pale yellow,
blue-green, and lime.

Beige with gray, pink, pale blue, aqua blue, and
orange melon.

Silver and blue.

Copper and brown.

Gold, silver, red, and white.

Black and gold.

Pink and gold.

Orange-red-brown, mustard yellow, light blue-green, white, and
clay silverish red.

People may have different favorite colors for clothes, housing
interiors and exteriors, furniture, cars, and flags. People may change
their preferences for favorite colors, foods, music or almost anything
during different times of their lives and they may have an
explanation for it or not. Some humans are color blind to certain
colors.

People have different opinions about the colors of car paint. Once
when Candi and Ben's mini-van broke down and they decided to buy
a new one, they spend one afternoon with the kids looking at the
vans and finally picked the one they wanted but the dealer said they
had to wait until the next day to pick it up. Ben came home the next
day with the new van but it was a different colored van than the one
they had picked out the day before. Since Candi was the one who was
going to be the primary driver, she had said that she wanted the blue-

green van. But Ben had decided that he preferred a dark green van and that is the van that he drove into the garage.

Candi asked Ben, "Where is my van?"

And Ben replied, "Candi, I drive the mini-van too and there is no way in hell that I am driving a van that is a fluffy-looking pearlescent blue-green color because I am a man and I am not going to be seen driving down the road in a van that is a fluffy-looking pearlescent mint-green color with a bunch of kids in it."

"Nobody is looking at you," Candi laughed at Ben.

"Nobody is looking at you either," Ben replied.

"Well, you like that pair of black sunglasses that has an orange and mint green stripe on them," Candi offered. "And you have some bright colored tee shirts."

"I like to wear some bright colors in clothes but that doesn't mean I want that color on a car," Ben said.

At first Candi was a little angry about it, but she got over it and actually learned to like the dark green van. Marriage can have surprises and life is a journey; this is what Candi's sister told her when she vented about the dark green van to her sister during a conversation over the telephone.

She reminded Ben about the new lamps that she had bought for their bedroom but that Ben made her put his samurai warrior lamp back on his side of the bed, so why couldn't she have the van of her color choice? He just laughed at her. She replied back to him: "I will never let you forget about the samurai lamp or the dark green van – you are a control freak!"

Ben replied: "You named all 3 kids the names that you wanted so let me win on some of the choices!"

Candi said: "Not totally true. We did discuss names."
But Candi decided to not start a fight. Then Candi and Ben looked at each other and started laughing because they really did not like to fight. A heart to heart talk can resolve differences.

Candi also read that some people liked green, brown, and blue cars and roofs on houses and buildings because from orbiting satellites, the earth-colored cars and roofs looked like grass, dirt, and water.

People also may have preferences for geometrical shapes such as lines, circles, squares, triangles, spheres, cones, or combinations or shapes. And many shapes are found in nature such as lines, circles, angles, and squares.

People often use nature in analogies or expressions to describe human behavior or human inventions. If someone is cursing 'a blue streak' it means that they are very mad. If someone is 'flipping out like a fish out of water' it means they are upset and not right. Blenders that whip smoothies have been called 'hurricane blenders'. Cars engines have 'horse power.' People who do outstanding things are called 'stars' while a person who does mean things may be described as 'mean as a snake.' The burners on top of stoves have been called the 'eyes' of the stove. 'Full throttle' means you are doing something fast, like when a boat or motorcycle is speeding.

At one time in my life I realized that I had been taking many things for granted and I was being too cynical and criticizing other people too much. For example, one time I was drinking a glass of orange juice and I realized all of the energy behind that glass of orange juice. Everything I was drinking or eating that I had gotten from the grocery store was the result of good human effort. Orange juice didn't happen by itself; human workers got out of their beds, went to work, did their jobs and picked or processed the oranges. Other human beings handled the operations or business part of the orange grove or juice factory. Artists designed beautiful packaging for the orange juice. Other human beings transported the oranges or orange juice. The human beings at the grocery store helped to stock the juice on the shelves at the store. The store manager made sure the electricity bills were paid in the store so that I, the customer, could shop in the store and see all of the products on the shelves. My boss was reliable in making sure that I received my paychecks in a timely manner so that I had money to go shopping. And I also give myself credit for getting out of bed and going to work so that I could get a paycheck. The world runs on universal energy and harmony; most everyone in the world is working hard and many processes are entwined or interconnected.

And all of the progress that humanity has made has not been easy. For all of the inventions that have brought humanity to the present day, many humans have died in the process. Madam Curie and Pierre Curie both experienced symptoms of radiation poisoning such as aching bones and malaise while researching radioactive elements and Madam Curie died of leukemia in 1934. When arsenic was added to paint to give it a green color, many people died from arsenic poisoning when mold grew on green wallpaper and released arsenic gas into the air. In 1908 Thomas Selfridge died while testing an airplane with Orville Wright. Giordano Brun was put to death in 1600 for teaching that the earth moved around the sun and Galileo was almost put to death for teaching the same concept. Joan of Arc was burned at the stake in 1431 because she wanted to wear pants as well as dresses but some controlling people in the church thought that women should only wear dresses. Astronauts have died in space maneuvers. Humans have died while building roads, water systems, bridges, buildings, and factories, or working in or on them. Human Samaritans have died while volunteering to help stranded motorists change a tire on the side of the road; they were killed by another vehicle crashing into them. A famous saying that describes setbacks of progress is 'One step up and two steps back.'

Scientists studied the earth's rotation around the sun for hundreds of years before many nations finally agreed on a solar calendar in the year 1582 because it was the most accurate calendar. Many religions still keep calendars based on the moon's rotation around the earth and are called lunar calendars.

Scientists studied electricity for 2400 years (from 600BCE until the 1780s CE) until electricity was harnessed and humans figured out how to produce electricity and use it. Benjamin Franklin of USA (1788) is credited as the inventor who finally achieved it. Then it took about 75 years until a feasible light bulb was invented for human use in 1879CE (current era). Thomas A. Edison completed the work of many scientists before him to create a long-lasting lightbulb.

After humans figured out how to produce power from electricity, the Industrial Revolution started in 1760CE in Europe with the invention of steel mills, power-driven machinery which enabled a decline in human manual labor. The Industrial Revolution caused human lives to change in many ways because humans had more time to invent new things instead of using human energy for basic survival such as producing foods to eat, weaving cloth by hand for clothing, bedding and window coverings, washing clothes by hand, making soaps by hand, feeding oxen, hunting, producing kindle from trees for fires for cooking and to heat water for bathing.

People in modern times enjoy hot showers and baths and think nothing about the history behind the invention of modern water piping, bathtubs, and clean warm water. Our modern bathrooms, kitchens, clothing, housing, transportation systems, communication systems, and medical care are luxuries that our previous ancestors did not get to enjoy.

Candi typed many of these ideas into the modern bible. She spent many hours at various libraries and book stores doing research. She tried to speak to as many people as possible about their ideas of God, prophets, miracles, morals, sins, rituals, and history versus the modern world and all of the progress that good humans have made. At one library, Candi started laughing to herself when she saw a woman who had fallen asleep at a computer station. The woman was middle-aged and Candi wondered if she might have been working on a college degree after going to work all day; maybe she had children and had to get up early to get them off the school. The woman snored a few times. 'I snore louder than her' Candi chuckled to herself.

Candi thought about sleep situations for a minute. She remembered a weird time that she could not figure out how it happened, but she simply was so deep in sleep that she rolled over and rolled off the bed and landed on the floor. Ben jumped up from the bed to help her. She was so thankful that she had not broken her back or neck. Weird things happen to people. One time she had a dream that a burglar had broken into their home and she starting yelling in her sleep 'Your ass is in trouble!'

Ben woke her up. He was laughing. "Who the hell are you yelling at?" She described her dream to him and told him about the burglar and that she had grabbed Ben's rifle and started going after the burglar.

Candi also remembered one time when they found Lee asleep on the family room sofa instead of in his bed. Apparently, he had gotten up to use the restroom in the middle of the night and for some reason went to sleep on the coach instead of in his bed!

Some reasons she compiled the new modern bible was because of the conspiracy of who tried to kidnap Valerie, the slander of the psychiatrists that ruined her life, the slander that ruined Shelley's life in an unfair divorce, and also because of the evil Bible verses. The evil verses and slander written on paper ruin peoples' lives for no good reason. Also, there were many news stories of babies and young children that had died from being left in hot cars in the summer time and news stories about bank and home robberies, drug dealings and deaths involving drug dealings. Maybe if preachers had a new book, they could talk about some modern issues from the pulpit in addition to issues that were taught 2000 and 3000 years ago. I am open-minded about God and I believe that all of the religious leaders of the past 3000 years have brought humanity to where we are today. So I admire all of the great messengers that I learned about when I studied world religions.

The Ten Commandments that Moses was given by Jehovah God were etched on a stone tablet. The Mormon prophets etched scriptures and other information on Plates of Brass. A Native American Indian named Chief Redstone of the Assiniboines carved peace pipes out of red stone found in Montana and Minnesota. The red stone was sacred to the Native American Indians and smoking herbs became a spiritual ritual. Later, humans recorded sacred writing on papyrus.

Explorers, inventors, scientists, royal families, philosophers, and everyday ordinary heroes also helped to shape civilization so some of these great names are also in the modern bible. If you think about it, people work in professions every day where they risk their lives to help other people. For example, police officers who are also called peace officers, fire fighters, astronauts, cosmonauts, vyomauts, ditch diggers for public water works, electricians, bank tellers, taxi drivers, airline crews, military personnel, and medical personnel – I revere these great heroes who are my fellow human beings as much as I revere the great religious leaders.

Many people in modern times think that the God spirit exists in humans of all religions.

One reason why people think the old bibles are the only truths is because when the old bibles were printed, it took a lot of effort to get them into print because the old paper writings had to be typed with the old manual typewriters. Now with the new modern word editors on laptop computers, books can be created in less time. So, why would it not be feasible for modern humans to come together, agree on the best scriptures and produce some new, updated religious books? If humans can embrace the latest cars, electronics, medical techniques, and food items then why can't the world update their religious books?

One good thing is that I was grateful that I lived in a country that had religious freedom. I began visiting various denominations of several different world religions and met many nice people who believed that the creator of the universe is called by many names and that there is no reason to kill each other over religions.

The war in the middle-eastern region around the Mediterranean between Jews, Christians, and Muslims has been going on for 3000 years now. Thousands of people have been killed worldwide over the issues in the middle-east. Many believers of the Middle-Eastern religions are being close-minded to the other spiritualities in the world that began with Buddha in the East on the Asian continent and with Great Spirit and Corn Mother in the West on the North American continent.

There were two world wars and many regional and civil wars and millions of combatants and civilians have died in the past 200 years.

Many people are questioning the imaginary boundaries that humans have created for themselves through human-made religions. Cultures around the world were separated for 3000 years but now with faster ships, airplanes, cell phones, and computer internet, people have been communicating better and more easily, and world cultures are being shared. Some people think that peace may be possible.

In the afterlife, it would be nice to connect with the souls of saints and relatives; some think it is possible and others think it is not possible but no one knows.

Human Messengers of the Great World Religions

Moses for the Jews,
Jesus Christ, Mary for the Christians,
Jesus, Mormon and Joseph Smith for the Mormons,
Onowutok, and Tamanend for the Lenape Native American Indians,
Mohammad for the Muslims,
Zoroaster for the Zoroastrians,
Sultan Sahak and Mithra for the Yarsan,
Mohammad and Jesus Christ for the Yazidi,
Moses, Mohammad, Nashtakin ad-Darazi for the Druze,
Bab and Baha'ullah for the Baha'i,
Mirza Ghulam Ahmad for the Ahmadiyya,
Aleister Crowley for the Thelema,
Jesus and Anne Lee for the Shakers,

Jesus, Ras Tafari Haile Selasie and Athlyi for the Rastafari,
Orunmila, Ifa (Unseen) for African Yoruba,
Siddhartha Gautama Buddha for the Hindus and Buddhists,
Veda Vyasa for the Hindus and Buddhists,
Nasadiya Sukta for the Hindus and Buddhists,
Krishna and Sai Baba for the Hindus,
Mohandas Gandhi for the Hindus,
Guru Nanak for the Sikh,
Mahavira for the Jain,
Confucius for the Confucians,
Laozi (Lao-Tze) for the Daoists,
Ngo Van Chieu for the Cao Dai,
Huynh Phu So for the Hoa Haoi,
Nakayama Miki (Oyasama) for the Tenrikyans,
Phineas Quimby for the New Thought Movement,
Charles and Myrtle Fillmore for the Unitarians,
Ron Hubbard for Scientology,
Paul Twitchell for Eckankar.

The Akasha Realm is the belief that there is a great universal consciousness that includes the Creator and every soul that ever existed. Maybe animals have souls, too. No one knows the exact answer as to what is beyond death, but the energy and heat leaves our bodies and goes back to universal energy of the divine matrix.

I am glad I studied world religions and philosophies. I am not an expert but I read enough to know that religious fighting is not necessary. Archaeologists have found evidence of divine reverence that existed in human civilizations before paper was invented such as cave drawings, artifacts in tombs, and buried totems.

Young people who are born today should not have to die in wars over religions that humans created 2,000 years ago. Young people might be enticed to serve in the military if they could be placed in noncombat positions only. Maybe wars could be fought with drones instead of live bodies. Militaries are important in order to secure countries but many people are opposed to the killing and violence.

Many people may not realize that human beings have existed for around 40,000 years. There is evidence that starches were ground by rocks, most likely by humans who were making the earliest unleavened breads.

Through excavations and carbon-14 dating methods of fossils, scientists and archaeologists believe that the first hominids were an ape about 4 feet tall and arose out of Africa about 4 million years ago; scientists called the fossil **Lucy.** About 1.5 million years ago during the Pleistocene Age the **Homo erectus** species emigrated from Africa to the Middle-East, Europe, and Asia. Then about 200,000 years ago another hominid evolved called the **Homo Sapien Neanderthals**. The Neanderthals were shorter and with a bigger skeleton and over 5 feet tall. Next Cro-Magnon called the **Homo Sapiens Sapiens** evolved about 40,000 years ago in Europe whose skin lightened to absorb more Vitamin D in the northern latitudes. Meanwhile, in Africa, as the gene for hair which covered the ape became suppressed, the skin became darker to protect the human from harmful ultraviolet light from the sun. The humans made their ways to Australia through Southeast Asia and to the North American continent through Siberia. The humans made specialized tools from animal bones which enabled them to survive. Fluted projectile points were attached to long sticks that acted as spears so the humans could kill animals and fish. Fruits, berries, and nuts were gathered from trees and bushes.

Excavators in North America believe that the first humans came onto the continent about 50,000 or 15,000 years ago because they have found buried artifacts such as fluted projectile points that were attached to long sticks to act as a spear along alongside bones of extinct large mammoth animals similar to a buffalo, feather headdresses alongside human bones, bone points made from deer antlers, bone pins, stone knives, pottery vessels, smoking pipes, stone slabs, and buffalo skins and bearskins with symbols carved or painted with berry juice. Radiocarbon dating has identified some of the artifacts to be 9000 years old and 4500 years old.

Also, palynologists who reconstruct past environments by excavating soil samples and study pollen and spores believe that the upper half of North America was covered by a huge ice glacier until about 10,000 years ago. The glacier advanced and retreated several times, causing the types of trees and plants in the forests to change. Scientists also believe that the first organism may have come from the ocean onto dry land.

Scientists have been studying blood types and chromosomes since the early 1900s CE. There are 33 human blood group systems that are internationally recognized but most humans fit into the ABO category with O, A, B, AB being the blood type with a + or – after the blood type for the RH factor. The other categories involve the presence of antigens on different chromosomes and much more. Blood is needed around the globe in order to save lives and to continue research. Consider becoming a blood donor. Type O Negative is a universal blood cell type; almost any human can receive Type O Negative blood cells. Type AB Plasma is a potential universal plasma for all humans.

Type O blood is the oldest blood type. 45% of humans have Blood Type O (from 40,000 years ago when humans were mostly hunters and meat eaters). 40% of humans have Blood Type A (from 25,000-15,000 years ago when Caucasian cultivators ate meats and whole grains). 11% of humans have Blood Type B (from 15,000-10,000 years ago when Mongolians of the Himalayan steppes ate meat and dairy). Less than 5% of humans have Blood Type AB which is the most recent blood type.

Archaeologists have classified the humans who came to the North American continent into 3 categories which are Paleoindians dated 11,000 years ago, Cloxis 9500 years ago, and Flosom around 8500 years ago.

The humans made their way from North America to South America. The ancient Mayan culture of Palenque in Chiapas, Mexico has been Radiocarbon-14 dated to 300 years ago.

When the Europeans and Christopher Columbus came to North America by way of the Atlantic Ocean in 1492 they brought with them the religion of the Middle-Eastern Mediterranean region that was of Egyptian, Greek, Roman, and Jewish cultures but there were millions of Native Americans consisting of at least 500 cultures and languages who practiced Native Spirituality. The Native Lenape Shaman symbols were recorded by a European Christian Protestant group called the United Brethren Moravian living among the Iroquois and Lenape Delawares. In 1822 in Kentucky, a man named Constantine Rafinesque who was born in 1787 in Constantinople (ancient Greek and Roman Byzantine city located in now Istanbul, Turkey) attempted to record the symbols of the Lenape into a book called the Red Record or Wallam Olum.

The Wallam Olum 400-1620 Current Era describes the native crossings from the Bering Strait from Asia to America, kachinas (spirits), sheets of ice, humans marching together, snakes, turtles, white eagles, wilderness, swamps, discovery, white owls, honesty, lineages (generations) of lives, evilness, fruitful fields, and white men coming onto the lands. Onowutok and Tamanend are among the names of great spiritual leaders of the Native American peoples.

    The earliest natives living on the North American continent had spiritual beliefs which were recorded as symbols and performed spiritual practices which were recorded as pictures on cave walls, pottery, and buffalo and bear skins and this evidence has been dated to be at least 10,000 years old. Land is set aside for the Native American Indians called Indian Reservations.

    Some of the names of the Native American cultures were Inuit Eskimo, Pueblo, Navajo, Chippewa, Iroquois, Dakota, Pawnee, Osage, Huron, Choctaw, Sioux, Miniconjou, Cheyenne, Lakota, Red, Yakima, Comanche, Crow, Palouse, Apachee, Toltec, Hopi, Natchez, Creek, Chiricahua, Lenape, Shawnee, Talegas, Delaware, Coloradas, Cochise, Cherokee, and more. The Native Americans and European settlers fought over lands and made negotiations from the 1400's to the 1800's current era.

    The European settlers who had formed 13 colonies fought for their independence from Great Britain in a war that lasted from 1775-1783 and it is estimated that there were at least 100,000 human deaths total from both sides of the war. The Boston Tea Party was a raid on a shipment of tea in the Boston Harbor by a group of people called American Patriots who were protesting high taxes imposed by the British Parliament. George Washington was commissioned by the Continental Congress to take hold of the militia units fighting against the British and he became the first commander of the Continental Army. On July 4, 1776, the Continental Congress put forth the Declaration of Independence for the United States of America. George Washington became the first president of the U.S.A.

    Since 1776, the United States of America has formed a prosperous nation for its people and offers freedoms to its citizens such as freedom to choose an occupation, to own land and property, to read books in all languages from all countries, to travel inside and outside of the country, freedom of religion, to dress as one pleases unless an establishment or institution requires a dress code to be followed, freedom of speech, and the right to bear arms (guns). People who value the freedoms of the United States should never forget the soldiers who died in military service for the country.

Because of disagreements, most Native American Indian tribes were forced off their lands and moved west in what is called the Trail of Tears from 1836-1839 but there are still Native American Indian lands in the eastern U.S.A.

Many United States citizens are concerned about the future of the country because there are too many large ethnic groups promoting the cultures and languages of foreign countries that could lead to confusion and hostilities.

The primary language in the United States is English. The English language consists of 26 characters and has derived over the past 2,000 years from old Germanic and French languages that used characters from ancient Roman and Greek languages. The English language does not require an object to be masculine or feminine. For example, a table that you place dishes on and sit at to eat has no gender and is not a man or a woman. English is more modern than Spanish or French, where nouns are masculine and feminine. People who advocate that English be declared the official language of the United States government are not being hateful or opposed to other languages but it is a fact that most citizens of the United States of America have been speaking English for over 200 years and it is part of the foundation of the culture. Many United States citizens do not want cultural wars to start inside the borders of the United States. To make English the official language of the United States is an effort to promote the stability and peaceful living of a great nation. The United States of America has offered humans freedoms and a good standard of living for over 200 years, is a peaceful way of life, and assists many humans in the world needing help.

There are people who hate the United States and other peaceful countries for no good reason. The author has personally spoken to a few people who said bad things of the United States, while at the same time, the people who said the criticism were enjoying the freedoms offered in the country that are protected by the U.S. Constitution.

All nations and all peoples are vulnerable to the actions of bad persons.

Each nation on earth has the capability to be a great, prosperous, and peaceful nation.

Most of the wars in the world have been fought between rulers who argue over lands, languages, money, and religion.

Some languages of the Middle East are Hebrew and Farsi and Tajik and have unique symbols. Chinese Mandarin consists of 27,000 symbols but 2,000 are most common. The Russian language uses characters similar to those in the ancient Greek, Roman, and Latin alphabet as well as cyrillic characters. The computers that used 8-bits were transliterating some Russian cyrillic characters which led to the formation of unicode in computers. Unicode in computers is enabling languages to remain spoken and typed in all parts of the world. Translators allow languages to be converted to other languages so people can communicate with each other.

There are over 2,000 languages used in the world and computer programmers have developed computer applications that translate languages quickly so humans around the world are now communicating with each other better and faster than ever before in the entire history of the world.

Candi also encountered a hacker on her laptop several times. One time the hacker took control of her document and added texts for several prayers that Candi assumed the hacker wanted to be included in the modern Bible. Another time the hacker erased her entire Word document but she luckily had copied the file to another USB thumb drive so she had a backup. Another time the computer hacker changed the entire font. Another time the computer hacker took control and locked her out of her own document and WORD would not let her save her document. One time Candi lost control and starting screaming 'God! Strike my hacker dead!'

"What is wrong with you?" asked Ben. "What are you screaming about? "

"It's the hacker again!" Candi said. "I'm not even connected to the internet and someone took control of my Microsoft document and they started typing!" So then Candi asked Ben if he would drive her around in their car for an hour while she sat in the backseat and typed on her document and she did not get hacked. They went through a drive-thru at a place called Scooter's to get smoothies. "Maybe it's harder for a hacker to find your computer if you are mobile," she told Ben.

Microsoft Word wants everyone on Word 2013 and 2016 which offer CLOUD technology but many people have gone back to WORD 2007 and WORD 2010 because of cloud hackers.
Hopefully there will be a solution to stopping evil hackers.

Candi also compiled another book called the CIVIC WORSHIP that contained samples of scriptures from major world religions. Then the hacking got worse. Candi asked many people for help regarding the hackers. She was told that hackers can hack your laptop by going through your cell phone or wireless optical mouse so she changed her phone number several times or took the battery out of her cell phone when she was typing on her laptop and she quit using the optical mouse. She was told that if you have a password for a modem internet connection, that a hacker could not get into her laptop. But still the hacking continued. Sometimes her editing document would shut down by itself and restart itself by itself; sometimes her document was intact but sometimes it was the wrong document or it was in a different font. Sometimes the screen went opaque and she lost control of the cursor; it was unnerving because she did not know what the hacker was doing. Other times when she was trying to upload a file to the self-publishing sites, the file would error out or the computer would never indicate a successful upload and the internet would go offline, or an export file message would appear; someone told her it could mean that someone was exporting her files from another network. One person told her to drive 5 miles away from her wifi zone to use her phone if she needed to do uploads or downloads in case the hacker was a nearby neighbor.

Candi felt like crying that another human being was interfering in her book project; she was not bothering anyone but another human was attacking her. How could humans be so mean to another human? Then she took her computer to geek squad experts who explained to her about the viruses which are mini-computer programs that computer hackers can place inside of an editing document or even inside the pixels of pictures. The programs of the computer hackers could gather personal information. The viruses could take over a person's entire laptop, tablet, television, refrigerator, security system, automobile, airplane, or cell phone without the knowledge of the owner. Many people believe that because of the damage that computer hackers can do, personal computers could be offered like the early models of personal computers - without any internal hardware components that allow access to the internet. People could buy personal devices that were connected to the internet or devices that were not connected to the internet.

Candi reset her cell phones and computers back to factory settings many times. Several times she paid techs to set her entire computer drive back to zeros and reinstall the Microsoft Windows operating system. But she thought the recovery system was all backed to the cloud server files so she did not feel that her computers were private at all.

One time someone must have hacked her smart TV also because a huge grid appeared on the screen and several minutes later the channel changed and she did not change it and there was a religious show on a channel that she was sure a hacker wanted her to see about the true existence of Noah's ark.

Fiber optics cable wiring could be removed from homes so people could not watch what a person is doing in every room of their house. The 'computer gods' are taking away the freedoms of privacy in homes.

If a person chose to have their money in a bank and requested that their information not be lifted to the internet cloud, it means that they could not use ATMs around the world but would have to go to the bank to remove cash from their account. The author of this book has interviewed many citizens of the United States who are thinking about starting banks that offer accounts that are private and not lifted to the internet cloud. Maybe a person could have two bank accounts – one for the internet and one not on the internet.

Internet Miracles & Dangers

Thanks to the hard work and ingenuity of physicists, scientists, computer engineers, technicians, manufacturers, programmers, analysts, and more, the internet, computers, satellites, and cell phones have transformed the entire world. Computers have enabled communication to be shared more easily around the globe. Data can be gathered, analyzed and shared more easily than ever before in human history. Information can be found almost instantly, whereas before computers it could take months to gather information. Computer graphics are enabling artists, musicians, and manufacturers to create more variety of products. Medical information can be shared quicker and more easily to help save lives. Humans can travel more easily to more places on the planet than ever before in human history. Law enforcement around the world can target and capture criminals. The checkout process at retail establishments and libraries has been made much easier because clerks can scan items quickly with bar codes and record information into computers and cash registers connected to computers so customer waiting lines have become shorter.

But because of evil computer hackers, many people do not want their bank accounts, medical history, cell phone, or car engines forced onto computer databases that are connected to the internet. Many believe that the internet should be optional. If you are inside an establishment and paying cash, you should definitely be able to order a pizza or buy a pair of shoes without having to give a telephone number, email, and/or a zip code; it should be optional because some people think that it is not right for manufacturers to know every product that a person is buying.

Many authors, artists, and engineers want computers that are not connected to the internet so that their creative ideas cannot be stolen.

Computer applications have been written that allow a hacker to use your telephone number, voice, picture, and emails on their computer devices.

Cell phones can be put in airplane mode which means that no signal is being received or sent.

Some people want to be GPS (global positioning point) located and some people do not. Some people have said that all humans are becoming like pawns on an electrical grid. People could use a tablet that is connected to the internet which could be used for research and purchases on the internet but carry a cell phone that is not connected to the internet so they can make plans in private with their family and friends. Purchases made on the internet could be made with a pre-paid plastic card that can be loaded and reloaded with money instead of a plastic card associated with their bank account.

Computer hackers can flip cars, run cars off the road and lock people in their cars, so many people want computers to be optional in car engines. Google Maps and Directions could be put in the dashboard.

Many people believe that forcing everyone onto the large cloud database that has been developed is wrong. The problem with the large cloud database is that a few hackers could ruin everyone's data on the cloud or the elite group of computer technologists could take advantage from their knowledge and access to everyone's data.

The author acknowledges to not know everything about computers and world affairs and is simply expressing opinions that have been shared by citizens of the United States of America.

The author spoke to a citizen who told her that she awoke in the middle of the night and a strange woman was standing outside her baby's doorway in the hallway of their home. Apparently hackers can shut off alarm systems.

Some people have theorized that there are smart buildings and smart houses that are involved in the production of movies without the occupant's knowledge. The occupants of the buildings, houses, or cities have the right to know if all of their life actions are being watched and monitored or recorded by strangers.

To offer consumers safe devices: Car manufacturers could offer cars with no internet in the engine or wheels. TV manufacturers could offer old analog TVs. Medical equipment manufacturers could offer hospital equipment and blood test analyzers that are not connected to the internet, Bankers could offer bank accounts that are not connected to the internet. Computer electronics companies could offer computers and word editors that are not connected to the internet for people who do not want to be connected to the internet, Beds can have canopy tops and pull-around curtains for privacy.

It may never happen that there will be a world language, so the best thing to do is to educate people to respect the different world countries, languages, religions, and cultures.

Most people on earth want the same things - to have a nice life with clean water, good food, a place to call home, family and friends, a craft or a job, and personal enjoyment. We definitely should not kill each other over languages, religions, or lands.

Many humans believe now is the time for stability and peace on earth. Many peaceful nations have aided groups of people who asked for help because they were being harmed by other humans. Most people on earth are peaceful.

While reading about sundials and how hard scientists worked to record the earth's revolution around the sun, Candi learned that the first solar calendar was established in 1582. The faces of most clocks have the numbers going from 1 – 12 around the right of the circle but Candi learned that there are also clocks that have the numbers going from 1 – 12 around the left of the circle. Imagine a person standing on the top of the globe in the northern hemisphere and looking down upon the earth and it is rotating to the left; that is why the sun appears to rise in the east and set in the west. If you think about it, clocks with the numbers going around to the left make a lot of sense for the northern hemisphere. For example, you imagine geographically on the globe where the time in California is 1am, Nova Scotia on the Atlantic Ocean side of North America is at 5am, and England 9am. A friend of Candi ordered her a clock as a gift with the numbers going around to the left and it took a few months to get used to it.

It is amazing to think about the sundials used to tell time by the ancient Europeans and Incas and Aztecs in South America and how far humans have progressed in the methods of telling and keeping time. Today in modern times we have stopwatches that can easily keep time in minutes or hours but in the past one method of keeping time was putting sand in an hourglass and the sand dropped through a tiny slit from the top portion of the hourglass into the bottom portion of the glass. When all of the sand had fallen from the top compartment into the lower compartment, an hour was up.

In the United States, a big issue is about the right to bear arms (guns). Most people are thankful for the freedom to be able to defend oneself from evil predators. Some problems are young people getting access to guns and careless actions of parents not securing the guns.

Some people think that our children are being exposed to violence in movies, TVs, and video games at very young ages and that can cause some children to commit violent acts as young ages, such as school shootings and gang violence.

A Baha'i told me that there are many names for the Spirit and peace may be possible due to the sharing of ideas over the internet.

Some names for the Spirit are JEHOVAH, YAHWEH, ALLAH, AHURA MAZDA, ROOG, CHUCKWU, ZEUS, JUPITER, DUC CAO DAI, TYR, JAH, WAKAN TANKA, UMNAAH, MAKEMAKE, KUNITOKOTACHI, BRAHMA, DHARMAKAYA, BUDDHA, VISHNU, SHIVA, MAHESH, KRISHNA, YAKSA, TSUKIHI, GOD, and more.

The movie Gattaca 2005 with Ethan Hawke and Uma Thurman states on the box that there is no gene for the human spirit.

I was sitting in my car at an intersection, waiting for the traffic light to turn green. I was pushing the seek button on the radio because I like to surf radio stations and I heard a Christian preacher saying that Christianity is the only way to God and if you do not give your soul to Jesus and be saved then you will burn in the fires of hell. Just then I looked up into the clouds and I saw a huge dragon shape reminding me of the Chinese Dragon Festival; I chuckled to myself and thought that many people in the world are Chinese Taoists, Asian philosophers of Confucian, followers of Japanese Shinto or Tenrikyo, Native American Spirituality, Vietnamese Cao Dai, and more. I am not crazy or psychotic but I really did see the shape of a dragon in the clouds at that moment. I pray for divine guidance everyday so maybe that is why I saw a dragon shape in the clouds. Also, I was so glad that I had studied world religions because it opened my mind and my heart.

I pressed the seek button again and it landed on a Spanish music station with a song that sounded good and had a good beat. I pressed the seek button again and it landed on a classical music station and I heard an orchestra. I listened for a few seconds and then I pressed the seek button again and it landed on a 1960's – 90's classic rock station. I think the seek button was a great invention because I love to listen to all kinds of music like classical, opera, jazz, country, R&B, hip-hop, mainstream pop, classic rock of 60s to the 80s, oldies from the 1920's to the 50's, alternative rock of 90s+, reggae, easy-listening, instrumental, acoustic, elevator music, movie themes, children's music, religious music, folk, mariachi, mamba, ye ye, chanson, even national and school anthems. Commercial ad jingles are fun. There are also many interesting talk radio stations. As far as music genre goes, people may categorize them differently.

Candi wished a manufacturer would offer a hand-held portable radio with a seek button so she could surf radio stations at home. She tried to find one but could not.

Music was sort of like an endorphin to Candi – her brain loved music. Candi guessed that music engaged her brain the way alcohol or marijuana engaged other peoples' brains. Music lovers should be careful not to let music and the right brain take control. If you feel yourself getting too swayed by the music, maybe you should turn off the music for a while. Candi also had a passion for reading books, which is a task done by the left brain.

Scientists say that learning to play a musical instrument is a task done by the left brain but the melody is understood in the right brain, so learning to play music stimulates both the left and right brains.

On one radio station I heard a Christian preacher saying that Jesus was better than Moses and I think that was a mean thing to say. Moses etched Ten Commandments into stone that were given to him from Jehovah God which taught the Jewish people good values and even the gentiles (a gentile was one who wasn't a Jew) respected the ideology of the Ten Commandments.

And one great thing about radios is that it is free for public listening. You can even pick up free television signals without subscribing to cable; you may have to move your television and antenna around your apartment or home to find the spot that has the strongest signal but if a signal can be found it can save you money. The signal can be higher towards the ceiling, midway between ceiling and floor, or lower to the ground; finding the spot where the signal is the strongest can depend the land elevation, if you are the first floor of a dwelling or higher, and if there are surrounding objects that could interfere with the signal.

Lee told his mother, "I do not like the idea of your book CIVIC, mom. Jesus is the only way." Candi replied to Lee, "I believe Jesus, John the Baptist, and all of the apostles were great heroes. Apparently, some Jewish priests ordered some Jews to be killed for working on the Sabbath, so John the Baptist and Jesus were great humans who stood up against the injustice. But I believe there are good people in all the world religions so I like the book with scriptures from many religions."

Lee asked Candi, "But, mom, do you still believe in Jesus?" Candi said, "Of course I believe in Jesus and God. King James Bible translators started using the word 'GOD' because it was becoming a popular word. 'God' is Dutch and 'Gott' is Germanic. Lee, nobody really knows what happened 2,000 years ago. I do not believe that God wants us to have wars and kill each other over religious beliefs. Did you know some people do not believe in God and they are called atheist?"

Lee said, "It is sad that some people don't believe in God and do evil things."

Candi said, "There are atheists who are good people. I think it is more correct to say that some people do not have good morals and do evil things."

Lee asked me again, "Mom! Do you still love Jesus?"

"Yes," I said. "And I still love the Smashing Pumpkins **1979** song and the Foo Fighters **Monkey Wrench**, too!" because I had recently heard them on the radio and he laughed.

While I was doing dishes, I thought about music and some songs that I had heard in my lifetime.

Our family lived in the United States so my parents listened to Frank Sinatra 1940 **Fly Me to the Moon,** The Shirelles 1959 **Mama Said**, Diana Ross and The Supremes 1960 **Ain't No Mountain High Enough**, The Shirelles 1960 **Will You Sill Love Me Tomorrow,** The Four Tops 1963 **Baby I Need Your Loving**, Andy Williams 1962 **Where Do I Begin**, Gerry and the Pacemakers 1964 **Ferry Cross the**

Mersey, Barbra Streisand 1965 **People**, Aretha Franklin 1967 **Respect**, The Beatles 1963 **I Want To Hold Your Hand, Let It Be**, Elvis1954 **Can't Help Falling in Love**, The Drifters 1967 **Up On The Roof**, The Carpenters 1969 **Close To You**, Bee Gees 1958 **How Can You Mend A Broken Heart**, Tommy James & The Shondels 1969 **Crystal Blue Persuasion**, The Sylistics 1971 **Betcha By Golly Wow**, Otis Redding **Sittin' on the Dock of the Bay**, Marilyn McCoo & The Fifth Dimension **One Less Bell to Answer**, Dionne Warwick 1968 **Walk on By, Message to Michael,** The O'Jays 1978 **Use Ta Be My Girl** and more. A lot of artists performed on TV on the Lawrence Welk, Ed Sullivan, and Bob Hope Shows. In the 1920s, there were many big swing bands like Glenn Miller, Count Basie, Duke Ellington, The Andrews Sisters and jazz musicians like Louis Armstrong.

Thomas Edison invented the phonograph to record human voices in 1877. I am glad I lived in the decades of recorded rock n roll music and I am sure there will be much more good song compositions after I die that I will miss, unless I will hear them in heaven.

In earlier times people gathered in large ball rooms in homes and listened to orchestra music like Mozart of Austria 1756, Beethoven of Germany 1770, Chopin of Poland 1810, Pachelbel of Germany 1653, Handel of Germany 1759, Brahms of Germany 1833, Vivaldi of Italy 1678, Saint-Saens of France 1835, Mendelssohn of Germany 1840, Kraft of Czech Republic 1752, Strauss of Germany 1864, Schubert of Austria 1797, Liszt of Hungary 1811, Tchaikovsky of Russia 1840, Rachmaninoff of Russia 1892, Pinghu of China 1871, Cowell of California 1897.

My older siblings listened to the Herman's Hermits of 1964, The Beatles 1963 **Hey Jude**, The Animals 1964 **House of the Rising Sun**, The Rolling Stones of 1965 **It's Only Rock 'N' Roll But I Like It** and **Angie**, The Doors 1965 **Riders On The Storm**, Bread 1972 **Baby, I'm A Want You**, Sonny & Cher **I've Got you Babe**, Isaac Hayes Hot Buttered Soul album 1969 **By the time I get to Phoenix**, Sergio Mendes Brazil 66 Equinox album 1967 **Fool on the Hill** a Beatle's remake and **Chove Chuva** Constant Rain) that our family learned about when we lived in the Azores Islands which is a territory of Portugal in the Atlantic Ocean.

There was so much music in our house that I was always listening to something good.

Then, when I became a teenager myself in the 1970s, I heard songs performed by groups such as Led Zeppelin 1979 **All of My Love**, **Stairway to Heaven**, Van Halen 1984 **Jump** and **Runnin' with the Devil**, Pink Floyd 1979 **Another Brick in the Wall**, Dan Fogelberg 1981 **Same Old Lang**

Syne, Elton John 1972 **Rocket Man** and **Tiny Dancer**, Debby Boone 1977 **You Light Up My Life**, Donny and Marie Osmond 1975 **A Little Bit Country, A Little Bit Rock N Roll**, Michael Jackson & the Jackson Five **Stop The Love You Save**, Gladys Knight **Midnight Train to Georgia, That's What Friends Are For** with Dionne Warwick, Elton John, and Stevie Wonder, Roberta Flack **Killing Me Softly, The Closer I Get To You**, Billy Joel **Uptown Girl, Piano Man**, John Denver 1972 **Country Roads, Leaving on a JetPlane**, Stevie Wonder **Isn't She Lovely, Cherie Amore,** the Commodores **Easy, Brickhouse**, Barry Manilow **Mandy** and **Copacabana**, Carole King **You've Got A Friend**, James Taylor **Fire And Rain** and **Up On The Roof**, Bread **Baby I'm a Want You**, Three Dog Knight **An Old Fashioned Love Song**, Chicago **If You Leave Me Now** and **25 or 6 to 4** meaning the song was written at 25 or 26 minutes til 4am), Carly Simon **You Belong To Me**, Dolly Parton **Here You Come**, Willie Nelson **On the Road Again,** Kris Kristofferson **Why Me Lord Story**, Doobie Brothers & Michael McDonald **I Keep Forgettin'**, Atlanta Rhythm Section **Imaginary Lover.** Allman Brothers **Ramblin Man**, Lynyrd Skynyrd **Sweet Home Alabama**, Fleetwood Mac **Rumors**, Rolling Stones **Beast of Burden**, Peter Frampton **Baby I Love Your Way**, Eric Clapton **Wonderful Tonight**, Marshall Tucker Band **Heard It In A Love Song**, Eagles **Hotel California**, Christopher Cross **Sailing**, Bee Gees **How Deep Is Your Love**, Seals and Croft **Summer Breeze**, Jim Croce **Time in a Bottle**, The Spinners **I'll Be Around**, Bill Withers **Ain't No Sunshine**, ZZ Top **La Grange**, Todd Rundgren **Hello, It's Me**, Paul McCartney & Wings **Band on the Run, Baby I'm Amazed**, and many others.

One of Candi's friends joined a Baptist church who forbad the teenagers to listen to any secular music on the radios and was holding a bonfire for them to repent and burn any albums or 45s that they owned. My friend wanted me to join him and burn all of my albums and 45s, but I declined. I do agree that some song lyrics are not very nice, but I wanted to keep my albums and 45s because I love the melodies and the music. I loved the Beatles songs **Drive My Car, Bluebird,** and **Good Day Sunshine** and did not want them on the bonfire. The people at the church were very nice people but they had some strict ideas.

Later in my 20s and 30s I listened to U2 1987 **With or Without You** and **Pride**, Steve Perry and Journey 1977 **Faithfully**, Foreigner 1984 **Waiting for a Girl Like You**, Michael Bolton 1991 **When A Man Loves a Woman**, Gloria Estefan 1987 **Rhythm is Gonna Get You**, Madonna 1986 **Vogue**, Jewel 1995 **You Were Meant for Me**, Bon Jovi 1986 **Livin' on a Prayer**,

Rod Stewart **Have I Told You Lately That I Love You**, Prince **Little Red Corvette**, Babyface 1993 **When Can I See You Again** and **Never Keeping Secrets**, Toni Braxton 1996 **Another Sad Love Song**, Boys II Men 1994 **On Bended Knee**, TLC 1994 **Creep**, Savage Garden **I Knew I Loved You**, SEAL 1991 **Crazy**, Sade **No Ordinary Love, Like a Tattoo**, Bee Gees **Still Waters**, Whitney Houston **I Wanna Dance With Somebod** ,Michael Jackson 1995 **Beat It, Billie Jean**, Monica 1995 **Before You Walk Out of My Life**, Janet Jackson 1986 **That's the Way Love Goes**, Maxwell 2001 **Lifetime**, Lenny Kravitz 1998 **Fly Away**, Bruce Springsteen 1987 **Tunnel of Love**, Garth Brooks **The Dance**, Wynonna Judd 1990 **Love Can Build a Bridge**, Vince Gill 1994 **Whenever You Come Around**, Amy Grant 1991 **Baby, Baby**, and many more. I even learned about hip-hop and rap music when it appeared in the late 1970s with artists such as Ice T 1991 **New Jack Hustler**, Eminem 2002 **Lose Yourself**. Some alternative rock I listened to was Nirvana 1991 **Come As You Are**, Metallica 1991 **Enter Sandman**, Green Day **Boulevard of Broken Dreams**, Jane's Addiction 1987 **Jane Says**, Third Eye Blind 1997 **How's It Going to Be** and **I Want You**, Smashing Pumpkins **1979, Tonight**, Foo Fighters **Monkey Wrench, Everlong**, The Cure 1989 **Lovesong**, Oasis 1993 **Champagne Supernova, Wonderwall**, 3 Doors Down 2000 **When I'm Gone**, Cranberries 1999 **Linger**. I heard B52s 1979 **Love Shack** from college days.

Some modern jazz musicians I heard were Kenny G 1987 **Champagne** and Dee Dee Bridgewater 1977 **Sweet Rain** and New Orleans Jazz. Bob Marley & The Wailers play Caribbean reggae **Is This Love.**

U.S.A. For Africa 1985 **We Are The World** song had 68 million views on YouTube. The song was written by Michael Jackson and Lionel Richie and raised $68 million to provide food and relief aid to starving people in Africa. The famine killed 1 million people.

The rock alternative band Green Day's song **Brain Stew** has opening notes that sound similar to Chicago's song **25 or 6 to 4**.

Both Ben and I do enjoy listening to children's songs with the kids with songs such as **If You're Happy and You Know It, Clap Your Hands, Three Little Monkeys Jumping on the Bed, Do You Know the Muffin Man?, Twinkle, Twinkle, Little Star, Baby Beluga** and **Baby Shark.**

We also like the old church hymns accompanied by organs, gospel groups, and modern spiritual rock and roll music.

There is good music, movies, books, entertainment, food, and sports games all around the globe in all of the various cultures such as South American, Middle-Eastern, Asian, Polynesian, African, Australian, North American, European, and Nordic.

As I drifted to sleep that night, a memory came back to me. My roommates in college and some others invited me to go to a bar with them one night so I went. All I did was have a beer and talk to some people. I didn't even dance that night. When Ben found out, he was angry and told me if I ever went to a bar again, he would break off our relationship, so I only went to one bar in all my 4 years of college, except I did go to 2 parties that I was invited to and one was at a fraternity house but it was in clean and good order and not like the trashy fraternity houses that I have seen in some movie scenes. That fraternity party was in the spring and it was a warm night, so the fraternity party was actually all across the front lawn and music was blaring from speakers set up in a window in an upstairs bedroom of the fraternity house. Ben attended a very strict Christian church during that time of his life and he was forbidden to go to any bars or drink any alcohol. I think Ben is a very good person but I wish he would lighten up a little. He thinks I am too wild but I think I'm a kitten.

CHAPTER 40

2011   *Ben admits that Candi is not crazy*

The mystery of who had tried to kidnap Ben and Candi's child was never solved. As Ben began to learn more about the computer technologies, he apologized to Candi. As a chemist, he actually thought for a while that Candi's problem was the chemistry in her brain.

But she believed a computer hacker or just an evil group of people may have been wreaking havoc in her life and she might have been correct, except for their house had burned down so they never knew. Maybe the psychiatrist was hired by the homebuilder to ruin Candi's image. Maybe the psychiatrist was hired by Candi's corporation to ruin Candi's image. Candi had lost most of her girlfriends over the years because they began to think that she was crazy; Candi was very sad about it.

"But you were crazy that time when you went shopping for 4 hours looking for the perfect pair of shoes when it isn't going to matter 100 years from now about what shoes you wore with that dress," Ben laughed.

"Well, I wasn't hurting anybody, except it did break our budget," I admitted. "Maybe that is the artistic side of me in my right brain," I replied. "But it isn't really crazy if I wanted to find a pair of shoes that I would use a lot. And you know that I have also bought clothes and handbags from the thrift store. Ben, remember, I was an orphan at the age of 12, so I've had to learn a lot of things on my own, making decisions for myself. It's not like I had a mother who took me shopping all the time who told me not to stress about clothes. I was going by magazines who say people have to be fashionable and I had to make a vogue pose." Candi also told Ben: "Ben, I've never called you crazy for saying that Satan the devil was in your parents' home when you were a little boy and made a shotgun go off when the shotgun was sitting in the gun rack because maybe it was a vibration in the wall from the floor above. Or, what about the time you shot a mocking bird down from a tree with a bb gun? You are calling me crazy but I could also call you crazy."

"You were crazy the time you brought home $400 of clothes for me to go through," said Ben.

"Well, I was trying to be helpful. You wouldn't go shopping and you had holes in the back of your shorts and you could see your underwear. But you really liked the cargo shorts that I picked out that had extra pockets on the legs to put things in," I said. "And remember you only kept 2 pairs of shorts and 2 shirts and I returned the rest back to the store. I'll never forget the saleslady who helped me; she was the same salesperson who helped me the day before and she looked frazzled when she saw all the items that I wanted to return." I laughed a small laugh. "Let's just start over today, okay?" I asked Ben. "Starting today, no more craziness."

We both laughed at each other.

Another thing about shopping that some people think is crazy but some people don't think is crazy is that if you find an item that you really love, for example, a shirt that you really like; some people will buy two of them in case they lose one or ruin one they will have a duplicate ready. Usually if I find a lipstick that I love, I will always buy two.

Ben's parents were still married and had been living in the same house for 45 years now; they were fine and wonderful people. Ben never really had to deal with as much anxiety as Candi; for example, during summers at college, Ben and many other students went home or on vacation with their families, but Candi had nowhere to go so she just stayed at college all summer. Emotionally, she had learned to survive on her own and her heart ached for the parents and the childhood that she had lost early on.

It is a fact that scientists believe that certain depressions or elations may be caused by the chemistry in the brain or by hormonal changes that cause reactions in the chemistry of the brain or from life situations that a person must learn to adapt to. Scientists are also still studying the vitamins and minerals present and needed in the body. It was believed that a small amount of lithium may be needed to stop violent or irrational tendencies. Buddhist philosophers and scientists have also helped humanity by suggesting that depressions and elations may be caused by people being unaware that they must use their left and right brains together to keep a balanced focus in their lives. People should be aware of their emotions and control their spirits; this is also a belief of the Scientology philosophy.

It is a fact that pharmaceutical geniuses have created many good medicines to make it easier while enduring colds and flus, antibiotics and antivenoms, epinephrine for when people have severe allergic reactions, and are trying to create formulas for birth-control and to stop aging processes so people can live healthier for a longer amount of time. Some scientific formulas may help increase serotonin levels in the brain. Serotonin is believed to be a chemical in the brain that my cause us to feel happiness and well-being. But Candi was still emotionally traumatized about the evil psychiatrists who had labeled her 'crazy' inappropriately after only knowing her for 10 minutes and prescribed for her to take Haldol, Ativan, Zyprexa, Tofranil, Fiorinal, Zoloft, Paxil, Lithium and Depakote in 1993.

Candi bought a pill book in 1999 that she saw at a drugstore and she highlighted the drugs that she had been prescribed, but then she got so busy that she did not have time to pick up the book and read it until 2005. She made a list of the drugs that had been prescribed for her in 1993. The book said that Zyprexa was not supposed to be taken with Ativan and Haldol was not supposed to be taken with Tofranil, and she had been prescribed all 4 drugs at the same time. She wished she would've known this in 1993 because she might have had a cause to sue the psychiatrist. Candi was glad that she took herself off of the psychiatric medications.

The book said that Zoloft was not supposed to be taken with Lithium and those two drugs had been prescribed for her the second time she was put into the mental hospital. Lithium is one of the naturally occurring universal elements, Candi learned.

People should read about the medications they are prescribed because there are many side effects to drugs and some drugs can cause your brain or body irreversible damages and even memory loss. Some drugs cannot be mixed with other drugs, even common drugs like decongestants because the mixture can be fatal which means that it can kill you. Some drugs cannot be mixed with alcohol or it can kill you or cause extreme side effects. Some drugs cannot be mixed with certain foods because the drugs will not work properly. People can have severe reactions to drugs or certain foods so if you are allergic to a drug or a food like peanuts or shellfish, you should have a medical id bracelet or always try to let your coworkers or family know that you are allergic to a drug or to foods like peanuts or shellfish in case you need help. A medical id bracelet may be more reliable than the memory of friends or coworkers. The Life Alert necklace can notify help with the press of a button.

Candi saw a movie called Michael Clayton made in 2007 by Tony Gilroy about a mental health patient who was actually not crazy but in a witness protection program, but the patient was tricked and was actually murdered by thugs who broke into his apartment and stuck a needle into his big toe near the toenail, killing him with a chemical that would later evaporate and be undetected by a medical examiner.

Candi was exhausted from being a busy working parent, confused by weird circumstances, and very worried about credit card debt. If the psychiatrist Jill River would have written Candi and Ben a check for $25,000 so they could pay off all of their bills and put some in a savings account, that would have helped alleviate some of Candi's anxieties but Dr. Rivers thought medications were the answer. Candi was very concerned about their credit card bills so she took a part-time job at a local grocery store but Ben told her to not worry; he had a more laid-back personality and reassured Candi that when the kids got older, they would be able to make $500 payments on the credit cards instead of $50 payments and the card balances would get paid off eventually. But one time Candi was so upset about a credit card late payment fee of $30 in addition to an over-the-limit-fee of $45 because the limit was over by $2 that she banged her fist on the kitchen table and said several curse words but thank goodness the children were not in the kitchen at the time. Ben told her to calm down; he was right. Candi said she hated credit card companies but Ben reminded her that the credit card company helped them to get the new lawn mower which they had needed. Candi tried to blame it on her hormones and hectic schedule but Ben said to stop attributing her anger on female hormones and a hectic schedule. Candi told Ben that the hormonal changes that women of child-bearing ages go through each month are real and do cause headaches, cramps, and moodiness. Then Candi put on some running clothes and went running for ten minutes to work out her frustration and came home and apologized to Ben for having an emotional moment. She put her small monthly dab of Dr. Lee ProgesterAll cream on her lower abdomen to avoid crankiness or hot flashes caused by a plummeting progesterone level at her age.

Candi and Ben were also making life insurance payments and each of their lives were covered for $500,000, so if either of them was to die, there would be insurance money that the surviving spouse could use to pay off the high credit card balances to maintain their lifestyle.

But Candi suffered from extreme anxiety regarding their finances and also from the mystery woman who had tried to kidnap their baby from their car in 1990; sometimes she would wake up in the middle of the night and pace the floor, praying for answers.

Candi also tried to write some songs and short stories, thinking that maybe she could sell some song lyrics or a novel and make extra money.

Ben surprised Candi by hosting a birthday party at their house to which he had invited her girlfriends with whom he had told his concerns. The friendships were amended and Candi was grateful to be reunited with her girlfriends. Lee, Valerie, and Will were out visiting friends. Ben thought it would be better if the children were not around when Candi and her friends were talking about the mental hospital and the state of Candi's mental health.

"I want to apologize to Candi and everyone," said Ben. "I was concerned about Candi's state of mind but now I realize that Candi is not crazy. I should have been more supportive. When our house burned down, that did it for me. The police believed it was arson. Something weird was going on but I don't think we'll ever get a resolution." Candi's sister had confidentially told Ben that they thought some type of mafia might have been trying to kill Candi to cover up an espionage ring if perhaps their home had been wired, so that is one reason why her family had put her into the mental hospital, so that she might be discredited if she had to be a witness. But they did not want to upset Candi any more than she was already upset, so that is why they did not tell her their thoughts.

"I am not crazy," Candi said to herself and to everyone.

Several of her friends told real stories related to computer hacking, identity theft, or possible espionage conducted with hidden cameras and listening devices in hotels, restaurants, and private homes. Some of the big techs offered music speakers that played music on demand that many believed were also used as listening devices to hear private conversations. Candi told her friends she was thankful that she had established a Facebook account on the internet so that she could reconnect with some old school friends and attend a high school reunion. "But then one time I was on my KDP Amazon publishing account for my book project and my computer said Waiting on Facebook and I was not on Facebook nor was the app downloaded to my computer so I think I got hacked from Facebook once! I even tried Norton LifeLock and got hacked despite a VPN because someone locked my computer with a message saying they loved skiing on the mountain slopes so I put that in my book. The hackers are so evil I cannot believe it.""

Ben even had picked up a cake from the bakery, complete with candles on top.

After everyone sang a popular happy birthday jingle, Candi fanned a magazine over the glowing candles to extinguish the candle flames. She had heard that most people do not realize that by blowing out birthday candles on a cake, it is similar to a person sneezing on the cake, so it is better to fan out the candle flames.

One time Candi had read that when you drink a particle of water, that particle of water has been recycled through the atmosphere for millions of years, even from another part of the earth. The same particle of water that you drink today could have nourished a plant or animal hundreds of years ago.

Everyone looked uneasy that Candi had fanned out the candle flames with the magazine instead of blowing them out like everyone else. Candi inwardly shrugged but managed to smile and say thank you to the guests.

The cake was delicious.

CHAPTER 41

2011   *Part-time Jobs*

The next month Candi sent her song lyrics and melodies to the U.S. Copyright office with the required payment and forms. She started networking in the art community. She made several friends and they went to open mic at several music shares at local churches, sports bars, and book stores. Someone told her that many artists start their own business by incorporating and keeping a post office box for their business. She signed a contract with a representative from a music company who was interested in her lyrics.

Candi had been attending classes to earn a degree in early childhood education while working as a waitress at the same time. When she completed her education degree she was hired at an elementary school not far from their home and she was very happy with her career change.

Ben also started a lawn-mowing business by himself. He put out flyers at church and at an Italian restaurant where they often went with the kids to eat. He mowed about 3 or 4 lawns a month and he charged $25 which included taking away the mulch. We had a woodsy area at the back of our yard that had some dirt erosion because of a nearby creek, so he dumped mulch in that area.

Their house and back deck needed some repairs and maintenance. They invested in leaf guards for their gutters so they wouldn't have to clean out the leaves each spring. At the hardware store they saw some lightbulbs that were multi-colored and low wattage, so they bought one of them and tried it out in a lamp on a small table while they were watching TV and they liked the colored shadows it created.

They were still making payments to pay off the credit card balances. They were going to focus on setting aside $50,000 in a retirement fund but they wanted to help pay for some of their children's college educations since the costs of college tuition were going up. They did not really have aspirations to travel a lot except to go on short trips within 500 miles of where they lived. They planned to put some money towards their children's college education loans to help pay them off.

CHAPTER 42

2012   *The Certified Letter*

One rainy spring day when Candi was out running errands, she dropped by the post office to check her PO Box and found the slip of paper indicating that she had to pick up a certified letter. Puzzled and wondering what it could be, she waited in line for 10 minutes and stepped up to the counter when it was her turn. She signed for the letter but did not open it until she was seated back inside her car.

The letter contained a check for two hundred thousand dollars and was from a music company that she had signed a contract with a year earlier.

"Yes!" she said to herself in the car, with a huge grin on her face. There would be no more money or future royalties from the songs; the contract was for the music company to own the rights to the 50 song lyrics that she had written.

When Candi got home and shared the good news with Ben, he had some good news for her. Judge Cameron, the judge that did not help Shelley to be able to see her children for many years, had resigned after being questioned by the media about the many mothers in divorces who had been denied supervised visits with their children.

CHAPTER 43

2013   *The Printer*

Candi and Ben were able to pay off all outstanding debts and open a retirement savings account with a substantial balance that would cover their retirement needs in addition to the SSN they would receive as citizens of the U.S.A.

Candi was able to finally negotiate a contract with a printer to print 500 copies of the modern bibles. The Good Book was the subtitle.

She went to the county license office to get a picketing permit. Ben went with her to buy a used van that was in good shape. Candi drove to the printer where the warehouse crew loaded the boxes of bibles into the back of the van.

That weekend she parked the van at corner of a parking lot near a busy street intersection after getting permission from the owner. When the lights were red, she approached cars and asked people who rolled down their windows if they would like a free copy of a modern bible which contained scriptures from many religions. Some people said 'yes' to which Candi gave them one of the modern bibles and some people said 'no'. Some people said 'No, a modern bible is blasphemy.' but Candi did not let it bother her. She did this on several weekends for two months and gave out 300 of the books.

Ben was a bit perturbed and told her that she should just try to sell the books, not give them away, but Candi was insistent that she give some free copies of her research.

Candi also paid a computer graphic artist and web designer money to develop a website for her non-profit. She also kept in contact with volunteer contributors and readers so in case the books made money she could compensate them for their time and expertise.

Over the next years Candi gave out the rest of the books. She told people "It's free research and I will send anyone a WORD doc to their email if they want to revise it and write scriptures of their own and get their own copyright."

Candi kept a record of contacts with whom she spoke to regarding the book and told proofreaders that she valued feedback, ideas, and suggestions for improvements and she hoped to compensate proofreaders for their time if the books produced revenue in the future. But there was little feedback but a lot of computer hacking. Some hackers kept exporting her files, which would make her irate. Candi had 30 police and IC3.gov cybercrime reports accumulated over 6 years. An accountant told her to dissolve the nonprofit and just try and sell her book as an independent author, since the nonprofit was not making any money.

During the time of her book project, Candi was invited to attend many church denominations and she tried to go to different churches and gave them of copy of the modern book she was trying to have published. She told one preacher who had told her that the King James Bible was the only true Word of God, "The King James Bible is 400 years old and King James did not have the resources to all of the world scriptures as we do today. Maybe you do not like the new bible now, but maybe someone will like it in 50 years, because the global community is getting more entwined each year."

For people who believe the King James Bible is the only truth, Candi typed a version with only Jewish and Christian scriptures called the King James Epiphany Bible.

She met a woman from Nigeria who attended a church based out of Nigeria, Africa in the United States, but the woman and her husband would sometimes have a church service in her home with friends. She invited Candi to the gathering several times and she enjoyed the sermons very much.

Then, Candi decided to send out WORD docs of her research to some of the preachers she had met who were interested in her book, in case they wanted to revise, rearrange, or add to the content and create their own worship book for their congregations. She also attended several bible studies in peoples' homes and Ben and the children went with her to one.

Once she saw a man and his daughter from Italy playing music with a cello and violin in a parking lot of a grocery store and she contributed $40 to their plight, as they had made a sign that said 'Cannot find work.'

During the course of her book project and working at the restaurant as a waitress, in addition to meeting people within the United States and on Native American lands, Candi met people from Canada, Japan, England, China, Korea, Vietnam, Philippines, Morocco, Ukraine, Russia, Estonia, Czech Republic, Lithuania, Sweden, Poland,

Bulgaria, Greece, Egypt, Israel, Lebanon, Iran, Kenya, Ethiopia, South Africa, Brazil, Venezuela, Costa Rica, Dominican Republic, Puerto Rico, Columbia, Honduras, Peru, Mexico, Spain, Italy, France, Germany, Australia, Nepal, India, Haiti, Guatemala, and Zimbabwe. She also met a few people who worked for the retail company Target in Congo, Africa and Walmart in Gabon, Africa that were in the United States for a few months who were on a business trip for the companies. There were several pilots and flight attendants who ate at the restaurant, many truck drivers since the interstate was a few miles down the road, many nurses and doctors, teachers, retirees, preachers, priests and nuns, students, chefs from other restaurants, car mechanics and salesmen, bankers, real estate professionals, engineers, construction workers, dentists, care-givers, dog walkers, insurance agents, musicians, entrepreneurs, retirees, babies, families, single persons, CBD salespersons, house cleaners, soap makers, police officers, computer programmers, pharmacist and pharmacy techs, hospice workers, school kitchen staff, school administration, bus drivers, and many more interesting people in many more occupations. Most truck drivers were men but Candi met a female truck driver who drove for a large cross-country trucking firm and she gave her a copy of the modern bible. The waitresses asked the man from Spain about the running of the bulls tradition and he said it was being outlawed in many places and becoming less popular because of cruelty to the bulls and the danger to the public. Candi also gave her book to a male customer who ate at the restaurant who traveled a lot between South America and the United States. One day a water pipe that piped in clean water burst in one of the bathroom sinks but luckily the dining room was not flooded. The manager turned off the water source to the sink and a plumber came the next day.

Candi also learned about several Unitarian and Unity congregations that had celebrations for the major holidays of many different religions because the congregation members were diversified and were of many different religions. She also learned about some Catholic churches that celebrate the life of Jesus and also invite Buddhist monks in to speak to the congregation. She learned through Mormon missionaries that there is a Mormon church on a Native Indian Reservation. Candi read on the internet that there is a Catholic church and a Buddhist garden on some Native Indian

Reservations. A Jewish synagogue hosted an ecumenical service with leaders from many religious faiths.

Many times, Candi experienced anxiety over the modern bible project, as she did not want to offend people. But she wondered, why is it necessary for the world religions to be focused on books that were written 400 – 4000 years ago? People have trashed or put into museums or archives old medical books and have written updated medical books. People have updated cookbooks with the latest recipes. Coffee percolators were reinvented and become brewers. Before bar code scanners were invented, when you checked out a library book, librarians would stamp a card with the due date and the card was placed in a little pocket located on the inside cover of the book. After bar code scanners were invented, bar codes that were located on a book's cover enabled librarians to click the scanner over the bar code to check the book out, recording the information in a computer. The bar code scanners also speeded up the checkout process in grocery and retail stores so customer waiting lines became shorter. Religious books could be updated to include some modern ideas, like when it is lightning do not take a shower and unplug electrical devices. Candi thought religions could include the messages of old scriptures as well as modern life discussion topics.

The religion that our parents raise us up in is like a habit because they are rituals that we do each day or week and become a fundamental part of our personalities. Most people stay in their same religion their entire life because it is a comforting ritual. Some people choose career paths that are similar to what their families or friends chose.

We can all share God in our respective religions. The unknown creator of the universe belongs to all life and all stars, planets, comets, asteroids, matter and anti-matter. Some think the enemy of believers of God is Satan who is the evil force against all good things-this has been a major belief in the scriptures of human religions for generations of time. Scientists who know physics have written that the anti-matter in the universe could overcome gravity and shred the universe so some think that there are two distinct opposing forces in existence. No one knows all of the answers except Our Creator.

CHAPTER 44

2017   *Good News*

The Good News is that God loves everyone.

Some other good news is that Candi and Ben, and their siblings and friends were blessed with grandchildren.
A great and true saying is that 'Children are tomorrow's future.'

Candi and Ben hoped that their grandchildren would grow into adults who were good, honest people, have faith in God, and care about and respect other people and other life forms and elements of the planet Earth.

Listening to the daily news, they learned about horrors taking place around the world and even in their own country. But they also recognized good works being done and tried to remain hopeful. That is a great tenet of the major world religions – that *good will prevail over evil.*

It is like looking at a glass of water half-full. Some people look at it like it is half-empty and are discouraged. But others look at it like it is half-full and still have some hope left.

Many good people in the world are trying to do good things.

Good people have a hard time understanding the minds of people doing evil.

Candi and Ben prayed to the Universal Mind of God for peace for future generations of people.

Shelley and Mike had gotten back together again, straight into each other's loving arms again after fifteen years of being apart. They were in love again and acted like the entire nightmare of their divorce had never happened. They said that they felt like they did when they had first fallen in love at the age of 19. Their children said that their parents were 'crazy' but in a good way and were glad for them. Everyone was happy for Shelley and Mike.

Shelley and Mike went to a bar called Electric Cowboy with some friends and were learning the steps of line dancing. Shelley invited Candi and Ben to go, but Ben didn't want to go. She was once again reminded of the memory when they were in college and he got mad when she went to a bar with some friends.

Ben said, "I am an adult and I do not dance in bars. That is for teenagers and younger people."

Candi thought for a second but she didn't want to remind him that he didn't want to go to any bars even while they were younger because she believed that maybe all people are on their own spiritual path so maybe God didn't want him to go to bars while they were in college. She finally said, "Well, everyone has a kid in their heart and I think it is okay for adults to go dancing in a bar. Shelley said this bar is for all ages. My problem is with the drunks and the cigarettes – that's mainly for the younger generation but I think it's okay if we go and listen to music and dance or have a martini like a Stoli martini or a Pina Colada. Don't you?"

"What is a Stoli martini?" Ben asked? "The only drink I know of other than beer is an Old-Fashioned and a daiquiri. My mom drank Old-Fashioneds before she came 100% to Christ and became a good Christian. Back in the day, when I was 15 my dad won a trip for two to Hawaii at his insurance company where he worked and they drank some alcoholic drinks on that trip."

"100% came to Christ?" Candi laughed and asked, somewhat cynically, with a questioning look on my face. "What about Moses and the Ten Commandments? That's at least 50%."

Ben just laughed.

Candi continued, "Stoli is a classic Russian vodka Stolichnaya that some people keep in the freezer. You can make a White Russian out of it with milk and Kahlua but a Stoli martini is made with a twist of lime and 2 or three green olives. A Pina Colada has rum, coconut milk, and pineapple juice and it started in Puerto Rico."

Candi begged him, "Please go with us to the bar just for an hour and hear the music. But we'll only have one drink and you are the designated driver." He finally said yes and they went but only stayed an hour because the cigarette smoke of the crowd was getting strong. Candi wished all bars would ban cigarette smoke to outside verandas and porches. But later Ben admitted that he had had 'sort of a good time.' He even danced a dance with Candi.

Shelley got a Singapore Sling and described it as containing bitters, gin, cherry liqueur, and grenadine. Her drink was garnished with pineapple and a maraschino cherry. Ben and Mike got ice cold beers, Miller Lite and Busch. There were free bowls of peanuts available. A man came to the bar and ordered a Bud Ice and asked if he could order a hamburger but that was not an option. The bartender told him the name of a place that had food, a bar to dance in, a billiards and ping pong room with arcade machines, and a bowling alley.

Candi told Ben again in the car that if his mom came 100% to Christ, then that included Moses and the Ten Commandments too because Jesus hung out at the Jewish synagogues and he also believed in the Ten Commandments. He didn't say anything. then he said something about the transmission of the car, that he hoped it wasn't going on the blink.

He said to me, "Do you know what is wrong with you? You think too much and you analyze too much." I thought to myself, that is what I was paid to do on my job as an information computer analyst many years ago. He said, "Just rest and enjoy the moment."

"I believe that Jesus spoke to Joseph Smith in America so I am 20% Mormon," Candi said to Ben but he just winked at me. Lord, he is so handsome; I love my husband, she thought to herself.

On one occasion when Candi and Ben were having a pizza party with their kids and their grandkids, Candi had a mild disagreement with her son Lee. Her granddaughter asked to have her slice of pizza cut up in small chewable bites. When Candi started to slice the pizza up in bites, Lee said, "Mom, do not cut her pizza slice up. Pizza is supposed to be eaten while eaten in the hand, and I want her to know the correct way to eat a slice of pizza."

Candi laughed and said, "Seriously, Lee? I'm sure I cut your pizza up in small bites for you when you were just 5 years old?"

Nonetheless, Lee proceeded to show his daughter how to eat a slice of pizza while holding it in his hand. His daughter frowned back at him but continued eating her small bites of pizza. Candi switched the conversation by asking her granddaughter how things were going at her school. Later the grandkids ate Haribo Gummy Bears.

Later when Candi was cleaning up the kitchen and Lee walked in to get a glass of milk out of the fridge, Candi said to Lee, "Lee, there is no reason why your daughter should have prevented from eating pizza cut up in small bites. If you are too strict with your kids all the time, they might rebel."

Lee said, "Mom, I just didn't want other kids to tease her because some kids are bullies. Now she knows the correct way to eat pizza. I taught her something. You are correct and it is ok if she eats her pizza in bites if she wants to but I just wanted her to know how to eat a slice of pizza by holding it in her hand. I love you, Mom." And he kissed Candi on the cheek.

Candi said, laughing and half-seriously, "I know you are the boss of your kids if we are in your home. But, if we are in grandma's home, does that mean that I am the boss who rules, or are you still the boss of your kids?' Both mom and son laughed.

"Who rules the nest?" Lee said, laughing. "Mom, thank you for being a good grandmother, but they are my kids so I prefer to be the boss for my kids all the time but if you have something important to say, feel free to voice your opinion because I think you are a good person."

Just then his 3-year child came into the kitchen and proudly said to Candi, "Grandma, I have 100% of my teeth in." And Lee said that she had gone for her dental check that morning. My heart warmed for several reasons, because my grandchild was so proud and gave me a big smile, but also because I remembered Ben talking about his mom committing 100% to Christ to me in a conversation that we had in the car recently. Maybe Jesus or God was trying to communicate back to me in percentages and letting us know about the power of spirituality in the world. (Don't tell this to a psychiatrist because they might say you are delusional and psychotic. But a magazine article said that everyone on the planet is delusional and psychotic about religious beliefs because there is no proof of any Creator except for what humans have come to believe over thousands of years.)

When they got home that night, they got a phone call from their daughter Valerie who was excited to go on a bachelorette party before her friend's wedding. She said they were going to Arizona for 2 days. Candi asked Valerie why the bride-to-be had chosen Arizona and Valerie said that they wanted to go ATVing in the desert and a guide would be with them so Candi and Ben should not worry. Their youngest child Will was busy working as an electrician and he was in a band. Then Candi and Ben went for a walk around the block to get some exercise and look at the stars. Ben slipped his hand in Candi's at one point and they looked at each other and smiled. They had been together for 37 years.

CHAPTER 45

2020   *Senior Years*

As they got older, Candi and Ben learned some senior jokes about getting older and sometimes it is harder to remember things.

Joke #1: Two seniors were driving in a car and the senior on the passenger side to the other: "You've been speeding for 50 miles now; did you know that?" And the other senior replied: "Am I driving?"

Joke #2: A man and his wife were sitting in their rocking chairs on a porch of their home. The man said to his wife: "I am going into the house to get us some ice cream." The wife said: "Well, write it down so you do not forget." So the man went into the kitchen of their house and made them bacon, eggs, and grits. He made two plates and carried them outside to the porch. When he handed his wife a plate, she said to him: "I told you that you would forget the coffee."

One day Ben came home from shopping with a new tee shirt which had something funny printed on it. The tee-shirt said 'This is my last clean tee shirt.' He handed me a tee-shirt which said 'If God made me ready to pop out of bed, I would be sleeping in a toaster.' That mildly offended me because I usually do get up on the first sound of the alarm on each working day although there have been instances on weekends which I was guilty of not being very willing to get up. But I did not say anything to Ben; I only laughed. I would probably have preferred a tee shirt that said 'I am as old as dirt.' Then he showed me another tee shirt that said 'Do me a favor. Quit talking to me.' We both laughed hard at that one.

One year Candi and Ben decided to try separate twin beds in the same bedroom because their sleep cycles were different. There were a few months when Candi kept waking up at 2 am so she put her twin bed in another bedroom so that Ben could sleep.

Candi read a novel called <u>The Law of Innocence</u> by Michael Connelly published in 2020 about a man who was framed for a murder. The book pointed out that a defendant is not innocent until proven guilty in the United States, as most people think, because a jury may decide whether the person is innocent or guilty. The only true way for a defendant to defend himself is to find and prove to the court the person who is actually guilty. It is possible that many innocent people have been sent to prison for crimes they did not commit.

They got invited to hear one of their nieces sing in a punk rock band and enjoyed hearing the original music of a song written by their niece. The band provided free ear plugs at the door that you could pick up as you paid the cover charge to enter for those whose ears could not tolerate loud, loud, loud music. Her niece also participated in a church choir and they attended a service to hear the choir and were impressed.

Candi received a text on her cell phone and a voice mail from her bank warning her that her bank account had been compromised and hacked and she needed to call them right away to discuss the issue. Candi had some errands to run so she decided to go to her bank in person, since her bank tellers and the manager actually knew her in person. When she got to her bank and spoke to one of the customer service representatives who knew her, they looked at her accounts and told her that nothing on her account had been flagged or compromised. The customer service rep told her that it was a scam and a computer hacker.

"Do you have any checking or savings accounts you could offer me that are not connected to the internet? I do not use the ATMs a lot and I do not use on-line banking so if I had an old-fashioned bank account I would like one," asked Candi.

"No, I'm sorry, all of our accounts are connected to the internet," the rep replied.

"Well, maybe I'll try to start my own bank and offer people accounts that are not even on the internet as well as accounts that are," said Candi, angry at the computer hackers of the world. Then she felt silly for blurting out her feelings.

Since they were empty-nesters and had lots of free time, sometimes they browsed the goods at thrift stores. Candi found a blouse that had puffed sleeves that were fitted with a band about midway down the sleeves and the rest of the sleeves led to open cuffs at the bottom that reminded her of some dresses from the medieval times but with a modern flair. In the art section of one store, Ben found a piece of pottery that he liked that we thought could have been Native American artistry because there were some pieces of turquoise and other stones imbedded in it. He found a turquoise ring that he liked and bought it.

Ben wanted to rent a boat on a lake one weekend so he and Candi spent a day at a nearby lake. Ben wanted to catch some fish, but he threw the fish back into the water because he did not eat fish.

"Why fish then?" she asked him.

"I like to catch them and look at them sometimes," he said.

Candi said, "You know what I read in a fishing magazine that I was looking at while I was waiting to get the oil changed in my car the other day? The article was talking about when people go deep-sea fishing and they catch fish that swim in deep waters – because the fish are removed from higher pressure levels to lower pressure levels, gases are released in their bodies that cause them to become bloated. So if the fishermen just throw the fish back into the water, the fish may not be able to swim back down to a low depth. The article was talking about an invention called SeaQualizer that has a weight on a cord and it sinks the fish back down to a low depth so they have a better chance of surviving. Or there is a venting tool made by Team Marine or Ohere that is inserted behind the pectoral fin to let the gases escape." She paused. "Fishing just to fish and throwing the fish back in if you're not going to eat the fish is not good for the fish."

One time Ben was in a silly mood and he secretly filmed Candi while she was cooking them a snack of grilled cheese sandwiches in the kitchen. He was sitting at the table and she thought he was just browsing through his phone apps, but he was filming her all the while he was sitting there. He showed it her and she thought she looked terrible in the video. That night they cooked popcorn and watched TV episodes of Seinfeld, The Big Bang Theory, The 70's show, Frazier, and CSI Miami, and Candi did not know that some popcorn kernel crumbs had fallen down the collar inside of her bathrobe. The next morning when they woke up and went to the kitchen for coffee, they saw a trail of popcorn crumbs leading from the bedroom to the couch. Ben said slyly "Uh oh, it looks like the popcorn fairy was here" and she nudged him on the arm and laughed.

Candi read about a company in Singapore that offered burials in a biodegradable pod that grew a tree where the loved one was buried and she began thinking about her final wishes when she would pass.

There was a knock on the door and it was a salesman named Omar selling purified water from a major corporation so they decided to try the home-delivered water service for a few months. They talked and he was a nice Muslim man.

Candi started listening to heavy metal rock, which she didn't really listen to in her youth. She started listening to it at night while lying in bed going to sleep if she slept alone in another room or if Ben stayed up later to watch TV. Some songs were AC/DC 1979 **Highway To Hell, Hells Bells, T,N,T,,** Alice Cooper 1972 **School's Out**, Black Sabbath 1970 **Paranoid, Iron Man**, Rush 1981 **Tom Sawyer**, Van Halen 1986 **Best of Both Worlds**, Motley Crue 1987 **Girls, Girls, Girls**. Alice in Chains 1992 **Rooster**, Badflower 2018 **Ghost**, Ozzy Osborne 2019 **Under the Graveyard,** Suzi Quatro 2019 **No Soul No Control**, Bad Wolves 2017 **Sober**, Filter 1995 **Hey Man Nice Shot**, Disturbed 2018 **Are you Ready**, Judas Priest **Living After Midnight**, Warrant 1990 **Sweet Cherry Pie**, Def Leppard 1983 **Love Bites**, I Prevail **Everytime You Leave**, The Scorpions 1982 **No One Like You**, Nickelback 2005 **So Far Away**, Shinedown 2018 **Monsters**, Greta Van Fleet 2021 **Heat Above**.

Candi heard in the news that there were over 7 billion people in the world and now analysts were concerned that there might not be enough food for everyone in the future.

Ben read that scientists were definitely sure that the moon was gradually moving away from the earth at about the rate of a few centimeters each year; scientists knew this from beaming laser beams at the moon and performing calculations each year. If the moon keeps moving away from the earth, one day the tides of the ocean could stop because the tilt of the earth could be lost and the earth might wobble because of loss of gravitation with the moon, causing tsunamis resulting in catastrophic losses at first and then stagnant seas. Scientists think that if the top layer of the ocean becomes stagnant, it could change the entire atmosphere of the earth and the outcome would be uncertain. It could one day mean the extinction of the human species. In addition, flesh-eating bacteria could cause the extinction of humans because such bacteria is becoming resistant to antibiotics. Also, there some fungi organisms on earth that are bigger than blue whales or elephants, making the fungi the biggest organisms on the planet. Scientists have recently notated that there are one-celled slime molds that have intelligence and can make decisions. The human spirit is hopeful which is why scientists are studying other planets and ways to extend human culture to another planet in addition to studying ways to improve life on earth for all people.

Also, if people keep killing each other on earth, maybe human error will be the cause of the end of humanity.

Humans have a choice; we can save ourselves from our own evil thoughts and correct our human errors. Humans need each other to have good lives.

CHAPTER 46

Year 3350

It was in the year 2900 that the polar ice caps were completely gone and scientists did not know if an ice age would reoccur. Much coastal land on the planet Earth was underwater. The sun had been getting hotter over the centuries. In the year 2032 the fire in the Pennsylvania mine finally extinguished on its own after burning for 80 years. In the year 2047 the fire in the Darvaza Crater in Turkmenistan finally extinguished on its own.

Captain Mark Kirk was sitting in the control room of the USS Starship Diamond browsing the control check logs preparing for his second voyage to the planet Mars, where a space colony had been established since 3300. One thousand humans were now living on Mars. The climate was still very cold. There was foliage surviving on the planet and the scientists were enthused about the progress of the ecosystem. Much of the plans were still underway and the success of the colony was still questionable.

On this voyage supplies were being sent to build the first religious chapel on the planet. Artifacts from every major religion on Earth were to be placed in the chapel. Kirk was a descendant of the typist of the books called CIVIC WORSHIP The Good Book, Saint Nicholas Infinity Bible, Queen Elizabeth II Bible after the monarch of England during the late 20th century. She also typed a new version of the King James version called King James Epiphany Bible. And a version called SPIRIT Infinity Bible and SPIRIT Infinity Book that had no references to WWI & II and some other civil wars. Candi Kirk had tried to improve relations among religious enemies a millennium before by being a volunteer typist on the project. Some Christians opposed the book and still used the King James version from the 1600s, but Mark Kirk had read Candi Kirk's new version and he was proud of his ancient relative.

Because of advances in healthcare, nutrition, personal fitness, and environmental science, the average human life span on earth had reached 100 years rather than 60-80 years.

In relation to the moon, the tilt of the earth was still holding in place.

<u>Each Person Matters</u>
There is a dignity and worth of every person in the relatedness of all of God's people. All lives matter.

WORLD COUNTRIES BY CONTINENT

<u>AFRICA</u>

Algeria	Malawi
Angola	Mali
Benin	Mauritania
Botswana	Mauritius
Burkina Faso	Mayotte (France)
Burundi	Morocco
Cabo Verde	Mozambique
Cameroon	Namibia
Central African Republic	Niger
Chad	Nigeria
Comoros	Reunion (France)
Congo-Kinshasa, Democratic Republic of	Rwanda
Congo-Brazzaville, Republic of	Saint Helena (U.K.)
Cote d'Ivoire (Ivory Coast)	Sao Tome & Principe
Djibouti	Senegal
Egypt	Seychelles
Equatorial Guinea	Sierra Leone
Eritrea	Somalia
Ethiopia	South Africa
Gabon	South Sudan
Gambia, Republic of	Sudan
Ghana	Swaziland
Guinea	Tanzania
Guinea-Bissau	Togo
Kenya and Mombasa Island	Tunisia
Lesotho	Uganda
Liberia	Western Sahara
Libya	Zambia
Madagascar	Zimbabwe

<u>ASIA</u>

Afghanistan	Malaysia
Bahrain	Maldives
Bangladesh	Mongolia
Bhutan	Myanmar (Burma) & Rohingya
Brunei	Nepal
Cambodia	Oman
China, People's Republic, Tibet, Hong Kong	Pakistan
China, Republic of Taiwan	Palestine
India (Andaman, Nicobar Islands)	Philippines

Indonesia (Sumatra)	Qatar
Iran, Islamic Republic	Saudi Arabia
Iraq	Singapore
Israel	Sri Lanka
Japan & Okinawa	Syria
Jordan	Tajikistan
Kazakhstan	Thailand
Korea, Republic of South	Timor-Leste (East Timor)
Korea, Democratic Peoples of North	Turkey
Kuwait	Turkmenistan
Kyrgyzstan	United Arab Emirates
Laos	Uzbekistan
Lebanon	Vietnam
Macau	Yemen

There is a natural boundary between Europe and Asia formed by the Caucasus Mountains, the Caspian Sea, the Ural River and the Ural Mountains. Therefore, many sources list the countries of Russia, Kazakhstan, Azerbaijan, Georgia, and Turkey as both in Europe and Asia.

The equator passes through 11 countries and the atolls of 2 countries. Africa: Sao Tome & Principe, Gabon, Republic of Congo, Democratic Republic of Congo, Uganda, Kenya, and Somalia. Asia: Indonesia, Maldives atolls, Kiribati atolls.
South America: Ecuador, Colombia, Brazil. The River Zaire crosses the equator twice.

ASIAN ISLANDS in DISPUTE
Kuril Islands (Japan, Russia, Ainu People)
Spratly Islands (China, Taiwan, Malaysia, Philippines, Vietnam)

EUROPE

Albania	Latvia
Andorra	Liechtenstein
Armenia	Lithuania
Austria	Luxembourg
Azerbaijan	Macedonia
Belarus	Malta
Belgium	Moldova
Bosnia	Monaco
Bulgaria	Montenegro
Croatia	Netherlands (Holland)
Cyprus	Norway, Svalbard, Jan Mayen Isle
Czech Republic (Czechia)	Poland
Denmark & Faroe Islands	Portugal & Azores
Estonia	Romania
Finland	Russia & Arctic Islands
France & Corsica	San Marino
Georgia	Serbia
Germany	Slovakia
Gilbraltar	Slovenia
Greece (Crete)	Spain & Canary Islands &

Guernsey, Isle of Man, Jersey (U.K.)
Herzegovina
Hungary
Iceland
Ireland
Italy (Sicily, Sardinia)

Basque & Catalonia
Sweden
Switzerland
Ukraine
United Kingdom (Great Britain)
Vatican City

NORTH AMERICA & CARIBBEAN

Anguilla (U.K.)
Antigua and Barbuda
Aruba (Netherland Islands)
Bahamas
Barbados
Belize
Bermuda (U.K.)
Bonaire Islands
British Virgin Island
Canada
Cayman Islands (U.K.)
Clipperton Isle (France)
Costa Rica
Curacao
Cuba
Dominica
Dominican Republic
El Salvador
Faroe Islands (Denmark)
Greenland (Denmark)
Grenada
Guadeloupe (France)
Guatemala

Haiti
Honduras
Jamaica
Martinique (France)
Mexico & Guadalupe Island
Montserrat (U.K.)
Navassa Island (U.S.)
Nicaragua
Panama
Puerto Rico (U.S.)
Saba
Saint Barthelemy (France)
Saint Kitts and Nevis
Saint Lucia
Saint Martin (France)
Saint Pierre and Miquelon (France)
Saint Vincent and the Grenadines
Sint Eustatius (Netherlands)
Sint Maarten (Netherlands)
Trinidad &Tobago
Turks & Caicos Island (U.K.)
United States
U.S. Virgin Islands

SOUTH AMERICA

Argentina
Bolivia
Brazil
Chile
Colombia
Ecuador (Galapagos Island)
French Guiana

Guyana
Paraguay
Peru
Suriname
Uruguay
Venezuela
Falkland Islands (U.K.)

PACIFIC OCEANIA

Australia (Norfolk Island, Kiritimati Christmas Island, Cocos Koeling Island)

French Polynesia (Tahiti and 1000 isles)

Polynesia (Tuvalu, Tokelau, Samoa, Society, Marquesus, Tudmotu, Mangareva, Tonga, American Samoa, Easter Island (Rapa Nui, Chile))

Melanesia (Fiji, Soloman Isle, Santa Cruz, Bismarck, Vanuatu, New Caledonia)

Micronesia (Guam (U.S.), Mariana Island, Marshall Island, Kiribati, Nauru, Palau, Wake Island)

Jarvis Island and Kingman Reef
New Zealand & Cook Island
Niue
Papua New Guinea (shares a border with West New Guinea of Indonesia)
Pitcairn Islands (U.K.)
Midway, Palmyra, Johnston Atoll (U.S.)
Baker and Howard Island (U.S.)
Wallis and Futuna (France)

<u>ANTARCTICA</u>
South Georgia and S. Sandwich Islands (U.K)
Bouver Island (Norway)
French Southern Territory
Heard and McDonald Islands (Australia)

Paulet Island has a large penguin colony.

The moon may appear different to humans on earth observing it from different latitudes.

There is an ecological balance in nature that pollution and harvesting is interrupting. Anoxic waters have depleted oxygen levels.

The five main oceans are Pacific, Atlantic, Indian, Arctic and Antarctic. The Caspian Sea and the Black Sea are the two largest inland seas.

There are 24 Time Zones. A new day begins at the 0° meridian in England. The international date line is at the 180° meridian in Pacific Oceania. If you go west from the 180° meridian you are in tomorrow's date.

www.worldclock.com

www.timeis

www.timeanddate.com

<u>THE GOLDEN RULE</u>

Baha'i Faith – Lay not on any soul a load that you would not wish to be laid upon you, and desire not for anyone the things you would not desire for yourself.

Buddhism – Treat not others in ways that you yourself would find hurtful.

Christianity – In everything, do to others as you would have them do to you: for this is the law and the prophets.

Confucianism – One word which sums up the basis of all good Conduct...loving-kindness. Do not do to others what you do not want done to yourself.

Hinduism – This is the sum of duty: Do not do to others what would cause pain if done to you.

Islam – Not one of you truly believes until you wish for others what you wish for yourself.

Jainism – One should treat all creatures in the world as one would like to be treated.

Judaism – What is hateful to you, do not do to your neighbor. This is the whole Torah; all the rest is commentary. Go and learn it.

Native Spirituality – We are as much alive as we keep earth alive.

Sikhism – I am a stranger to no one; and no one is a stranger to me. Indeed, I am a friend to all. God is within everyone.

Taoism – Regard your neighbor's gain as your own gain and your neighbor's loss as your own loss.

Tenrikyo - All human beings in this world are the children of God.

Unitarianism – We affirm and promote respect for the interdependent web of all existence of which we are a part.

Thelema, Wicca – If it harms none, do what you will.

Zoroastrianism – Do not do unto others whatever is injurious to yourself.

SOME MUSIC COMPOSITIONS

Mozart:
Syphony No. 40 in G minor, Symphony No. 25 in G minor,
Symphony No. 38 in D,
Symphony 36 in C,
Einekleine Nachtmusik,
Requiem,
Magic Flute,
Violin Sonata No. 26 in B-Flat major, Piano Concerto No. 21 in C Major,
Clarinet Concerto in A Major,
Flute Concerto No. 2 in D Major,

Beethoven:
Ode to joy, part of Symphony No. 9 in C sharp minor
Septet Op. 20
Moonlight Sonata No. 14 Op. 27 no. 2
Symphony No. 3, No. 4, No. 5
Air, Violin Sonata No. 9,
Fur Elise
A melody of Tears & Silence
Adagio

Chopin:
Nocturne No,2, No. 20 in C Sharp
Nocturne Op. 9 No. 2
Waltz Op. 64, Marche Funbre,
Prelude No. 4, Fantasie Impromptu

Pachelbel:
Canon in D

Bach:
Toccota and Fugue in D Minor

Handel:
Hallelujah Chorus, Messiah

Brahms:
Lullaby

Vivaldi:
Four Seasons (1723CE)

Saint-Saens:
Rondo Capriccioso, Second Piano
Concerto, First Cello Concerto,
Danse Macabre, Samson and Delilah,
Third Organ Symphony, Carnival of
The Animals

Mendelssohn:
Violin Concerto E Minor OP.64

Richard Wagner:
Ride of the Valkyries (Took Wagner 26 years to complete it. Based on Odin's daughter in Norse mythology.)

Richard Strauss:
Spring, Four Last Songs.

Schubert: 600 Leider (Songs)
Symphony No. 5 in B-flat major
Der Erlkonig D328 (1815CE)
Nacht und Traume D827 (1875CE)
Serenade

Tchaikovsky:
Waltz of the Flowers, Swan Lake
Antonin Dvorak:
Song to the Moon
Carl Orft:
O Fortuna
Josef Szalai:
Csardas-Vittori Monti:
Claude DeBussy:
Claire de Lune
Edvard Grieg:
Peace of the Woods
Johann Strauss:
The Blue Danube
Gioachino Rossini:
4-part overture with finale
King Henry VIII of England 1500:
Greensleeves
Koji Nakano of China 1974:
 Spring Breathes Double Concerto with Chinese Orchestra
Salzburg Festival is an opera and music festival held in Austria each year.
TOP 100 BILLBOARD HITS U.S.A./U.K.
He's Got The Whole World In His Hands 1927 was sung by Laurie London of England and became an international hit. In 1929 Tiptoe Through the Tulips by Al Dubin (lyrics), Joe Burke (music), and Nick Lucas (Guitar). The song was also released in 1968 by Tiny Tim. Ray Charles sang Georgia On My Mind in 1930. In 1934 Richard Rodgers and Lorenz Hart released Blue Moon, based on the phenomenon when the moon looks blue because of particles in the atmosphere. In 1935 Fred Astaire and Ginger Rogers sang Cheek to Cheek in the movie Top Hat. Somewhere Over The Rainbow 1938 Judy Garland. In 1939 the Andrew Sisters sang Beer Barrel Polka which was also called Roll Out the Barrel in Britain. The song was popular during WW II. The World Will Sing Again was another British song that help Brits through WW II. Jimmie Davis and Charles Mitchell sang You Are My Sunshine in 1939 and the song melody was popular for a hundred years and sung by many music artists. In 1951 Hank Williams sang Hey, Good Lookin. In 1952, Rock Around the Clock was a song written in 1952 by Max C. Freeman and James E. Myers in the 12-bar blues format. The most popular rendition was by Bill Haley and His Comets in 1954. The song was liked in England and other countries. In 1956 Elvis Presley sang Love Me Tender. Elvis had a daughter named Lisa Marie Presley who sang Over Me in 2013. Elvis had a grand daughter named Riley Keough who was an actress. Elvis was a Caucasian man. Couples get married in Elvis Chapel, Las Vegas, Nevada.Tea for Two 1950 with Doris Day. In 1957 Danny and the Juniors sang At the Hop, a doo-wop song. Chances Are by Johnny Mathis 1957. Splish Splash by Bobby Darin 1958. Louie Louie by The Kingsmen 1960. Since I Fell For You by Buddy Johnson and sang by Lenny Welch 1963. It's My Party by Lesley Gore 1963. Easier Said Than Done by The Essex 1963. Ferry 'Cross the Mersey by Gerry & The Pacemakers 1964 a hit in the U.K. and the U.S.A. Light My Fire and Riders on the Storm by Jim Morrison & The Doors 1965. Baby Elephant Walk by Henry Mancini 1961. Our Day Will Come by Ruby & The Romantics 1962. Surfin USA by Beach Boys. Afrikaan Beat by Bert Keampfert. Unchained Melody by Righteous Brothers 1965. Heart Full of Soul by Yardbirds 1965. Impossible Dream 1965 Jim Nabors as Gomer Pyle. Good Lovin by Young Rascals.Smoke on the Water by Deep Purple 1968 about a casino that burnt down. Wild Thing by The Troggs of the U.K. written by Chip Taylor of the U.S.A.1966. Born to Be Wild and A Magic Carpet Ride by Steppenwolf 1969. The House of the Rising Sun and Don't let Me Be Misunderstood by The Animals 1964. These Boots Are Made for Walkin by Nancy Sinatra. Baby, I'm Yours was written by Van McCoy and sung by Barbara Lewis in 1965. Build Me Up Buttercup by The Foundations

1968. By the time I get to Phoenix was written in 1965 by Jimmy Webb and it has been recorded by many vocalists. Mr. Tambourine Man 1965 Bob Dylan. California Dreamin' by Mama & the Papas in 1965 classified as psychedelic pop.Please Release Me by Engelbert Humperdinck 1966. What A Wonderful World by Louis Armstrong in 1967. What the World Needs Now is Love by Burt Bacharach and Hal David 1965 sung by Jackie DeShannon. Rainy Days and Mondays by the Carpenters 1965. People 1964 sung by Barbra Streisand was a Jewish singer and the song says that people who need people are lucky. In 1964 the Beatles of England released I Wanna Hold Your Hand, Drive My Car, In My Life 1965 about memories of people and places. I Want You Back by Michael Jackson & the Jackson Five and his sister Janet Jackson who were very famous, I Heard It Thru The Grapevine was a Motown hit in 1966 by Marvin Gaye and 1967 by Gladys Knight & The Pips. Sound of Silence and Bridge Over Troubled Water by Simon & Garfunkel. I Started A Joke 1968 by The Bee Gees. Otis Redding sang The Dock of the Bay in 1967 with guitarist Steve Cooper. Grazing in the Grass by Friends of Distinction 1969. The Rolling Stones sang You Can't Always Get What You Want and the first band members in 1962 were Mick Jagger, Brian Jones, Keith Richards, Bill Wyman, Charlie Watts and Ian Stewart. But Ronnie Cam and Charlie Cam have also played with the band. In 1967 Procol Harem of England released A Whiter Shade of Pale. These Eyes by The Guess Who. In 1968 Marvin Gaye and Tammi Terrell sang Ain't Nothing Like the Real Thing. Raindrops Keep Falling On My Head by BJ Thomas in 1969 and written for the movie Butch Cassidy and the Sundance Kid. Both Sides Now by Joni Mitchell 1969. Proud Mary 1969 by Creedence Clearwater Revival. Space Oddity by David Bowie 1969. Spirit in the Sky by Norman Greenbaum 1969. Suspicious Minds by Elvis Presley 1969. Fire & Rain 1970 James Taylor. Everything is Beautiful in its Own Way 1970 Ray Stevens. Morning Has Broken, Jesus, King of Trees, and Lady D'arbanville 1970 by Cat Stevens. If I Could Read Your Mind Love 1970 by Gordon Lightfoot. War by Edwin Starr 1970. Donna Summer On the Radio in the 1970s. Let It Be, Day After Day, The Long and Winding Road by the Beatles 1970. Oooo Child by Five Stairsteps 1970. Me & Bobby McGee by Janis Joplin 1971, America released a Horse with No Name 1971 and Ventura Highway. Marvin Gaye released Mercy Mercy Me (The Ecology) and What's Going On in 1971. Chicago released 25 or 6 To 4. Summer Breeze by Seals & Crofts 1972. Elton John and Bernie Taupin wrote Harmony and Rocket Man in 1971, Philadelphia Freedom in 1975 and Belfast in 1995. Ain't She A Honey by Don McLean 1971. Imagine 1971 by John Lennon describing peace and Strawberry Fields about a children's home in Liverpool, England. A section of Central Park in New York City is dedicated to the memory of John Lennon. His 2nd wife, Yoko Ono, is still living in the building she lived in with John Lennon until he was shot to death outside the home in 1980. She is 85 years old. Rising by Yoko Ono 1995. How Long has this been going on? 1974 by Ace. You Light Up My Life 1977 by Debby Boone. Two Out of Three Ain't Bad by Meatloaf 1977. Stairway to Heaven1971,Rock and Roll Song, Love, and Kashmir by Led Zeppelin. Lean On Me 1971 by Bill Withers. Lost Inside of You by Barbra Streisand and Kris Kristofferson duet 1976, Never Been To Spain by Three Dog Night 1971. If & Diary by David Gates & Bread 1972. Drift Away 1972 John Henry Kurtz and 1973 Dobie Gray. You're So Vain by Carly Simon 1972. Puppy Love 1972 by Donny Osmond. Wildflower by Skylark 1972. The Reverend Al Green sung Let's Stay Together in 1972. Daniel by Elton John 1973. Knockin' On Heaven's Door 1973 by Bob Dylan. Jackie Blue by Ozark Mountain Daredevils 1974. Love Will Keep Us Together by Captain & Tenille, Margartaville by Jimmy Buffett and the Coral Reefers Band, Reelin In the Years by Steely Dan, Lonesome Loser by Little River Band, Listen to the Music by Michael McDonald and the Doobie Brothers, Before the Next Teardrop Falls by Freddy Fender 1974. Keep on Smiling by Blackberry Smoke 1974. Who Loves You by Frankie Valli & the Four Seasons 1975. Landslide by Stevie Nicks and Fleetwood Mac 1975. Bohemian Rhapsody by Freddie Mercury of Queen 1975. Annie's Song by John Denver 1975. Baby, I Love Your Way by Peter Frampton 1975. Evil Woman 1975 by Electric Light Orchestra. All By Myself 1975 Eric Carmen. Boogie Fever by Sylvers 1976.Living In The Past by Jethro Tull 1976.'96 Tears' by Question Mark & The Mysterians. At Seventeen by Janis Ian 1976. In 1976 the Greek Orchestra Emmetron released Zorba The Greek Dance. In 1976, A Fifth of Beethoven by Walter Murphy and The Big Apple

Band, Shower The People you love with love 1976 James Taylor and Up On The Roof (In the lyrics: At night the stars they put on a show for free) and You've Got a Friend written with Carole King. Lovely Day by Bill Withers 1977. Paradise by the Dashboard Light by Meat Loaf 1977. Dust in the Wind by Kerry Livgren of Kansas in 1977. Baker Street by Gerry Rafferty 1977. King Tut 1978. Wheel in the Sky by Journey 1978. Werewolves in London by Warren Zevon. Boogie Wonderland 1979 by Earth, Wind & Fire. My Sharona by The Knack 1979. Another Brick in the Wall by Pink Floyd. Roxanne by The Police 1979. Knock on Wood by Amii Stewart 1979. Sailing by Christopher Cross. The Arrows sang a song I Love Rock n Roll in 1979 in the U.K. Joan Jett & The BlackHearts released the same song I Love Rock n Roll in the U.S.A. in 1981. Another One Bites the Dust 1980 by Queen. Same Old Lang Syne by Dan Fogelberg 1981, In 1983 Stevie Ray Vaughn sang Pride and Joy and a blues song Texas Flood. Love Bites & Let It Go by Def Leppard in 1981. Private Eyes 1981 by Hall & Oates. Should I Stay or Should I Go? By The Clash 1981. Eye of the Tiger by Survivor 1982. Endless Love and Upside Down by Diana Ross 1982. Closer to Fine by Indigo Girls, Dirty Laundry by Don Henley 1982. Eclipse of the Heart by Bonnie Tyler 1983. True by Spandau Ballet 1983. If I Could Turn Back Time by Cher 1983. Missing You by John Waite of Britain 1984. We are the World by Michael Jackson a song compilation sung by many popular worldwide music artists 1984 was written by Michael Jackson, Lionel Richie, and Kenny Rogers and produced by Quincy Jones and Michael Omartian. Take on Me by A-ha 1985. Stevie Wonder who is blind wrote a song about the planet Saturn, Love's In Need, and a song called I just called to say I Love You in 1984. Black Butterfly & Silly & Let's Hear It For the Boy 1984 and I Love Your Smile by Deniece Williams. I Can't Wait 1984 by Nu Shooz. I wanna know what love is by Foreigner 1984. Holding Back the Years 1985 Simply Red. Everybody Wants to Rule the World 1985 by Tears for Fears. Tears for Fears also recorded a song called Mad World that was written by Ronald Orzabal. Janet Jackson sang Escapade about escaping after a workweek. In 1985 Falco of Austria sang Rock Me Amadeus about Mozart the musician. Livin' On A Prayer 1985 and You Give Love A Bad Name by Bon Jovi tells about relying on faith to get by. Walk Like An Egyptian 1986 by The Bangles. Only Human by Human League 1986. One Step Up 1987 about one step up and two steps back by Bruce Springsteen. Shattered Dreams 1987 by Johnny Hates Jazz. Heaven is a Place on Earth by Belinda Carlisle 1987. Band on the Run by Paul McCartney & Wings 1987. Journey released the love ballad Faithfully in 1988. Another Day in Paradise about the homeless 1989 by Phil Collins and the Genesis Band. High Class Girl by Joe Bonamassa is a blues guitarist who opened for B.B. King. End of the Line by Traveling Wilbury's 1988. Alive by Pearl Jam. From a Distance 1990 sung by Bette Midler and written by Julie Gold is a song saying God is watching. I've Got Love on my Mind by Natlalie Cole. Natalie Cole was Nat King Cole's daughter. Unbelieveable by EMF 1990. Hold On 1990 Wilson Phillips. Walking in Memphis Marc Cohn. Don't Dream It's Over by Crowded House, Steady Commons, Sandra Eakes and San Rah Lees, Kayla Taylor who sang to jazz music, Dominic Gaudious who played guitar and didgeridoo. Eric Clapton wrote a song called No More Tears in Heaven 1992 for the movie Rush 1991 but it reminded him of his son who fell to death after falling out a window of a New York apartment building. I Can't Make You Love Me 1991 by Bonnie Raitt. I've Been Thinking About You 1991 by Klass & Londonbeat. No Ordinary Love by Sade 1992. Together Forever and Never Gonna Give You Up 1993 by Rick Astley from England. Creep 1993 by Radiohead. In 1995 Tracy Chapman sang a song Give Me One Reason about getting out of a homeless shelter. Stay I Missed You by Lisa Loeb 1995. Vogue by Madonna a female Catholic singer who used an icon from her church as her singing name. Everything I Do I Do It For You by Bryan Adams 1996. The Prayer by Celine Dion & Andrea Bocelli duet, Matteo Bocelli son of Andrea. In 1994, Joan Osborne released 'One of Us' asking questions about God. In 1994 Soundgarden sang 'Black Hole Sun.' In 1994 Melissa Etheridge sang 'Come To My Window'. We Got the Beat by the GoGos, Songbird by Kenny G who played the saxophone, Parachute by Sean Lennon, Too Late for Goodbyes by Julian Lennon, Wicked Game by Chris Isaak, Walking on Broken Glass & Why by Annie Lennox and the Eurethmics, Careless Whisper by George Michael, Crying by KD Lang, Step by Step by New Kids on the Block, Up All Night by Widespread Panic, Who Will Save Your Soul and We Were Meant to Be by Jewel, Rhythm is Gonna Get You by Gloria Estefan, Call Me by Blondie, Rush Rush by Paula Abdul, Danger Zone, House at Pooh Corner, Celebrate Me Home by Kenny Loggins, Lady in Red by Chris De Burgh, Only Wanna Be With You by Hootie & The Blowfish 1994. You Gotta Be by Des'ree 1994. Kiss From A Rose by Seal 1994. Lightning Crashes 1994 by Live. In 1995 Alanis Morisette sang the song Ironic and You Oughta Know. Bryan Adams sang Summer of 69 in 1996. Crash Into Me, #41, What Would You Say by Dave Matthews 1996. I Am Barely Breathing 1996 was released by Duncan Sheik. Toni Braxton sang There's No Me Without You in 1996. I Believe I Can Fly by R. Kelly. In 1997 British alternative rock band The Verve sang Bittersweet Symphony. Chumbawamba of England released Tubthumping. In 1997 the Backstreet Boys released Quit Playing Games With My Heart. In 1998 the B52s released Mesopotamia. I Knew I Loved You by Darren Hayes & Savage Garden 1999. Lee Ann Womack sang I Hope You'll Dance in 1999. Steven Tyler sang I Don't Want to Miss a Thing in 1998. Michael Bolton sang That's What Love is All About. Breakdown and Free Fallin by Tom Petty. My Hero by Foo Fighters 1998. I'll Be 1998 by Edwin McCain and Misguided Roses. In 1999, Christina Aguilera released Genie in a Bottle. This is How We Do It by Montell Jordan 1999. I Try by Macy Gray 1999. In 2000 Nelly Furtado of Canada sang I'm Like A Bird. Around 2000, Irish rock band U2 released It's A Beautiful Day, In God's Country, Peace On Earth, and a song called 'In the Name of Love' about civil resistance in the United States that led to social change for the betterment of all people. U2 also released Where the Streets Have No Name. Drive by Incubus 2000 says Whatever Tomorrow Brings I'll Be There With Open Arms and Open Eyes. Here Without You 2001 and Love Me When I'm Gone 2003 by 3 Doors Down. A Moment Like This by Kelly Clarkston who won the first American Idol singing contest on TV. In 2001 Train released Drops of Jupiter. This Year 2002 is a song about having an incredibly good year with the planets lined up for you written by Leah Andreon, Martin Frederiksen, and Billy E. Steinberg who also wrote a song called True Colors about determination and surviving unhappiness sung by Cyndi Lauper in 1986. Hard to Handle by the Black Crowes 1990. Hybrid Theory and Numb by Linkin Park 2000. Irresistible by Jessica Simpson, Don't Know Why by Norah Jones, Fleetwood Mac released 'What's the World Coming To?' in 2003 questioning why people tell lies. Toxic 2003 Britney Spears. Seven Nation Army 2003 by White Stripes. British singer James Blunt released You're Beautiful in 2004. Coldplay sang Spies in 2000 and Speed of Sound in 2005. Home by Michael Buble 2005. We Belong Together by Mariah Carey 2005. Hey There Delilah 2006 by Plain White T's. Apologise was released by Timbaland in 2006 about troubles in a relationship. No Air by Jordin Sparks and Chris Brown in 2007. Home by Chris Daughtry 2007. Bleeding Love by Leona Lewis 2007. Kanye West sang Heartless in 2008. Beyonce sang Halo in 2008. Akon is a musician from Senegal, Africa who sang Right Now (Na Na Na) in 2008. Matt Nathanson sang Come On Get Higher in 2008 saying I miss the sound of your voice. Duffy sang Mercy 2008. Everlong 2009 by Foo Fighters. John Mayer sang Wheel in 2003, Daughters in 2003, Heartbreak Warfare in 2009. Ellie Goulding Lights 2009. Party in the USA 2009 Miley Cyrus. Firework 2010 Katy Perry. The A Team 2011 Ed Sheeran. Radioacitve by Imagine Dragons 2011. I Won't Give Up 2012 Jason Mraz. Mirrors by Justin Timberlake 2013. All of Me by John Legend 2013. Animals 2014 by Maroon 5. All About That Bass by Meghan Trainor 2014. Let Me Love You 2014 Mario. There's Magic in the Air 2014 Magic System. Ride by Twenty One Pilots 2015. Rihanna from Barbados in the Caribbean Islands sang Love on the Brain in 2015. What Do You Mean? 2015 Justin Beiber. Lights Down Low 2016 Max Feat Gnash Julia Michaels sang Issues in 2017 saying do not judge me and I won't judge you because we both have issues so let us listen to each other. Born This Way 2017 by Lady Gaga. What About Us? 2017 by Pink. Feel It Still by Portugal The Man 2017. Tghayarti by El Far3i 2017. Sit Next to Me by Foster the People 2017. Attention by Charlie Puth 2018.In My Blood by Shawn Mendes 2018. The Middle by Zedd, Maren Morris, and Grey 2019. I'm Coming Home by Skylar Grey, Diddy – Dirty Money and Gentleman's Rule. Electricity by Dua Lipa 2019. Blankets of Sorrow by Bear's Den 2019. Tik Tok by Ke$ha 2020. Stay With Me by Sam Smith, Without Me by Halsey, Ocean Eyes by Billie Eilish, Who's in Your Head by Jonas Brothers, Vices of Vanity, KT McCammond, Leah Catherine Thompson, Fly by Sugar Ray, Say So by Doja Cat, Heat Waves by

Glass Animals, Chandelier by Sia, On the Floor by J Lopez & Pitbull. Cold Heart by Elton John and Dua Lipa 2021. Butter by BTS 2021. Celtic Women.
Go Easy by Adele 2021.
Songs with the theme of support: Reach Out I'll Be There by the Four Tops 1965. Got to Be There by Michael Jackson 1972. I'll Be Around by Spinners 1973. Rembrandts in 1994 for the sitcom FRIENDS and the Week End in 2017 an R&B version. I'm Your Angel by R. Kelly and Celine Dion 1996.
Some songs with the word CRAZY:
Crazy by Patsy Cline 1962, I Go Crazy by Paul Davis 1977.Crazy For You by Madonna1985, Crazy by Seal 1990, Crazy by Bobbie Eakes and Big Trouble1987, Crazy by Aerosmith 1993, Crazy by Gnarls Barkley 2006. I Get Crazy by Niki Minaj with Lil Wayne 2009.
Some songs about money are: Money, money, money by the Swedish Group ABBA, For the Love of Money by the O'Jays, and Money by Pink Floyd.
Some songs about saying HELLO:
Hello, Goodbye by the Beatles 1967, Harmony by Elton John and Bernie Taupin 1973, Hello, It's Me by Todd Rundgren 1972, Hello, Hello by Mitch Allan and Tomorrow Band 2002, Just By Saying Hello by Sonja 2013.
Some songs about Time: As Time Goes By 1931 by Herman Hupfeld, Colour My World 1970 by Chicago, Jim Croce sang Time In A Bottle 1973.Long Time by Boston1976. Far Behind 1993 Candlebox. Times Like These by Foo Fighters 2002.
Some songs about Love: Till the End of Time by Perry Como 1945. Blueberry Hill 1950 Fats Domino. Fly Me to the Moon by Bart Howard sung by Kaye Ballard 1954 Frank Sinatra 1964. I Love You Baby by Frankie Valli. I Only Have Eyes For You 1959 The Flamingos. Sealed With A Kiss by Brian Hyland 1960.Angel Baby by Rosie and the Originals 1960. Can't Help Falling In Love by Elvis Presley 1961. Please Mr. Postman by the Marvelettes 1961. I Can't Stop Loving You by Ray Charles 1962. I Left My Heart in San Francisco by Tony Bennett 1962. He's so Fine by The Chiffons 1963. You Really Got Me by The Kinks 1964. My Guy by Mary Wells 1964. My Girl by Temptations 1965. This Diamond Ring by Gary Puckett 1965. Help Me Rhonda by Beach Boys. I've Got You Babe by Sonny & Cher 1965. How Sweet It Is To Be Loved By You by Marvin Gaye 1965, Ain't No Mountain High Enough & by Diana Ross and the Supremes 1966. When a Man Loves a Woman by Percy Sledge 1966. How Can I Be Sure by The Rascals 1967. Leaving on a Jet Plane by John Denver 1966 and Peter Paul & Mary in 1967. The Look of Love by Burt Bacharach 1967. Message to Michael and I Say a Little Prayer for You 1967 Dionne Warwick. Hello I Love You by the Doors 1968, Hooked On A Feeling by BJ Thomas 1969. Love Can Make You Happy by Mercy 1969. One Less Bell to Answer by Marilyn McCoo & 5th Dimension 1969. Where Do I Begin? 1970 by Andy Williams.I Need You by America 1971. Help Me Make It Through The Night by Sammi Smith and Kris Kristofferson 1970. Reach Out and Touch by Diana Ross 1970. Ain't No Sunshine by Bill Withers 1971. Betcha By Golly Wow by Stylistics 1971. Where is the Love? By Roberta Flack 1972. Brandy by Looking Glass 1972. Marlene by Todd Rundgren 1972. Free Bird Lynyrd Skynyrd 1973. Angie by the Rolling Stones 1973. Radar Love by Golden Earring 1973. Feelings by Morris Albert, Andy Williams 1975. Come and Get Your Love by Redbone 1974. Mandy by Barry Manilow 1974. Always and Forever by Heatwave 1974. Feel Like Makin Love by Bad Company 1975. Somebody to Love by Queen 1976. Evergreen by Barbra Streisand 1976. So into You 1976 Atlanta Rhythm Section. Baby Come Back by Player 1977. Wonderful Tonight by Eric Clapton 1977. Give a Little Bit by Roger Hodgson of Supertramp 1977. I'm In You 1977 Peter Frampton. I'm Gonna Make You My Wife 1977 The Whispers. Kiss You All Over by Exile 1978. Count On Me by Jefferson Starship 1978. You Don't Love Me Anymore 1978 by Rose Royce. Use Ta Be My Girl by The O'Jays 1978. Just The Way You Are 1978 Billy Joel. Heartbreaker by Pat Benatar 1979. Lady 1980 by Kenny Rogers. How Much I Feel by Ambrosia 1980. Stop Draggin My Heart Around by Stevie Nix 1981. Always On My Mind by Willie Nelson 1982. Send Her My Love by Steve Perry & Journey 1983. Tell Me If You Still Care by The SOS Band 1983. Jeopardy by Greg Kihn 1983. Owner of a Lonely Heart by Yes 1983. I'll Wait by Van Halen 1984. Silly by Deniece Williams 1981. What About

Love by Heart 1985. By The Time I Get to Phoenix sung by Isaac Hayes or Glen Campbell. Bruce Springsteen and the E Street Band released Tunnel of Love in 1987. My Heart Can't Tell You No by Rod Stewart 1988. In 1974 Dolly Parton released I Will Always Love You and Whitney Houston sang it in 1992. Smokey Robinson sang Cruisin in 1994 and Huey Lewis and Gwyneth Paltrow sang it in 2006. Lovesong by The Cure 1989. Only Love by Wynona Judd lyrics by Cindy Holman 1992. Because You Loved Me by Celine Dion 1996 written by Diane Warren.

B52s sang Love Shack and Summer of Love that says Be in Love with the Love in 1986. More Than Words by Extreme 1990. Kiss of Life 1992 sung by Sade says an angel was by her side because something heavenly led her to you. Achy Breaky Heart by Billy Ray Cyrus 1992. I'll Always Love You by Babyface 1993. 7 Whole Days and Another Sad Love Song by Toni Braxton 1994. Right Here Waiting For You by Richard Marx 1995. Before You Walk Out My Life by Monica 1995. Love Song by Sara Bareilles 2007. 'Only Love.' by Wynonna Judd 1993. So Amazing by Luther Van Dross. I'll Be Your Angel and Take It To Heart by Michael McDonald 1990, That's What Love is All About by Michael Bolton 1987. Tainted Love by Soft Cell in 1981 which was a remake from Ed Cobb 1964. Anniversary by Tony Toni Tone 1993. Nobody Knows by Tony Rich and Kenny Edmonds Babyface 1996. What I Got by Sublime 1996. That's My Girl by Usher 1997. I Could Not Love You More 1996 and My Lover's Prayer by the Bee Gees. For You by Kenny Lattimore 1996. I'll Be There For You by the Moffatts. The Game of Love by Santana 2002. Home Life by John Mayer 2003. I Could Fall In Love by Selena 2010. You're My Wonderwall by Oasis 2014. Water Under the Bridge 2015 by Adele. Closer by The Chainsmokers 2016. Greatest Love Story by Lanco 2017. Never Be The Same by Camila Cabello 2018. Someone You Loved by Lewis Capaldi 2018.This is it by Scotty McCreery 2018.Blinding Lights by The Weekend 2019. Died in Your Arms by Cutting Crew 1986 12:38 minute long-version at Rockpalast 2014. Adore You by Harry Styles 2019. If I Didn't Love You by Jason Aldean and Carrie Underwood.

Some songs about Happiness: Doo Wah Diddy by The Exciters 1963 and Manfred Mann. I Got You I Feel Good by James Brown 1964. No Stress by DJ Laurent Wolfe 2008, Happy by Pharrell Williams 2013, Don't Worry Be Happy by Bobby McFerrin 1988, Happiness by Need to Breathe 2016.

Some songs about MUSIC: I Believe in Music by Mac Davis 1971. Music by Madonna 2000.

Some songs about dancing: Save the Last Dance For Me by The Drifters 1960. Dancing in the Street by Martha & Vandellas 1966. Dancing in the Moonlight by Toploader 1970. Tiny Dancer by Elton John 1971. Dancing Queen by ABBA 1976. Get Down On It by Kool & The Gang 1981. Last Dance by Donna Summer 1978. Into the Groove by Madonna 1984. I Wanna Dance With Somebody by Whitney Houston 1987. Step In The Name of Love by R. Kelly 2003. Can't Stop the Feeling by Justin Timberlake 2016. Levitating by Dua Lipa 2021.

Some songs about the weekend:

Thank God It's Friday by R. Kelly 2003.

Saturday Night's Alright for Fighting by Elton John 1973. Saturday Night Fever by the Bee Gees 1977.

Some songs for a party:

Happy Birthday To You, At the Hop by Danny & The Juniors 1958, Let It Whip by Dazz Band 1982,Fiesta Forever by Lionel Ritchie 1983, That's What I Like About You by The Romantics 1979, I Wanna Rock and Roll All Night by KISS 1975, Rock and Roll song by Led Zeppelin, Rock With You by Michael Jackson. Fiesta by R. Kelly, Backyard Party by R. Kelly, Celebrate by Kool & The Gang, Light My Fire by The Door1996. All Summer Long by Kid Rock 2007. Good Time by Niko Moon 2021. Uptown Funk by Brass Heart Band 2014. Chicken Fried by Zac Brown Band 2016. 24 Magic by Bruno Mars 2018 of Hawaii.

Some songs about rain: Singing in the Rain by Arthur Freed 1929, A Rainy Night in Georgia written by Tony Joe White sung by vocalist Brook Benton in 1970. Have You Ever Seen the Rain by John Fogerty & Creedence Clearwater Revival 1971. Showdown by ELO 1972. I Can See Clearly Now by Johnny Nash 1972. Raindrops Keep Fallin on My Head by BJ Thomas. Georgia

Rain by Trisha Yearwood. Purple Rain by Prince. Axel Rose of Guns N Roses sang November Rain 1991.

Songs about the sun: Good Day Sunshine & Here Comes the Sun by the Beatles 1966, Crystal Blue Persuasion Tommy James & the Shondells 1969,Walking on Sunshine by Katrina and The Waves 1985,Don't Let the Sun Go Down On Me by Elton John 1992.

Soak Up the Sun by Sheryl Crow 2002, SunGoes Down Kenny Chesney 2004. Beautiful Dawn by James Blunt 2004.

Some songs about Keep On Keepin On: Keep on Keepin On by Len Chandler 1964, Tangled Up in Blue by Bob Dylan 1975.

Genres of Music

1800s: Some names from the 1800s were George W. Johnson who sang The Whistling Coon in 1891, George W. Johnson who sang The Laughing Song in 1898, Arthur Collins who sang Hello Ma Baby in 1899. In 1912 WC Handy sang Memphis Blues.

1920s-1930s Big Bands called jazz and swing bands and jazz solo artists were popular in the USA. Benny Goodman, Duke Ellington, Artie Shaw, Glenn Miller 'In the Mood', Miles Davis, Louis Armstrong were popular. The Entertainer by Scott Joplin1902 is a famous ragtime piano song. In the U.S.A. in the 1920s, Billie Holliday was a female jazz singer and Lana Turner was a famous female actress and singer. Marlene Dietrich was a famous German singer and actress in the 1920s. Claude Gordon 1916 was a famous trumpeter from Helena, Montana. Harry Fox from California was a vaudeville actor who invented a ballroom dance in 4/4 times called the Foxtrot that is similar to the waltz. Harry Fox appeared in the silent films Beatrice Fairfax and the biopic The Dolly Sisters.

A biopic or biography is a movie that is based on a true story.

Arthur Murray started a dance studio in the 1920s in the U.S.A. and began teaching dancing lessons. He had a contract with Colombia Gramophone Company to produce vinyl records about dancing. He took business courses at Georgia School of Technology in Atlanta, Georgia (Georgia Tech). He organized the world's first radio dance. The Georgia Tech school band played 'Ramblin' Wreck From Ga. Tech' the school's alma mater and some other songs that were broadcast by radio to 150 dancers that danced on top of the roof of the Capital City Country Club. Arthur Murray had over 200 dance studios.

In the 1940s-1960s singers in the USA were Bing Crosby, Andy Williams, Frank Sinatra (New York, New York & My Way), Doris Day, Patsy Cline (Crazy), Dean Martin (That's Amore), Ray Charles (Hit the Road Jack), Connie Francis (Where the Boys Are), Eddy Arnold (Make the World Go Away), Andy Williams (Where Do I Begin), Bobby Darin, Lulu, Tony Bennett, Johnny Mathis (Chances Are). Marilyn Monroe (I Wanna Be Loved By You),Victor Borge was a pianist from Denmark in 1920 and died in Connecticut USA. Liberace was a famous pianist in the U.S.A. in the 1950-1960s. His parents were Polish immigrants.

1950 DOO WOP ROCK

Bill Haley & His Comets, Danny and the Juniors, Mills Brothers, Platters, Temptations, The Drifters, The Shirelles.

COUNTRY MUSIC

A main venue for country, bluegrass, or folk music is the Grand Ole Opry House in Nashville, Tennessee. Famous singers are: Fiddlin' John Carson in 1923, Jimmie Rodgers, Ray Price, Vernon Dalhart, Dave Macon, Porter Wagner, George Jones, Hank Williams, Hank Williams, Jr. his son, George Strait, Jimmy Dean, Loretta Lynn, Johnny Cash, Lynn Anderson, Tammy Wynette, Buck Owens, Merle Haggard, Roy Rogers and Gail Davis, Naomi and Wynona Judd, Willie Nelson, Waylon Jennings, John Denver, Glen Campbell, Ronnie Millsap, Dolly Parton, Kenny Rogers, Emmy Lou Harris, Linda Ronstadt, Tim McGraw, Alan Jackson, Garth Brooks, Randy Travis, Vince Gill, Amy Grant, Shania Twain, the Eagles, Carrie Underwood, Charley Pride, Reba McEntire, Faith Hill, Kenny Chesney, Keith Urban from Australia, Martina McBride, Taylor Swift, Jason Aldean, Lady Antebellum, Mark Wills, Scotty McGreery, Maren Morris, Pam Tillis, Nate Fortner, Travis Benning.Some country songs:

I Walk the Line by Johnny Cash 1956.

Your Tattoo by Sammy Kershaw 1958.

Mustang Sally by Wilson Pickett 1965. Family Tradition by Hank Williams Jr. 1982. We're Supposed to do that now and then by George Strait 1990. Do I Ever Cross Your Mind by Randy Travis 1990. Thunder Rolls and The Dance by Garth Brooks 1990. Love Can Build a Bridge by Naomi and Wynonna Judd 1990. Should've Been A Cowboy by Toby Keith 1993. Go Rest High On That Mountain by Vince Gill 1994. Strawberry Wine by Deana Carter 1996. You're Still the One by Shania Twain 1997. She's Got It All by Kenny Chesney 1997. This Kiss by Faith Hill 1998. Remember When by Alan Jackson 2003. How Do I Live? By LeAnn Rimes 2003. God's Will by Martina McBride 2003. Trisha Yearwood 'Georgia Rain' in 2006. All Summer Long by Kid Rock 2008. The House That Built Me by Miranda Lambert 2009. Lady Antebellum 'Need you Now' 2010. Like A Back Road 2017 Sam Hunt U.S.A. Nothing Like This by Rascal Flats 2010. Colder Weather by Zac Brown Band 2010. Remind Me by Brad Paisley and Carrie Underwood 2011. Got My Country On by Chris Cagle 2011. Blown Away by Carrie Underwood 2012. Lee Brice 'I Drive Your Truck' 2012. Burnin' It Down by Jason ALdean 2014. Yeah by Joe Nichols 2014. The Weekend by Brantley Gilbert 2016. Most People Are Good and One Margarita by Luke Bryan 2017. Humble and Kind by Tim McGraw 2015. Somewhere on a Beach Dierks Bentley 2016. I Lived It and God's Country by Blake Shelton 2017. Greatest Love Story by Lanco 2017. Burning Man by Dierks Bentley 2018. Best Shot by Jimmie Allen 2018, Space Cowboy by Kacey Musgraves 2019, The Joke by Brandi Carlile 2019, Fairview Union, Chris Lane, Sam Hunt 2019 Kinfolks. One Man Band by Old Dominion 2019.The Ones Who Didn't Make It Back Home Justin Moore 2019,Donna Taggert, Hard Times 2014, Chris Janson Done 2019. Meant to Be by Bebe Rexha. Half of My Hometown by Kelsea Ballerini. The Good Ones by Gabby Barrett. Stayin Out of AA by Walker Hayes 2021, Thinking Bout You by Dustin Lynch & MacKenzie Porter. Slow Down Summer by Thomas Rhett 2021.

BLUEGRASS

Remington Ryde, Deer Creek Boys, and Old Crow Medicine Show, Avett Brothers.

ACAPELLA QUARTETS

The Big Chicken Chorus is a men's quartet in Atlanta, Georgia. Others are Gold City and Primitive Quartet.

1950s Rock N Roll

Rock n Roll music originated the USA in the 1950s & 60s from African American rhythm and blues, gospel, country, bluegrass, swing bands, and tin pan alley piano players. The Apollo Theater in Harlem, New York is a famous venue.

USA musicians were Everly Brothers, Iggy Pop, Elvis Presley, Little Richard, Otis Redding, Buddy Holly, Chuck Berry, Carl Perkins, Robert Johnson, Muddy Waters, Howlin Wolf, Bill Haley and His Comets, The Hollies, The Turtles, The Grateful Dead, The Cascades, The Boys Next Door from Chicago, Illionois, The Swingin Pros a college band at the University of Georgia 1968 with John Havrilla. Around 1970s and 1980s were The Monkees, David Cassidy, Mamas & the Papas, Blue Oyster Cult, The Ventures, Roy Orbison, Neil Diamond, REO Speedwagon, Supertramp, Night Ranger, Jimmy Hendrix who was a famous guitarist, The Police, Steve Miller Band, Stray Cats, Styx, England Dan & John Ford Coley, Jackson Browne, Carly Simon. The Ed Sullivan Show in New York on CBS TV channel from 1948-1971 and Steve Allen on NBC in 1956 featured live performances with a variety of music including Elvis Presley, the Beatles, the Jackson Five, the Rolling Stones, magic acts, sketch comedy and comedians, and jugglers, and acts with animal trainers.

MOTOWN R&B

American Motown started in Detroit, Michigan by African American Berry Gordy in 1959 and featured rhythm and blues also called R&B, doo-wop, soul, pop, and disco of African Americans. Lou Rawls and Quincy Jones were famous music producers, singer, and film producer. Motown musicians or R&B musicians of other record labels were Duke Ellington, Nat King Cole, B.B. King, Ella Fitzgerald, Isaac Hayes, Stylistics, O'Jays with Eddie Levert, Walter Williams, William Powell, Bobby Massey, and Bill Isles, Diana Ross and the Supremes, Jackson Five, James Brown, The Temptations, Curtis Mayfield, Isley Brothers, Dionne Warwick, Roberta Flack, Funkadelic,

Herbie Hancock, Toni Braxton, Gerald and Sean Levert, Beyonce Knowles and Destiny's Child, Usher, H.E.R., Childish Gambino.

Some R&B hits: Money by Barrett Strong 1960. Will You Still Love Me Tomorrow? By the Shirelles 1961. Hit the Road Jack 1962 by Ray Charles, Keep on Keepin' On by Len Chandler 1964. Sunny by Bobby Hebb 1963. Ooo Baby Baby by Smokey Robinson & the Miracles 1965. Respect by Aretha Franklin 1967 and Who's Zoomin Who, All Along the Watchtower by Jimi Hendrix 1968. What Does It Take to Win Your Love by Jr. Walker & All Stars, Ain't No Woman Like the One I've Got by Four Tops 1972. Isn't She Lovely? By Stevie Wonder 1976. Low Rider by War 1976. She's a Brickhouse by Lionel Richie and the Commodores 1977. Everyday People by Sly & the Family Stone. Nobody by Keith Sweat 1996.

Come Back To Me and Let's Wait Awhile by Janet Jackson 1986.

Michael Jackson released Beat It and Billie Jean in 1982 and Man In The Mirror in 1987 and Earth Song. Michael Jackson had a daughter named Paris Jackson who had her own band called SoundFlowers. Ain't Nobody by Chaka Khan 1983. Purple Rain, When Doves Fly, and The Most Beautiful Girl In The World by Prince and The Revolution 1984. My Lovin' by En Vogue 1992. I Wanna Know by Joe 2000. All My Life by K-Ci & JoJo 2010.When Can I See You by Babyface also called Kenny Edmonds 1993. Count on Me by Whitney Houston & CeCe Winans 1996. On Bended Knee, A Song for Mama by Boyz II Men 1995.One Sweet Day by Mariah Carey 1995.Do I Ever Cross Your Mind? By Brian McKnight 1997. American Woman by Lenny Kravitz 1998. Lifetime &This Woman's Work by Maxwell 1997. Differences by Ginuwine 2001. Wishing on a Star by Rose Royce 1996. Sittin' Up in My Room and Have You Ever by Brandy 1995. Creep & Waterfalls by TLC 1994. Can We Talk? By Tevin Campbell 1993. Walking Away and 7 Days by Craig David 2001. Angel of Mine by Monica 1998. I Swear by All-4-One 1998. We're Not Making Love No More by Dru Hill 1997. Yeah! Ft. Lil Jon, Ludacris by Usher 2004. How You Gonna Act Like That by Tyrese 2002. Golden by Jill Scott 2004. Heartless by Kanye West 2008. Over and Over by Nelly 2004. Charlene by Anthony Hamilton 2009. Blurred Lines by Robin Thicke 2013. Breathin and God is a Woman by Ariana 2018. Old Town Road by Lil Nas X 2019. Panic At the Disco I Made It 2019.

ROCK BANDS USA

Rock bands in the 1970s-2000s: Led Zeppelin, Ted Nugent and Amboy Dukes, Bon Jovi, Pink Floyd, Steven Tyler and Aerosmith, Guns N Roses and Axel Rose, Foreigner, Boston, REM and Michael Stipe, Todd Rundgren & Utopia, Queen, Grand Funk Railroad, Poison, New York Dolls, Kiss, U2, Coldplay, Kings of Leon, Humble Pie, Scorpions, Molly Hatchet, Backstreet Boys, Twenty One Pilots, Rockin Roundup Band, Country River Band, Matchbox Twenty, Chris Anderson Band, Joyce Manor Band.

SOUTHERN ROCK

Southern rock bands were Allman Brothers, Charlie Daniels, Marshall Tucker, Lynyrd Skynyrd, Atlanta Rhythm Section. Duane Allman played a slide guitar. Tres Hombres was a small local band in Warner Robins, Georgia that played at a Mexican eatery.

La Grange by ZZ Top 1973. Midnight Rider by Allman Brothers 1972. Can't You See by Marshall Tucker 1973.

ALTERNATIVE ROCK

 In the USA, a genre of music called alternative played band music that was not considered to be 1970's rock such as like the Rolling Stones who sang 'Beast of Burden' or Aerosmith who sang 'Dream On'. A new alternative sound was like the bands of Smashing Pumpkins, Foo Fighters, Red Hot Chili Peppers, Incubus, Nirvana,The Cure, REM and Michael Stipe a college band that started at University of Georgia released Everybody Hurts in 1993, The B52s a college band that started at the University of Georgia, the Fray, Jane's Addiction, Nine Inch Nails, Third Eye Blind, Blind Melon, Godsmack, Live, Collective Soul, The Wallflowers, Oasis, Beck, Green Day, The Naked and the Famous, Tomorrow, Perfect Circle, Circle from Finland, Jet from Australia, Arctic Monkeys and Bastille from England. Some of these bands played in New York, Los Angeles, and Washington D. C. Some famous alternative songs: '1979' and Tonight, Tonight by Smashing Pumpkins released in 1996. Big Empty by Stone Temple Pilots 1994.

Everlong and Monkey Wrench by Foo Fighters 1997. Enter Sandman & Fuel by Metallica 1991. In Bloom, Come As You Are by Nirvana 1991. Definitely Maybe by Oasis 1994. Everything Zen by Bush 1994, Hemorrhage (In My Hands) by Fuel 2000. How's It Gonna Be by Third Eye Blind 1996. December & Shine by Collective Soul 1995. Brain Stew by Green Day. Machinehead by Bush. One Headlight by Jakob Dylan and The Wallflowers 1996. Jakob Dylan is Bob Dylan's son. Found Out About You by Gin Blossoms 1996. The TV music theme to The Big Bang Theory by Barenaked Ladies. By the Way by Red Hot Chili Peppers 2002, Runaway Train by Soul Asylum 1992.Brick by Ben Folds Five 1997. Loser by Beck 1994. It's Been Awhile by Staind 2001. Never Too Late 2007 by Three Days Grace. So Far Away by Nickelback 2005, Patience by Chris Cornell 2016. Two High by Moon Taxi 2017, Ain't No Rest by Cage the Elephant. Some alternative music was also called funk or punk. **Famous funk bands** the Ramones, Patti Smith, Stooges and Iggy Pop, Matchbox Twenty, Ben Folds Five, Pistols, Pere Uber, Flowers of Romance, Raincoats, Pink, Slits, Clash, Chain Smokers, Bad Brains, Everlast, Spin Doctors, Trash Talk, Zero Point Energy.

HEAVY METAL ROCK

Heavy metal bands were AC/DC, Metallica, Alice Cooper, Black Sabbath, Pearl Jam, Alice in Chains, Motley Crue. Tom Sawyer by Rush 1981. Best of Both Worlds by Van Halen 1986. Girls, Girls, Girls by Motley Crue 1987. Alice in Chains released the song Rooster in 1992. AC/DC released Hells Bells and Highway to Hell in 1994. Ghost by Badflower 2018. Under the Graveyard by Ozzy Osborne 2019. No Soul No Control by Suzi Quatro 2019. Sober by Bad Wolves. Hey Man Nice Shot by Filter. Are You Ready by Disturbed. Living After Midnight by Judas Priest. Sweet Cherry Pie by Warrant. Rock of Ages Def Leppard.T.N.T. by AC/DC.Everytime You Leave by I Prevail. No One Like You by The Scorpions. Monsters by Shinedown 2018. A Little Bit Off by Five Finger Death Punch 2020. Heat Above by Greta Van Fleet 2021.

CANADA

Blood, Sweat & Tears 1968. Anvil is a heavy metal band.Sarah McLaughlin sang ballads. Neil Young from Toronto wrote Old Man 1971 and also was a movie producer and screenwriter. Isabelle Boulay sang 'Parle Moi'. Nelly Furtado of Canada sang I'm Like A Bird. 'Home' by Michael Buble who named his son Noah. Theory of a Dead Man band from Delta, British Colombia sang Livin' My Life Like a Country Song in 2001.

ENGLAND

British rockers in the 1950s-2000s were Tommy Steele, Wee Willie Harris, Cliff Richard and the Shadows, Teddy Boy, Lonnie Donegan, The Vipers, Skiffle Group, Ken Colyer, Chas McDevitt, Marty Wilde, Adam Faith, Bill Fury, Joe Brown, Johnny Kidd and the Pirates, Alex Korner, The Troggs, Cyril Davies, the Quarryman who became the Beatles, the Animals, the Rolling Stones with Mick Jagger and guitarist Keith Richards, Brian Jones, Bill Wyman, Charlie Watts, Ian Stewart, Ronnie Cam and Charlie Cam, the Yardbirds, Jethro Tull. Roger Daltrey and the Who, Badfinger who were the first band signed to the Beatles' Apple Records Label. XTC, Freddie and the Dreamers, Wayne Fontana and the Mindbenders, Herman's Hermits, Yes, Engelbert Humperdinck, Tom Jones, Freddie Mercury and Queen, Dave Clark Five, Elvis Costello, Deep Purple, Def Leppard, Elton John, Iron Maiden an English metal band, Amy Winehouse, Leona Lewis, Des'ree, Ed Sheeran, Liam Gallagher and Noel Gallagher, Oasis, Spandau Ballet, Dua Lipa. Music was recorded in Liverpool, Manchester, Birmingham, and London. The four Beatles were Paul McCartney, John Lennon, George Harrison, and Ringo Starr and they were very famous. George Harrison sang My Sweet Lord in 1970. The End of the World and Bring Me Sunshine were written by Arthur Kent and Sylvia Dee. Bring Me Sunshine became the anthem (signature tune) of the comedy duo Morecambe & Wise of BBC in the U.K. Soul II Soul is a British R&B band that released Back to Life in 1989. Bear's Den. John Entwistle a bass guitarist of the Who started a foundation for teen cancer, animal welfare, and music education. Russell Watson. Shirley Bassey 1953. Cutting Crew 1986. Radiohead 1985. Manfred Mann from England sang Blinded By the Light 1996, a remake of Bruce Springsteen's song.

GERMANY

La Bouche was a German and American dance duo based in Germany in 1994. Apparat is a German electronic musician. Milli Vanilli were a German R&B duo in 1988. Zedd is a Russian-German music producer who sang with Americans.

IRELAND

Some famous Irish rock bands were U2 1976, The Cranberries 1989, Enya.Snow Patrol released the song Chasing Cars in 2006. Take Me To Church by Hozier 2013.

ITALY

Domenico Modugno sang Volare 1958

SWEDEN

Roxette sang Listen to Your Heart in 1988. Albatraoz is an electro house hip-hop band 2012.

FINLAND

Apocalyptica is a Finnish band.

DENMARK

Volbeat, Mo, Trentemoller, Kaspar Bjorke

NORWAY

Sissel Kyrkjebo, Jaga Jazzist, Burzum,
Wardruna, Ulver, Dimmu Borgir, Royksopp, A-Ha.

HOLLAND (Netherlands)

Borja Catanesi guitarist

ICELAND

Sykur, Asgeir, John Grant & The Czars,
Of Monsters and Men, Sigur Ros & Jonsi,
Kaleo, Bjork, Emiliana Torrini (Italy and Iceland) Lord of the Rings song

RUSSIA

Sonic Speed Monkeys is a Russia band that also plays in India and England. Dmitri Hvorostovsky is a Russian operatic baritone. Anna Netrebko is a Russian operatic soprano who lives in Russia, Austria, and New York City.

FRANCE

In France, Christophe sang Aline in 1965. Lara Fabian sang 'Je T'Aime'. Lara Fabian and Patrick Fiori sang 'L'Hymne a L'Amour' together. Lara Fabian also sang a duet with Dmitri Hvorostovsky the Russian opera singer. Edith Piaf was a famous French singer who became an international star in the 1930s.

LEBANON

Yasmine Al Massri a singer and actress who has lived in France and USA

PALESTINE

Mohammed Assaf

ISRAEL

Ofra Haza, Arik Einstein, Idan Raichel, Achinoam Nini David Broza, Aviv Geffen, Omer Adam, Sant Hadad, Netta Barzilai, Berry Sakharof, Shlomi Shabat, Dana International, Yehudit Ravitz, Eyal Golan

JORDAN

Omar Al-Abdallat, Toni Qattan, Tawfig Al-Nimri, Lobo Ismail,
Adham Nabulsi, Aziz Maraka, Diana Karazon, Mais Hamdan, Ilham al-Madfai, Rania Kurdi, Mahmoud Radaideh, Naser Mastarihi, El Far3i, Nedaa Sharara

ZIMBABWE

The Soul of Mbira, traditions of the Shona People, was recorded by Paul F. Berliner in 1973 and 1995. Musical notes were from drums and metal nails flattened on wooden boards, and singers.

West Africa

Foli is a Malinke musician.Burna Boy is from Nigeria. Akon is from Senegal.

TRINIDAD

Nicki Minaj is a famous rapper & model who was raised in New York.

AUSTRALIA

Helen Reddy sand I am Woman in 1971. Keith Urban is a country singer who moved from New Zealand to Australia. Crowded House Band 1985, Men At Work, INXS, Johnny O'Keefe, Jet, an alternative rock band. AC/DC a heavy metal band, and Empire of the Sun. For King & Country. Split Enz is a group from New Zealand.

HIP HOP & RAP

Hip-hop music started in Bronx, New York. Hip-hop is rhyming lyrics to music and may include break-dancing. Some lyrics are angry. Some famous hip-hop or rap artists called rappers are Ice-T, Aaliya, R. Kelly, Eminem, Kidd Rock, Snoop Dogg, Ludacris, P. Diddy, Felicia Pearson, Cassidy, Kendrick Lamar, Kanye West, LL Cool J also called James Todd Smith, Jay Z, Drake, Queen Latifah, and Aint Afraid. Ahmad Balshe also known as Belly is a hip-hop artist born in West Bank, Palestine and raised in Canada. Ayo & Teo are rappers from Ann Arbor, Michigan.

Jude Abaga also known as M.I. Abaga is a Nigerian hip-hop producer.

Some hip hop songs: Hey Ya! by Outkast 2003. U Can't Touch This by MC Hammer 1990. Play That Funky Music by Vanilla Ice 1990. Not Afraid by Eminem 2010.

Watcha Say by Jason Derulo 2010. Roxanne by Arizona Zervas 2019. In Chile, Ana Tijoux of Makiza is a hip-hop artist.

REGGAE / TROPICAL

Jamaican reggae musicians are Bob Marley, Toots and the Maytals. Reggae includes offbeat lyrics and staccato chords. Bob Marley sang Is This Love? in 1978.

Cuban music artists are Camila Cabelo, and Gloria Estefan. Jencarlos Canela is a Cuban American singer and actor.

Puerto Rico musicians are Roselyn Sanchez and Residente also called Rene Juan Perez.

DISCO or discotheque music is a type of dancing music as in the U.S.A. movies Saturday Night Fever with John Travolta and Karen Lynn Gorney and Grease with John Travolta and Olivia Newton John, the music of Chaka Khan, Donna Summer, KC & The Sunshine Band, Yvonne Elliman, Gloria Gaynor, Bee Gees, and Prince. The Bump and the Hustler were popular dance moves to disco music.

Laura Wright and Anthony Padilla were dancers who performed in Las Vegas. Anthony Padilla was also a comedian. Jody Watley is an R&B dancer and singer.

Rumba is a Cuban dance move that became famous in the 1930s. Mambo is a dance move popular in Africa and Europe.

Zumba is a dance designed for body workouts for cardio fitness, weight loss, and weight management.

Electronic music is played on keyboards that have computer parts that can recreate the sounds of guitars, drums, cymbals, trumpets, organs and pianos all by playing a keyboard. Christopher Cross produced a CD called Sailing with electronic music.

PAKISTAN

Tere Bin by Atif Aslam 2006.

INDIA

Famous Women Singers: Lata Mangeshkar, Sunidhi Chauhan, Asha Bhosle, Shreya Ghoshal, Monali Thakur, Alka Yaguik, S. Janaki, Usha Uthuy.

Famous men: Ravi Shankar, Amrit Maan, Koi Fariyad, Raghupati Raghava

Famous bands: Varanasi, Indian Ocean, Avial, Kerala, Tripwire, Black, The Works, Shillong Soulmate, Zodiac, Khiladi, Asylum, Garden of Thorns.

CHINA

When My Dear Come Again 1937, The Wandering Songstress 1937, Four Seasons Song 1937, Night Jasmine 1944 by Li Xianglan, Shanghai Night 1946 by Zhou Xuan, Ali Mountain Girl 1947 by Zhang Che, Jasmine Flower 1947 by He Fang, Fine Wine and Coffee 1972 by Teresa Teng, In That Distant Place by Wang Luobin, Out of the West Pass, Childhood 1979 by Lo Ta-yu, Nothing To My Name 1986 by Cui Jian, Silence is Golden 1988 by Leslie Cheung. Li Ronghao is a famous singer. Some famous bands are Black Panther 1987, Hang on to the Box 1998, Silver Ash 2000,

River of Sorrow by Min Hui Fen, Wei Li 2000, Joyside 2001, Snapline 2005, Hanggai 2004, Tengger Cavalry 2010.

ASIA

In Taiwan, Jay Chou is a male singer and Joey Yung is a female singer.
In Mongolia The Altai Band 2015 with Altal Kal, The Hu sang Yuve 2016.
In Cambodia, Sin Sisamouth and Ros Sereysothea were musicians in 1970.
In Thailand, The Impossibles were musicians in 1970.
In Vietnam, Trinh Cong Sow was a male musician and Khanh Ly was a woman musician.
In the Philippines, Wally Gonzales and the Juan De La Cruz Band were popular.
Lang Lang is a Chinese musician.

KOREA

In South Korea, Shin Jung-hyeon was a male musician in the 1960s – 1970s. Beast Highlight songs: Yoseop Yang sang Caffeine 2012. Produced by Jun Hyung. Fiction 2011. BTS 2013. Apink singing on rainy days 2018. Big Bang K POP. Jessica Jung 1984 Song Divine. Shock 2011 Japan and Korea. Bad Girl 2009 Japan and Korea.

JAPAN

Malice Mizer, Beat Crusaders, Band-Maid, Kin Ki Kids, Tokyo Jihen, Cute, Tokio, Oblivion Dust. Baby Metal is a kawaii metal band.
Chiemi Eri was a woman who recorded Rock Around the Clock in 1955.
Keijiro Yamashita was a male musician and Michiko Hamamura was a woman musician. Carol and the Cools, the Black Cats, Peppermint Jam, Guitar Wolf, and Akiko Urae and Take Blue Angle were popular musicians. Anthem and BOW WOW were heavy metal bands.

SPANISH & Mexican MUSIC

Ranchero classic mexican music may include accordion, bajo sexton, bass, drums, and saxophone. Manuela Vargas was a dancer that performed on the Ed Sullivan Show in 1966. Danna Paola sang a song called Mundo de Caramelo about candy. Ritchie Valens sang La Bamba in 1958. Danny Flores, El Groupo Uzziel were Mexican musicians.
Other popular artists are Sergio Santos Mendes and Brazil, Los Rockets, Los Crazy Boys, Jose Feliciano, Carlos Santana, Julio Iglesias and his son Enrique Iglesias, the Refrescos, Pistones, Emilio Sancho & Los Nikis, Ivete Sangalo, Selena Gomez, Luan Santana, Jorge & Mateus, Bruno & Marrone, Roberto Carlos, Joao Neto & Frederico, Joel Marques, Los Tigres Del Norte, Pesado, Nuevo Leon, Ramon Ayala, Intocable, Los Cadetes de Linares, Los Alegres de Teran, Los Tucanesde Tijuana, Los Rieleros del Norte, Los Huracanes del Norte, Los Angeles Azules, Remmy Valenzuela, Ulices Chaidez y Sus Plebes, Los Corceles De Linares, La Septima Banda, Edwin Luna y La Trakalosa de Monterry, Christian Nodal, Regulo Caro, Banda Carnaval, Gerardo Ortiz, Romeo Sautos, Marc Anthony, Calibre 50, Banda los Recoditos, Romeo Santos, Nicky Jam, Shakira, el Bandero, Cumbias.El Jarabe Tapato 'Mexican Hat Dance.'
Lani Hall was a woman who married A&M records founder Herb Alpert of Los Angeles who had a band called the Tijuana Brass and Herb Alpert and Brazil. Janis Hansen of the United States sang with Herb Alpert also. The band had a Latino jazz sound. Spanish Flea song.
Maluma also named Juan Luis Londono Arias was a music artist from Columbia who signed with Sony Music.
La Ley is a famous band in Chile formed in 1987 that included Beto Cuevas, Andres Bobe, Rodrigo Aboitiz, Luciano Rojas, and Mauricio Claveria. Some of their famous songs: Desiertos, Tejedores de Ilusion, Prisioneros de la Piel, and Aqui for Warner Music Mexico.
La Movida Madrilena was a music clubhouse for bands after the death of dictator Francisco Franco in Spain in 1975. Tomeu Penya 1992 Sirena album.

COLOMBIA

Jose Salgado & Valery Salgado singing The Prayer in Spanish language

PERU

Joe Moraya guitarist The Good, The Bad The Ugly

EASY LISTENING MUSIC

Tubular Bells by Michael Gordon Oldfield of U.K. Tangerine Dream and Edgar Froese of Germany 1967.Secret Garden of Ireland and Norway 1996. Kenny G of U.S.A. 1986. Bonne Nuit French Lullabies by Jane Woodruff and Jana Minter 1995.

Where I Stand by guitarist Nick Gaudious 1996. Enchantment by Charlotte Church of U.K. 2001.Passion: The Love Album by Placido Domingo. 2011.

RELIGIOUS MUSIC

Some Jewish music artists in the 2000s were Six13 and Max Stern. Max Stern Song of Moses Ha'azinu was 32 minutes long. The Vienna Boys Choir of Vienna Austria has 100 choristers. Christian music artists- 1972 Doobie Brothers 'Jesus is just alright' -1980s - 2000s: Brandon Heath, Kari Jobe, Casting Crowns, Mercy Me, Tenth Avenue North, Aaron Shust, Newsboys, When You Speak by Jeremy Camp, TobyMac, Steven Curtis Chapman, Mary Mary, Yolanda Adams, Patti Labelle, 'Believe For It' by CeCe Winans, Babbie Mason, Kirk Franklin, Judy Jacobs, Muzeel Fairley, Jars of Clay, Northpoint InsideOut Band, Mandisa, Nichole Nordeman, Natalie Grant, Petra, Switchfoot, 'Redeemed' by Big Daddy Weave, Francesca Battistelli, Phillips, Craig & Dean, Hillsong Worship, Selah, Oak Ridge Boys, Paul Cardell, Laura Story, Third Day, Christy Nockels, Nathan Pacheco, Chris and Conrad, Rich Mullins, Johnny Diaz, Michael W. Smith, Nate Fortner, Lighthouse, and more. Some songs: Brandon Heath 'Give Me Your Eyes' 1997. Chris Tomlin 'God of this City' 2008. Kari Jobe "I Am Not Alone' 2013. Mercy Me 'I Can Only Imagine' 2000. Amy Grant 'Better Than A Hallelujah' in 2010. Natalie Grant 'Your Great Name' in 2010, Plumb 'Need You Now' in 2013. Sara Groves 'Tent in the Center of Town' about Christian tent revivals. Jon Thurlow 'Jesus You're Beautiful' in 2010. John Stringer's That's Love in 2015. Sanctus Real Lead Me 2010. Josh Groban 'You Raise Me Up 2003. The Booth Brothers, The Three Bridges, The Browders, Soul'd Out Quartet, Collinsworth, Exodus, Legacy 5, Sounds of Jericho were famous Christian gospel acts. Gospel acts could be a capello (acapello) quartets sung in harmony with no musical instruments or with music. Bob Dylan wrote Knockin' On Heaven's Door in 1973. Hallelujah by Lee Dewyze 2011. Lift Your Heads Weary Sinners by Crowder 2015. Like You by Tauren Wells 2018. God is With Us 2021 by For King & Country. So Will I by 100 Billion X 2018. That Was Jesus by Zach Williams and Dolly Parton 2019. Jesus is King by Kanye West 2019.One Day by Cochren 2019. Every Step by Covenant Worship 2020. Peace Be Still by Hope Darst 2020.Truth Be Told by Matthew West. Sparrows by Cory Asbury 2020. Believer by Rhett Walker 2020. Eric Clapton and Luciano Pavarotti sang Holy Mother with the East London Gospel Choir in 2020. Zealand Woship. Run to the Father by Cody Carnes. God Turn It Around by Jon Reddick, Jesus Knew by Al Holley, Jesus is Coming Back by Jordan Feliz.

In 2000 Cat Stevens (Yusuf Islam) was a Muslim musician who wrote a song called A is for Allah as it is spelled in the English language. Allah means God in the Arabic and Farsi languages. Gott means God in German. Dieu means God in French. Elohim means God in Hebrew.

Cat Stevens was drowning in the ocean off the coast of England and prayed to God to save him and he would devote his life to God. When he was recovering in the hospital, his brother gave him a copy of the Quran and that is when he was became Muslim.

Pandit Jaitly, Aparat, Jagjit and Chitra Singh offer Hindu music.

Apsaras offer Thai and Japanese music.

Demis Roussos was born in Egypt to a Greek family. Demis Roussos and his band Aphrodite's Child created an album entitled 666 based on the Book of Revelation in the King James Bible. Other bandmates were Loukas Sideras, Silver Koulouris. Other contributors to the album were Michael Ripoche, John Forst, Daniel Koplowitz, Yanni Tsarouchis, and actress Irene Papas. Vangelis is another Greek composer.

Juju is music of the African Yoruba religion with guitars and drums.

CHILDREN'S MUSIC Famous children's music artists were Pete Seeger 1919, Captain Kangaroo 1950-1960, Mister Rogers and Sesame Street 1980, Baby Beluga by Raffi of Canada, Egypt, and Armenia 1948, and Ziggy Marley of Jamaica 1968. Some famous children's songs are Lullaby and Goodnight, Twinkle, Twinkle Little Star, The Wheels on the Bus, Three Little Monkeys

Jumping on the Bed, Itsy Bitsy Spider, This Old Man, If You're Happy And You Know It Clap Your Hands. Do You Know The Muffin Man Who Lives on Drury Lane? The Farmer in the Dell, The Chipmunks are animated music for kids and also included Christmas songs.A song called Earth Boy in 1962 by Roy C. Bennett that has an Asian sound is heard in Girls, Girls, Girls an Elvis movie. The Lion King movie song Hakuna Matata means No Trouble in Swahili.Baby Shark by Pink Fong had billions of reviews on YouTube. In 2015. People whisper to avoid waking up a sleeping baby.

MUSIC AS REQUIEMS

Deep Purple wrote Contact Lost, Echo's Children wrote Columbia, Eric Johnson wrote Bloom for Columbia for astronauts who died in the 1963 Apollo fire and Challenger 1987 and Columbia 2001 Space Shuttle explosions.

BIBLIOGRAPHY

1. The Red Record, The Wallum Olum. The Oldest Native North American History
Copyright 1993 by David McCutchen, Published by Avery Publishing Group.
2. King James Bible 1611.
3. The Book of Mormon, Published by Intellectual Reserve, Inc., Copyright 1981. The
Church of Jesus Christ of Latter Day Saints, Salt Lake City, Utah, USA.
4. The Koran, translated by N.J. Dawood. Copyright 1990 by Penguin Group, London &
New York.
5. The Divine Liturgy of St. John Chrysostom by Rev. Protopresbyter Jon Magoulias,
Copyright 2000, Double Eagle Publishers.
6. The Holy Piby, by Shepherd Robert Athlyi Rogers, Copyright 2011 by White Crane Pub.
7. Introduction to African Religions Copyright 1975 by John S. Mbiti,Praeger Publishers,
London, England and Ny, Ny 10003.
8. The True Saint Nicholas by William J. Bennett, Copyright 2009, Howard Books, NY.
9. Be Thou There, The Holy Family's Journey in Egypt by Gawdat Gabra, Copyright 2001,
Published by The American University in Cairo Press.
10. Mother Theresa, The Joy in Living, Copyright 1996, by Jaya Chalika and Edward Le Joly,
by Viking Penguin.
11. Avesta, The Religious Book of the Parsees, by Arthur Henry Bleeck in 3 Volumes,
Copyright 2005 by Adamant Media Corporation.
12. Kitabi-Aqdas by Baha'u'llah, 1953 translation by Shoghi Effendi.
13. The Adi Granth the Holy Scriptures of the Sikhs, by Dr. Ernest Trumpp. 2010.
Originally published in 1877 by Munshiram Manoharial Publishers.
14. Shinto, Japan's Spiritual Roots, by Stuart D.B. Picken, Intro by Edwin O. Reisenhauer,
Copyright 1980 by Kodansha International Ltd. Thru Harper and Row Publishers, NY 10022.
15. Kojiki, by O no Yasumaru. by Basil Hall Chamberlain, Copyright 1882, Perfect Library.
16. Ofudesaki Sixth Edition by Tenrikyo Church Headquarters, 1993.
17. Tao Te Ching, Copyright 2015 by Thomas Miles, Avery Publishing Group.
18. The Wisdom of Confucius, Copyright 1938, 1966, 1994, Edited and translated by Lin
Yutang, Published by Random House.
19. The Lotus Sutra by Gautama Buddha, Translated by Hendrik Kern, Copyright 2012, Alex
Struik cover design.
20. Cao Dai Faith of Unity, Copyright 2000 by Hum Dac Bui, M.D. with Nagasha Beck,
Published by Emerald Wave.
21. Bhagavad Gita, Translated by Stephen Mitchell, Copyright 2000, Three Rivers Press, NY.
22. Hindu Scriptures, Translated by R.C. Zaehner, Copyright 1992, Alfred A. knopf, Inc, NY.
23. Singing the Living Tradition Copyright 1993, Unitarian Universalist Association, Boston,
Massachusetts 02108
24. Left Brain, Right Brain, Fourth Edition, By Sally P. Springer and Georg Deutsch,
Copyright 1981, 1985, 1989, 1993, Published by Freeman and Company, New York.
25. The Four Agreements Wisdom Book by Don Miguel Rulz,Copyright 1997, Published by
Group West, California USA.
26. Encyclopedia of Evolution by Stanley A. Rice Ph.D.Copyright 2007, Facts on File, Inc.,NY.

This fictional story of the book was typed in Cambria font, size 11.

The book title page was typed in Chiller font, size 48 and Segoe UI, font size 20.

The chapter headings were typed in Calibri font, size 14.

The chapter descriptive headings were typed in Bookman Old Style font, size 11.

This sentence and the description of the fonts above is typed in Calibri font, size 11.

Photo images of paper curls are credits of ek inyalgin and dimitar gorgev at www.dreamstime.com.

www.ingramcontent.com/pod-product-compliance
Lightning Source LLC
Chambersburg PA
CBHW070445120726
47910CB00003B/941